Taking the Reins

Laurie Twizel

Chapter One

Elsa removed the poultice from Connor's pus-filled hoof, and screwed her face up at the mess and smell that greeted her from his abscess.

"Well, it sure *looks* like it's doing the trick," she told him, as she gave him a pat for standing so quietly. She knew he must still be uncomfortable despite the painkillers and antibiotics she had hidden in his feed, as the infection had spread up his leg.

She fitted him with a fresh bandage, growling every so often at him to stop fidgeting, and taped it firmly around his hoof. He nuzzled her for treats, and she willingly slipped him a slice of carrot.

"Anything for my brave little soldier," she told him, planting a kiss on his soft, velvet nose.

She let herself out of his stall and strode down to the far end of the row of brick built stables where Timber Bear waited patiently, her earlier jaunt on the horse-walker having calmed her a little, and smiled.

She often smiled these days where Timber Bear was involved, but not so much where the other horses were concerned. Elsa's boss and good friend, Sophia Hamilton, had suffered a run of bad luck recently, and their competition calendar was somewhat empty.

It had been looking desolate until a new owner had turned up one day unexpectedly and entrusted in their care his two young event horses. Their arrival had been a bittersweet occasion for Elsa; the circumstances in which they had relocated from their previous, top-class rider Frederick Twemlow, something she still found difficult to reflect upon. They were quality types and Sophia was confident she would get their campaign underway very soon, but it was still early days and she was careful to get to know them properly and not to rush them or herself.

Since this had left Elsa with more time to ride her own feisty little mare, the chestnut had certainly calmed down a little and put much more effort into her work at home, and Elsa couldn't wait to get her out and about to put all their hard work into practice. She was prepped to perfection for her next event, and Elsa knew that their imminent success or failure was all in her hands.

Elsa was just sweeping up the last of the dropped hay and muck from the cobbled stableyard before she retired for the evening to her cosy cottage and a long, hot shower, when she heard Sophia's bedroom window fly open.

"Elsa!" Sophia called urgently. "*Elsa*!"

Elsa looked up as Sophia leaned out the window fresh from her shower. Her washed hair was tied up in a towel, and another she held tightly around her.

"What is it?" Elsa frowned.

"Just come up here, *now*!" Sophia hissed, looking frantic.

With an amused smile, Elsa did as she was told. She let herself in to the Hamilton's farmhouse, and skipped the stairs to Sophia's room.

"What's the matter?" Elsa pushed open the door to her boss standing in just her underwear in front of her floor length mirror, a pile of dresses discarded on her bed.

"Please," she sighed in frustration, "will you help me choose and fit into a dress?"

"Yes sure," Elsa replied slowly, a mixture of confusion and amusement washing over her.

"And do you mind doing late night check tonight?" Sophia pleaded, as if her loyal groom might actually decline. "I know it's my turn, and you don't get many evenings off, but..."

"Of course not," Elsa grinned. "I assume all this is for something very important?" She scanned around the absolute turmoil of Sophia's usually spotless and organised bedroom;

the discarded clothes and the makeup scattered everywhere. "And not the dinner you are booked onto with Ava and I this evening?"

Sophia's eyes widened, and her hands flew to her mouth. "Shit! Is that tonight? I had completely forgotten. I can cancel?"

"No, don't be silly!" Elsa laughed. "I'm just teasing. I mean I've been slaving over the meal all day, but no doubt we'll be able to eat your share," she told her with a wink.

"Elsa...don't make me feel bad." She groaned. "I'm already stressed enough."

"I'm *joking,*" Elsa laughed. "So where might you be off to which is obviously much better than hanging around with us?"

"Just dinner..." she replied coyly, her cheeks reddening. "With Harry."

"Wow!" Elsa beamed. "And about bloody time, too!"

Harry was their local and rather good-looking young vet, and he and Sophia had been making eyes at each other over routine visits for quite some time. Or rather, Elsa had amusingly observed them both staring shyly at the floor whenever they had to engage in conversation, their feelings for each other blatantly obvious to everyone except each other.

"But I totally forgot about dinner with you two!" Sophia whined. "I feel awful, and I was really looking forward to it. But when Harry asked me, well... my mind went blank, I couldn't think of anything other than to not faint! Honestly, I can cancel?"

"No, you will not!" Elsa laughed, persistent. "Especially not after how long it's taken you two to finally get together!"

She smiled gratefully. "I'll cook next time," she promised.

"It's a deal," Elsa winked. "And tonight...should we expect you back?"

"Yes! Of course!" Sophia was mortified. "Elsa who do you take me for? And even if I wanted to...well...you *know*

Harry."

"Oh, yes I do," Elsa rolled her eyes. "Not going to go anywhere fast that one, is it?"

Elsa quickly checked her lasagne wasn't burning as she heard a car engine arrive out in the yard. Cecil barked and ran to the door, waiting patiently for the knock. His hackles were restrained and his tail wagged excitedly; he always knew who the visitor was long before he saw them.

Elsa swung open the front door and greeted Ava with a huge smile.

"Hey, girl!" They embraced in a friendly hug, as Cecil excitedly struggled to be a part of it. "I hope you've brought wine?"

"Oh, copious amounts!" Ava laughed, holding up two chilled bottles of white. "It's Aussie, of course," she added with a wink as she went straight to the fridge. "So it's bound to be good!"

Elsa smiled fondly. She and the bubbly Australian had built up a strong friendship, ever since Elsa had dropped off Sophia's previous top horse, Nobby, to fellow competitor Frederick Twemlow, and Ava was his groom there to receive him. The circumstances of their meeting being another painful memory for Elsa, as most things were where Frederick Twemlow was involved. So she was glad at least something good had come of it.

"Smells delicious!"

"It's just lasagne," Elsa replied, taking two wine glasses down from the cupboard. "It's almost ready. And Sophia can't join us tonight, so there's more for us!"

"Oh, shame," Ava replied honestly.

"I know, but she's got a hot date!" Elsa could not conceal her excitement, and Ava waited expectantly. "With Harry, the vet!"

"No way!" Ava exclaimed, having heard all about the pair's

previous shy exchanges from Elsa. "That's awesome! And about bloody time!"

"I know!" Elsa grinned, passing her a glass of wine. "So, how are you? How's work? You look exhausted." Elsa mentioned, with some concern. "You know you didn't have to come tonight; you could have cancelled."

"I'm fine," Ava insisted, taking a large, grateful sip of her favourite wine. "And work is going great; all the horses are on top form. But it's been manic at the yard."

Elsa nodded, she had suspected that was the case as she'd been trying unsuccessfully to meet up with Ava for weeks. Elsa supposed that for people with normal jobs, the last thing they wanted to do when they got home was *talk* about work. But grooms, lived, breathed and slept horses, and Elsa was often still to be found out on the yard on her day off, much to Sophia and Petra Hamilton's disapproval.

"We've two working pupils coming," Ava went on, curling up on the sofa, her bare feet tucked underneath her. "Well, I say working pupils, but not in the typical sense. One has been riding quite successfully in France for the last few years, and is moving over here and wants to be based with Fred to see what he can pick up from him. He sounds like a nice guy. The other...well, she sounds like a right stuck up bitch. She's a show jumper, fancies a change of scenery apparently."

Elsa's eyes rose at the sound of venom in the voice of her usually indifferent friend.

"Oh, honestly, Elsa," Ava sighed. "She's not even arrived yet and she's already stirring up trouble. She's got a list of requirements as long as my arm...*no,* as long as my *body*! If she thinks I'm running around after her, she's got another think coming!"

"Oh, geez, I don't envy you."

"You're so lucky working for your best friend," Ava told her.

"It does have many good points," Elsa agreed. "What does

Frederick make of it?" She still struggled over saying his name, and silently cursed herself. She'd have thought he would be out of her system by now.

"Very little, which is typical of him," Ava rolled her eyes. "In fact, he's been very accommodating. I shouldn't be surprised, though. I looked her up; she's extremely beautiful, talented and successful. I think he's a little in awe of her."

Elsa felt her stomach lurch. She busied herself retrieving plates and cutlery, hoping Ava wouldn't notice her sudden discomfort as she prepared the salad garnish. But nothing much slipped past Ava.

"Shit, sorry," Ava mumbled feebly.

"No, it's fine," Elsa cut her off, taking a large gulp of her wine. "It's nothing to do with me."

"If it's any consolation, I've heard some awful things about her, although I can't be sure if they're true of course, but I'll see for myself soon enough."

"Like what?" Elsa peered into the cosy living room, intrigued.

"Massive staff turnover, treating her grooms like shit, not particularly nice to her horses," Ava trailed off with a wave of her hand, as if there were lots more that she simply didn't have enough time to go through them all.

"How has she managed to become so successful, then?" Elsa frowned.

"Her parents have pots of money apparently," Ava replied. "As soon as one horse breaks or refuses, it's quickly replaced. They're probably paying Fred to have her, whereas the other guy will have to earn his keep."

"Wow," Elsa replied, glad that her own exposure to this side of the equestrian world had been so sheltered.

"Yea, but if it is true, her true colours will show soon enough and she won't last five minutes at ours. There's no flies on our Freddy; there'll be no pulling the wool over his eyes." Ava told her confidently, detesting her already. "She'll be gone in a shot."

"I heard Frederick had a good run at Howarth the other day?" Elsa quickly changed the subject, desperate to get the unwelcome images of Frederick mingling with pretty girls, off her mind. She took a deep, silent breath. She had to stop feeling like this about him; what they'd had was fleeting and minor, and she knew she had to get over it. She couldn't let it keep eating her up; she doubted Fred was wasting his time sitting at home thinking about her, and he was free to mingle with whoever he wanted. But that didn't stop it hurting.

"He did," Ava nodded. "Not enough to win but both horses finished on their dressage score and it was a big step up for them. I think a few horses are going to go to Kya Fisher over winter for some schooling. Depends how much room she's got."

"Oh, I'm sure she'll find room for Frederick," Elsa nodded, hating the sound of her bitterness. Kya Fisher was a locally-based international dressage rider. She was also beautiful, elegant, kind and charming, both on and off a horse.

"She's a bit old for him, Elsa, so don't worry about that," Ava replied, not bothering to hide her amusement.

"You would never know to look at her."

"Well, trust me, Fred doesn't look at her, so you've no need to worry about that, either."

"I'm not worried about anything," Elsa replied, checking the lasagne again and using the rush of escaped steam from the abrupt opening of the oven door a good excuse for her increasingly reddening face. "I told you; what he does is nothing to do with me."

Ava bit her lip as she watched her try to busy herself. She felt bad for her friend, but sometimes equally as bad for her boss. She had always been a loyal employee, and she wasn't about to change that now, but as far as she was concerned they had both handled the breakdown of a potential blossoming romance, like adolescents.

When Elsa's alarm went off the next morning, she reluctantly dragged her wine-fuddled head from its short sleep and went downstairs.

"Hey," Ava smiled, stretched out on the sofa underneath one of Cecil's blankets. "Thought I'd head out with you and say hi to your lot before I left."

They made their way out into the crisp morning air. Elsa threw all the morning feeds that she'd made up the night before into her wheelbarrow and began the walk along the stable block, before all the horses started kicking their doors.

"So, yours are not doing so well?" Ava probed cautiously as they stopped to feed the first horse in the line. Drop Kick – by far the noisiest horse on the yard – had quietened down a lot since he had moved stables to be immediately next to the feed shed, meaning he was the first to get fed.

Elsa shook her head. "Pretty much everything is lame; it's ridiculous." She paused as she patted the big, filthy grey, disinterested in her now he had his food to tuck into. "This one is back in light work after his escapade with the stock fencing, at least. The only plus side is I've been able to ride Bear lots. She's really coming on; I can't wait to get her out again!"

"Well, that's something!" Ava beamed. "It's only right that you get to reap some of the rewards, with all the hard work you put in at home."

"I feel like a bit of a fraud while Sophia is so frustratingly low on horsepower; I'm just the groom, after all." Elsa shrugged.

"Ah, you're so modest!" Ava laughed. "You're not a fraud; and you deserve it more than anyone!"

Elsa wasn't sure about that, and although she enjoyed nothing more than getting Bear out and about to events, she harboured none of the dreams and aspirations that Sophia did. And it troubled her greatly that Sophia wasn't getting the runs she needed to reach the success she craved.

"With all your new riders appearing, Michael Patricks might be persuaded to take his horses back?" Elsa queried, biting down on her lip.

"Michael would *never* do that," Ava shook her head fiercely, and Elsa felt herself relax a little. "How are they getting on, anyway? I do miss them; they were such easy characters."

"They've settled great," Elsa nodded enthusiastically, quickly making her way down the row so that Ava could see them. "Sophia and I are absolutely in love with them."

"And with Michael Patricks, too?" Ava queried with a wink.

"Oh, he's a dream, isn't he?" Elsa giggled, referring to the tall, handsome silver fox. "There's no pressure from him, and although he obviously wants them out running, he is happy for Sophia to take her time. He's always alone, though..."

"Oh, there's no *Mrs* Patricks, Elsa," Ava cut her off with a smile, patting Cali first and giving Dusty a huge kiss. "But tell you what, if he was twenty years younger I'd make damn sure it was me!" she exclaimed, and Elsa could not contain her laughter.

"So, when am I going to bump into you again?" Ava asked her, as they made their way across the yard to her little car.

"I'm not sure," Elsa sighed. "Sophia has some entries lined up, but it all depends on soundness and the ground. She's not going to risk any of them now if she's not one hundred and ten percent happy with the ground."

"Sounds sensible," Ava nodded, and embraced her in a hug. "Well, then, so long. Let me know how you get on with Bear at the weekend."

Chapter Two

The lorry was parked ready in the yard, and Elsa's little mare walked enthusiastically up the ramp, standing patiently while Elsa tied her up and fastened the partitions against her.

"I'm coming!" Sophia called, hurrying from the house. She thrust a slice of toast in her mouth as she struggled into her jacket.

Elsa smiled appreciatively as she started the lorry engine. Ever since Sophia's own competitions calendar had dwindled considerably, the extra time Elsa had been handed meant she had taken the plunge and affiliated Timber Bear to the world of eventing. Sophia had insisted that she needed a groom, and duly stepped up to the mark.

"Another late night, was it?" Elsa teased, as she rolled the lorry out onto the lane. "That's twice this week that you've been out with young Harry. Must be keen."

"Shut up, Elsa," Sophia mumbled good naturedly, fumbling with her seat belt in an attempt to hide her reddening face.

Elsa was so used to driving to events alone, that the company was both strange and nice, and made the journey appear much quicker. Normally she chatted away to Cecil, or sang along to the radio at the top of her lungs. Either way, Cecil often spent the journey looking at her in disdain.

Elsa took her place in the lorry park, and left Bear in Sophia's capable hands while she located the secretary's tent. They had just enough time to work in before Elsa's dressage test, as she had quickly discovered that while Bear needed time to settle before Elsa could get on, too much time and she would start to get herself worked up.

When she returned to the lorry, Sophia was looking stricken.

"What?" she froze in her tracks, and Cecil barked.

"She only has three shoes on," Sophia replied, holding up a twisted piece of metal. "I found it lying in the shavings; she must have pulled it off during the journey. God knows how, I barely heard her move."

"She is a mare of many talents!" Elsa groaned. "I just wish one of those was eventing." She grabbed the lead rope and turned on her heel.

"Where are you going?" Sophia called after her.

"To find the farrier!" Elsa called back over her shoulder.

"Who's meant to be the groom here?" Sophia shouted back, hands on hips as the pair of them were quickly out of sight.

Me, thought Elsa, as they weaved through the lorries back towards the secretary's tent. Locating the farrier in the first place, and then the precious time they would eat up while she probably danced all over him while he tried to shoe her, was not the start to the day she needed, and Sophia would only panic.

Elsa could have kissed the aging farrier as he quickly nailed on another show, and Elsa jogged her back to the lorry to find Sophia had all the tack laid out ready.

"You get changed," she told Elsa. "I'll get her studded and tacked up."

"Don't worry about boots; I've barely any time left to warm up," Elsa called over her shoulder as she climbed up into the lorry without argument. Of course, nothing was ever stress-free and straight forward with Timber Bear.

Bear was understandably forward in the dressage, and Elsa struggled to contain her. Maintaining the trot was difficult when Bear just wanted to canter the whole test. She thought being asked to halt was a good opportunity to try and rear, but Elsa managed to nip that in the bud before her feet managed to leave the floor. She was grateful that the extra time she'd had to ride recently meant she had got to know her little mare's tricks a lot better, and try to keep a lid on them until they were out of the arena, and she was surprised to discover that the judge's thought she hadn't disgraced herself too badly.

"Wow, you worked hard to pull that off, didn't you?" Sophia commented from under raised brows, as they exited the arena and walked straight back to the lorry.

Elsa nodded, gratefully taking the water that Sophia handed to her on this warm day. But Sophia hadn't seen anything yet, as the real battle with Bear began as soon as the fiery chestnut laid eyes on a show jumping pole.

There was not much time between dressage and show jumping, and Elsa kept her walking around the lorry park until it was her turn to go in, desperate not to let the enthusiastic Timber Bear see the excitement that was going on in the warm up rings until the last minute. Elsa popped her over what should have been a simple cross pole to warm up, and was grateful that Sophia was on hand to put it back together as Timber Bear duly trashed it. She was too busy watching what was going on around her that Elsa wasn't sure she'd even recognised her rider had pointed her towards a jump.

Second time round and she wasn't going to make that mistake again, clearing it by a country mile, so Elsa decided to be brave and try the oxer, and again she flew over it.

"Impressive!" Sophia beamed. "She's getting better each time!"

Elsa did not want to tempt fate, and was silent until the steward called her in. With a click of her tongue, Timber Bear sprang into action. Elsa had found that the poles fell more freely when she tried to hang onto her, and tried to remember Frederick's words from when he had accompanied them at Nelson. *Frederick,* she sighed, trying to push the sudden thought of him aside. They were most unwelcome when she had a course of fifteen jumping efforts fast approaching her. She relaxed her reins, letting Bear go. She had found it easier to utilise the little chestnuts fast pace and use the whole of the grass jumping paddock, and she would easily make the time without cutting corners and risking setting her up wrong for the fence.

It worked without fail until they were three quarters round, when Bear decided it was now a race and took hold through the double, having both parts down. A sharp half halt before the next, a wide oxer, and Elsa had her back enough to clear it.

Elsa couldn't help but be annoyed at herself as she left the ring on an long rein. Why couldn't she find it in herself to ride as well as she had the day that Frederick's gorgeous blue eyes had been peeled on her? She always felt deflated that she couldn't use Bear's endless energy to their advantage. But there was no time to dwell on it as cross country wasn't far away, and Elsa had not even had time to walk the course. She had planned on doing it before dressage, but where horses were concerned things rarely ran to plan.

Sophia removed Bear's tack, and offered her some water and hay while Elsa hurried off to try and walk the course. From memory, it was quite straight forward, and as usual she didn't expect to make it round anyway. When she returned, her confidence spiked a little as she observed Sophia leading her calm overgrown pony around the lorry park, and hoped that maybe her arms would have a rest today from being yanked out of their sockets for five minutes of hair-raising galloping.

They tacked Bear up and tightened her studs. Sophia legged Elsa up into the saddle, and she attached her air jacket for extra safety. As they neared the warm-up ring, Timber Bear was already on her toes. She sprang over the practice jump like a stag, and as the starter counted her down, Bear reared her way into the start box, and exited it like a bullet from a gun.

"Come on, girl!" Elsa encouraged, crouched forward in her saddle as they cantered to the first, a simple but up-to-height log that Timber Bear cleared with ease.

"Good girl!" she beamed, patting her already warm neck as she regathered her reins and kicked on. All her worries disappeared, and she was having the time of her life - as was Timber Bear - until the mare slammed on the brakes three from home.

"For fuck *sake*!" Elsa growled, turning her away and asking for canter again. She had thought she'd had everything required to get her over; rhythm, impulsion, *determination*, but Bear obviously felt otherwise. Presented the second time and feeling Elsa's crop on her shoulder, she flew over it and they cantered up the hill with no signs of tiredness at all. She cleared the hay rack, popped the tyres, and then there was just the last.

Having not expected to make it this far, Elsa was elated and felt sure they would fly the simple roll-top with ease. But she had paid little attention to the positioning of the finish just past the lorry park. Timber Bear clocked it, and five strides out she decided she would quite like to go home now.

"No!" Elsa growled, feeling her put on the brakes. "No! *No*!" But not even a sharp smack down the shoulder with her stick could encourage Timber Bear forwards, and she kicked out in protest. It was too late for Elsa to salvage any impulsion to get over the simple fence now, and she resigned herself to another refusal. She sighed as she turned Bear around to attempt it again. Bear tried to rear; her focus now fixated on the lorries, but Elsa was expecting this and turned her sharply off balance, kicking her on before she had time to try again. They cantered a circle, and Elsa wondered whether it was even worth approaching again or calling it a day, but Bear had already regained her exuberance and she bounded up to it enthusiastically, popping over it and galloping to the finish as if she had not even noticed the lorries.

"She's so frustrating!" Elsa exclaimed as she met Sophia just through the finish, patting the little mare's lathered neck nonetheless.

"You got round, though," Sophia tried, although she felt that frustration with her. "She's improving all the time. Come on, if they were all easy we wouldn't bother doing it."

Elsa nodded, giving Bear a genuine pat as she slid from the saddle and immediately unfastened her girths. She took the saddle from her as they walked back to the lorry park. She couldn't blame Bear for any of their round, it was always up to the rider to work harder and improve and convey that through to whatever horse they sat on, to ensure they were prepared for whatever they faced them at. No matter how angry at herself she was for letting them down, Elsa's first thoughts were always for the welfare of her horse, and she quickly set about sponging her off once back at the lorry, as Sophia offered her water.

"If she wasn't fit enough and getting tired, I'd pull her up," Elsa went on, debriefing her round for her own benefit. "But she showed no signs of struggling, she just suddenly throws in the towel and switches off. She's so easily distracted."

"She's a baby as far as eventing is concerned." Sophia reasoned. "That will improve every time you come out."

"I know, I know," Elsa sighed, scraping off the excess water. "You're right, of course. But I get so annoyed at myself."

"Why don't you get her out to some clinics or group lessons," Sophia suggested.

"As if I have the time or money for that," Elsa rolled her eyes, but knew that was unkind. Sophia was only trying to help. But there was only one person who had made Elsa ride round the cross country with the determination and skill that she knew she possessed somewhere inside her, but she knew that was a no-go.

"Frederick has some coming up," Sophia grinned, as if reading her mind.

"No way," Elsa cut her off quickly, chucking Bear's sweat

rug over her quarters.

"Why not?"

"I'd be the last person he'd want there, and I wouldn't know what to say to him," she replied feebly. "I said all I could, and he wasn't interested."

"Well, you're going to bump into him at some point," Sophia told her. "You and Timber Bear might even be competing against him soon."

"Give over!" Elsa scoffed.

"I'm being serious!" Sophia declared. "Frederick's a professional, and I think the pair of you should just suck it up, clear the air and continue on a purely professional basis, to avoid the many awkward moments that are bound to come from you bumping into him at events, and allow you to attend any clinics or lessons or whatever he's hosting."

Elsa slowly nodded, and forced back the heavy lump in her throat. She didn't want a *professional relationship* with him, she wanted a personal one. And every time she tried to tell herself she was over him, she knew it was a lie. She couldn't face seeing him and gazing into those deep, blue eyes without wanting to run a mile from him yet fall into his arms at the same time.

"You still like him, don't you?" Sophia murmured quietly, as she slowly began to bandage Bear's tail.

Elsa nodded without hesitation. *It's nothing to be ashamed of,* she told herself.

"Oh, geez," Sophia rolled her eyes. "Come on, let's get boxed up and get home."

They hit the road, and covered the first few miles in silence as Sophia tapped away at her mobile phone. Eventually she looked up, and beamed across at Elsa.

"Right, that's that, then!"

"Huh?" Elsa frowned.

"Timber Bear is finding her feet now and throwing her weight around, and you need someone from the ground to tell you what you need to do, and *make* you do it. You know…a gorgeous guy, beautiful eyes, masculinity and authority shining through…" she broke off laughing at Elsa's face of fear. "Relax, it's not Frederick - I respect your wishes. But I want to treat you, Elsa, and I'm not going to take no for an answer, so I'm treating you to a clinic with Craig Ellis."

Elsa looked at her in surprise. "Really?"

"Why not?" Sophia shrugged.

Craig Ellis was a local show jumper who had competed internationally and had a protégé of students - Sophia being one of them - but it was hard to get onto his books and obtain a slice of his precious time.

"No, I can't…" Elsa faltered. She didn't deserve *this*.

"Yes, you can!" Sophia waved her mobile towards her. "Because I already text him to book you on, and he's *already* confirmed. So, no backing out. Get the show jumping nailed and I reckon she'll grow into an awesome little cross country horse in her own time. Once she calms down she'll carry herself nicely on the flat, too."

Elsa couldn't stop smiling. "Thanks so much. And I *promise* I'll pay it back."

"That's OK," Sophia shrugged, with a smile. "And no, you will not. What are friends for?"

Elsa grinned, and gave sleeping Cecil an affectionate rub.

"So, you promise you will turn up?" Sophia probed hesitantly

"I *promise*," Elsa smiled. "We will get so much out of it."

"Good. Now that you've promised; I'll inform you of the only catch." She anxiously bit her lip. "Which wasn't intentional, I may add, but it was the only availability he had."

Elsa looked at her expectantly.

"It's being held at Frederick's yard," Sophia smiled sweetly, and Elsa felt her heart fall.

Chapter Three

Timber Bear had turned into a monster by the following weekend, which Elsa put down to the sudden spell of colder weather which had crept over them, and she debated over whether she should take her.

"She's definitely a Bear today," Elsa growled in frustration at Bear's refusal to stand still to have the mud brushed from her tail. She kicked out, narrowing missing Elsa's kneecap, and she responded with a firm slap across the mare's rump. Bear jumped with a start, and turned her head to gaze at Elsa with her sulking face on.

"She's not herself," Elsa sighed.

"*Go,*" Sophia insisted. "You are not backing out, so stop looking for excuses."

And so Timber Bear was loaded up, and Elsa felt the lorry swaying as the mare's hooves struck the walls as they departed down the driveway, and she sensed it was going to be a *long* drive to the Twemlow stables.

Elsa joined the small row of parked, visiting lorries and had barely climbed from the cab before Ava was beside her.

"Hey, girl!" the Australian beamed. "Glad you could make it. And well done on your run last week!"

"Thank you," Elsa smiled. She had told Ava all about her round as soon as she had returned home, and Ava had found lots to feel positive about while Elsa was tired and struggling.

"Do you tack her up inside the lorry?" Ava asked, helping Elsa with her equipment in the tack locker. "Or you getting her out first?"

"Inside," Elsa replied, with a roll of her eyes. "She's on one this morning. Nothing is ever easy with this one."

"Even more credit to you, then," Ava smiled, taking the lead into the horse compartment.

Elsa followed. She widened the partition so that they had room to get to Bear, and she felt like a grateful spare part as Ava fussed over the highly-strung chestnut and started removing her travel rug and boots. Elsa's heart was pounding so fast, and she had no idea why she was so nervous. Whether it was the thought of mixing with the high calibre of riders that Craig's clinics attracted, or whether it was the prospect of bumping into Frederick; she wasn't sure which filled her with the most fear.

"How're things here?" Elsa asked, trying to take her mind from it as she rolled up Bear's tail bandage.

"Yea, busy!" Ava replied, and Elsa couldn't help but notice how tired she looked.

"Here, pass me that," she replied, trying to prize Bear's tack from her.

"Don't be silly," Ava replied with a gentle laugh. "You go and get yourself ready."

"But Frederick won't like it if he sees you helping me, while he's paying your wages!" Elsa argued. She was so happy to catch up with her friend, but she couldn't have her getting into trouble with her boss on her account.

"Ha, that's tough!" Ava laughed, smoothing down the saddlecloth on the chestnut's sleek coat. "I've already told him he won't be paying my wages much longer if he doesn't pull them working pupils into check."

Elsa hesitated in the door to the living area as she pulled on her jodhpurs, eager to hear more.

"Honestly, Els," Ava went on, bridling the obliging mare. "They've only been here a few days and they're already doing my head in. The guy is OK, but he's French...he has funny...*ways*. The girl? Well, don't even get me started! She is self-centred, opinionated, righteous, arrogant..." She trailed off. "Shit, I shouldn't be saying this. Walls have ears, don't they?"

"Stand your ground," Elsa smiled. "I'm sure Frederick

would rather lose them before he loses you."

"Hope so, but I wouldn't dare push my luck," Ava shrugged. "I'll keep doing what I'm told, within reason, but if that girl dares talk to me again like I'm something she's just scraped off her shoe, she's going to get a slap!"

She pulled the stirrup iron down the leather with such frustration that the noise made Bear jump, and she looked around in alarm.

"Shit! Sorry, girl!" Ava soothed her, and was quickly forgiven once she produced a mint.

Fully kitted out and as ready as she'd ever be, Elsa duly led the intrigued Timber Bear outside. She had a quick look around at her surroundings, gave a shrill whinny, and was content when the horse tied to the lorry next door whinnied back.

"I'll walk you to the outdoor jumping arena, then I better get on." Ava told her as she legged her into the saddle and adjusted her girth. "Craig is in the house drinking coffee with Frederick, so you might as well walk around and he'll be out soon."

Elsa took a deep breath and nudged Timber Bear on. She was the first one out, and the first thing she noticed was how high the show jumping course was set at. She hoped the poles were going to be lowered before she and Bear were asked to tackle them.

"Don't look so worried," Ava laughed, as they parted. "Craig is great. Smile, and good luck!"

She wondered whether Frederick might come and watch them ride, and the thought immediately made her sit straighter in the saddle. She would love to meet his eye across the rail, receive his -hopefully – approving glance.

She looked up as another horse entered the arena, a plain-looking dark bay whose tall rider's long legs wrapped around his sides and made him look small, even though Elsa thought he must be a good seventeen hands.

He nodded politely at Elsa and cut across the end of the arena to fall into step beside her. She felt her heart quicken; he oozed professionalism and she felt so inferior beside him, she wished he'd leave her alone. She stole a look at him without moving her head too much, and observed he was exceedingly handsome. Timber Bear's stride quickened as she silently observed her new friend.

"Hey," he smiled across at her. "I'm Clement."

"Elsa..." she stammered, hoping he hadn't noticed her looking, as she hissed at herself to pull herself together. "Nice to meet you."

"Likewise," he nodded, and she gazed openly at his horse. He sat so lightly, and although he barely had any contact, it carried itself so nicely under him.

"Impressive horse you have there." She told him, despite it looking plain.

"Thank you," he smiled sincerely. "He is lovely, but he is young and just finding his feet. We expect great things of him."

Elsa nodded slowly, not sure that Bear could ever be compared to him.

"Yours is a pretty little thing," he replied, eyeing Bear with something Elsa could not determine as just politeness or general interest. "Is she young?"

"Yes..." Elsa shrugged. "And no. She's eight; but she has raced since a two-year-old, only recently retired." She paused and nodded towards the course set up around the arena. "So, she is very young where all this is concerned."

"Ah, but lots of life experience," Clement smiled encouragingly. "And you cannot put a price on that. These horses are often over looked, but of course they have so much to give after racing."

"My thoughts exactly," Elsa smiled warmly, as the remaining two riders joined them.

Craig strode out a couple of minutes later, and Elsa

recognised him immediately from the equestrian magazines, and the very rare occasions that show jumping was ever shown on national television, and she suddenly felt very privileged and undeserving to be in his company. He was quite short, with thin, blonde hair, and walked slightly bow-legged. Although he hadn't officially retired from show jumping, he spent more time these days teaching than he did competing.

"So, guys!" he addressed them all. "Welcome! I want you all to spend fifteen minutes warming up as you would before jumping either at a show or at home, and then we'll all pull into the middle and introduce ourselves and have a chat through the warm up, and so on. OK?"

It was a rhetorical question, Elsa observed, as her fellow riders picked up their reins with a confident nod, she felt her world crumbling around her. She had *no* idea how to warm up for jumping to an international show jumper's standard, especially when their eyes were on her, *judging* her. Some days Bear was easy, but most days she wasn't, and Elsa was just happy if she managed to stay in the saddle.

She picked up her reins, praying that Timber Bear didn't show her up, and found her own space in the arena. She tried to block from her mind that her every move was being observed, and just get on with it.

She nudged Bear into a trot, and the mare responded with a fly-buck and a kick, desperate to show off her athleticism to her new audience, and Elsa noticed her fellow riders give her a wide berth whenever they needed to pass her.

Be a stronger rider, Elsa demanded of herself, and she put her leg on with much more meaning, pushing the mare into her bridle. She did some circles, Bear often arguing with her on the bend required, one eye always on her fellow riders so that she could follow their lead. Eventually they cantered, and Elsa expected a rodeo.

Elsa received a rodeo, and there was nothing she could do

about it. Bear launched forward on the first long side, displaying a variety of lunges and kicks and airs above the ground that made Elsa feel quite sea sick. She noticed the others watching in a mixture of awe and disgust as the feisty little mare - by some miracle - failed to unseat her. Elsa eventually managed to retrieve her head from between her knees and perform a circuit of decent canter before she had to bring her quickly back to walk before she slid helplessly from the saddle since her legs had turned to jelly.

"How to get the instructors attention?" she murmured breathlessly to Bear, as now everyone's eyes were certainly on her.

"Right, bring them in," Craig called, and while the other three stuck together, Elsa noticed that nobody wanted to stand too close to her. And while she was grateful from a safety aspect, her mare's behaviour and Elsa's inability to conquer it made her want to burst into tears. She felt sick to her stomach as Craig approached her first.

"What a cracking little mare," Craig grinned, and Elsa immediately felt herself relax a little. "She sure doesn't like being told what to do, does she?"

Slowly Elsa shook her head. Her mouth was bone dry, and she was glad that it was another rhetorical question that didn't require her to speak.

"You're Elsa, right?"

She nodded again. Good guess, considering the other three were guys.

"Sophia speaks very highly of you," he went on, "and I can see why."

Elsa felt her cheeks reddening, and she twisted a lock of mane between her damp fingers.

"Let me guess; ex racehorse?"

She nodded again. "Is it that obvious?" she croaked.

"Well, definitely a thoroughbred," he smiled, "which would be my preferred horse had I chosen to pursue the road of eventing. Speed, stamina, character, toughness."

"She's certainly got all those four," Elsa replied, and heard the gentle laugh of her three fellow riders.

"Is she always like this, at home and when you take her out to jump?" he scratched his head.

"She's always got bundles of energy," Elsa nodded. "She's not fed much and she mostly lives out. I'm learning to contain her a lot better at home, but out…well show jumping normally clocks up a cricket score. But I'm not sure if she's losing her focus because she knows the cross country is next."

Craig nodded intently. "You have a very good, secure position, so well done. We're going to try some trot poles, then canter poles, and build them up to make a grid. Everyone here will benefit from that," he told them, as he moved onto Clement.

Even though Elsa could practice trot and canter poles at home with ease, she knew that Bear would show her up as soon as she was away from home, and true to expectation, Timber Bear found trotting poles immensely exciting and refused to trot to begin with, but there were no moves that she could throw that Craig hadn't met before, and his instruction quickly had her settled into a decent rhythm. While Clement navigated the simple poles with ease, Elsa couldn't help but think his horse looked far from plain, and as Craig put up raised canter poles, he navigated them with exceptional expression. But there was something about the rider that put Elsa off a little.

She thought him rude when Craig gave him instructions and a couple of times he questioned them, but Craig appeared unperturbed. And the way Clement looked down at his fellow riders when Craig put up the grid and asked Clement to demonstrate before the other riders had their turn, Elsa wanted him to send every pole flying.

Bear had apparently had enough of showing Elsa up, and snapped her legs up tightly for each element, trying her hardest to get the striding right, that even Craig looked impressed.

"Very good," Craig told her honestly, as she and Bear flew down the grid clearing all six elements in style, the last pole standing at a good three and a half foot. "We'll leave it there with her for that one; she really tries her heart out when she buckles down." He paused, and met Elsa's eye as she pulled back into line. "Seriously, I can see she's hard work, but don't give up. She's got huge potential."

"Thank you," the words came out at barely more than a whisper, and she suddenly felt very emotional. Words like that from a highly-regarded international show jumper suddenly made the little mare's arm-wrenching antics worthwhile putting up with.

I wouldn't swap her for the world, Elsa thought, giving her a well-earned pat as Clement was plucked from the line up to demonstrate how to ride the first section of the course Craig had erected for them. His dark bay really did ooze class, and Elsa was openly gaping as they executed it perfectly and drew back into line beside her.

When she eventually looked up to the rider, she realised Clement was grinning at her. She had no desire to boost his ego any further, but she couldn't escape without saying anything.

"He really is a lovely horse," she croaked, embarrassed. "Is he yours?"

"He really is," Clement agreed, casually giving him a pat. "But unfortunately he's not mine, although I do hope to keep the ride while I am here."

She frowned, unsure what he meant. "Do you event? I'm not sure I've seen you on the circuit."

"I do," he smiled, as if he got this question a lot. "But I am new to this...circuit. Hence I hope I will be partnering Darcy to a few events. He actually belongs to Frederick Twemlow; I've recently joined him as a kind of working pupil."

"Oh, I see," Elsa felt her heart display its familiar lurch at the mention of *that* name. She'd thought Ava had said the working pupil was French? "Are you French?" she queried with a frown.

"Well observed," his dark eyes sparkled, and she felt like a fraud. He didn't sound French, but she should have guessed purely from his name. "My father is French, and I've been living there the last few years, but I was actually brought up here."

"Oh, I thought I detected the hint of an accent," she lied, and had to look away. She was useless at detecting anything like that.

"How about you?" he smiled, and she felt like he was looking down on her even more since he had name-dropped *Frederick Twemlow*.

"No, I'm not French," she frowned, thinking it a stupid question.

"I didn't mean that," he replied in amusement. "I mean, do you event, or show jump?"

"Oh! We event - well, we try," she smiled sweetly. *I'm just a groom,* she wanted to tell him, but the words stuck in her throat.

"I used to have a little horse that looked just like her," he smiled fondly. "We represented France on the Young Rider teams. We won silver at the European Championships, in fact."

"I see," she mumbled in reply, feeling like she really shouldn't be here with these people at all.

"It was a smashing little horse," he went on, but trailed off as they watched the third rider come to grief and send poles scattering everywhere, waking Bear up from her snooze.

Elsa had lots of exercises and praise to take home with her, and she was so glad Sophia hadn't let her talk herself out of coming. She walked Bear off and quickly untacked her back at the lorry, suddenly wanting to be out of here and back on the road.

"Will I be seeing you again?" Craig Ellis asked, as Elsa loaded her little mare and closed the partition on her.

She jumped, having not heard him approach, and went down the ramp to join him.

"I might be tempted to join another one," Elsa smiled, nodding eagerly. "It's been really insightful, thank you."

"No problem," he told her. "Let me help you with that ramp."

She stepped back and the pair of them easily lifted the ramp. It was fastened and she was ready to go. She hesitated. "Tell me, though," she began sheepishly. "Are most of them held here?"

"Oh, yes, as many as I can," Craig replied, as if that would seal the deal, but Elsa's face told him otherwise. "Frederick and I have been friends for years; we help each other out where we can, and the facilities here are great." He waited, but Elsa bit her lip as she stared blankly ahead. "Is that a problem?" Craig probed, bemused. Most people *loved* coming to Frederick Twemlow's plush yard.

"No, no, not at all," Elsa replied quickly, breaking herself away from her thoughts. She was surprised and even a little hurt that she had not got a look at the man in question herself, although with each day that passed she found herself with less that she wanted to say to him.

"I'd better go," she told him, wondering where Ava had got to, too. Probably held up with her ever-increasing workload, Elsa thought with a hint of sadness. She'd call her as soon as she got home, and check that all was OK. "Thanks again."

Chapter Four

"Connor *is* sound, isn't he?" Sophia looked thoughtful.

"Sound as a pound," Elsa nodded, feeling her excitement rise already. "Didn't you listen to anything Harry said the other day," she teased. "Or were you too busy gazing helplessly into his eyes?"

"Stop it!" Sophia replied coyly. "Of course I was listening..."

"And gazing helplessly into his eyes," Elsa finished for her, and Sophia couldn't even deny it. Her recent relationship with their local vet was going really well, and it had been a very silver lining to the recent cloud hanging over her yard with her horses' recent health issues that meant Harry had to regularly visit them.

"Sound enough for a run around Hastings?" she mused, as the pair of them gazed across the yard at the gelding grazing in the paddock. As they watched, a hiding pheasant took flight, putting the wind up Connor and he took off at full pelt across the paddock, bucking and kicking and squealing as he went.

"I'd say so!" Elsa laughed, and they high-fived each other like only true high school friends could.

Once he had slowed down enough for Elsa to catch him, she put him on the horse walker so that he could get his exercise in a more controlled environment. There was no way she was risking any more undue injury when their string was already so fragile.

Dusty looked out over his stall door expectantly as Elsa approached him. Dusty was a beautiful, kind horse, and Elsa had taken to him as soon as he'd stepped foot off the Twemlow lorry. As Ava had handed his leadrope over, she had told Elsa how much she would miss him, and Elsa knew that she'd meant it. She gave him a quick brush over before saddling him. He kept himself so clean that he really was a dream to look after.

His stable mate Cali kicked her stable door impatiently. She was younger and a little less experienced than Dusty, but Sophia and Elsa loved them equally. Sophia's smile was so wide every time that she sat on them, and Elsa knew they really were so lucky to have them both. Frederick had produced them both beautifully, as one would expect.

Elsa went to the tack room and flipped the switch on the back of the kettle. She took her phone out of her pocket and selected Ava's number.

"Hey!" she beamed when Ava answered. "You OK to talk?"

There was rustling, and Elsa waited. "Yea, erm…" she hesitated. "Yea, sure. Why not?"

"I can call you later, if you'd rather?" Elsa told her. "I was just having a cup of tea and thought I'd check in."

"Ah, a cup of tea!" Ava sighed. "The chance would be a fine thing."

"Is everything OK?" Elsa frowned. "Honestly, if you're busy, I can call you back later?"

"No, it's fine," Ava insisted.

"Talk to me," she probed. "What's up?"

There was another sigh and another hesitation. "Wait a sec," Ava mumbled, and Elsa waited as she listened to the rustling and footsteps, the slam of a door, and then the line was suddenly clear again.

"Sorry I didn't catch you after the clinic the other day," she told her, sounding strained.

"Or answer your phone when I called you in the evening?" Elsa smiled.

"I'm sorry, Else, I got an early night. I was exhausted." She declared. "I'm not sure how much more of this I can take!"

"What the hell has happened?" Elsa demanded gently. She

had never heard her friend speak with anything but fondness towards her job.

"Oh, it's probably nothing really," she sighed. "I'm just being over dramatic, I guess, and over sensitive."

Elsa frowned, and turned away from the noise of the boiling kettle. "It's not nothing if it is affecting you so badly." She would never use over dramatic or over sensitive as words to describe Ava.

"It's these new arrivals," she began after a moment's hesitation. "Well, one in particular."

"Clement?" Elsa frowned. "I met him at the clinic, seemed arrogant and up his own arse…"

"No, he's fine," Ava quickly cut her off. "It's the girl, *Portia,*" Ava slurred over her name with such contempt. "She's only been here five minutes, and already strutting around like she owns the bloody place. And she's *so* demanding. I already told Fred I wouldn't be her groom, but it seems she has other ideas. I'm being worked into the ground, Else, I've never felt so exhausted."

"Wow," Elsa murmured, unsure of what to say to make it better as she ran her hands through her hair. "I thought you'd been quiet the last few days, but I didn't realise how much strain you were under."

"And it's not just the work, Elsa," she went on, needing to unload on someone before she cried. "I love being busy, under pressure, and thrive on hard work, but she's such a *bitch.* She never asks you to do anything, just tells you, bossily, while she's looking down her perfect snout at you. And nothing is ever good enough. You can do something to the best of your ability, and it be absolutely fucking perfect, and she'll find fault in it," she broke off and growled in anguish. "She's *awful,* Elsa, you'd hate her, I'm sure of it."

"It does sound like I would," Elsa agreed. "Especially as she seems to enjoy making your life difficult. What does she look like?" she asked after a pause, the uneasiness of such a self-assured woman living and working in such close vicinity to Frederick making her feel uneasy. She knew it was nothing to do with her, but it suddenly mattered if she was pretty.

"Oh, *beautiful,*" Ava drawled, as if that made it ten times worse. "Well, on the outside, anyway. Flawless makeup, tonnes of money, all the latest designer gear. Looks down at you like a piece of shit, personality of a gold fish, refuses to lift a finger around the yard and isn't particularly pleasant even to her horses. Sure living up to everything I've heard about her."

"Shit, I'm sorry to hear that, Ava," Elsa told her sincerely. "What does Frederick say about it?" She flittingly closed her eyes as she forced out his name.

"He doesn't see any of it, as soon as he's about she's all fluttering eyelashes and sweet as. She's really vile, Else." Ava sighed, and Elsa really felt for her. She dread to think what would happen if someone of that character started sharing Sophia's yard, and giving Elsa orders. She'd like to think she had been best friends for so long with Sophia that she could tell it to her straight, but you could never be sure when people were reliant on something to bring in more income. Although she couldn't imagine Frederick ever needed the income so badly that he would see his Head Girl treated so badly, so he must be blinded by beauty, Elsa decided bitterly.

"Anyway, what's new with you?" Ava asked, trying to sound cheerful.

"We're off to Hastings this week," Elsa told her, unable to keep the excitement from her voice. It felt like such a long time since she'd been out to a proper event.

"Us too!" Ava squealed. "Yay, we can finally meet up at another event."

"Yup!" Elsa laughed. "I guess you'll be much busier than me, though. We're only taking Connor to ease him back into it, then next week Dusty and Cali are making their debut."

On Harry's last visit, the young vet had taken bloods from

Merlin, who on his last outing had been stressed, lethargic and simply not himself, and they suspected he had suffered some bruising in a topple on the lorry. Young Ruby had changed shape dramatically throughout the season and had subsequently suffered some back trouble from her saddle not fitting as well as it should. Although there were no immediate events lined up for either of them, at least Elsa and Sophia were feeling much more positive.

"I'm so excited for you both," Ava told her, as she knew how hard the pair of them worked, and no one deserved it more than they did. "How's the new one?"

"Candy? Sophia has taken her cross country schooling a couple of times and apparently she was *perfect;* jumped everything and flew through the water without a second glance. Sophia might get her out to school around Wellington before their event there, otherwise she'll wait until next season. She's in no hurry with her."

"The arrival of Michael Patrick's has really taken the pressure off you," Ava agreed, knowing how vital the extra horsepower had been to Sophia. "I've got to go, but hopefully we'll cross paths at Hastings? We can talk properly then?"

"Definitely," Elsa replied, sensing the need in her voice. "I'll come and find you, and I'll have time to give you a hand if you're busy?"

"Thank you," Ava told her, heartfelt.

Prepped for his travels, Connor eagerly hauled Elsa up the ramp into the lorry, his excitement evident at finally being allowed out to a party. Elsa had bathed and brushed the gelding until she could see her reflection in his sleek, dapple grey coat. They had decided that although only taking the one horse, Elsa would travel him early in the morning and spend time getting him reacclimatised to the showground, while Sophia stayed behind and schooled the youngsters at home, so that he was nice and settled in by the time she arrived later to work him in for his dressage.

Elsa's offer of help to Ava played on her mind. She did not regret it, as they would always help each other out, but Elsa's stomach churned at the possibility of bumping into Frederick again, and it was inevitable if she was grooming his horses. She was torn between the lesser of two evils of grooming Frederick's, or those belonging to his evil working pupil, if she was as bad as Ava had described. Elsa suspected she was, as Ava was not known for any over-exaggeration. She normally just said things how they were - nothing more and nothing less.

As Elsa swung the lorry around the country lanes, she couldn't help thinking that maybe Frederick wouldn't be there at all, so she didn't need to worry about avoiding him. Just because Ava was attending, it did not mean that it was with Frederick. Especially as Hasting's weren't running any big classes, she may well just be there with Clement or Portia, or their other working pupil. Ava had not mentioned it anymore, and she had seemed so stressed that Elsa hadn't liked to ask, but she couldn't wait to see her.

She turned the radio up as she hit the dual-carriageway. The roar of the engine was loud, and the passing traffic even louder. Cecil yawned and curled up even tighter, and she was certain he held his paws over his shaggy ears as she belted out a love ballad. She went to take a deep breath, ready to hit a high note - much to Cecil's disgust - and gasped. *Smoke.* She was certain she could smell smoke.

She looked fearfully to Cecil, and he confirmed her worst fears as he sniffed the air and quickly got to his feet with a deep growl.

"Fuck! *Fuck!*" she mumbled, trying not to panic as she looked for a safe place to stop. But she was running out of time, she realised as the smoke forced her to cough. It was quickly filling the cab. She switched the radio off and only then heard the extreme extent to which the struggling engine was screaming at her, and knew she had to get out. She was slowing as quickly as she safely could, desperate not to cause alarm to her precious cargo in the back. As cars passed her on the dual-carriageway road, they beeped to get her attention at the thick, black smoke billowing from her lorry.

"I know! *I know*!" she hissed, putting her hazards on and accepting she wouldn't make it to the next layby. There was no time. She screamed as the engine gave an almighty bang and the lorry cut out, and she eased onto the grass verge, unable to get completely off the fast-moving road, the suspension only cushioning the bumps a little.

Her hands were shaking as she took her mobile from her pocket and dialled 999, trying to scramble one-handed through the small cut-through into the living. Cecil followed, his hackles raised and barking furiously at the smoke that quickly surrounded them.

"Fire brigade, please!" she demanded of the operator. "And police, too. Quick - my lorry is on fire!"

"OK," the operator replied calmly. "Is anyone hurt?"

"Not yet! Please come quick!" she sobbed, unable to believe this was happening to her. "I'm on a main road. My horse is inside!"

"OK, we are dispatching the fire brigade for you now. I need you to tell me exactly where you are."

As she looked behind her, she could barely see the cab anymore it was so engulfed in smoke, and she yelped at the intensity of the fire taking hold. She couldn't escape seeing the flames lap up against the windscreen, and fear took hold of her. She desperately tried to think of the last signpost they'd passed, but her mind was whirring with the urgency of needing to get Connor safely out.

"Rosegate, I think?" she stammered. "Heading towards Hastings."

"OK, we have a motorway patrol vehicle in that area, he is going to try and locate you." The operator told her in a

calmness that no way mirrored her own. "The fire brigade are also on their way."
"I need to get my horse out!" she sobbed, grabbing for the door handle through to the horse area, as the smoke quickly filled the living. She felt her stomach fall as she realised she would have to unload her excitable horse onto a main road. Even if she got him safely out of the lorry before it became a totally blazing inferno, they would surely get hit by the fast, passing traffic?
"Someone will be with you shortly," was the last promise she heard as she shoved her phone in her pocket. She stumbled over the rugs and equipment she had thrown on the floor, the smoke thickening and clouding her view. Cecil was barking, frightened and trembling and not wanting to leave her side. Before she had even got to the door of the horse area she could hear Connor thrashing about, panicking as the smoke reached him. She couldn't believe how intense the heat was already, and she coughed, struggling for breath.
She pushed open the outside door, hoping the fresh air would clear the smoke, to be greeted by a short, balding guy reaching out to her.
"Are you OK?" he demanded. "I've stopped the traffic - you need to get out!"
"My horse!" she cried, jumping out and glad that he caught her as her shaking legs gave way. As she peered around to the back she realised in his quick thinking he had straddled his huge lorry across the two lanes to stop the traffic. People had climbed out of their cars to watch in horror as the scene unfolded before them, but no one knew what they could do to help, and left the lorry driver to it.
"I've got the ramp," he shouted, already running to undo it, as if reading her mind. "How many nags you got in there?"
"Just the one," Elsa called back, not even caring about the smoke anymore as she climbed back inside. All she could think about was getting Connor to safety.

She scrambled back through the living, over all of their gear to get to her horse. As soon as she swung open the door to him, she could see how terrified he was, his head up in the air as far as the lead rope would allow, as his legs thrashed against the sides. She tried to sooth him, desperately trying to untie his leadrope, which she would have done by now if her hands weren't shaking so much. And once she got him out onto the tarmac, what did she do then? She needed to call Sophia, to call for backup. She hit speed dial on her phone, it was on loud speaker in her jacket pocket.

"Hey, Elsa!" Sophia answered cheerfully. "Everything alright?"

"No!" Elsa cried, dropping the rope as her hands just wouldn't seem to work. "Lorry is on fire! I'm on the roadside…" she got knocked back against the wall as Connor, realising he was almost free, reared up, and her phone slid from her pocket. She saw the illuminated display, but it was just out of reach and Connor was her priority.

She could barely see a thing through the smoke, until the ramp hit the floor and the lorry driver was unfastening the partitions to get to her.

"Get it out! Get it out!" he shouted urgently. "Before the whole thing goes up!"

She could hear the sirens and see the building traffic parting for the police to reach them. She hoped they would silence their sirens before they reached her, save from scaring her already terrified horse any further. She took a deep breath, praying that Connor's lead rope stayed within the feeble grip of her sweating palms. She gave him a tug, told him she meant business.

We have to get out, she implored him. *You have to behave.*

With a snort, he bounded down the ramp beside her, and she tried with all her might to hold him and reassure him at the same time. Cecil barked up at them from the foot of the ramp, and Elsa shouted at him to be quiet. But Connor's gaze was

transfixed on the loud sirens accompanying the bright blue lights, and his whole body trembled as he refused to take the final step from the lorry.
Elsa frantically signalled for them to be quiet, her hands waving everywhere as she struggled to keep Connor contained, and they cut the noise. The officers were out of the car as soon as they parked. Cecil barked at them, threatening them not to come too close as he dashed back and forth across both empty lanes of the carriageway, snarling at anyone who tried to pass him. Elsa called him back, well aware of all the eyes upon her as half of her lorry was already engulfed in flames, but everyone just stood watching, totally helpless.
"How many more are inside?" an officer rushed towards her, readjusting his hat in what she was certain was an attempt to hide his nerves.
"None," Elsa gasped, a huge sense of relief as all four of Connor's hooves finally hit the tarmac. "No people and no animals." She paused, as a sudden thought occurred to her. "But we have gas canisters on board!"
"Is the horse injured, can you walk him away down the carriageway? There's a layby just a hundred yards further, but we won't let the traffic past until this is out and safe. We need to get you out the way, in case it blows."
"He's fine, I think," Elsa nodded, leading him around in a circle and gazing quickly over him. "Just shocked." Her limbs were on autopilot, she wasn't sure how she was still functioning.

Connor was dripping in sweat, and as his hooves repeatedly left and pounded the tarmac, she wasn't sure how much longer she could hold onto him.

"I need a bridle otherwise I'm not going to be able to hold him." She implored with the officer. "Please can you check inside?"

He cautiously approached the living door, but even from a distance Elsa could tell it was a no go. The whole thing was on fire, and she felt sick to the very pit of her stomach.

"We'll escort you up the carriageway," the officer told her, indicating to his car, and clearly keeping his distance from the highly-strung animal. "We need to get you out the way."

Her attention was stolen by more sirens and blue lights, and she prepared herself to fight with Connor. But he seemed to sense he was safe now and the fight had left him. She patted him relentlessly, telling him over and over what a good boy he was. His ears pricked, he gazed into the distance, and Elsa felt her knees trembling as she tried to lead him past the raging lorry, unsure of how much longer they were going to hold her up.

"Do you have breakdown cover? Someone will need to come and get you." The officer was talking to her, and Elsa suddenly wished for the practicality of the lorry driver to be back by her side instead.

"Yes," she replied a moment later. "But I don't have the number; it's in the cab," she sobbed as she eventually persuaded Connor past the burning lorry as the fire fighters unreeled their hose to fight it, but the cab was almost completely burnt out and she could see that there would be nothing left of it, just a black, burnt-out shell.

"We will call for someone," the other officer told her from the window as he crawled the police car alongside her, keeping himself inside the safety of it away from the horse.

"I can ring my boss, she's still at home. But how long will they take to come? Shit!" she broke off, frantically patting her pockets and finding them empty. "My phone – I dropped it in the lorry!"

She turned to the footsteps behind her, and saw the friendly lorry driver jogging to catch her. He held out her phone to her, a little battered but still working, and she clung onto it gratefully.

"Sorry, I had to move my lorry to let the emergency services through. I picked this up for you, just before the whole thing went up in flames." He told her, and she could have kissed him. "Someone called, Sophia? I told her where you were, she said she'll send help."

"Thank you *so* much," she frantically wiped her stinging eyes. "We both might be still inside where it not for your quick thinking."

"It just went up so quick; can't quite believe it myself," he rubbed his furrowed brow as they both observed the carnage behind them. He held out his arms to her. "Come here, lass."

She gratefully accepted his hug, he rubbed her arm and promised her she'd be alright now. He grabbed the rope just as Connor backed quickly into the police car, and it did not go unnoticed how the policemen cowered.

"Horse all right?" the lorry driver asked her.

"I think so, yea," she nodded. "But there's nothing can be done here anyway. He's standing and breathing so for that I am thankful."

"My wife has got horses," he told her, a shiver running down his spine despite the intense heat coming their way. "This would be her worst nightmare…and mine."

"Thank you so much for helping," she told him. "I can never repay you."

"Anyone would have done the same," he shrugged. "Is there anything else I can do to help?"

"I don't think so, thank you. I hope he'll quieten down if I can just keep him walking."

"I'll stay out of your way, then," he told her. "All the best, and good luck."

She nodded gratefully and watched him walk away, before being distracted by more sirens and blue lights behind them, and Connor threw his head up in the air with such force he almost took her with him. She tried frantically to calm him, but she couldn't determine what was shaking most from her hands or her voice, and Connor stomped all over her. She was desperate to get him away from the carriageway, despite the stopped traffic, a scared horse of his size and strength could easily get away from her, and the consequences didn't bear thinking about.

"Can you move that thing along to the layby?" the officer called to her, looking concerned.

That thing? She had just risked her life to save him, he was not just a *thing*.

"I've only got one pair of hands!" she snapped back at him. "I'm kind of struggling here; do you want to bloody take him?"

She wasn't sure how long she kept him walking up and down the length of the lay-by, but it felt like forever. Each time she asked him to stand, he tensed and tried to watch the fire-fighters pouring gallons of water onto the inferno, so she kept him walking. She wiped away the sweat from her forehead, finally letting the tears tumble down her blackened face. The police officers stayed with her - but not too close - and for that she was glad.

The officers radio beeped, stealing her attention. Through the muffled receiver she determined the officers who had the traffic stopped, were escorting a rescue lorry though to pick her up. Her sigh of relief was audible. They both turned to look down the carriageway, and sure enough blue lights were escorting - at a snail's pace - a huge lorry past the activity and flames. She squinted to read the name scrawled across the front of the familiar paintwork.

"Frederick Twemlow?" she gasped. "Ava is here!" she told Connor, patting his lathered neck as he pawed at the ground and snorted. "Ava is here!" she turned to the policeman, looking as relieved as she did that her horse taxi had arrived. "Ava is here!" she told him.

She steadied Connor as the lorry pulled to a halt before them, and looked up to meet Ava's smiling, friendly, comforting face gaze back at her. She felt her heart skip a beat as Frederick Twemlow stared briefly back instead. Were this any other situation, she had so many things she wanted to shout at him for, but they and her anger were suddenly all gone. All the time she had spent worrying about avoiding him; she had now never been so grateful to see him. He was ashen faced as he jumped quickly down from the cab. She struggled to hold back her tears as he hurried towards her, his expression full of concern. Cecil's hackles were up and he snarled, recognising the new arrival immediately.

"Leave him, Cecil," she scolded him feebly, and he whined and came to heel. "He's come to help us."

He was so glad to see her in one piece after the shock when the police had escorted him past the lorry; now that the fire had been extinguished it was just a burnt out black shell awaiting recovery. She could easily not have been standing before him - or her horse - and he just needed to hold her. He could not bear to think about how he'd be feeling had she not got out in time. He'd been swearing at being stuck in traffic when Ava called him, frantic because Sophia had been on the phone to her. Fear had rocked him when he'd finally been able to make sense of her, and it had felt surreal when the police vehicles had escorted him through the miles of queuing traffic. He could barely believe his eyes at the sight of her.

"Are you OK?" he implored, putting his arm around her and letting her sob into his shoulder. "Here, give me him." He gently prized the lead rope from her filthy hand and gave Connor a pat to let him know he meant no harm. "It's OK, Elsa," he whispered. "I'm here, it's OK."

She looked up, helplessly wiping her eyes and acutely aware that she was just smudging more thick, black soot across her face. "Where's Ava?" she craned around him, expecting to see her jump from the lorry any minute.

"It's just me," he shrugged, apologetic although not sure why. "Are you OK? Are you hurt at all?"

"No," she shook her head, wishing she could shake away her tears, too. But she couldn't help it, she was shaking like a leaf, and her bruised body suddenly stung from the scrapes she had encountered while trying to release her panicking horse inside the lorry. Her adrenaline had not allowed her to notice before, but now that Frederick was here, she didn't need to be strong anymore. "I was so scared, Frederick."

"I know," he soothed her, instinctively pulling her into his chest again, as he surveyed the blackened shell before them. "What happened?"

"I don't know," she shrugged helplessly. "One minute I was driving along happily singing, the next minute there was a bang, and it's up in smoke." She helplessly let out a strangled sob. "It was so quick; I barely had enough time to get us all out. Thank God I only had Connor."

"Please don't cry, Elsa," he murmured, instinctively wrapping his arms tighter around her. "I can't cope when you cry. I want to be able to make you stop, but if anything I think I'll make you cry even more."

"Don't flatter yourself." She fell easily into his arms. She wanted to snuggle into his shoulder and cry herself to sleep, and hope that when she woke up this had all been a horrible nightmare. But Connor tugged on the leadrope and impatiently pawed the ground, reminding her that this was very much a real situation.

He took in a deep breath of her scent. Her hair smelled like coconut once past the bonfire smell, and he recognised a hint of perfume underneath the sweat and soot. The smell of burning rubber and fuel was overwhelming, and he really felt for her. She had black smears across her face, her loose hair clung to her face with sweat, but he still thought she looked beautiful, and he was so relieved she was safe. "Come on," he tenderly kissed her blackened forehead. "Let's get him loaded."

"Do you think he'll load?" her eyes widened in panic. "Wouldn't blame him if he never wanted to go inside a lorry again."

"They are surprisingly resilient to these sorts of things." He squeezed her shoulder, not wanting to let her go. "We'll get him loaded," he insisted. "Then once we get to Hastings he can settle in his stable and a vet can check him over."

She took hold of Connor's leadrope while an officer assisted Frederick with the ramp and partitions. Whinnies sounded from inside, and Elsa felt Connor relax at the realisation that he was no longer alone, and with his head held high he whinnied back and pawed the ground.

Frederick stepped back, ready for her, but Elsa was frozen to the spot. *What if it happens again?* The thought filled her with fear, and a cold shiver ran down her spine. *What if next time I am not so lucky?*

"He trusts me, every time he follows me up that ramp." She mumbled, realising they were watching her expectantly. "The least I can do is keep him safe."

"He still trusts you," Frederick murmured, coming to her. "And it was you that led him to safety."

Her hands were still shaking as he easily prized the leadrope from her. He patted the geldings neck, dripping with sweat, to soothe him.

I'm a friend, Frederick told him. *You can trust me, and I'm going to get you out of here.*

Connor nudged him in the chest, as if to tell him he was eager for this to happen, and Elsa bent down and gathered her scruffy dog in her arms as Frederick turned Connor towards the waiting ramp, and the big gelding walked straight inside without any hesitation.

Elsa breathed the biggest sigh of relief and she just wanted to crumple to the floor and let the tears flow now that they were safe. But she needed to be strong. A policeman approached her, but Cecil barked and snarled at him and he quickly backed up.

"Does she need medical assistance?" the policeman turned helplessly to Frederick, concerned but not getting too close. "Maybe it's the fumes?"

"She'll be fine," Frederick insisted, watching silently as she placed her filthy, scraggly dog in the immaculate living area of his luxurious lorry. "Thank you for your assistance today."

"And you, too," the policeman nodded. "Lucky you were passing, eh? We should be able to get this cleared up quickly and the road reopened. We'll be in touch about the lorry."

"I'll let her know," Frederick nodded, shaking his hand. He wondered why Elsa hadn't reappeared from the side of the lorry, and he went round to look.

She leant back against his lorry, knees bent and face in her palms, and he felt a piece of his heart float away to join her. He watched her for a moment before he went to join her.

"He's safe, Elsa," he murmured, gently removing her hands from her face, and holding them tightly in his against his chest. "He's happily eating his hay and making friends with my lot, like nothing has happened. You're safe, Cecil is safe. It's going to be OK, so let's get out of here."

She nodded, squeezing her eyes shut in an attempt to stop the tears. She wondered if her heart rate would ever return to normal. "I know, but we were so close to not being OK. It was terrifying, Frederick."

"I can imagine," he replied, "but you mustn't think like that."

She looked so fragile, like she would fall down and smash into a thousand pieces at any moment, and he couldn't bear it. Instinctively he scooped her up into his arms and carried her along the lorry, easily as if he carried her around every day. She'd no idea how he lifted her, but she remembered the magnificent, strong body that lay under that shirt.

He lifted her up into the passenger seat of the lorry. He didn't want to let go of her but they needed to get going. She clung to his shirt, noticing how filthy she had made him as he gave her a final hug. She felt so safe in his arms, and she let out a gentle sigh as she sank back into the leather seat.

"Thank you," she whispered, not daring to open her eyes

and stare into his, she kept them firmly closed.

"Shhh," he soothed, gently trailing his hand down her cheek.

She felt cold once his touch had left her, and she shivered. Her t-shirt was wet with sweat, and she felt filthy. She couldn't wait to get into the shower and wash away every feeling and scent of smoke and fire. She heard the click of her door shutting, waited for the click of the driver's door opening, and then sensed him beside her again.

Her head was pounding, and she put her hands to her ears and squeezed her eyes shut to try and block everything out. She was only vaguely aware of the engine roaring to life and the smooth ride as he eased the lorry forward onto the carriageway.

Chapter Five

When Elsa opened her eyes, she took a moment to realise where she was. She stretched out, and surveyed the blonde haired beauty sitting beside her, staring at the road ahead of him. They were off the dual carriageway, and driving a main country road that Elsa didn't recognise at first. Cecil stretched out on the cushion of the cut-through behind her, his tail wagging when he looked at Elsa, quickly ceasing and turning to a snarl when his gaze flickered to Frederick. She patted the seat beside her, and he eagerly jumped down to join her, his head in her lap as if he couldn't quite figure out what had happened but was just glad that they were all safe.

"Why are you driving?" she eventually asked.

"How do you mean?" Frederick frowned, briefly turning to look at her.

"Driving the lorry," she repeated, remembering how she had liked accompanying him while he was driving, because she could gawp shamelessly at him without him noticing while he had to keep his own eyes on the road.

"What am I doing driving my own lorry?" he repeated, amused.

"Well, yes," she shrugged. "Ava always drives it. When I saw the lorry coming I..." She trailed off, and turned to look out of the window.

"You hoped it was Ava?" he finished for her.

"Well, I *thought* it would be Ava," she replied. "I wasn't going to say I *hoped*." She fought away fresh tears, thinking that right now was the perfect time to have it out. "Do you know how many times I've *hoped* I'll bump into you, wished I could see you? Wished that you would just answer my call, or - even better - *call me*?"

"Let's not talk about that now," he murmured, not taking

his eyes from the road.

She'd thought she could stop caring about him - forget about him even - but his touch had ignited feelings within her that she had done her best to eliminate. She realised not for the first time that she had helplessly failed.

"Let's not ever talk about it, shall we?" she retorted. "Let's just carry on avoiding each other at all costs."

"If that's what you want," he said quietly.

"Of course it's not what I want!" she cried, her frustration with him as raw as ever.

"Well, at least I know you are OK now," he replied a moment later, with a wry smile.

"Huh?" she glared at him.

"Elsa is back," he told her. "The real Elsa, the fighting Elsa. You had me worried back then."

He knocked her off guard, but she realised that he always did. She never really knew where she stood with him, and even when she thought she knew him, she found him impossible to read.

"Why were you so nice to me, if you don't care?" she murmured.

"*Care*?" he slammed his fist down on the steering wheel, making her jump. "For fuck sake, Elsa!" he shook his head in disbelief. *How could she be so stupid? How could she think he could ever stop caring?* "You have no idea, do you?"

"How am I meant to have any idea, if you don't bloody talk to me?" she hissed, making Cecil bark, and Frederick regarded him suspiciously.

He couldn't bear to look at her, because just the sight of her broke him down. He wanted to turn around right now and take her straight back home to the comfort of his house. He wanted to be *nice* to her - that thing she found so difficult to understand - for the rest of their days, but they were not compatible. She didn't need him, for a start, she was strong enough on her own and he'd only bring her down.

"How are Cali and Dusty?" he asked her casually.

"*What?*" she gaped at him, incredulous. She wanted to reach across and shake him, make him look at her and see into her eyes. Properly *see* what he was doing to her. "Is you reminding me what you did for us with Michael Patricks, your way of rubbing salt in an already sore wound?"

"No, of course not," he frowned. "I was merely asking how they were. They are nice horses; I miss them."

She went to speak, but she felt the lorry slowing and she realised they were here. They pulled into the show ground, and Frederick parked the lorry in silence. She knew she shouldn't have snapped, after everything he *had* done for her, but she wouldn't apologise, either. Even when the engine switched off, neither of them moved. Elsa didn't want to ever climb from the cab, to ever leave his company, despite how hostile it was. She just wanted things to be back to how they were, when they had shared their fleeting special moments that she knew would be ingrained in her memory forever.

"We'll get the vet to check him over," Frederick told her softly, breaking her from her wayward thoughts.

"Cali and Dusty are fine," she whispered. "Thank you for asking."

Slowly, he nodded. "It's understandable if Sophia doesn't want to ride him today, so I can get Ava to run you both home. I'll go find the vet," Frederick told her, his hand already on the door handle, and there were no words she could think of quick enough to stop him.

So, this is it, she told herself. *Another chance wasted.* She watched him leave, and she wanted to collapse into a heap of tears. One look at Cecil told her to pull herself together. His quiet but ever-present snarling had ceased as soon as Frederick exited the cab. He was such a wise dog, why didn't she just listen to him and his evident dislike, and shove Frederick Twemlow firmly from her mind, once and for all?

She sat rooted to her seat, wondering if her legs would hold her up when she jumped from the cab. She felt so drained; she wished Frederick's strong arms were still here to be wrapped around her. Ava's presence at the passenger window broke her from her thoughts. She had swung open the cab door before Elsa even had a chance to gather her senses, and thrown her arms around her friend.

"Bloody hell, Elsa! Look at the state of you!" she declared, her voice muffled in Elsa's hair. "I'm so glad you're OK, I was so worried. I've been looking out for you ever since Fred said he was on his way to get you."

"Oh, Ava!" Elsa sobbed, fresh tears flowing. "I was so scared. It was awful."

"I can only imagine," Ava soothed her. "Come on, let's get you out, and Connor. You can have a shower and freshen up, and I'll get you a cup of tea."

"The good, old, trusty cup of tea, eh?" Elsa gave a small smile.

"It'll sort you right out, I promise!" Ava told her with a laugh, and climbed back down from the cab.

Cecil jumped eagerly outside, and looked up at her expectantly. Elsa had no choice, and she reluctantly climbed down. Once the ramp was down, she was relieved to see Connor's ears pricked as he gazed at her over the partitions, seemingly none the worse for wear after the mornings events.

"We don't have a stable," Elsa suddenly realised. "We were only bringing Connor anyway, and our times were quite close together; we thought he could just stay on the lorry."

"That's OK, you can have one of ours," Ava smiled.

"You sure?" Elsa frowned.

"Of course. I would have let you anyway, but Fred already offered one up."

Connor strolled down the ramp and had a look around him, seeming to have enjoyed his trip in the plush lorry. Elsa peeled off his filthy and wet travel boots and chucked them on the floor. They were so trashed, she suspected he'd never be wearing them again.

"We're on the furthest block of temporary stables," Ava told her, taking his leadrope before she could object. "I'll get him settled while you take a shower. Come and find us when you're ready."

Elsa watched them leave before stepping gratefully into the living compartment. Despite the cosiness of the shower and the lukewarm water that soon ran out, she thought it was the most welcoming shower she had ever taken. She lathered herself with a bountiful supply of Ava's shower gel and watched as black water swirled down the plughole. Her now clean skin was evidently bruised and battered, but she could deal with that. She was safe, as was her horse and dog, and that was all that mattered. At least their lorry could be replaced.

She located Ava's clothes - easy when they were scattered throughout the lorry - and pulled on a pair of jeans and fresh t-shirt, glad that they were near-enough the same size, and went to find her horse.

Connor quickly settled and was tucking into a haynet, making new friends with his neighbours through the metal grills that separated the stalls. Although the vet examined him and declared him fit and well, Sophia had sensibly withdrawn him, as neither horse nor rider would be in the right frame of mind after their morning trauma.

While Frederick would be competing all day, his young working pupil had almost finished his third ride, and Ava was planning to take him home once Frederick had finished with his first two, which meant there would be room on the lorry for Connor, too.

"How come Frederick was driving?" Elsa asked Ava quietly, as she helped tack up a young gelding who insisted on trying to trample all over the pair of them. "I thought it would be you."

"We're running two lorry loads today," Ava told her. "We

brought the first lot over together, then I stayed with them and he went back for the second."

"Short of grooms?" Elsa asked from under raised brows.

"As ever," Ava confirmed. "Especially if the new resident witch scares them all away. So you know that job offer I'm always trying to tempt you with..."

"No way," Elsa quick cut her off, gazing in the direction of Frederick. "If I'd ever thought about it before, I definitely wouldn't be now. Plus, there are no witches at Sophia's, resident or otherwise."

"Why does it matter that it was Frederick?" Ava asked a moment later, making Elsa pause from fastening the tendon boots. She stood up, and met Ava's eye as she plaited his tail.

Ava waited, but Elsa didn't speak, just stood staring at her biting her lower lip.

"I mean, honestly, why does it matter?" Ava went on with a shrug. "So, you went out together a few times, and slept together, so what? Either there's still something between you, feelings and emotions that neither of you can talk about and it's making it awkward. Or you'd both laugh it off as one of those things, and merrily go your separate way behaving as adults, because you know you're going to be bumping into each other all the time."

"I would like to think we are taking the moving on like adults route," Elsa told her, crouching back down to fasten the last boot, and hide her face from her friend's scrutinising stare.

"I think I'd disagree," Ava told her. "Neither of you are behaving maturely about it, Elsa."

"He's ready," Elsa refused to meet her eye as she stood up, and instead turned away to let herself out the stall. "I'm going to get some chips."

There was a queue at the catering van, and even though Elsa had no horses she had to rush off to prepare, she was impatient none the less.

"Ah, we meet again," came a familiar voice behind her. "I

believe you're the one to blame for leaving me with the ghastly Christine Forrester's horses."

"I'm sorry?" she spun around, not in the mood for small talk. Clement gazed at her, his thick dark hair flopping against his forehead. He was tall and lean, and he towered over her.

"Sorry, that was my poor attempt at making a joke to break the ice," he looked embarrassed when she didn't respond.

She glared at him. Did he not have *any* idea how dearly she wished Christine Forrester hadn't taken her beloved Nobby from her. Joking or not, she hadn't the energy to put him straight.

"I heard about your awful start today," he told her sincerely.

"Hasn't everyone?" she snapped, and immediately felt bad. But she didn't want to have to relay the story again; she just wanted to be able to forget about it.

"Yes. You look like you could do with cheering up." He hesitated, wishing he could start again."How about I buy you a drink?"

"I'm only getting a can of coke and a scoop of chips - an eventing grooms staple diet," she shrugged, turning away as she gathered her order up from the counter.

"I meant later," he told her, blocking her way.

"I know," she croaked, staring at the floor. He seemed nice, and he seemed genuine - if a little arrogant - but weren't they all? And maybe she would have liked to have gone for a drink with him, were he not employed by Frederick. But she had no intention to get involved in any sort of triangle, while the only one who was always on her mind was his boss.

"Well, let me buy your chips and coke." He tried again, wondering what she found so offensive about him. Her look of fury had not gone unnoticed when he mentioned Nobby, but was she really still holding that against him? "Let me say sorry about the horses?"

"Honestly it's fine. There are no hard feelings." She told

him, feeling guilty. Of course it wasn't just the horse, but there was no way he could even begin to comprehend her situation. "If anything, we got the better deal." She tried not to look at him, to not notice how good looking he actually was, but she still observed his dark hair, his thin, attractive face with its gentle stubble.

"Maybe another time, then?" he prompted, and as Elsa met his eye she noticed the hurt and confusion that flickered across his face.

She wanted to nod, but she prevented herself, remembering how awful her last romantic conquest had panned out. She hesitated, staring helplessly at the floor as she dragged her toe through the short grass. She went to leave, but Clement's hand lightly on her arm stopped her. He took a pen from his coat pocket, and gently prized a napkin from her grip of food. He folded it over and leaned against the food counter as he scribbled down his number.

"I can sense you are not going to give me your phone number," he gave a gentle smile. "But if you change your mind about the drink, or fancy dinner, give me a call. I would love to join you for dinner one night, and maybe you could even show me around my new local area?"

She wished it were a rhetorical question, and she wouldn't come across as so rude in her silent response. She did not move. She wanted to take the napkin from him, to tell him now she would happily take him up on his offer if only for friendship, but also desperately didn't want to get involved. But his dark eyes searched her, and he gently tucked the napkin back between her chips and can. The only eyes she wanted romantically roaming her were gorgeous, soft and blue.

"See you around," she mumbled, hating herself, and she turned and left, feeling his eyes burning into her back with every stride she took.

Elsa shared her chips and drink with Ava, in between

getting horses ready and handing them over to their rider, and taking them back and cooling them off. It was a busy morning, and Elsa was grateful as it gave her little time to reflect on her horrendous beginning to the day.

"Hold this one for me, will you?" Ava passed her a bay gelding's reins, and fastened his girths. Elsa waited for her to take him back, but she started to walk away.

"Where's he going?" Elsa called after her. "The working pupil?"

"Oh no," Ava smiled sweetly. "He's for Frederick; you can hand him to him. I just need to go and get one from the show jumping."

His breath caught when he saw her. She had showered and changed her clothes since he had picked her up this morning - probably indulging in the facilities of his lorry if he knew that Head Girl of his - and still she looked perfect. She gathered the gelding's reins in one hand and stood in front of the saddle, ready to give him a leg-up and see him on his way.

"I appear to have a new groom," he hesitated.

"Just earning my lift home," she replied, careful not to meet his eye.

He stood watching her intently. She sensed him about to speak, but he stopped himself and ran his tongue along his lower lip. His ocean blue eyes searched hers, and put her on edge.

"Please, Frederick, *stop*," she breathed.

"Stop what?" he murmured.

"Stop *looking* at me like that," she sighed, her heart threatening to pound right through her chest. "Unless you intend on doing something about it." Her confusion at his actions tormented her.

He slowly nodded, but still he did not move.

"Do you want this bloody leg-up, or not?" she snapped, Ava's earlier words about their behaviour, playing on her mind.

Slowly, Frederick raised his shin to her, and she legged him up into the saddle. He didn't look at her again as he found his own stirrups and in the blink of an eye had walked the gelding away. All that Elsa could do was stare helplessly after him, and wish that the sight of him did not fill her with butterflies and such emotion.

Ava gave her a knowing smile as she returned. "Well?"

"Please do *not* put me in that situation again, Ava."

"I've no idea what you're talking about."

"Ava!" came a demanding screech along the row of stables. "Ava!"

They both turned in the direction of the screech, as a perfectly turned out creature waltzed towards them.

"Where is my horse?" she demanded. "You were supposed to have it ready for me *now*!" She glared at them from underneath perfectly shaped eyebrows that accompanied a perfectly shaped face.

It? Elsa's eyebrows rose sternly, and suspected that this new arrival could only be Portia. She suspected that if she actually stopped sneering at them, and instead smiled, she was quite stunning. But she glared at them with such contempt, her leather-gloved hands resting on her slender hips, her tailored show jacket hugging her tiny waist. Her breeches were bright white, and there was barely a speck of mud on her long, black, polished leather boots with their diamante encrusted tops. Elsa very much doubted she polished them herself; she looked the type that would have a maid for things like that.

Elsa watched Ava sigh, and her heart broke for her. Her friend looked thoroughly beaten.

"This one needs to be ready first, for Frederick." Ava tried to maintain her calm, nodding towards an occupied stable.

"Well, he won't mind waiting," Portia replied, waving her hand dismissively. "So, saddle mine first."

Ava didn't move, and she and Elsa gaped at her.

"*Please,*" Portia snarled sarcastically, as if she really shouldn't have to worry about her P's and Q's with the *groom*.

Ava cleared her throat, refusing to back down. "Last time I looked, Frederick paid my wages, so you'll have to wait." She folded her arms defiantly across her chest.

"And last time *I* looked," she hissed. "*You* were the travelling groom! So saddle my horse...*now*!"

"Or, you could send for your own groom to do it?" Elsa suggested.

"Excuse me?" she glared at Elsa. "Who on earth are you?"

"Ava's assistant for today," Elsa couldn't conceal her smile. *An assistant who is not going to do what she's told by you,* she wanted to add, but stopped herself.

"Well, you can saddle my horse then," she snapped. "Off you go…chop, *chop*!"

Elsa didn't move. "Don't you *dare* talk to me like that," she kept her voice level. "Is this how you treat people in the show jumping world? Because that's not how we treat people around here."

She glowered at the pair of them in absolute disbelief that they weren't moving, and even more so that they dared to answer her back.

"You're hardly busy," she snarled.

"Come on, Ava," Elsa tugged her away before claws came out. "Let's go and *busy* ourselves preparing Fred's next horse."

"This is not the last you'll hear about this!" she jabbed her pointed finger towards Ava, and Elsa silently dared her to touch her. There was no way this skinny little thing stamping her feet before them would ever be a match for the petite yet stout, hard-working Australian.

"Wow," was all that Elsa could say as they strode down the aisle, out of earshot.

"She really is something, isn't she?" Ava said, stopping outside the stall of a big chestnut gelding.

"Well, thinks she is, at least," Elsa replied, instinctively picking out a body brush from the grooming box. "How on earth do you put up with that?"

"It's getting tiring, I can tell you," Ava sighed, sitting down on the tack trunk. "My patience is definitely wearing thin."

Elsa slowly nodded; she could quite believe it. "You're a much better person than I am, to have lasted this long without saying anything."

"I need this job, Else," Ava ran her hand through her hair, and looked thoughtfully at her. "OK, well I don't. I guess I could give her a piece of mind, quit my job on principle or probably get the sack, and I could find another job easily, here or back home, which would probably please my mother...but they're *my* horses, Elsa. Why should I give them up because I can't tolerate a spoilt brat for a few months? Nowhere else in the world would be *my* yard, with *my* Fred - despite what you may think of him - *my* routine and reputation, *my horses...*" she trailed off, and Elsa could see the hurt in her eyes.

"I get that," she sat down beside her. "Of course I do, but you've changed since she's been around. You've lost your spark, your energy, your ability to always look on the bright side of life. You shouldn't have to put up with one single person doing that to you. Not when you work bloody hard and Fred would be a fool to let you get pushed out."

They sat in silence for a moment, neither of them wanting to get to their feet again. They hadn't stopped all morning. But tack was ready to be packed, and Ava reached out for a sweat sheet dumped on the floor and tangled with hay and straw, she shook it out before folding it neatly away.

"Shit like this gets on my tits!" she spat. "That awful cretin will *not* tidy up after herself."

Elsa bit her lip as she watched her. She wanted to tell her she needed to talk to Frederick, but hadn't Ava been saying those exact same words to her for the last few weeks?

She sighed. *Frederick*. He would be back soon, his dreamy

blue eyes looking for his next horse.

"Is this one up next?" she nodded towards the chestnut, and Ava nodded.

"I can get him ready, if you need to go assist Frederick?" she offered.

"It's OK," Ava smiled. "Fred's got Daisy assisting him. He's keen on her."

Elsa looked up sharply. She hated the way that the mention of any female name alongside Frederick's made her feel uneasy. Her turmoil did not go unnoticed on Ava.

"Keen as in she gets on with her job and she's bloody good at it; Fred likes that." Ava told her.

Slowly, Elsa nodded. "Of course." *It's none of your business!* The voices in her head reprimanded her.

The chestnut was groomed and saddled in no time, and prized away from his haynet to be taken to his rider.

"He's the last one, then we'll be off," Ava told her as she led him away. Elsa waited behind and began packing the tack lockers and bandaging the first ones to be travelling.

"He keeps looking at you," Ava mentioned later as they packed up a tack box, when Clement must have strolled past them for about the fifteenth time. "He looks like a little lost puppy."

"I'm not interested," Elsa replied.

"Why not?" Ava's brows rose in surprise. "He's gorgeous."

"I know, and don't get me wrong, I wish I was, but…" she trailed off.

"Frederick?" Ava finished for her. It was more of a statement than a question.

Elsa sighed. "Has he ever…you know…mentioned me?"

Slowly Ava shook her head. "But he's not likely to, to me, is he?" she added quickly, seeing her friend's hurt. "What did you talk about earlier?"

"Nothing much," Elsa admitted. "I was a little in shock, I think, at the whole thing."

"I'm not surprised," Ava replied, thinking the whole event had been the stuff of nightmares. "You did very well. I'm not sure I would have been so practical."

"Oh, you would have," Elsa argued. "Instinct just kicks in, doesn't it? And you do whatever you can when you are faced with your prized possessions burning to a crisp in front of you, if you don't act fast."

There was silence. Elsa felt fresh tears threatening as her mind replayed over the horrendous events of the morning, and she fiercely willed them away.

"Frederick was very good, though." Elsa murmured, as if that would make her feel any better.

"I can imagine he would be very practical in times of a crisis," Ava gave a small smile. She imagined were she ever unfortunate enough to be alone in a burning lorry, she would like practical, quick-thinking, *brilliant in a crisis* Frederick to be the one to come to her rescue, too.

Chapter Six

Elsa was retrieving Timber Bear from the horse walker when the unfamiliar lorry screeched to a halt outside the old dairy farm gate, only clocking their yard at the last minute.

"Not expecting anyone, are you?" she asked Sophia, eyes raised.

"Nope," Sophia replied, stopping beside and dropping her haynet to the floor as the pair of them watched the lorry carefully navigate the tight turn into their yard. It drew to a halt before them, neither of them recognising the dark-haired woman that drove it, who jumped down from the cab.

"Here OK?" she beamed across at them. "Heck, you can move it wherever you want; I'm sure you're much better at reversing the bloody things than I am!"

Sophia and Elsa didn't move, just stared at her in confusion. She was probably in her early thirties, petite and with a round face and straight dark brown hair that was tied back into a pony tail. She looked from one to the other, and frowned.

"Fred told you I was coming, right?"

Elsa felt her heart fall. *Frederick*. Why could she never seem to get away from him?

"No," Elsa replied through gritted teeth. "Have you come to pick up Michael Patricks horses?" They were the only ones she could think of, whom Frederick would have influence over. She ran a hand through her caramel hair in disbelief that her nightmare could relive itself so soon. "I can't believe Michael didn't tell us."

"What are you chatting about?" the older woman asked. "I'm Clement's groom. I'm dropping off his lorry for you to use until you sort yourselves a replacement."

"You're *what*?" Sophia gaped.

"Fred insisted," she shrugged. "He already has two, so

Clement won't be short of transport; he can borrow one of them. He said you're to keep it as long as you need," she paused as she scratched her head. "Can't believe he didn't tell you, though."

"No way!" Sophia quickly insisted, as it began to sink in. "We *cannot* accept this. Please get back in that cab and take it away."

"No way," she held her hands up in protest. "Clement gives my orders, and now…unluckily for us both, Fred gives his. If you have a problem with it, take it up with one of them. I'm just the middle woman."

She looked relieved as a familiar car pulled into the yard. "Oh, look! My lift home is here already!"

"Ava!" Elsa shouted, as it pulled to a halt. "You make sure this lorry goes back, right *now*!"

"No way!" Ava smiled innocently as she wound down the window. "Nothing to do with us. Would love to stop, but I've got to get Daisy home. Clement is a slave driver; not at all like Fred! I'll catch up with you soon, yea?" She gave an enthusiastic wave, and as Daisy settled into the passenger's seat, Ava's foot was to the floor and they were away before Elsa could reach them.

"I can't possibly accept this," Sophia spun to face Elsa, her hands on her hips. "There is no way I can be indebted to Frederick, or Clement. *You* will have to call Frederick, tell him to send them straight back to take it away. Or we'll drop it back at his yard…*asap*!"

"Me?" Elsa repeated, agape. "*We*?"

"Yes, *you*," Sophia insisted. "You've been looking for an excuse to talk to him!"

"No, I haven't!" Elsa retaliated, but she could feel her cheeks reddening.

"Well, call Clement, then?" Sophia changed tact. "You must have *his* number?"

"Oh, must I?" Elsa retorted. "And why might that be?"

"Well, haven't you?" Sophia tried to hide her smile. The puppy dog eyes Clement had been making at her at Hastings had been the talk of the lorry park, and Sophia had heard about it from several reliable sources.

"Yes," Elsa mumbled.

"Well, there you go, then!" Sophia beamed, triumphant.

Elsa waited until Sophia was up on board Cali, and she had a quiet moment, before locating Clement's number and hitting the *Call* button. It rang for some time, and for a brief moment Elsa thought luck was going to be on her side and she'd be able to escape by just leaving a message.

"Hello? Clement speaking," he sounded out of breath.

"Ah...hi...hello," she stammered, closing her eyes at how ridiculously and unnecessarily nervous she suddenly felt. "It's Elsa."

"Ah, Elsa..." he purred. "Finally."

"Finally?" she mumbled. "Listen, this is just a quick call, as I am incredibly busy. Sophia insisted I call you to tell you we will be bringing your lorry back immediately. It's a very kind and generous offer, but one that we cannot accept."

"It was nothing to do with me," Clement insisted. "Fred was adamant that I use his and lend mine out. He's my boss now, you'll have to take it up with him. It's out of my hands. But if you feel like thanking me, you could always join me for that drink?"

"If it's nothing to do with you, I've no reason to thank you, have I?" she retorted, and she immediately ended the call.

Shit! What did I just do? Her reaction had been totally rude and unnecessary, and not at all like her. She felt awful and wished she hadn't let her nerves get the better of her. She immediately found his number and hit the call button, but this time he did not answer, and she could not form the words together to leave a message.

"He won't accept it back," she told Sophia. "He said it was Frederick's doing, and I'm to call him. Which I am *absolutely not,* by the way," she added quickly, before Sophia could make any more demands of her. "Not even if you offered to quadruple my salary, would I call him, OK?" She gave her boss a dark look, and strode off to resume her yard duties.

"Guess we might as well use it, then!" Sophia shouted happily after her.

Having known her for so many years, Elsa could tell Sophia was more nervous than usual about their impending stay away trip to Wellington. Campaigning Michael Patrick's horses was a massive step up for the both of them. Sophia had never been fully entrusted by an independent owner before who wasn't already a family friend. She had everything to play for; if Michael didn't like what he saw, he could take his horses away the next day and they would be back to square one. With all the turmoil their yard had suffered recently, Elsa couldn't think of anything worse.

They had decided against taking any of Sophia's other horses, so that Michael and his charges could get her full attention. Also she didn't wish to over-compete any of her horses and risk injury, especially when her string was already so fragile.

Elsa spent extra time turning them out. Michael Patricks could turn up to see them at any moment, so she wanted them looking immaculate for when he did. Although he didn't call into the yard very often, Sophia was in regular contact with him through telephone calls, and Elsa often stood and recorded bits of schooling sessions or jumping lessons on her phone to send to him later. He loved seeing and hearing about his horses' progress, and was very excited to see them out at the weekend. Elsa thought they couldn't have wished for a nicer owner, but the fact that she had Frederick to thank for it still weighed her down.

The drive to Wellington was smooth and comfortable and flew by, Clement's lorry being much more modern and nicer to drive than Sophia's previous older model. The seats were leather, and Elsa had covered the passenger seat with a clean throw before she'd allowed Cecil to climb up onto it. The only thing to dampen her spirits was the persistent rain that insisted on falling. They had waited with baited breath for the announcement that Wellington would indeed be running, the ground staff pulling out all the stops to ensure the course and grounds were up to scratch for the competitors. Elsa was so glad they hadn't cancelled, even while she was waiting stationary at the entrance, ready to be towed onto the lorry park. It felt like so long ago that she'd left home, when she was finally parked and ready to unload into the deep mud.

Elsa quickly located her stabling, and they were the last in the outside row of temporary, plastic green stables assembled on a field that was holding up much better than the lorry park, despite the rain. She chucked some shavings in and filled the water buckets before unloading her charges.

"Hey, babe!" Ava called as she passed, her arms stacked with rugs. "Barbie at ours tonight," she told her with a smile, running off again before Elsa had a chance to decline.

But Elsa had already decided she would not decline, because despite her discomfort of bumping into Frederick, she had been thinking about it a lot over the past week and knew that Ava was right. They were adults that had parted company, and they needed to move on respectfully. She couldn't stand living in fear of seeing him, or talking to him, or even of having feelings towards him still, because - unless she changed career - she would spend the rest of her days living in fear. She wanted to enjoy herself; she wanted to have a beer with everyone else and enjoy being away at shows again.

Elsa had just reached her lorry when she observed Clement; his hands thrust in his pockets and head down against the drizzle as he strolled purposely across the lorry park. He was long-legged and covered the ground easily. She took a deep breath, and before she could talk herself out of it, she chased after him.

"Hey!" she called nervously, as she almost caught him up.

He stopped and turned with a frown.

"I thought...maybe...you'd let me get *you* that drink. Later?" She shrugged, a nervous bite to her lip. "Peace offering?"

"It's OK," he replied coldly. "I don't need sympathy drinks." He turned away, but she gently grabbed his arm, stopping him.

"I never expected that you did. How about a thanks for letting us borrow your lorry drink?"

"Not necessary, that was all Frederick's doing." He began walking away. "Maybe you should thank him?" he shouted back over his shoulder.

"OK!" she jogged to catch up with him. "Maybe you would like an I've-been-a-totally-unnecessary-bitch drink?"

He stopped and turned to face her, and she didn't realise she had been holding her breath until she released it when he finally broke into a smile. "I don't think I've ever tried one of them before."

"Well, let me introduce you," she winked. "They're surprisingly tasty."

"I'm sure they are." He murmured as his eyes searched hers.

"My lorry, later?" she offered, stumbling over the use of *my*. "Sorry, I can't offer much more," she shrugged, embarrassed.

"Sounds great," he nodded. "After all, I hear you have quite a nice little lorry that has got an exceptionally comfy sofa and a working TV. Maybe even some wine chilled in the fridge?" he teased.

"Ah," she stopped him, smiling sweetly. "It was all sounding fine up until the wine, but I must confess I've already drunk it. It was lovely, if it's any consolation. And don't worry, I will replace it by the time your lorry is returned."

"Worry not," he laughed. "I was sorry I came across as being so rude; I'm not in the best of moods today and I shouldn't have taken it out on you."

"I was the one that came to apologise," Elsa replied, and broke off. "Is it anything I can help you with?"

He gave it a thought for a brief second, his eyes glazing over her, before slowly shaking his head. "No, just one of those things."

"Well, I actually need to hack Cali and try and calm her down a little," Elsa replied cautiously, not sure where she wanted this to lead. "Would you like to join me?"

He held her gaze for a moment, and slowly nodded. "I'd love to."

"Great!" she clasped her hands together. "Let's go before this rain starts to piss me off too much."

They fell into stride side by side as he stole curious glances at her. She was so intriguing, and he wasn't quite sure what to make of her.

Cali and Dusty were tucking into their hay and absolutely fine, that Elsa felt bad tearing Cali away from her beloved stablemate and disturbing the peace. Clement introduced her to his weekend rides, who were as happy as hers, and Elsa recognised the groom brushing a big bay.

"Elsa, meet my loyal groom, Daisy." Clement smiled.

"I believe we have already met," Daisy thrust her hand towards her, and Elsa eagerly shook it. "Only briefly, though. Sorry, I would have introduced myself then, but I was under Ava's strict instructions to dump the lorry and run. She said you'd never accept it otherwise."

"She was right," Elsa told her with a smile.

Elsa quickly brushed Cali off and tacked her up, deciding that just her snaffle bridle and jumping saddle would be enough for their stroll around the estate. When she rode back to meet Clement, she smiled to see that he had groomed and saddled his own horse despite Daisy's persistence that she do it for him.

"Must be a nice change for Ava to have you around the yard," Elsa began and quickly stopped herself, knowing it wasn't her place to talk ill of Portia. The two of them might even be friends.

"How so?" he enquired, as Daisy swung him into the saddle and the pair of them strolled across the parkland, side by side.

Elsa pretended not to hear him, and bit her lip. "So, are you feeling confident for the weekend?" she quickly changed the subject, feeling Cali's initial excitement at her new hacking buddy wearing off, and her beginning to settle.

"Yes," he shrugged, but he didn't look convinced. "Why not? I have good horses, and for that I mostly have Fred to thank, but still things don't go my way.

"Maybe this weekend?" she smiled encouragingly.

"Maybe."

"So, how long has Daisy worked for you?" she asked a moment later, twisting a lock of Cali's mane between her fingers.

"Eight years," he replied, barely having to think about it. "She moved over to France with her young family, just down the road from me. She didn't really want horse work, but speaking no French, that was all that was on offer in my village."

"She must have enjoyed it if she moved back over here with you?"

"I think she was getting a little weary with the French way of life, a little homesick," he told her. "I think the day I told her I had accepted a position here with the one and only Frederick Twemlow, ad asked her to come with me, she was relieved more than anything. I don't think she'd have ever left otherwise."

"Do you think you'll go back to France?" Elsa probed. "Is this a temporary visit or...something more permanent?"

"Are you trying to get rid of me already?" Clement smiled. "Or hoping I am staying?"

"I am not trying, nor hoping anything," she smiled sweetly back. "It was merely a question."

"Let's go for a trot," he looked straight ahead. "Then we can canter back through the park."

Dusty was up first for his dressage, which suited Elsa fine as she handed him straight over to Sophia and then took Cali for another walk around the estate so that she didn't create merry hell at being left alone at the stables.

Elsa observed Frederick warming up down the far end of the grass warm up arena, and she was happy that she had already resolved to keep Cali far away from her fellow competitors, so she stuck to schooling in the opposite end to Frederick, and tried to get her mare to concentrate.

Frederick observed her, and didn't know whether to go to her or avoid her. He personally wanted to go to her, of course, but he only wanted to do what she wanted of him, and he expected she wanted him to stay well away. He sighed; women were so very confusing.

He nearly went to her twice, but quickly stopped himself. He felt his mount hesitate underneath him, unsure of what was being asked of him, and he immediately felt guilty. Just the presence of her across an arena made his riding fall apart. He decided he was safe when he saw Sophia return on foot, and swallowed his pride.

"Mum's walking Dusty back to cool him off and put him away," Sophia called to her groom. "Thought you might like to stay and watch Cali's test?"

"Oh, brilliant, thanks," Elsa smiled, bringing the mare to a beautiful square halt.

"She is still as feisty as ever, I notice," Frederick's smooth voice purred.

"Who, Elsa or the mare?" Sophia smiled sweetly, and Elsa

shot daggers at her as she tried to avoid Frederick's eye.

She felt her pulse quickening as she slid to the floor, glad that Sophia was here with her.

"Cali, of course," Frederick smiled.

"Yes, but doesn't she move so beautifully?" Sophia gushed.

"She does," Frederick replied, and as his eyes gazed longingly over Elsa, Sophia wondered whether he was still talking about the mare.

"It's all credit to you, of course," Sophia went on. "I know it's all your doing, and I'm just the passenger."

"Nonsense," Frederick smiled modestly. "I like to give all my horses a good, thorough grounding, but any successes you both reach are fully down to you."

Elsa thought this an understatement, but she wouldn't boost his ego any further. All his horses went beautifully on the flat; having been produced by Frederick one wouldn't expect anything less.

Elsa watched him nudge his mount back to work, and when she could finally peel her eyes from him she helped Sophia into the saddle.

"See, wasn't that bad, was it?" Sophia pressed.

Elsa simply rolled her eyes, refusing to rise to it. Sophia walked the little mare on, and Frederick fell into step beside her. Elsa left them to it as Frederick kindly gave her pointers on how to settle the mare, and she was suddenly aware of a presence behind her.

"Hello," the gentle voice broke her from her thoughts, and she turned to greet Michael Patricks. He wore dark red corduroy trousers, and a crisp, ironed shirt with polished, brown leather shoes despite the mud. "They've quickly forged a great partnership, haven't they?" he nodded towards where Sophia now worked in the mare alone, her expressive movement obtaining glances from all directions.

"She's a super little mare," Elsa nodded in agreement. "Did you see Dusty's test?"

"I did, yes," he smiled. "It was very pleasing. I watched it from the stands with some friends, who were very complimentary of Sophia."

"It was a very strong test," Elsa beamed with pride. "It will put them right in contention for a placing."

"Dusty's very good across country," Michael reassured her. "He's a real workhorse. But he's not always so respectful of the show jumps, although I know Frederick has put a lot of work into that phase with him, with the help of that show jumper friend of his, Craig something or other..."

"Ellis," Elsa finished for him. "I can highly recommend him."

"Do you event?" he looked surprised.

"I try," she shrugged, wondering why she always felt like such a fraud when someone asked her that. "I have an ex-racehorse," she added quickly, and he nodded as though he understood, even though she knew he couldn't possibly.

When she was sufficiently warmed up, Sophia made her way to the collecting ring. Elsa ran a towel around the mare's mouth, splashed some more oil on her hooves, and she was quickly ready to go.

Elsa was very much looking forward to Sophia's and Cali's first appearance. She liked Michael, and Elsa was relieved to have him on board and take the strain off their other horses.

Whatever Frederick had said to the pair of them definitely did the trick, as Cali remained attentive to her rider for ninety percent of her test and pulled off some very expressive movements. Michael was beaming throughout, and he clasped his hands together in glee as she executed her final halt and saluted the judges.

"Ah, this is what it's all about, isn't it?" he beamed at Elsa. "To see your young horse that you work bloody hard for, pull out all the stops and start to shine."

"Sure is," Elsa whole-heartedly agreed. As far as she was concerned, they were all her children and she was always both excited and apprehensive to watch them perform.

Elsa left him to debrief with Sophia and took Cali to walk her off. She liked to be left to get on with her work. While so many owners liked to be hands-on, and Elsa was often glad of another pair of hands to help, she didn't like to be hindered while her only priority was to get her horse comfortable again.

Plus, there was somewhere else she needed to be. She had been rather unsettled ever since hearing the news that Portia would be accompanying Nobby this weekend. And although it hurt to watch and half of her really didn't want to, she felt that she owed it to Nobby. After all that he had done for Sophia and herself, she wanted to keep an eye on him and make sure he was OK, even though there was nothing she could do about it either way. She saw Portia's groom leg her up into the saddle, just as Elsa was returning Dusty from his walk. She gave them a couple of minutes to get ahead, before grabbing Cecil from the lorry and following them down to the dressage warm up arena.

Elsa couldn't help but be critical, because try as all Portia might, she was not a rider of Frederick Twemlow's calibre, nor was she a patch on Sophia. She sat nicely, but that was about the only pleasing thing to meet Elsa's eye. She was not a soft rider, but instead she harshly tugged and kicked, and she over-expressed all her movements. Frederick was admired by fellow competitors and spectators alike because he just appeared to sit there and do nothing and get the best out of his horse, whereas Portia was a long way off replicating that. Elsa had already looked her up on the internet, and while her riding style may have got her many results on the toughly-competitive show jumping circuit, on her huge, fired-up warmbloods, Elsa couldn't fathom how she could ever nurse a tiring horse around an imposing cross country course. But she would see, and she hoped for Nobby's sake that she was proven wrong.

Elsa had ridden Nobby many times, and although she had

never ridden him in the tense environment of a dressage test or taken him across a big, solid cross country, she knew him inside out and the softly-softly approach won him round every time. He wasn't getting any softness from Portia, and the overall picture was quite vicious. He looked uncomfortable and miserable as she hauled on his mouth and jabbed her spurs in his ribs. Elsa could maybe understand had Nobby been a strong, man's ride, but she knew first hand he was far from it. He was as gentle as a lamb, and tried his heart out for his rider, but during their test they suffered several miscommunications where poor Nobby stood no chance of understanding what she meant. She felt certain that were Portia allowed a whip, she would have used it on each occasion; her fury towards the low scores was etched across her face as she took it out on Nobby. When she thought he was moving too forward, she jabbed on the reins, not allowing him to move forward freely. Nobby shortened, his confusion evident, and she booted him. He shot forward in surprise, not used to such heaviness, and was harshly reprimanded for that, too.

Elsa didn't want to watch, but she couldn't seem to prize her eyes away. The moves she did pull off, Elsa begrudgingly agreed they were executed very well, but she could not find solace in that and her mind was a whir of the few bad moves. She looked around for Frederick, but she could not see that he was there, and she envisioned him asking Portia afterwards about her test, and her spinning him some cock and bull story about how the low scores were all Nobby's fault.

She kept her distance as they excited the ring, and her heart broke for Nobby as he didn't even receive a pat from her for his efforts. She slid from the saddle and chucked her reins at her groom, and Portia strode away without even a second glance back. Elsa clenched her fists at her sides, preventing herself from going to him and she hoped Portia's groom was nicer than the vile rider. She knew it was none of her business and she tried to shove away the tears that pricked her eyes. She crouched down and pulled Cecil into her chest, and let him lick away the solitary tear that escaped her.

Slowly she meandered back to the stables, checked that Dusty and Cali were warm enough, and had enough hay and water. She wished she could replicate the joy she had felt earlier after their tests, but she knew she wouldn't settle until she had checked Nobby. She detoured past the Twemlow stables on her way back to the lorry, praying that Ava was there to give her the chance to just look in on him to put her mind at rest.

As she cautiously approached, Portia's snarling words hit her ears like a brick of ice.

"He's a bit of a stubborn brute, isn't he?"

Elsa craned around the end stable, and watched as she fluttered her perfectly mascaraed eyelashes up at Frederick. "Not really a lady's horse."

"Well, Sophia managed well enough with him," Frederick replied simply. "I find him quite enjoyable to ride."

"That *Sophia* had a long time to get to know him and she bumbled along at a snail's pace, so I've heard," Portia scowled. "Plus, she probably doesn't know what a *decent* horse feels likes."

Elsa felt her blood pressure rising. She itched to stomp right over there and give her a piece of her mind, wipe that smirk off that pretty girl's face, but she shouldn't be eavesdropping. It was not her place to speak up, but she wished that Frederick would.

"She has a few," Frederick replied evenly, and Elsa wished she could tell whether he were smiling or not. Even though the thought made her sick, she wished she could tell whether he was smitten with the pretty little thing, whether she had him wrapped around her finger, whether he was blinded by her and thought she couldn't do any wrong.

"And she'll do very well with them," Elsa heard him say,

and she smiled gratefully, but she couldn't hear any words that followed as the noise of activity increased, and she decided that was probably a blessing.

She turned, and carried on her walk through the temporary stabling, resigned to the fact she would have to wait a while longer to see Nobby. Head down and hands driven into her pockets, she didn't hear Clement calling after her, until the hurried footsteps sounded immediately behind her as he jogged to catch her up.

"Hey!" he frowned. "Are you OK?"

She hesitated before nodding. "Sure," she replied, not even convincing herself.

Clement waited for her to go on, falling into step beside her.

"I just watched Portia and Nobby's test," Elsa explained. "I kind of wish I hadn't. He is amazing and I adore him. He doesn't deserve to have *her* riding him."

"No, no horse does," Clement agreed. "Where are you heading now?"

"Just back to the lorry," she shrugged.

"Maybe I could come with you?" he suggested. "You look like you could do with that drink right now."

"Sure," Elsa shrugged. She wasn't really in the mood for company, but she could hardly turn him away from his own lorry. "Why not?"

"And maybe you could help me with my horses, too?" he gave her his best *I'm totally helpless* look. "Daisy has run off to catch up with an old friend, and left me to my own devices."

Elsa felt her cheeks reddening as she remembered the moment she had asked Ava to cover for her while she supposedly caught up with an old friend, in actual fact accepting Frederick's offer of dinner. Those days seemed so long ago now, when in reality they really were not.

"How do you guys cope without us?" she murmured.

"We simply can't," he grinned. "So, horses first, drink

second?"

Elsa happily busied herself aiding Clement washing and drying, and rugging-up his horses, and was a little anxious once she'd run out of jobs to do. Before she knew it the horses were away and tucking into their hay, and there were no other jobs she could busy herself with. They were strolling across the lorry park, and she could spot her lorry easily, painted up with Clement's sponsors' logos. Her hands shook as she unlocked the door, and she felt weird stepping back to welcome him into his own lorry. Her breath quickened as her mind involuntarily took her back to the time she'd shared a night with Frederick in Sophia's old lorry.

Even though she desperately wanted to make amends after their inauspicious start on her behalf, she couldn't help but wonder what he wanted from her. Although his exceptional good looks had not gone unnoticed on her, she was in no fit state of mind to consider anything other than friendship, and the last thing she wanted was to lead him on.

"I thought you drank my reserves?" Clement observed the fridge contents with a smile. He cracked open two beers and passed her one.

"Oh, I did, but I never come away to an event without restocking," she replied.

"Good girl," he murmured, and looked around at the interior, overly impressed. "*Love* the colour scheme you've got going on here," he told her, his eyes sparkling. "This really is a most fabulous little lorry you've got yourself here. Tell me, did you choose the interior yourself?"

Laughing, she tossed a cushion at him. "*Stop* it," she told him. "We really are so grateful, OK?"

"I'm teasing," he smiled and patted the seat beside him. "Come and sit down," he said gently.

She nodded and did as he said, waiting for him to speak.

"I'm in a new area, I don't know anybody, I have no one to hang out with. I could do with a pretty girl by my side to show me around. Someone funny, easy to talk to, to join in the lorry for a beer," he raised his bottle to her. "Someone I can call a friend. Is that too much to ask?"

"Not at all," she smiled, feeling guilty at the relief that rushed through her. She wondered if he was just what she needed to get Frederick off her mind, but she was nowhere near ready for that yet, and was glad instead to have a new friend.

He watched her for a moment, considering her carefully. He had asked Ava about her as soon as he'd realised the pair of them were friends, but Ava had pulled a face and warned him off. Trying to get anything out of Ava that wasn't about a horse was like trying to get blood out of a stone, and he'd known then that there was obviously someone else involved. He had quickly formed a good idea of who, although only time would tell if his suspicions were correct. But he didn't mind; he had meant what he said, and Elsa was kind, funny, hardworking and generous - everything he'd look for in a friend. Hopefully they could help each other out.

Chapter Seven

Elsa was up at the crack of dawn - along with most of the other grooms - to feed her horses. It was important when away at events, that her horses kept the same routine that they were used to at home. She took Cecil for a walk around the estate and grabbed herself a tea and a bacon sandwich, before shutting him back up in the lorry while she got to work. He didn't mind, he was used to being a lorry dog and she couldn't risk him running off while she was trying to work, or getting in people's or horses way.

She plaited them both while they ate their hay, brushed the dust and shavings from their sleek coats, and tacked up Dusty ready for his show jumping. Elsa jumped on board, and Dusty remained his calm, laid-back self as she walked him down to the warm up arena and began working him in.

"Feeling good?" Elsa smiled as Sophia approached, having just walked the course with her trainer Derek, and Sophia nodded excitedly.

"Lovely course, much like the cross country. I couldn't have asked for a better first event for them. How's he feeling?"

"Much like the usual," Elsa shrugged, sliding from the saddle.

"Lazy?" Sophia laughed, taking his reins. "He'll perk up as soon as he sees a coloured pole."

Elsa could see her confidence shining through after her strong dressage. Michael Patricks had assured her that there was no pressure at all on her. This was just their first outing and she was to take it easy, to continue to get to know her new horses, and most importantly, *enjoy herself.* While Elsa knew that Sophia was relieved at his words, she was competitive by nature, and she would not be taking it easy just for the sake of it.

Elsa couldn't stay and watch their round, and she left Derek to sort the practice jumps for her while she went back to fetch Cali. She was dismayed to see that Cali had rolled in the short time she'd been away, and she sighed as she grabbed a brush to remove the fresh shavings, and redone a couple of loose plaits.

She tacked her up and walked her around the estate a couple of times to try and calm her down before working her in. She was working nicely by the time Sophia had finished her round on Dusty with one pole down and a few time faults because he had really not woken up as much as Sophia would have liked.

Sophia's start times were tight, and she hopped straight on to Cali. Elsa walked Dusty back to the stabling on a long rein, taking the long way around the estate. By the time she was back he was cool enough to be put straight away and have the dried sweat brushed from him. She rugged him and mucked out both her stables, and returned to the show jumping arena just as Sophia was going in. Elsa watched from the rail as Cali took hold right from the outset, clearly fresh and excited but not giving Sophia too much of a rough ride. They both kept their cool enough to finish on just two poles down.

"Perfect!" Michael Patricks clasped his hands together and went to her as soon as they exited the arena, and Elsa didn't think she'd ever seen an owner so happy to get eight faults. "You rode her so well, a couple of baby mistakes but it's early days. How did she feel?"

"Great! Really pleased with her," Sophia slid from the saddle and handed the reins to Elsa before answering Michael in detail, and Elsa led the mare gratefully away.

Nobby had show jumped early and so Elsa had missed his round, but the talk in the stableyard informed her he had gone clear, one of only a few to do so. Although Sophia had rated the course well, it appeared it didn't suit many of the horses attending Wellington this weekend.

Dusty was keen to be out again, and she checked his studs and greased his legs before handing him straight over to Sophia. Cali started box walking and calling out at the departure of her stable mate, and Elsa struggled to get her ready without many cross words being spoken. Eventually she left her and went to the finish, jumping in glee to hear that Sophia was three quarters of the way round, clear and bang on the time. Dusty flew over the last, full of running, and Sophia galloped him through the finish, slapping his neck triumphantly. Elsa was waiting with water and she hurriedly removed his tack and cooled him off, which didn't take long as the persistent drizzle had re-reared its ugly head.

Elsa wished she was busy around Nobby's start time, so that she was too pre-occupied to worry about what was occurring out on the course. But she had a bit of a wait until Cali's cross country, being one of the last to go for the day. She'd already walked them out for a pick of grass, so she found herself wandering down to the course to the best vantage point to catch as much of Nobby's round as she could. She was glad in a way that she'd been so busy all morning she'd had little time to think about him. She remembered her torment when she'd first scanned the list of entries and seen Portia's name partnering Noble Mission, but there was nothing she could do about it.

She watched them in the warm up ring, burying herself amongst a small crowd of other spectators so that she wouldn't stand out and have them notice her, and she felt her heart crumble at the sight of them. Portia walked him beside Frederick who sat astride a huge, dapple grey. Elsa noticed the way the beautiful young woman smiled at him with her perfect white teeth and her perfect complexion, and felt a stab of jealously.

Why couldn't it have been her? Why had she always been so happy at being a groom, that she'd never had her own aspirations of reaching the dizzying heights of top level eventing. She could have applied to be a working pupil at Frederick Twemlow's glorious yard, she could have been sitting astride Nobby while she gazed helplessly into her boss's ocean blue eyes, and most importantly she would let Nobby's head go and not hold him as tightly as this girl desired. She would let him show off his expressive free walk that ate up the ground with seemingly minimal effort. Her riding made Elsa feel quite sick. And the way Frederick smiled back at her, totally oblivious to anyone else around them, made her feel quite sick, too.

How could he fall for her? Her heart screamed. She wanted to run up to him, drag him off that beautiful horse and shake him. Make him look at her instead, and see that other creature for the vile person that she really was. But there was nothing vile about her when she gazed adoringly at Frederick. She looked sweet and perfect and as though butter wouldn't melt.

Stop it, Elsa barked at herself. It was nothing to do with her and she needed to snap out of this. But still she could not peel her eyes away as Portia gathered Nobby's reins up even tighter and pushed him into a trot. She held heavily onto her reins, and Elsa wished Frederick would say something to her. He did not ride at all like that so how could he condone it? But he wasn't even looking anymore as they moved to separate areas of the warm up and did their own thing. While Frederick's horse looked comfortable and relaxed as they floated effortlessly around the arena, Frederick barely seeming to move a muscle, Nobby's stride was choppy. He gave many indications that he was not happy. Elsa noticed him try to toss his head to evade the heavy contact and receive a firm tug in the gob. He swished his tail and she stuck her spurs in him to get him moving more forward, but he struggled when she held him so tightly.

Elsa's heart broke for her former charge, her kind-hearted, laid-back, genuine Nobby who would hunt all day long in only a snaffle and try anything his rider asked, if they asked nicely. She didn't think she could watch their round, but she owed it to Nobby.

She noticed Ava appear over at the rail and Frederick drew to a halt alongside her. They exchanged words and Ava made some tack adjustments, and then he made his way to the start box. Portia was starting a couple of horses after Frederick. Once Frederick had left, she pushed him into canter, and Elsa observed that at least she let him go a bit, and he seemed to relax. She turned him towards the roll-top warm up fence, and sat deep as Nobby excitedly pulled her into it. *This is what I live for,* he exclaimed as he ballooned over it with far too much enthusiasm, pulling her out of the saddle and earning himself her crop brought down across his flank. He kicked out in protest and she angrily turned him much too sharply and made him do it again from just a stride out. Unprepared and taken by surprise, Nobby only just made it with no help from his rider.

Elsa kept her distance when they were called to the start box, and watched her circling as the starter told her the time left. Elsa knew Nobby inside out, he would stand or walk calmly the whole time, only actually getting excited once the starter counted you down from ten and he entered the start box. But he was on his toes already, he looked confused as Portia held him back but kicked him on at the same time. He began to jog, and she sat smiling as if that was how she wanted him; all fired up and wasting precious energy that he would need at the end.

When the starter got to ten, she turned him into the box. He lurched forward and she smiled, restraining him until the very last second and he exploded onto the course.

Elsa thought she set off much too fast, but she reminded herself that it was nothing to do with her, and Portia would have been briefed on how to ride the course. But it was common knowledge that this was the biggest course that Portia had tackled since coming to work for Frederick – and therefore probably in her life - and Elsa was surprised if this was how Frederick had instructed her to ride it.

Nobby cleared the first at a blistering pace, his rider's petite frame crouched low up his neck and keeping the weight off his back. Elsa knew the jumps she wanted to see them at, and she let them disappear out of sight as she cut across the course to jump six, the narrow hedges.

She waited around for him there, and breathed a sigh of relief when she saw them come charging up the hill towards them. Elsa heard Portia vocally trying to steady him as she sat tall in the saddle, and gave him a tug to bring him back to her. His stride shortened, he rounded, and she thought in that brief moment they really did look the part. Nobby's ears pricked, and Portia's concentration was fully on the fence. Elsa determined she had nerves of steel; an undeniable confidence. He breezed over the first one, landed promptly, perfect three strides on an angle to the second, and he brushed through the top of the forgiving brush, not giving it an inch more than he had to. As soon as they landed, Portia's spurs were into his side, and she was pushing him on.

No pat, Elsa thought sadly, observing them gallop into the distance. *No scratch to the neck, no words whispered into his ear to reassure him he was a good boy.* Nobby lived for praise; he tried endlessly to please, but Elsa suspected he'd stop jumping for her eventually if he had no idea he was doing well. Her clenched fists shoved deep into her pockets, she meandered across the field to the combination of solid picnic tables that were not testing individually, but the line taken between them needed to be right.

The first thing Elsa thought when she saw them coming towards her, was how tired Nobby looked, and how determined his rider looked. She was not surprised, for they'd travelled the whole way at a blistering pace, and must be well up on the time. She wondered even whether they'd incur penalties for going much too fast.

She could hear his heavy breathing as he stomped up to the first fence, and thought surely she'd have to pull him up. She observed him back off, but Portia wasn't having any of it and growled at him to get on. He just about made his stride; thought twice about chipping in an extra short one, and somehow hauled his heavy, tiring frame over the solid table.

But he pecked on landing, and Portia wasn't expecting it as she was fixed firmly on the second element. She needed to turn him to get the line, but his nose was almost on the ground and she missed her moment as she was thrown onto his neck.

Take the long route, Elsa willed, wondering if she even knew what it was. Instead Portia sat up, yanked him round and kicked him on. But there was absolutely no way he'd make the fence from there.

Pull him up! Elsa wanted to scream, but the words wouldn't come out. Portia clearly had no intention of pulling up; her eyes never leaving the second element.

Poor Nobby didn't stand a chance. She set him up all wrong and he couldn't get his stride. Portia had his head yanked in so tightly that Elsa doubted he had even seen the fence.

"Let him go!" Elsa shouted furiously. She didn't care that the handful of spectators turned to look at her, for they looked as bewildered as she did, though she suspected Portia wouldn't listen anyway. Nobby would have helped her out if she let him have his head, but she held on to him so tightly. He was over-bitted, too, and his eyes rolled in terror and he tried to force his mouth open despite his tight flash noseband clamping it shut.

She yanked on his mouth with all her weight, her spurs digging in his sides as she forced him to take-off despite both of them being dangerously off balance, and Elsa felt her heart stop.

He was never going to make the stride, but he was genuine and bold, and his desire to please his jockey shone through.

He tucked his front legs up tightly, but it wasn't enough. His knees whacked the front of the table and he slid over the top, twisting sideways mid-air and sending Portia flying out the side door.

Elsa was frozen to the spot as she watched Nobby roll over in the mud. Portia was blocked from her sight by the jump, but Elsa didn't care about her. As Nobby struggled to get up, Elsa sprang into action, instinctively sprinting to him and grabbing his reins before the fence judge did.

"It's OK boy," Elsa told him soothingly, running her hand down his neck, lathered with thick sweat. "You're alright. *Please* get up; you can do it."

Trusting he was safe with her he stuck his front legs out, shakily found his footing and with a deep groan he hauled himself up.

"Good boy!" Elsa patted him, relief flooding her while Nobby looked around, as if confused to have fallen despite doing all he could to prevent it.

Portia was also up on her feet, her perfect make up splattered in mud, but otherwise no worse for wear. She pushed the medic's comforting arm away.

"I'm fine!" she spat furiously. "Get off me!"

She marched towards her horse, her face full of fury as she glared at Elsa.

"Get away from my horse!" she roared, and shoved her roughly in the chest, causing Elsa to lose her footing and sending her sprawling into the mud.

Portia snatched his reins and yanked them heavily, startling him and sending his head high up in the air. His studs cut up the ground as he tried to back away, but Portia held tightly and cracked her whip across his shoulder.

Elsa thought her heart was going to explode through her chest as she shakily tried to get to her feet to stop her.

"You stupid, *bloody* horse!" Portia shouted at Nobby, onlookers horrified but no one willing to confront her. "What the *fuck* did you do that for?" She brought her crop down on him again, and he reared in terror and broke away from her. He backed away, but he didn't know where to run. Loyal Nobby would have never left his rider. Elsa neared him, she held her outstretched palm flat and watched the flicker of recognition cross his gorgeous face. She felt her blood boiling as a tear ran down her cheek. She watched him slowly relax, and he allowed her to take his rein.

"What the *fuck* are you doing?" Portia turned on her again. "Who *are* you?"

"Don't you *dare* treat him like that *ever* again - do I make myself clear?" Elsa rounded on her, and she watched as Portia's eyebrows rose in surprise at the confrontation. "Everyone else might be afraid to stick up to you, but I am not. Lay a hand on him again, and I will knock you into the middle of next week!"

"Lay a hand on him?" Portia stood tall to her, tauntingly. "That brute needs a meat cleaver taken to him and packed into a tin of dog food."

Elsa had never been so offended in all her life. She clenched her fists and stepped towards her, and immediately felt Ava's hand on her shoulder pulling her back.

"Thanks for catching him, Else," she said gently. "I'll take him from here."

Elsa slowly nodded. She never wanted to let go of him again, but she wasn't his groom anymore. She was trembling as Ava gently prized the reins from her hand. The medic's and stewards hovered, wanting the heated situation to resolve itself without having to step in.

"Walk back with me?" Ava offered, desperate to stop this confrontation.

"Or how about *I* walk back with *my* horse and *my* groom," Portia retorted, poking Elsa in the chest. "And you climb back into whatever hole you just climbed out of."

Even though her words were a blur, the poke was the final

straw for Elsa. "I'll smack you straight back into that hole if you lay another finger on me," she shoved her away, towering above the pretty blonde.

There was an interrupting cough, and they turned to face the steward. "Please could you clear the course?" she asked nervously.

"Of course!" Ava replied, hastily leading Nobby away, and her arm was around her friend's waist, pulling her away before she could object.

Elsa noticed from the corner of her eye Portia about to follow them, but the medic took her arm. "If you have other rides today, you need to come with me," the medic told her sternly. "I need to check you over and declare you fit to ride."

Elsa could see she was still fuming as she reluctantly turned away with the medic.

"I'm *so* glad you shoved her!" Ava told her when they were finally free, Nobby walking eagerly - if a little stiff - at their side.

"I don't know where my nerve came from, Ava," Elsa replied, her voice shaky. "That's not like me at all."

"Well, she deserved it." Ava smiled.

"Of course she did!" Elsa replied without hesitation, quickly swiping away her angry tears. "How can anyone get through life treating horses like that, and talking to people like that? Actually, I am amazed at the restraint that I *did* show."

"Thank you for sticking up for Nobby," Ava told her quietly.

"I could never *not* stick up for Nobby," Elsa replied. She observed her sudden silence as they walked. "Could you?"

"It worries me, but I don't think I could have done that." She replied quietly, with an anxious bite to her lip.

"But she's a cruel bitch!" Elsa gaped at her.

"Oh, I know she is. We all know she is, except..." she broke off and looked away.

Elsa took a deep breath, knowing what she was going to

say. "Frederick?"

Ava nodded. "It scares me the hold she seems to have over him. He's supposed to be the boss, yet most of the time it seems to be the other way around. If I stepped out of line, Else, I honestly think she could have me fired."

"Frederick would never do that!" Elsa gasped.

"I would have believed you a few weeks ago," Ava replied. "But not now, Elsa. Something's happening, and I don't like it. I don't know what and I don't like it at all."

Silently, Elsa took her hand, and Ava smiled in appreciation. Elsa hated seeing her so downcast, and she'd certainly been that the last few weeks.

"Well, I've got your back," she smiled eventually. "Sophia isn't going to sack me for standing up to a bully, so I'll happily fight your corner."

"Thanks, Else," Ava smiled gratefully, squeezing her hand. "I'm just hoping she'll give up soon and bugger off, leave us in peace. Many more falls like that and it'll be sooner rather than later."

Elsa gave Nobby a grateful pat. "Keep up the good work, boy," she told him sadly.

As they rounded the temporary stable yard and turned into the Twemlow aisle, Elsa felt her heart quickening at the sight of Frederick bent over his horses' hoof as he tightened its studs. He looked up and fleetingly locked eyes with Elsa, his expression quickly turning to confusion.

"Sorry for leaving you, boss," Ava apologised. "But Nobby required my attention."

"Yes, of course," he replied. "Is everything OK?" he looked from Ava to Elsa, trying to read the solemn expressions of either them and failing. "Has something happened?"

"He fell at the picnic tables."

"Oh blimey, is he OK?" he glanced quickly over him for any obvious knocks and scrapes.

"*He's* fine," Ava replied awkwardly. "At least *physically*, I think. But..." She broke off as Frederick's hands flew to his face in panic.

"Geez, Portia! Is she OK?"

"She's OK, but..." Elsa replied, frowning at his concern. She felt her temper rising at Mr Cool, acting genuinely concerned about the wickedest woman on the circuit. *Was he serious?*

"She's with the medic," Ava sighed. "But she's fine."

"Thank God," he visibly relaxed. "What happened?"

Ava went to reply, but Elsa stepped ahead of her.

"What *happened*?" Elsa replied, hands on hips as she boldly squared up to him. "Is that Portia hammered that poor horse into the ground until he couldn't give anymore, and he had no option but to fall! And *then*, once she'd got to her feet, she took her stick to him!"

Frederick glared at her, switching those blue eyes to Ava as if waiting for conformation.

"I didn't see it all," Ava shrugged helplessly. "I was grooming for you, remember?"

"She *whipped* him!" Elsa spat.

"I'm sure she thought he just needed waking up or something," Frederick replied defensively., running his hand through those soft, blonde curls. "Come on, Elsa, you don't ride with a stick?"

"*Ride* with one, yes, but I don't use it from the fucking ground to wrap around an exhausted horse's head!"

Frederick's eyes rose, but he calmed himself. "I know you are *precious* about that horse, Elsa, but Portia is a good rider, well-respected on the show jumping circuit and earning respect on the eventing circuit, also."

"She will not earn anything near respect behaving like she did just then!" Elsa refused to back down.

"You two seem to have got off on the wrong foot," Frederick told her. "But you do not need to worry about her, or Nobby, or anything. She knows what she is doing; she would not be competing from my stable if she did not."

"I can't listen to this!" Elsa replied in disbelief. Raising her palm to him, she turned on her haunches and left, unable to even glance at Ava and Nobby on her way past if she was to keep what was left of her heart intact. Nobby was the most genuine horse she'd ever met, he deserved better than this and there was nothing she could do about it.

She went to check her horses, taking deep breaths to calm herself down. She would always put her horses before any guy, but how did Frederick still unwittingly have the power to make her want to punch him *and* rip his clothes off at the same time.

Eventually, it was Cali's turn to go across country, and Elsa was grateful that at least she would get to watch one of Sophia's rounds this weekend as well as have something to take her mind off Nobby. Cali was on fire as she tore around the warm-up, and Elsa hoped Sophia had much more control than what it looked. Elsa thought her nails would be bitten down to the quick before she'd even made it to the start box if she didn't find some more brakes soon.

Under Derek's expert tuition, Cali was eventually calm enough to tackle the practice fences, taking the roll-top several times on a twenty-metre circle, that laid any doubts of Sophia's control firmly to rest. Once called to the start box, Sophia didn't dare to halt the mare once, and kept her walking circles, changing direction often so that she didn't begin to anticipate or switch off. And as the starter counted her down she left the start box like a rocket, barely slowing to take the first fence, and both Elsa and Michael gasped in unison.

"You'd never think this is their first outing," Michael shook his head, as she cleared the second and third in a similar style and headed down the hill out of sight.

"She's done a fair bit of cross country schooling with her," Elsa nodded. "But quickly came to the conclusion that this is just her. She'll steady up when she has to come back up the hill and then Sophia will hold her firmly from there."

Michael nodded intently, and they waited with baited breath for Sophia to reappear. Of course, Elsa was right, and Cali was travelling much more acceptably as she came back into view, and Sophia set her up for the brushes. She got the first element perfectly, but was slightly off the line she needed for the second. Although Cali flew it, she did so too much to the side, taking the flag with her.

"That's going to be close, isn't it?" Michael winced, watching the back of her as she thundered towards the next fence, and cleared that without any trouble.

But Elsa was watching the fence judges deliberate, and sensed it wasn't good news.

She was waiting at the finish line with sugar lumps, and saw the look of disappointment on Sophia's face as she pulled up from what should have been her second of two perfect clears for the day.

"What was the verdict?" she winced.

"Jumped outside of the flags," Elsa shrugged, feeling that although the judges had quickly decided against them, they could not be argued with on this occasion. "So, penalties."

"I thought as much," Sophia nodded, as she slid from the saddle and gave a Cali a well-earned, hearty pat. "Oh well, we both live to fight another day."

Elsa nodded and began walking the mare away as Sophia stripped her saddle off. It was still disappointing, nonetheless, but there was hardly time to dwell on it as she set about cooling her horse down.

Chapter Eight

"Coming for a beer at ours?" Ava called down the aisle.

Elsa hesitated from scrubbing out the plastic feed bowls. "I can't drink," she replied feebly, "I've got to get my two home tonight."

"A lemonade, then? I won't take no for an answer," Ava added, hands on her hips as she stared her down. "Plus, you can't leave yet if you've only just fed. So, you've time for one."

"I just think I'll want to punch her when I see her," Elsa sighed, running her hand through her loose hair. "I've barely calmed down." She wasn't sure she wanted to be anywhere near Ava's employer or his new awful rider.

"Hey, same here!" Ava told her. "Which is why I need you there, to stop me. Safety in numbers, and all that."

"OK," Elsa gave in under her stare, knowing she couldn't avoid them forever. "I'll just see to my two then I'll be over."

Dusty and Cali had eaten up some time ago, but Elsa knew it wouldn't hurt to leave them a while longer. Plus, the exodus of the lorries from the field was causing problems in the deep mud, and Elsa knew she wasn't going to get out of here quickly. The tow-tractors were hard at work as the queue of stuck lorries grew, and Elsa reluctantly trudged to the Twemlow lorry.

"Portia still isn't back," Ava was unable to conceal her smile as she passed her a can of lemonade. "Apparently the stewards are speaking to her."

"Bloody good job!" Elsa replied. "Hopefully they throw the book at her."

"No doubt she'll flutter her eyelashes at them and promise not to do it again, and everything will be OK," Ava rolled her eyes. "Frederick is in the lorry, talking with owners. He hasn't said much on the matter."

Elsa saw her approaching from a distance, and waited

anxiously. She looked furious, walking quickly. She looked up and hesitated as she saw the small congregation laughing and chatting outside the Twemlow lorry.

The lorry door flew open and Frederick stepped out. Elsa wondered how the mere sight of him still took her breath away, when her emotions towards him were currently not very pleasing. But he always managed to do that to her, and she hated herself for it. He didn't even notice her as he looked straight ahead and locked eyes on Portia. She struggled to read the expression that flittered across his face, and frowned. Although he had broken into a smile by the time Portia looked up and noticed him, the first look had not been particularly warm.

"*Dangerous riding*?" Portia snarled at him. "Did you hear about what that cretin said to me?"

"I know," Frederick sighed, backing off. "Maybe it was a little fast."

"I was checking my watch, Fred," she bit back. "I was right where I wanted to be."

"Well, there's no right or wrong answer," he shrugged. "The stewards just have a different opinion to you on that."

"Because I was right, and they are wrong! How *dare* they! I shall be appealing; this won't be the last they hear about it!

"You got off lightly, really," Frederick ran his hand through those glorious blond curls, and Elsa thought he looked half scared of her. "Rotational falls kill people, Portia."

"It was never going to be a rotational if that stupid friend of your rubbish groom hadn't been shouting at me, trying to distract me! Is that the only way that girl she works for can win classes?" she spat bitterly. "To have her groom distract all the competitors."

Elsa launched forward to attack, but Ava quickly stopped her.

"Stop, Portia," Fred said gently. "That's unfair."

"Sorry," she purred eventually, with a flutter of those long eyelashes and the flash of that perfect smile, and Elsa could see she almost had Frederick eating out of her hand.

She felt sick to her core. *How could he not see her for who she really was?*

She noticed Frederick glance awkwardly in her direction, no doubt praying she hadn't heard, but the words had smacked her ears crystal clear. Slowly, he shook his head, and she regarded him with nothing but hatred. He was a coward, why else wouldn't he stand up to her? She couldn't help thinking were that Clement's behaviour, he would be out on his ear in a flash.

Frederick looked away first, but Portia glared straight at Elsa with a look of her own pure hatred.

With a bite of her lip, Elsa turned away. Her hands shook as she took a long gulp of her drink. When she reluctantly looked back, Frederick and Portia had their backs to her as they talked animatedly with some owners who had appeared, Portia's arm tightly around his waist and Frederick doing absolutely nothing to fend her off.

She felt Clement's presence by her side before she heard him, and was grateful for the distraction as she turned to face him.

"Well done for standing up to her," he murmured.

"I couldn't just stand there and watch her treat him like that." Elsa shrugged, guessing that everyone must have heard about it by now.

He nodded knowingly, but did not speak. She found her gaze being involuntarily drawn back to the entwined couple. Portia was laughing and smiling as if nothing had ever happened, as if she didn't give two hoots that Nobby was probably mentally scared for life by her brutality. She kept touching Frederick's arm, and he didn't even try to move away. Elsa felt her stomach churn, and peeled her eyes away as she realised Clement was watching her.

"Come," he extended his arm to her. "Let's take a walk."

Her mouth was so dry she could not speak, but she linked her arm through his and allowed him to lead her slowly away.

"That horse gets the best care," he murmured a moment later, as they left the busy lorry park behind in favour of the extensive, peaceful parkland. "You know that, don't you? Ava makes sure of it. She is a bloody good groom."

"I know," Elsa croaked, nodding. She was so grateful that of all the people he could have looking after him, he had Ava.

"So try and forget about it, and enjoy yourself," he smiled.

She nodded, and forced a half-hearted smile that she did not feel. She didn't think she would ever forget the image of Portia taking all her anger and her crop to her darling Nobby, and if she ever got her by herself she'd love to give her a taste of her own medicine.

She removed her arm from his. "Actually, Clement, I'm just going to go," she told him, unable to meet his eye. "Thanks for being...*nice*. But I'm just going to get going."

She turned and sped away, and felt him watching after her as she stumbled through the mud and back onto the lorry park. She just wanted to get packed up and out of here. She had not eaten all day, and for that reason alone was glad that she was not allowed a drink, or who knows what words may have come out of her mouth. Her restraint amazed even herself. She normally *loved* being away at events, and she felt as things were starting to look up for Sophia, she deserved to be able to let her hair down, and she shouldn't let Portia and Frederick ruin it for her. She needed to move on. Maybe she needed someone handsome, nice and caring - like Clement - to help her get over all this stuff. But right now all she wanted was to go home.

She stopped only when she reached her lorry, and sighed, letting her face fall heavily into her hands. She hadn't asked for any of this, yet in some way it was all her own doing. But how did she make herself stop caring about someone who obviously didn't give a toss about her?

"Elsa!" she heard the familiar voice before her, and spun around as Clement jogged through the squelching mud to catch up with her. He couldn't just leave her when she looked so troubled, especially when she was about to hit the road in a twelve tonne truck.

She observed his hurt look, as his eyes searched her face for an explanation. She lost her footing slightly and fell back against the sleek bodywork of his plush lorry, squeezing her eyes tightly shut to hold back the threatening tears.

"Elsa..." he murmured.

He reached for her arm, and she wasn't sure if it was because he believed she might fall if he didn't. But he didn't let go, and stepped closer to her. Her heart was beating overtime as she felt his breath on her forehead. She prized open her eyes, having never seen him so close before, and not wanting to miss out. She had to look up, he was so tall. He really was so handsome, she affirmed, starting at his soft, dark hair, longer on the top and cut shorter on the sides, and thinking it as lovely as Frederick's soft, blonde curls in its own way. She realised her mind had always been so clouded with thoughts of Frederick, to realise how attractive Clement was, and he *really* was. She wondered, would she always compare guys to Frederick? But those chiselled looks, the strong-set jawline, the piercing dark eyes that were staring straight into her own. He was perfectly shaven, perfectly preened, and as he subconsciously ran his tongue along his lower lip, she thought how wholly kissable they looked. His eyes searched hers, but she was fixated on his lips. She realised he was still holding her; a firm, authoritative hold that made her threatening tears and all the troubles of the day just want to melt away.

He dipped his head towards her, and she smelled the slightest hint of beer on his breath. She took a deep breath; she could kill for a beer right now.

"What are you doing?" she murmured, her eyes never leaving his lips.

"What I've been trying to pluck up the courage to do for a while now," he whispered, smiling. She closed her eyes as his lips met hers, so softly and respectful, and she found herself responding. She wasn't sure if without the turmoil and emotion of the day's events, whether in her right mind she would have shoved him away and demanded he not be so stupid, but her arms were around his neck, as her tongue gathered momentum and passionately joined with his.

"I thought you just wanted to be friends?" she murmured, as he pulled away to catch his breath.

"I do, Elsa, I really do, but I've also been wondering how it would feel to kiss you," he replied.

"So, how does it feel?" she giggled, her stomach fluttering.

"Absolutely bloody fantastic," he whispered, brushing his lips teasingly against hers.

"I think you should try it again," she told him, her bottom lip clamped between her teeth. "Just to be sure."

"Of course," he murmured, and his arms were around her as his lips covered hers, and she felt his smile widen along with her own with every moment that passed.

What the fuck are you doing, Elsa? Something inside her screamed. *You have enough problems!* But she tried to ignore it as his hard body pushed against her, into the even harder body of the lorry, and she resisted the urge to wrap her legs around his waist, aware that they were in the middle of a muddy lorry park where anyone could see them.

But we are a few steps from the comfort of a very luxurious lorry... she thought. But she didn't want him to stop kissing her *like that*.

"What the *fuck* do you think you're doing?" came a roar from behind him, and Elsa's eyes flew open, certain that this voice was not in her mind. Not at this moment, anyway.

She wasn't sure if Clement pulled away of his own accord,

or if Frederick grabbed him first, it all happened so quickly. But one minute he was warm against her, the next he was ripped away from her and she saw the look of fear on his face as he was thrown into the mud on his knees as if he was a man of only half his size.

Elsa caught her breath as Clement struggled to his feet. She locked eyes with Frederick for only a second before he had launched furiously towards Clement and sent him sprawling into the mud with a single punch.

He stood over him as Clement rolled over, clutching his bloody nose with his muddy hand. He was covered in thick mud, and as Elsa's shock subsided she felt herself bubbling over in a fury to match Frederick's own. She reached down and grabbed Clement's elbow to help him up, but her hands slipped with all the mud and she felt Frederick grab her arm as she struggled. She straightened up to him, shoved him as hard as she could in the chest and watched him barely move. He shook his head at her; a mixture of fury, hurt and confusion clouding those blue eyes which she remembered as being only beautiful.

"Go on, punch me, too!" she screamed at him, shoving him in the chest again, but her strength evaporated. She was aware they had accumulated a few stares from neighbouring lorries, and she felt humiliated.

Frederick looked furious as he held her easily by the elbows, but she felt it fading as he looked her in the eye, and she wondered what he might do next. He had no right to intervene, in *anything* she was doing.

"I'd never hurt you, Elsa," he whispered. "*Never*."

"Shit," Clement scrambled up unaided, as the blood would not stop. "I'm sorry, boss," he shrugged, helplessly looking from Frederick to Elsa. "I had no idea…" he trailed off.

"*You* have nothing to be sorry for," Elsa sneered, suddenly feeling like a drunk who had very quickly had to sober up. "*He* is the one with the problem." And she freed herself from his hold to poke Frederick meaningfully in the chest.

Frederick closed his eyes, his remorse building and his fight gone, and for a moment Elsa felt sorry for him.

"I'm going to go and, well...get cleaned up," Clement told them, backing away.

Elsa nodded. She wanted to go with him; to help him and make sure he was OK, but she wasn't finished here, yet. She saw a spectator reach out to him, ask if he was OK, and she was grateful and wished they'd all go with Clement and leave her and Frederick alone.

"Well, a bloody well done for making a total fool out of yourself!" she turned on Frederick, her arms folded resolutely across her chest. "What the *fuck* are you playing at?"

He took a deep breath before opening his eyes, and looked right at her. "I can't control myself when it comes to you, Elsa." He mumbled, running his hands through his blonde curls.

"Well, you're going to have to fucking learn, aren't you?" she snarled, suddenly hating his guts more than she thought she ever could. "I opened up my soul to you, Frederick, and you weren't interested! So, you can't have it both ways!"

"I know," he sighed. "I'm sorry, I don't know what came over me."

"Oh, I do!" she retorted. "You're a control freak; you want to have your cake *and* eat it."

"That's not me, Elsa."

"Yes, it is!" she cut him off. "All this time you spend trying to make people believe you are an honest, genuine guy, when you're nothing but a fucking fraud! You don't want me, but suddenly you don't want anyone else to have me? While all the time you and that vile piece of shit you have working for you are all over each other. She took her whip to Nobby earlier, but you don't give a shit about that, do you?"

"Don't try and make this about her, Elsa," Frederick told her.

"Why not?" she shook her head sadly. "I heard what you were both saying about us. You've changed, Frederick. The old Frederick had principles and would have stood up for us - especially Sophia - no matter what your feelings towards me are."

"My feelings towards you, Elsa, have always remained the same."

He looked pained as he said it, and for a moment she felt like she could believe him. But his actions spoke loudest of all. She could never forgive him for this. She felt confusion wading through her, trying to make sense of it all.

"People change, Elsa, circumstances change," he went on, barely able to look at her. "But my feelings towards you have never changed."

"Bullshit!" she cut him off with venom.

"You have no idea what I'm going through!" he furiously grabbed hold of her arms and shook her as his eyes bore into hers. "No fucking idea!"

"Oh, I'm *sorry*!" her sarcasm forged ahead. "Is poor little Freddy having a tough time in his otherwise perfect life, with some beautiful, stuck up bitch hanging on his arm, his luxurious mansion, his stableyard of half a million pound horses and his endless pot of family money - are you looking for *sympathy*?"

"No!" he spat, and she froze in fear. As she looked into his eyes, they weren't as blue or beautiful as she remembered. He looked worn out, the rings around his eyes making him look much older than he was. He looked *beaten*, she thought, and she felt her heart twist in pain.

"Let go of me, please," she whispered, as a tear rolled down her cheek.

He took a deep breath, wanting to wipe it away and wrap his arms around her. Everything he was feeling; only she could make it better. And that pain that he could see, deep in her eyes, that she did so well to keep hidden, he knew only he held the key to making that go away.

"Please, hear me out?" he breathed.

She shook her head. "I don't want to hear another word you've got to say."

She yanked herself free from his hold, and turned, making her way unsteadily to the lorry door. He couldn't bear to watch her walk away from him, and instinctively launched at her.

"Elsa!" he shouted.

His grip took her by surprise, and she fell against the hard body of the lorry. He was so dangerously close to her, and she took a deep breath of his familiar aftershave that usually sent the butterflies fluttering in her stomach. But they didn't want to flutter today.

"Get off me!" she snarled. "And don't you *dare* come after me! Do I make myself clear?"

He nodded, and could do nothing but watch her leave. He stood staring at the lorry door long after she had slammed it shut behind her.

Elsa couldn't cope with anymore humiliation, she just wanted to keep her head down and get away from Wellington unscathed. She scooped Cecil up into her arms and fell down onto the sofa in an exhausted heap.

She didn't know how long she had been lying there when she heard the catch click on the lorry door. She opened her eyes, for a fleeting minute thinking it was Frederick come to apologise and pour his heart out to her. But Cecil remained calm, and his heckles remained down, so she knew it could only be one person.

Ava opened the door with caution, unsure of what she was going to find inside. She hoped it wasn't a bloodbath inside – for Clement's sake – as the interior of his lorry really was very lovely. But from what she'd seen so far, Clement himself had been the only one to shed blood, and plenty of it, so maybe he was to blame. Maybe they had all kissed and made up again, but she wasn't sure that her eyes wanted to see the consequence of that, either. Word got round very quickly at places like this, especially if you were going to have a punch-up in the lorry park, but Ava wasn't sure how much of it had been exaggerated to her as she'd sped across the lorry park to her friend's lorry. Most of it, she hoped.

She took a deep breath before slowly opening the lorry door, and let out an audible sigh of relief. Elsa lay huddled on the sofa with Cecil. She had obviously been crying, but her mud-covered boots had been kicked off just inside the door, and what filled Ava with the most relief, was that the interior of Clement's lorry was still *immaculate*.

"Elsa..." Ava began quietly, struggling to remove her boots without getting mud everywhere. "Rumour has it there was a little fight." She took a deep breath. "Are you OK?"

Elsa sat up straight, wiping her eyes as Cecil jumped to the floor, hoping the new arrival might feed him.

"What the fuck is wrong with me?" she mumbled. "Why can't I just stay out of trouble and focus on my work? Events are meant to be such a happy time for me."

"You've done nothing wrong, Elsa," Ava reassured her. "Fred's the one with the problem. You're single, and Clement's a good looking guy."

Great, Elsa thought, so people knew about the *whole thing*.

"But I didn't want a guy ..." she sighed. "I *don't* want a guy. I just want to be good at my job and get on with that in peace. I've brought all this on myself, I know." She wiped her eyes as fresh tears threatened.

"No you haven't," Ava insisted, wrapping her arms around her. "Boys are just stupid, that's all."

"I can't believe he *punched* him," she shook her head.

"I can," Ava replied. "Not because Fred's nasty or violent, but because he's been out of sorts recently. And I've seen the way he looks at you. Don't try and make sense of it, I told you; boys are stupid. Come on, let's go get you packed up and these horses loaded, and get the hell out of here."

"Have you seen the queue to get towed out of here?" Elsa retorted as she peered out of the window to see the ever-growing backlog of already loaded lorries the tractor boys were trying to tug off the estate. "Looks like it's going to be a long night."

Chapter Nine

Elsa wasn't sure how she managed to drag herself out of bed the next morning, and must have hit the snooze button on her alarm several times before she finally got up. It had been late when she had finally packed all their stuff and made it to the front of the queue to be towed off the mud-bath lorry park, and she had been on the road for a few hours.

She showered quickly and headed straight out onto the yard before even consuming toast and coffee, the horses banging impatiently at their stable doors as soon as they saw her arrive. She regretted now not loading the wheelbarrow up the night before, but she had been too shattered by the time she'd eventually made it home to do anything other than put the horses to bed.

She flicked the switch on the kettle on the way past, and tried to serve up the feeds as quickly as possible to make the banging stop. When they were all made, she loaded the wheelbarrow up in order and pushed it along the row of stables, making sure they were all fed and satisfied before she went back to fill haynets.

When she went back to the kettle she found Minty the yard cat sitting on the worktop, purring and meowing just out of Cecil's reach, much to the shaggy dog's disgust.

"OK, OK," Elsa sighed, giving in and going to the fridge to feed them both before she finally got round to coffee.

She checked the whiteboard as she took her first sip, and saw that she was in for a busy day.

"No rest for the wicked," she murmured, stroking Cecil behind the ears.

Cali and Dusty were to spend the day in the field, but Sophia had to exercise the other horses in work that had missed out the last couple of days, and Elsa needed to hack

Timber Bear and Drop Kick. She already felt her bones aching with exhaustion just at the thought of it. She hadn't even cleared out the lorry yet and put the washing on.

"I'm having a lesson on Thursday with Derek," Sophia told her as she took Connor's reins. "Michael Patrick's is coming to watch."

"Don't you worry," Elsa winked, reading her mind. "I will have the yard spic-and-span by then."

"Thanks, Else," Sophia smiled, as Elsa legged her into the saddle. "I'll help of course, it's just it's still early days with him, I was nowhere near the placings at Wellington."

"Stop panicking," Elsa cut her off. "He absolutely *loves* you. And even if he had been with us for ten years I would have the yard looking tip-top for his visit."

"I know you would," Sophia replied. "He mentioned he has a close friend who works for a firm of shaving manufacturers, and that he would put in a word for me to get sponsorship. Can you imagine? I know shavings aren't as exciting as fancy clothing or whatever, but it would save me *so* much money, it would really help out."

"Soph, that's amazing!" Elsa exclaimed. "Our first real owner and first real sponsorship package."

"Yea, I mean I don't want to jump the gun, but how cool would that be?"

"You've worked so hard for this," Elsa told her sincerely. "You thoroughly deserve good things to come your way."

"*We* have worked so hard, don't you mean?" Sophia corrected her. "We're a team, Elsa, and there's no way I could achieve any of this without you."

"Oh, go ride your horse!" Elsa insisted, clicking her tongue and encouraging Connor to walk on. "Before I start getting all emotional!"

Elsa was back into her routine by midweek, and while she tried to forget the mess of last weekends events, they were never far from her mind. She knew she owed Clement an apology, or at least an explanation, but she couldn't bring herself to call him, and she had no idea what she would say if she did. The longer she left it, the harder it was to pick up the phone. And as for Frederick, her fury was still raw and she was more than happy not to lay eyes on him or Portia for a long time. But that didn't stop images of him keeping her awake late into the night; reminders of when he was carefree and happy, and *loving*. She longed to see that side of him again, but she never again wanted to see the side of Frederick she had witnessed at Wellington.

Just Cecil and I, she told herself. *That is how it should be.*

Even though their season had not worked out as she and Sophia envisioned, it had had its good points and its bad. Elsa was almost glad it was starting to wind down as she was looking forward to her well-earned winter break. But first, she had brownie points to earn.

"I want to congratulate you, Elsa," Michael Patricks told her sincerely, taking her hand between his, and she was surprised at how soft they were. "My horses have never looked so well, and I am so pleased now that I made the move to Sophia and yourself."

"Well, I try my best, Michael," she replied modestly. "They are my pride and joy."

She finished saddling Dusty and led him outside, ran the stirrups down the leathers and held him for Sophia to get on.

"Can I get you a chair?" she asked Michael as she returned to his spectator position at the manège gate.

"Oh, no. I'm fine, thank you," he smiled appreciatively. "I sit down all day."

The chance to sit down at all during the day would be a fine thing, Elsa thought, and she leaned against the gate alongside Michael as they watched Derek warm horse and rider up first, before properly putting them through their paces.

He had set up a couple of tricky combinations for them to jump, designed to get Dusty thinking more forward, and

Dusty was willing and genuine as he made light work of them all as soon as he realised what his rider wanted. As they began to cool off, Elsa departed to saddle Cali, and Derek adjusted the combinations and added more poles in his quest to slow her down. She had plenty of enthusiasm, it just needed curbing.

"I know I am biased, but I believe them to both be fantastic horses," Michael confided in Elsa as she returned to watch with him. "Dusty is a little slow, a little cautious at first, he will only do something for his rider once he has established a firm bond, a firm *trust*. Cali, on the other day, will do anything to please. She is eager for her rider to like her. I think early on, Cali will shine, but in the long run, Dusty will be the better horse."

Elsa smiled as he went on. He was so passionate about his horses; never big-headed or boasting, just generally intrigued and behind them one hundred percent of the way to see what they could achieve.

"I have a proposition for the both of you," Michael told them, once Derek had departed and Elsa and Sophia were rugging the two horses ready to turn them out. They both stopped what they were doing, and looked up in interest.

"You both work hard, you're a great team and it really is a privilege for me to have joined into it," he smiled, and they waited with baited breath for him to go on. "I really was so disheartened to hear about the lorry incident," he paused, and looked straight at Elsa. "It must have been terrifying."

She felt a lump in her throat as she nodded, and bit down hard on her lip, willing herself not to well-up. It had been the very worst experience of her life so far, to believe a horse in your care was going to burn to death in front of your eyes.

"It was," she forced the words out.

"It is very nice of Clement to lend you his. I have only met him a handful of times but have heard only good things about him."

Elsa felt her cheeks reddening, and hoped she could blame it all on the emotion of the lorry fire were Michael to get suspicious.

"My father is trying to secure another one," Sophia told him awkwardly. "But the insurance company are being a bit…slow."

"That's where I hope I can help," he clasped his hands together enthusiastically, and he had their undivided attention. "I have funded a new lorry for you - well, I say *new*, but I mean second hand, and I can assure you it will do the job - and I have arranged for it to be delivered tomorrow afternoon. It has been painted up with my company's logo, and will be kept here for your sole use, while you are contracted to ride my horses."

Sophia's hands flew to her face. She wasn't used to hearing all this business talk of logo's and contracts, but she believed he had just given her a lorry.

"Are you sure?" she gasped.

"Of course!" Michael beamed. "We'll see how the rest of this season pans out, then see if we can't arrange a more permanent sponsorship package to kick off next season."

Elsa couldn't believe their luck, and she wanted to throw her arms around him and plant the biggest kiss on his cheek, but she hastily reminded herself that this was the most professional relationship they had *ever* had, and she didn't want to be the one to ruin it. The only downside was the reminder that she had Frederick to thank for all of this, and she didn't want to be thinking of him right now, and ruining her good mood.

"I'm going to leave you in peace now," he told them. "I'm sure you have lots to be getting on with and I don't wish to hinder you any further. Mind if I call in sometime next week?"

"Call in whenever you want," Elsa told him. She could get used to visits like this.

"I'm *so* relieved!" Sophia clasped her hands together, as

they both watched his car depart down the drive. "Dad is really struggling with the insurance company, and we can't *keep* taking advantage of Clement's generous hospitality."

Elsa felt her heart sink as she mentioned the tall, dark Frenchman.

"Talking of whom..." Sophia added cautiously, as she sensed the sudden change in mood. "I think *you* should be the one to drive his lorry back, and make sure you see him."

"No," Elsa sternly shook her head. "I can't."

"You must!" Sophia insisted.

"Well, I won't," Elsa shrugged. "I can't see him. My name will be mud at that yard."

"Even more reason for you to go. Chance for you to explain and clear your name," Sophia told her, not backing down.

Elsa groaned as she realised she would not win this one. "This new bloody lorry had better be worth it!"

"Oh, it will be!" Sophia smiled sweetly at her, and skipped joyfully across the yard. But Elsa suddenly could not meet her enthusiasm, and desperately tried to think of a way out of it.

Elsa sank back into the sofa and put her feet up on the coffee table. Cecil snuggled on her lap, but she warned him not to get too comfy as this was just a quick break while she sorted out her predicament. She held a coffee in one hand and her phone in the other, her thumb hovering over the call button on Ava's name. Eventually she pressed it.

"Ava, *darling*," she purred as soon as she answered, not giving her a chance to speak. "How about you and Daisy come on over later and I'll cook you dinner?"

"Sounds great," Ava replied, immediately detecting the sarcasm she had laced the word *darling* with, and Elsa could feel her smiling through the phone. "What's the catch?"

"Aha," Elsa smiled, cutting to the chase. "One of you has to drive Clement's lorry back afterwards."

"Is he expecting it?" Ava asked.

"He will be, once you tell him. I was supposed to call him, but no way."

"Oh, come on, Else!" Ava replied. "At least give him a call? The poor boy has been dying to hear from you; he has absolutely no idea what he's done wrong, and has been keeping his distance from Frederick in case he strikes again."

"Yea, well I don't think you are entirely innocent, are you?" Elsa retorted.

Silence. Elsa smiled. Silence was what she was relieved to hear; it meant she had caught Ava out and all her speculation had come to fruition.

"I think you owe me," Elsa went on when Ava still did not reply. "Don't you? You're supposed to have my back, but where were you when Clement suggested we take a little walk? You knew what was on his mind. Were you *trying* to set us up?"

"Trying?" Ava sounded offended. "It bloody worked, didn't it? He kept asking about you and I thought a little distraction would help you get over Fred, now that he has seemed to move on with...well, you know. OK, so it backfired, and I *totally* underestimated Fred's reaction."

"You sent him after us?" Elsa gawped down the phone.

"No way, Else!" Ava replied. "I would *never* do that."

"I know you wouldn't," Elsa sighed. "So, I'll see you and Daisy tonight at eight for dinner."

Elsa let the casserole cook on a low heat while she did her afternoon yard duties. It had been her Grandmother's favourite recipe, and a staple food of young Elsa's when she had been growing up. She was certain that once Ava took a bite she would see that there were no hard feelings between them.

Cecil was barking as soon as she stepped out of the shower, and she pulled her dressing gown around her and descended the stairs in lightning speed.

“You’re early!” she beamed as she pulled the door open to them.

“Well, didn’t want to do anything else to get into your bad books, did I?” Ava grinned, thrusting a bottle of wine towards her.

“No, of course you don’t,” Elsa ushered them in, wanting them off her doorstep before Sophia saw them.

“Oh *my*,” Daisy took a deep breath of the kitchen’s glorious aroma. “That smells delicious. What is it?”

“Casserole,” Elsa smiled proudly.

“Casserole?” Ava repeated, eyebrows raised. “What, is it winter already?”

“Might as well be, the weather we’ve been having,” Elsa retaliated, shivering for good effect. “But if you’re going to pick holes in it, you can always go without.”

“No, no! I’ll have some,” Ava replied quickly. “I’m starving.”

“Right, well, it’s almost ready,” Else replied, heading towards the stairs. “I’m just going to go and get dressed.”

“Isn’t that what you wear to greet all the guests you have over for dinner?” Ava frowned, and Elsa shot her a scowl.

“Daisy doesn’t want to hear *anything* about it,” Elsa warned, taking the stairs two at a time.

She didn’t need to tell them to make themselves at home, as when she had returned they were both sitting on the sofa in front of the TV; legs curled up underneath them and Cecil sitting cheerfully in between them. They each held a small glass of wine while they took it in turns to scratch behind his ears.

Elsa went straight to the kitchen and dished up three generous servings of casserole and dumplings, and a small bowl for Cecil, which she guessed he would probably have licked clean before she even made it back to her chair.

“So, dare I ask…” she began as they all tucked in. “How are things at yours?”

"Well, Portia is still furious at the officials and taking it out on everybody who dares so much as to even look at her funny," Ava replied with a shrug. "Clement is just keeping his head down and trying not to wind Frederick up. And Frederick, well...he's just Frederick, not saying much at all. Portia has no idea why the two of them were fighting at all, and I denied all knowledge, but to be honest if she isn't at the centre of something then she's not really interested."

"You're quite the little minx, aren't you?" Daisy leaned forward in her seat with a wide smile, and gave her a wink. "But Clement aside, tell me what's the secret to bedding Frederick Twemlow, hey?"

"Woah!" Elsa cut her off. "Firstly, myself and Frederick are...well, *nothing*. Secondly, I *never* meant to lead Clement on, so please make sure you tell him that for me, won't you? And thirdly," she rounded on Ava. "How much have you bloody told her?"

"Elsa, if you expect a favour from someone, they need the full story!" Ava replied defensively.

"Oh, she told me *everything*," Daisy told her with a mischievous wink. "But it was a long drive over here and we were running out of things to talk about. Plus, this was much more exciting than *anything* going on back at the yard."

Elsa felt her cheeks reddening as she took another mouthful of dumpling.

"And *also*," Ava replied, determined to have the last word. "After you got poor Clement into a fight and left him lying on the floor covered in mud and bleeding, poor Daisy here had to mop up his nose!"

"I did," Daisy affirmed with a strong nod. "That was a first, I can tell you. Did quite a good job, if I do say so myself, but I draw the line at mending his broken heart."

Elsa couldn't help but join in with their laughter, and had to take another long gulp of wine.

"Seriously, though," Elsa told them when they had all

finally stopped. "I do hope Clement is OK?" she looked expectantly from one to the other. "I really didn't mean for *any* of this to happen."

"Ah, he'll be fine!" Daisy waved her concern away with a smile. "Don't you worry about him. His ego is a bit bruised and battered, but I'm sure he and Fred will patch things up, too."

"I bloody hope so," Elsa murmured. Could she ever forgive herself if they didn't?

"How was it?" Sophia dared ask the question as they passed in the tackroom. She had noticed Clement's lorry was gone as soon as she'd crawled out of bed and peered out of the window, leaving the space free for her new arrival later on. She clasped her hands together excitedly. It wouldn't be as nice as Clement's luxurious model, but it would be her own for as long as Cali and Dusty were performing well.

"Fine," Elsa shrugged, unable to meet her eye.

"Have you patched things up?" Sophia probed, reaching for a saddle off the rack.

"Absolutely," she replied, a little too quickly. "Everything is dandy...all patched up."

Sophia narrowed her eyes at her. She put the saddle down and stood waiting, her hands on her hips. "You didn't go, did you?"

Reluctantly, Elsa shook her head. "I'm sorry, Soph," she sighed. "I know you have my best interests at heart. Well, that and the fact that you probably couldn't be bothered to drive it all the way back yourself," she smiled sweetly. "But I just couldn't do it. I can't go there...I can't *see* them; *either* of them."

"Oh, for crying out loud, Else!" Sophia retorted, raising her hands in the air in frustration. "This is never going to sort itself out unless one of you is the bigger person! And that's not going to be either of them, is it?"

Elsa's eyes bore into her back as she watched her stride

away. *Since when was this her problem?*

She decided a fresh burst of country air to clear her mind could not come soon enough, and she saddled Bear and headed out past the grazing cattle towards the river, anything to tear her mind away from unwelcome thoughts of Clement and Frederick tussling in the mud. Bear began to jog when she anticipated a canter, and Elsa made her walk until her excitement had evaporated. The little mare felt on fine form, and Elsa hoped they would fit another couple of events in before the season was over, at least. Her smile had returned by the time they wandered back into the yard.

"Why don't you take the rest of today off?" Sophia suggested, as she strode the short distance back from the paddocks with a headcollar slung over her shoulder. "I can manage the ridden ones by myself, and the others can have a day out in the field."

"Are you sure?" Elsa frowned, dismounting and stripping her tack off.

"Of course," Sophia smiled. "I wouldn't have suggested it otherwise. All the stables are made up ready, aren't they? So, Mum can help me get them all in."

"Well, if you're sure," Elsa shrugged, already thinking how lovely it would be to put her feet up all day. She turned Bear out in the sand paddock, watching her kick up the sand as she rolled.

"Of course! And I'll feed in the morning, too, so don't hurry back."

"You sure?" Elsa looked at her suspiciously, following her to the haybarn.

"Of course!" Sophia busied herself stuffing haylage into a net, wishing she would just go. "You deserve a lie in."

"Right...OK," Elsa nodded.

When Sophia looked up, she was still there, looking at her suspiciously. "You're finished, aren't you?"

"Guess I am now," Elsa nodded.

"Well, get yourself home, then!" she laughed.

"Not sure what I'll do with myself, with all this spare time on my hands."

"I'm sure you'll find something," Sophia told her with a wink.

Elsa sunk back onto the comfy sofa and put her feet up on the coffee table. Despite their dry run recently, she had been looking forward to a day off, and the coffee mug warmed her hands as she contemplated what film she and Cecil were going to watch. He stretched out beside her, his head resting on her lap, and she couldn't help feeling that despite everything, her life was simply perfect.

Cecil's head shot up as her mobile phone began to ring, dragging her from her thoughts, and she ruined Cecil's comfort as she fidgeted to retrieve it from her jeans pocket.

Ava flashed up on the display, and Elsa answered the call with a smile.

"Hey!"

There was rustling before Ava eventually spoke, and she sounded a little breathless.

"Hey, Elsa. How's it going?"

"Good," Elsa nodded, her smile subsided. "Is everything OK?"

"Is it your day off?" Ava asked, ignoring her question.

"Yea," Elsa smiled. "Just curled up on the sofa with my favourite boy. What are you doing?"

There was a pause before Ava answered, amid more rustling and distant voices. "I'm loading Clement's horses," there was another pause. "He's leaving, Elsa." Ava added, her voice sounding strained. "It's all kicking off. Fred has sacked him."

"What?" Elsa's breath caught, certain she must have misheard her amongst the increasing rustling. "Seriously? What for?"

"Well, he had a whole list of stuff, but I'm telling you it was all bullshit." She paused, Elsa heard her take a breath. "I think it's really about seeing you two…you know...the kiss...the fight?"

Elsa closed her eyes, her serenity ruined. "*Pig*!" she spat, and tried to calm herself as she gathered her thoughts. "It can't be that, Ava," she eventually spoke again. "Mr Cool would never sack someone because of a girl, a girl who he has made it quite clear he wants no involvement with. There must be more to it – Clement must have done something."

"He hasn't…" Ava insisted, and Elsa waited as more rustling muffled the receiver. "He is beside himself, Else."

"Why are you telling me?" Elsa probed, not unkindly. "It's really nothing to do with me, it's their business."

"I'm telling you because… Clement mentioned you; he had some stuff he really wanted to say to you, but he didn't feel that he should. He is just going to leave, without saying a thing."

"Maybe it's for the best," Elsa sighed.

"Well, I don't think it is," Ava snapped. "Which is why I'm telling you. He's really upset and he could really do with some kind words from someone that means something to him so that he doesn't leave here on awful terms hating all of us."

"So, what should I do?" Elsa asked, not wanting to hear the answer.

"For fuck sake, Elsa!" Ava despaired. "You should go and catch him, quick! He asked me to sort the horses while he quickly packs. He's staying in the West wing. I think it would mean a lot to him if he could see you before he goes, get some things off his chest."

"Isn't the West Wing Frederick's?" Elsa frowned.

"Yes." She hesitated. "He's staying with Frederick."

"He's not staying in the staff accommodation?"

"No, definitely been staying with Frederick." Ava's tone was short, and Elsa really felt for her. She'd had enough on her plate recently without this. "That's partly why it's all so awkward and he's having to leave quickly. I don't think he's even found somewhere else to go yet. He might even go straight back to France."

Slowly Elsa closed her eyes as she tried to process it. She didn't want to get involved, but Clement had turned into a firm friend in the short time they had known each other, and she wished him well. Maybe it wouldn't hurt to say goodbye, and ensure him that there were no hard feelings.

"If he drives off in a state, before anyone has had a chance to calm him down," Ava tried one last time. "And something terrible happens to him and his horses, I don't think I could ever forgive myself if I hadn't even tried..."

"OK, *OK*!" Elsa gave in, dragging herself to her feet and Cecil jumped to the floor with a whine. It was her day off after all; she had nothing else to do. "But what if I bump into Frederick, Ava? I can't face..."

"You won't," Ava promised, cutting her off. "He's out all day."

She ran a brush through her hair and changed into a clean t-shirt. Despite not wanting to make herself appealing to Clement, if he really was going straight back to France and she was going to be his last memory of their little country, then she wanted it to be a good impression. She didn't want him sitting at home in his chateau in years to come, reminiscing that the only one who had come to wave him off looked like she'd been dragged through a bush hedge backwards.

She started her trusty little Fiat and began the cross country drive to Frederick Twemlow's impressive estate. Suddenly hoping she made it there before Clement did depart, she put her foot down.

Despite having had plenty of time to think about it, she still had no idea what she was going to say to him by the time she pulled to a halt beside Frederick's plush lorry. Her heart fell as she noticed Clement's wasn't parked beside it, and feared she was too late. She hoped it was backed out of sight on one of the smaller yards, or maybe Daisy had driven it away and Clement was still packing. Having driven all this way she didn't want to have missed him. One last brief check of herself in her tiny interior mirror and she climbed out of her rusting little car. Taking a deep breath, she started walking past the immaculate yards - where she would normally be heading - towards the big house, and suddenly felt in very foreign territory.

Chapter Ten

The West Wing looked out onto the well-kept landscaped gardens, and was more of a house in its own right than the extension of the Twemlow mansion she had envisioned it was. Her hand hesitated over the big, brass door knocker, and she stalled as she noticed Frederick's Range Rover parked in the four-bay open fronted old cart lodge.

He's gone out, she told herself, *of course he doesn't have to have taken his car…or his lorry.* Ava's words played on her mind. This whole thing made her feel uncomfortable, but she had come this far, and with a shaking hand she rapped the knocker against the unnecessarily wide front door, and nervously waited.

She heard footsteps in the hallway and straightened herself in preparation for the door swinging open - ready to fight - but then she froze.

He looked *gorgeous.* Those soft, blue eyes stared straight at her, his thick blonde, springing curls that she instantly remembered what it felt like to run her hands through them. Any attempt at a sentence stuck in her throat as she observed how casual he looked. His blue denim jeans sat low on his hips, his shirt untucked and unbuttoned halfway down his chest. The sleeves were rolled up to his elbows and his expensive, chunky watch sparkled on his tanned wrist. He wore slippers that she thought might suit him were he puffing on a cigar. He didn't look at all as though he had just sacked someone.

"Elsa," Frederick Twemlow purred. "What a lovely surprise."

She remembered the hatred that had raged through her the last time her eyes had rested on him, the pent up fury that had spilled out from him as he'd punched Clement into the mud, and she so desperately wanted to hate him now. Yet standing before her, he looked nothing like the Frederick from Wellington lorry-park, the one who had been a stranger to her, and instead just like the Frederick she had used to know. For a moment she had to remind herself of the real reason she had come here.

"Where's Clement?" she eventually managed.

"He's taken his horses for a gallop." He frowned. "Ava has gone with him; they'll be gone at least a couple of hours."

At first Elsa didn't know what to say, and a cold shiver ran through her as she immediately realised what her friend had done.

"Is everything alright?"

"You haven't sacked him, have you?"

"Who?" Frederick's brow furrowed.

"Clement!" Elsa ran her hand through her caramel hair in frustration.

"What on earth has got into you?" Frederick asked in amusement, his arms folded across his chest as he leaned casually against the oak door frame, and her heart gave a familiar pang. "Of course I haven't sacked him! Who on earth told you that?"

"Ava," she mumbled in embarrassment, reeling at what her so called friend had done to her, with a thousand questions swirling around in her head. "That little..." she quickly stopped herself, and let her gaze fall to the floor. Frederick didn't need to know about it, and she desperately wondered where her hatred towards him had evaporated to. "I should go."

"Or you could come in?" he stood back from the door, holding it open so that she could peer into the impressive hallway.

No! Her head screamed, arguing ferociously with her heart. *Don't go in! You haven't come here to see him!* But she wanted to, more than anything. She didn't think she could ever have the willpower to just turn and leave, walk straight back down the drive without even a second glance in his direction. After his actions at the weekend, she knew that was all that he deserved. But she knew there was an untold story somewhere, and her curiosity wanted her to get to the bottom of it. And she *needed* to see him; she needed to see this insight into his life he was offering her if she were to ever figure him out.

The hallway wasn't stately-home impressive - she assumed that was saved for the main entrance around the front of the main house - but it was more than just an annex. It was bigger than any room in her cosy cottage, with oak panel stairs right in front of her and a door off to the kitchen to the left, which Elsa followed Frederick through. The kitchen was large, with a marble-top island and more cupboards than Elsa could shake a stick at. It was immaculately kept, and Elsa looked around herself in awe.

"Do you even cook?" she asked, eyebrows raised. "Or is all this just for show?"

"I like to cook," his soft blue eyes twinkled in amusement, "when I can find the time. It's a good way to unwind. Drink?"

She looked up and her eyes settled on him, and she realised he had asked her a question. She nodded, her mouth bone dry. He opened the fridge, and she couldn't help but notice at how well-stocked it was, and as she peeled her eyes back to him she realised he was still waiting for her answer.

"Just water is fine," she lied. She was dying for a glass of wine, even though the day was still young.

She watched as he ignored her, reached for the bottle of white wine in the fridge door and unscrewed the cap. She licked her lips as he poured her a generous glass and passed it to her.

"I said water," she smiled, as she took it from him. Her palms were sweating so much she prayed the glass didn't slip from her grip and smash on the flagstone floor. "It's barely even lunch time. Are you trying to get me drunk?"

"Drunk, no," he smiled. "To relax a little? Of course."

She took a larger than she intended gulp of wine, and sighed as the cool, crispness hit the back of her throat.

"Please," he stilled her shaking hand. "Why are you always so nervous around me?"

She jumped at his touch. She looked from his hand, those perfect fingers gently gripping her slender wrist, up along his muscled arms, until her gaze fell on his eyes. "Because you put me on edge," she whispered.

"You have brought yourself here, Elsa," he trailed off, as though he were going to say something else but thought better of it.

"Yes, under false pretences," she replied. "Which is probably just as well, as last time I came here willingly to see you, you didn't want to know."

He dropped her hand and turned away, and she saw the hurt flicker across his face, and it filled her with confusion. She watched him as he poured himself a glass of wine, and gazed out of the window across the gravel drive as he took a sip. He leaned forward against the sideboard, and she had an overwhelming urge to walk behind him and slip her arms around his waist, and hold him tightly. But she stilled herself, and pulled out a barstool at the island, not trusting her legs to hold her up much longer.

"Are we just going to keep ignoring it forever?" she eventually spoke, her heart pounding fast as she waited for his response.

"Ignoring what, Elsa?" he turned around to face her. His question caught her, she didn't want to say it out loud. She just wanted him to be able to look at her and see the turmoil within her, that he had created, whether he had meant it or not. But most of all, despite how much she wanted to hate him right now, she wanted him to put everything right.

"What are you doing here, anyway?" he broke her from her thoughts. "Have you come to see him?"

"Ava told me you'd sacked him."

"Did she now? And why would she tell you that - to get you all worked up and storming around here to give me a piece of your pretty mind."

"No, not exactly," she mumbled. "She told me you were out, and Clement was in here packing, and he wanted to see me before he left."

"Well, you got the wrong house, for a start," Frederick told her in amusement. "Clement doesn't live here; he has an apartment in the staff quarters."

She raised her eyebrows at his use of the word *apartment*, imagining the spacious living area he had been allocated. She had been suspicious when Ava had told her he lived with Frederick, but she hadn't questioned her because she was her friend. Why would she lie to her?

"She's well and truly fooled you, hasn't she?" Frederick smiled, as if reading her mind. "I thought the pair of you were friends?"

"We were...*are*," Elsa gulped. "But she's set us up, hasn't she?"

"And why would she want to do that?" His blue eyes searched hers from across the kitchen.

"You tell me, she's your Head Girl." Elsa gave a feeble shrug. She bit her lower lip as she tried to figure out what went on in Ava's head. She knew Elsa currently detested Frederick and never wanted to lay eyes on him again, so why had she sent her directly to him?

"Yes, and she's your friend, which means more right now."

"So is Clement, so are you going to sack him?" she demanded, because she could *really* hate him if he said yes.

"Of course not!" Frederick implored, the suggestion absurd, and Elsa let out her breath. He turned to look back out of the window, and she hated not being able to read his expression. "He wanted to leave, I had to almost bloody beg him to stay. What would people say if it got out that I'd punched my protégé?"

"Is that all you care about, what people think?"

"No, of course not!" Frederick replied, spinning around to face her angrily. "But this is my livelihood, Elsa."

"I think you'd manage to survive if this all went wrong," she snapped curtly. "I'm sure you could tap your parents up for a bit more cash to try something else." She knew she was being unfair and out of line, and she saw the hurt flash across his sad eyes.

She almost felt bad, but she forced herself to remember everything she hated about him. But it was helpless; just one look at him and she wanted to fall into his arms.

"It's not like that," he murmured. "It's not like that at all."

"What is it like, then?" she whispered. "Talk to me, Frederick."

She placed down her wine glass before she dropped it, and got to her feet. Slowly she made her way across to him, and he made no attempt to move as she ran her palm softly down his cheek. He reached up and took her hand in his, his eyes roaming hers until they fell on her mouth.

He wanted to kiss her so bad, but he knew she must hate him right now. And he didn't blame her; he had treated her badly and he couldn't promise to treat her any better now. He took a deep breath of her scent, her coconut-smelling soft hair. She looked as beautiful as ever, even more so when she was angry at him.

"Why did you punch him?" she whispered, taking a deep breath of his familiar aftershave that awoke the butterflies in her stomach.

"Because I couldn't bear to see him touching you," he murmured, still holding her hand as her thumb subconsciously stroked his stubble. "I can't bear to think of anyone touching you."

"Yet you," she retorted matter-of-factly, "can't bear to touch me."

"Oh, I want to do more than just touch you, Elsa," he told her. "But you deserve better than me. I'm not good for you."

"You have no idea what's good for me," she replied, fighting back a tear. "So, do you know how it feels for me, to stand here before you, wanting to hate you, but simply being unable to? Wanting you to touch me and hold me and make me feel worthwhile, knowing that you don't want to?"

"You don't need me to make you feel worthwhile, Elsa," he whispered. "You are perfect; you are beautiful, funny, intelligent, and you are more than worthwhile and you know it."

Frederick's lips were on hers, taking her by surprise as he dropped her hand and his hands grasped her cheeks. He was eager and rough, yet gentle and kind, and she felt her stomach flip somersaults as her lips parted to welcome him. She pushed her body against him, and he encouraged her into his rock hard chest.

"I do want you, Elsa," he told her huskily, his hands skimming over her shoulders, quickly down her arms and clasping the bottom of her t-shirt, as he lifted it off over her head. "I always want you!"

He dropped it to the floor and her arms wrapped around his neck. She could already feel his erection, pressing into her through his jeans, and she smiled. She grasped the collar of his shirt as he kissed her, her fingers working their way down his buttons as she fumbled to unfasten each one. She slipped it off over his shoulders, his hands briefly happy to part from her as it fell to the ground, and she rejoiced as her palm fell on his warm, hard chest.

She felt him hesitate, and he pulled away. She took a deep breath as she waited for the *We shouldn't be doing this* line.

"Come to bed with me?" he murmured.

She playfully rolled her eyes, as if she'd say no to him now. She didn't care of the consequences, or who else was involved in his life to make things so complicated. She needed him and she wanted him to need her, too.

He took her hand, leading her back through the kitchen to the hallway, and she eagerly followed him, her heart pounding fast and hard with adrenaline. She followed him closely up the stairs, along the landing to the end, and he pushed open a door to his immaculate, spacious bedroom, as if she would have expected anything else.

His bed was not perfectly made, but he had made some effort with the crisp, whiter-than-white sheets. He stopped her just inside the doorway, and pulled her into him, his lips not wanting to be parted from her for more than a minute.

"Are you sure?" he murmured, tracing kisses along her neck as she tilted her head to accommodate him.

"As sure as a sure thing," she murmured back, and she meant it. Moral dilemmas and maintaining her dignity could shove off right now. If only for half an hour, she would worry about them after.

He easily scooped her up, carried her to the bed and dropped her down in the centre, hovering above her with a knee between her legs, and the other beside her. She smiled up at him, wanting this to last forever, but also wanting to hurry him in case he changed his mind.

He expertly unclasped her bra and shoved it to the side. She gasped as his tongue found her hardened nipple, and he licked and sucked at it sending tingles to her groin. She wanted to be out of these jeans, but his knees pinned against her prevented her.

She reached forward for his belt buckle, and unfastened his jeans. He helped her slide them over his hips and she felt his intake of breath as she ran her fingers around the waistband of his boxers, and slipped her hand inside, taking a firm, eager grip of his cock, and quickly stroking it to full hardness.

"*Elsa...*" he murmured helplessly, as he nibbled her ear. He grabbed the waist of her jeans and hoisted her up, easily sliding them over her petite rear and down her slender, perfect legs. He traced kisses along her inner thigh, leaving her squirming beneath him as he peeled her jeans off over her ankles, and tossed them to the floor. She clasped hold of the bed sheets as his lips neared her groin, and subconsciously parted her legs for him.

"I've missed you, Else," he murmured, skimming his thumbs over her hips bones as he hoisted her up towards him.

Her mouth was so dry she could not reply, nor did she want to tell him how much she had missed him or how often she thought about him.

He was hungry for her, he could barely wait any longer. He always thought about her, and how he had messed up when she had tried to apologise. But he was stubborn, as was she, and there was no way he'd back down of his own accord. And now here she was, lying on his expansive bed and looking as delicious as ever, and he couldn't wait to devour her. And he needed to do it before she realised what a stupid thing it was to be getting reacquainted with him, and made her excuses and left.

He didn't think he'd ever have got the chance to see her like this again, and while half of him wanted to make the most of it, the other half didn't think he could wait that long. His hands slid underneath her perfect rear and she hoisted her hips up towards him, aching for his touch. Her sex was tingling just at the thought of everything she wanted him to do to her. Her heart was aching at how much she wanted to hate him, but she couldn't. While she thought she should be running a mile, instead she was arching her body towards him, wanting to feel more of him.

He ran his thumbs inside the waistband of her panties, sliding them delicately down her thighs and off over her ankles. She was at his mercy, totally naked before him. She reached forward and slid his boxers off, and laid back as he stepped himself out of them, licking her lips as his erection sprang towards her.

He leaned towards her, and she laid back in the soft duvet, gazing up at him. His ocean blue eyes searched hers, and the gentlest of smiles tugged at his lips.

"What?" she murmured, feeling embarrassed under his scrutinising gaze.

"You're so beautiful," he whispered, his eyes roaming what they could of her body as he hovered above her.

She giggled shyly and tried to twist her body away from him to hide, even though he had seen her all before. But his knees held her tight, and she could barely move. She stilled, and there was silence except from her pounding heart that threatened to burst through her chest at any moment.

Leaning back, Frederick gently prized her folded arms from across her breasts, his strong hands around her slender wrists as he moved them above her head. As the weight of his body brushed against her throbbing sex, she had a sharp intake of breath.

She closed her eyes and his lips were suddenly against hers. She felt so good with his weight pressed hard against her. He held her wrists with just one hand as his mouth parted from her warm, moist lips, brushed down her neck as his other hand kneaded her breasts. She groaned and writhed against him, and he shuffled between her legs and she felt his erection probing at her folds.

Her breathing quickened as his tongue lapped at her hardened nipple, quickly skimmed across her stomach, and she cried out as his head was buried between her legs. She bucked against him, his tongue feeling glorious against her, and knowing she was so wet for him, so ready for him to fill her. She sensed his eagerness too, as he stopped her from reaching for his cock even though she desperately wanted to. He hooked his arms under her knees, dragging her towards him, and she observed the hunger etched across his beautiful face as he swiftly entered her, making her cry out in a glorious mixture of adulation and shock.

His arm was around her back; he held her firmly off the bed and close to him and she grew accustomed to the size of him inside her. She involuntarily whimpered as he withdrew, and she braced herself as he swiftly entered her.

"Relax," he murmured, biting her ear a little harder than he intended to.

She felt him stretching her; she wasn't sure how she could accommodate all of him but it felt glorious and painful both at the same time, and she didn't ever want him to stop. She obeyed him, and felt her muscles relax around him, as he lay her back down on the bed and began his assault of eager, quick thrusts, her arching towards him to feel more of him each time. Her fists clenched the crisp bed sheets, her eyes closed as he didn't hold back.

He watched her as she chewed her bottom lip, tilted her head back and he couldn't resist biting her neck as he hungrily drove into her. He didn't think he would get this chance with her again, and it had been all he'd been thinking about since the last time. He prized her fists from the bed, his thumb and fore-finger easily holding her slender wrists. He felt his orgasm brewing; amazed at himself he'd managed to last this long already. He sat back and pulled her onto his lap, lifting her up and down with his strong arms to meet his every thrust. He gently bit down on her shoulder and she let out a low groan, feeling him bruise her and not caring a bit. Their sweating, entwined bodies slapped together and she felt herself nearing the point of no return.

"I'm going to come," she whispered, her eyes closed and head back, her breasts bouncing against his chest. He took a hardened nipple in his mouth and sucked hard, anything to make him last a bit longer as he slammed helplessly into her.

He felt her muscles convulsing against his cock as she bucked against him, losing any remaining control of her body as she gave herself to him entirely. He tilted her back, she trusting him to hold her as she slowly came back down to earth, wanting to satisfy him. With a groan he drove into her with all his might one last time, slamming her down on his lap as he emptied himself into her.

She fell against his chest as they slowly got their breath back, and he held her tightly, never wanting to let her go. Eventually he withdrew, and gently pulled her down beside him as he stretched out in the gloriously large bed, pulling the crumpled duvet over the pair of them. Her back was to him, and she felt his breath on the back of her neck, as gently he toyed with her nipple in the palm of his hand. She felt his lips brushing softly across her shoulder blade and couldn't conceal her smile. She felt sore but satisfied and she wouldn't change it for the world.

He drew his hand up to his lips and kissed it softly. She deserved the world and he only wished he could give it to her. He nudged her neck with his nose and she tilted it for him. He observed the faint red mark he had left, one of many, and kissed it gently.

"I am sorry," he whispered, feeling her heart pounding.

She nodded and pushed herself further back into his warm cocoon, and wondered if he was talking only about the intimate moments they had just shared, or the much broader picture. Suddenly exhausted, she closed her eyes and fell asleep in the safety of his muscular frame.

She yawned and stretched out in the warm, huge, soft bed and smiled as she observed the beautiful, blue eyes staring back at her.

"Do you not have to be anywhere today?" she asked him.

"No, it's my day off," he planted a gentle kiss on her forehead.

"Did Ava know that?" Elsa narrowed her eyes at him.

"Of course, she's my right-hand man. I tell her most of my plans."

"Wow, she asked me if I had a day off today, too," Elsa

replied, thinking aloud. "She really did plan this down to the infinite detail; knowing neither of us would have to rush off quickly somewhere."

"Unless of course, you want to rush off somewhere quickly?" he murmured, looking uncertain.

"I could stay here forever," she told him, holding his gaze.

Stay, then? His heart implored him to ask aloud. *Stay forever?* But he couldn't. It was far too complicated in the real world than it all seemed while they were lying between the sheets.

"Can I get you anything to eat?" were the words that escaped his lips instead, and she looked at him in surprise.

"I hadn't really thought about food," she murmured.

"You grooms never do," he replied, peeling back the bed covers and getting to his feet. "I've no idea where you lot get your strength from, really."

She propped herself up on her elbow as she watched him pick up his crumpled jeans from the floor and cover his splendid body. She felt a little sad, wondering if she would get to see it again. Even though she suspected she may not, she had no regrets at all about coming here.

She watched him leave the room, and then dragged herself up and paced across to the en-suite bathroom; stopping on the way to admire the view over the whole of his stable yard to the left, and his parent's stately gardens to the right. A groom lunged a horse in the outdoor arena, but from here Elsa could not see who they or the horse were. Realising she was standing naked at the window, she quickly tore herself away.

The bathroom was white and silver with marble top around the huge sink basin, the expansive shower that could almost house a horse. She stared at herself in the mirror, and smiled. She felt *amazing*. Her hair was ruffled around the back and she dragged her fingers gently through it, before tying it up in a tight bun on top of her head. Although she wanted the scent of him to remain on her forever, she really wanted to test whether that shower was as glorious as it looked.

She turned the temperature up and spun the dial, and watched half of the shower ceiling cascade with water droplets down onto her, and smiled. She could get used to this, she thought as she stepped underneath it. It was nothing like the tiny little bathroom back at her cottage where she regularly smacked her limbs against the glass every time she tried to shave her legs.

She wasn't sure how long she had been in there, but as she wiped the water from her face and turned, she saw Frederick standing in the doorway, smiling as he watched her.

"Enjoying yourself?" he smiled.

"Oh *yes*," she replied, suddenly feeling self-conscious that she was totally naked before him, and he clothed. "Why don't you come and join me?" she found herself asking, and felt her heart racing as she waited for his decision.

"I thought you'd never ask," he murmured eventually. Tracing his tongue along his bottom lip, he unfastened his jeans and stepped out of them, standing before her in just his pants. She couldn't help but look, as he stepped towards her. She outstretched her arm, her pointed finger digging into his chest bringing him to a reluctant halt.

"You can't come in here with *clothes* on," she told her.

Smiling, he dug his thumbs into the waistband of his underwear and slid it down and off over his heels. She didn't even try to hide the fact she was taking in the whole, glorious sight of his erection.

She felt herself shaking, despite the heat of the water, as he stepped towards her. His hands brushed her shoulder, skimmed across her collar bone and rested on her neck, as he tilted her head up to meet his lips.

He kissed her gently at first, his tongue becoming more forceful as his lust intensified. He *needed* her. She made him feel alive and complete, and he spent every minute that she wasn't here, wishing that she could be. His hands skimmed down her back and cupped her cheeks and in one swift move he hoisted her up and her legs were around his waist.

"I *need* you, Frederick," she gasped. "*Please.*"

He felt his heart skip a beat as her words danced in his ears. But she must know he was no good for her. She was intelligent, after all, one of the many things he loved about her.

Her back slammed against the rock hard wall, but she didn't care. He held her firmly, but it wasn't easy with the cascading water. Her drenched hair clung to her face, and he thought she'd never looked so beautiful. He kissed her lips, her neck, traced along her shoulder and she groaned deeply as her breasts pushed against his chest. He anchored her firm, poised his cock at her folds, and as he steadied his arms around her he drove hungrily into her.

She cried out, welcoming every inch of him as she wrapped her legs tighter around him.

He thrust quickly, eager to satisfy her and himself, but well aware how much her drenched skin slipped in his palms, and worrying about how long he could hold her. His mouth covered hers, he was so hungry for her and he didn't like to be rough but he just couldn't help himself.

Her breath was short as her muscles clenched. He groaned as she felt him nearing his orgasm. She bit down on his shoulder as she felt herself erupt around his greedy cock, and her hips bucked against him as she accepted all of him.

"Oh *God*, Elsa!" Frederick gasped, unable to hold back any longer, and his fingers dug into her cheeks as he pounded gratefully into her and unleashed. "Oh *God*!"

He held her tight for a moment as she collapsed against him, breathless and fulfilled. She let out a low moan as he withdrew, and her jelly legs slid from him, grateful that he held her tightly when she could easily have just collapsed in a spent heap in the shower. His eyes bore into her so intently that she felt shy and nervous. *What happened now?*

She shivered, having been under the water long enough now. Frederick turned it off and planted the most tender of kisses on her wet lips.

"Come on," he murmured, lifting her easily from the shower. He pulled a crisp, white towel from the heated rail and wrapped it around her. She closed her eyes as she snuggled into its warmth, and she was in his arms within moments, as he carried her out of the bathroom and across the bedroom.

He placed her down on the huge bed, and she could not move under his huge frame as he hovered above her.

"Have you had enough yet?" he brushed his lips teasingly against hers.

"I don't think I could ever have enough of you, Frederick," she breathed.

"Well, that makes two of us, then," he murmured, tracing kisses down her neck, and she writhed beneath him as she half-heartedly struggled to be free. His lips paused, and she heard his breathing. She lifted her head to observe him, chewing his lip as he stared intently at the slight red marks he had left on her.

"Shit, Elsa," he murmured.

"What's wrong?" she frowned.

"I hurt you," it was almost a whisper, as he traced his finger softly across her breasts, up her chest, across the marks on her shoulder and neck.

"It's fine," she murmured, remembering the surges of passion that had spiralled through her with his every touch, rough or not.

"It's not fine," he told her.

She stilled his hand, trailing her fingers across his knuckles, and placed his hand against her neck. He pulled her into his chest, and held her so tightly she thought for a moment he might suffocate her.

"I must admit, you are more accommodating than the last

time I saw you," he murmured teasingly.

"What the hell had got into you?" She remembered her fury and hatred towards him, and how she believed it wouldn't subside for months.

"Me?" he laughed. "What the hell had got into *you*? I mean…*Clement*?"

"Yes, Clement! He's kind, genuine, good looking, funny…" she sighed.

"As well he may be, Elsa," Frederick replied quietly. "But he's not for you."

"How do you know who is for me?"

"Do you want to go to bed with him?" he asked her seriously.

"No," Elsa admitted after a pause, her cheeks reddening.

"Then why kiss him?"

"I was intrigued." She shrugged. "I was grateful for a bit of attention, I guess."

"He's not for you, Elsa." Frederick shook his head.

"So, who is for me?" she confronted him bitterly, not sure she wanted to hear his answer. She could already sense him backing off, his overriding reluctance at any important discussion between them.

Me! His heart screamed. *Can't you see? Me!* He took a deep breath and couldn't meet her eye. Instead he pulled her closer to his chest, and kissed the top of her head, immediately feeling his temper disintegrate.

"You deserve the best, Elsa," he told her, his heart breaking to know that he was far from that.

Her eyes shot open at the sound of banging underneath their window and she spun to face Frederick. He lay on his back, with his arm still around her like he didn't want to let her go no matter how uncomfortable it might be for him. His eyes were open, and he stared blankly at the ceiling.

"Is that the door?" she murmured.

"Just ignore it," Frederick replied, pulling her in closer to his chest.

She sighed as she rested her head on his chest. But the banging on the door continued.

"What if it's important?"

"It won't be important," Frederick told her, but he did not look at her.

"*Frederick*!" the familiar voice snarled, and Elsa froze. *Portia*.

She sat up, staring at him as she waited for an explanation, but he continued staring blankly at the ceiling.

"*Frederick*!" Portia was louder this time and more ferocious. "Open the bloody door!"

"What does she want?" Elsa breathed, feeling nauseas at the sound of her voice.

"She probably wants to ask something about one of the horses," Frederick told her, but something told her not to believe him. "I'm sure she can figure it out herself."

"It could be something serious," Elsa bit her lip as she struggled to hold back her emotion. "Maybe you should go to her?"

He didn't reply, and she was conscious of his thumb brushing over her shoulder. She had an urge to wrap her arms protectively around him, but something told her to back off.

She waited in silence until Portia got bored. She heard the growl of frustration, the final slam of the big, brass, door knocker and the stamp of feet scrunching on gravel as she made her way back down the drive. She waited until total silence resumed, and looked at him again. He looked emotionless, and she waited for him to speak.

She sensed his hesitation, as though his mind was struggling for the words to string a sentence. She wouldn't hold her breath. Even through their unexpected intimacy, she could feel his distance. Something had changed, and she wished she knew what it was, but he wasn't the same cheerful, friendly, bouncing, unflappable Frederick that had knocked on the door of her lorry in what felt like a lifetime ago.

She took a deep breath. "Are you and her together?" she forced the words out.

"No, Elsa."

"Don't lie to me," she warned. "I see how she is with you; she's all over you."

"I wouldn't lie to you," he told her simply, even though there were things he couldn't tell her and wished he could.

"You do nothing to fend her off. You seem quite taken with her."

"I would not be lying here with you, Elsa, were I supposed to be in a relationship with Portia, or even harbouring any feelings towards her. Give me *some* credit." He even looked offended and she marvelled at the cheek of him. But it was his deep sadness that troubled her the most.

"You've stuff on your mind, haven't you?" she realised once it was too late that she'd asked the question aloud.

He turned slightly to look at her, as though surprised, before slowly nodding. "Tremendous amounts, but…"

"But it's none of my business, I know," she cut him off. "Sorry."

"Don't be sorry," he looked hurt. "I wasn't going to say that. I won't bore you with the details, but there is a lot going on, yes."

She nodded, feeling as though she was only scratching at the surface of a very deep wound. "They are things that are out of your control, aren't they?" she went on boldly. "And you don't know how to handle that."

"Something like that," he replied slowly. "You're good at reading people, Elsa."

"I'm not, actually," she replied. "But I would like to think I know you, even if just a little bit."

He rolled over to face her, propping himself up on his elbow. "You know me better than most," he held her gaze, studying her. "Yet I don't really know you at all, do I?"

"You could have, if you'd wanted to," she murmured, feeling the raw hurt come flooding back. She wanted to cry, as she knew deep down this wasn't the reconciliation that she'd hoped for.

"You can do better than me," he told her. "I am filled with admiration for everything that you have achieved in your life, and everything you continue to achieve, and I am no match for that. I am not deserving."

She wanted to laugh out loud at the absurdity of his comment, but the noise stuck in her throat, and all she managed was a feeble gulp.

Chapter Eleven

"Had a nice day off?" Sophia beamed as she offered Elsa a cup of tea.

Elsa nodded, pausing from mucking out Connor's stall, and gratefully accepting the tea.

"Get up to much?"

"Just headed into town to browse the shops," Elsa shrugged, unable to look at her.

"Buy anything nice?"

Elsa spun to confront her, waiting for the smirk. But Sophia looked at her blankly. *She couldn't know,* Elsa thought. There was no way she could know, and she wanted it to stay like that.

"What?" Sophia frowned, wondering what she had said to achieve such a *look*. When Ava had called her, asking if Elsa could have the day off so she could take her out for some well-deserved retail therapy, Sophia had thought Elsa would at least enjoy herself. She rarely took the chance to have any time to herself.

"Nothing," Elsa mumbled.

"So, did you?" Sophia shrugged.

"Did I what?" Elsa repeated, her cheeks turning red. *Could she really tell?*

"Buy anything nice!" Sophia sighed in exasperation. "Seriously, Elsa! What's got into you?"

Oh, you don't want to know! She thought, her cheeks definitely red now. She took a deep breath. "No, nothing took my fancy," she told her, turning away to grab the broom. "Maybe next time, hey?"

Her mobile phone was pressed closed to her body in her jeans pocket, and she pulled it out every time she thought she detected the hint of a vibrate, or the sound of a text. Her heart fell every time she looked at the blank screen, or read a contact's name that wasn't *Frederick*. She sighed, she knew she only had herself to blame, but why did she let herself get so worked up over him? Why couldn't she just accept it for what it was - a fabulous one-night stand - and walk away?

She scrolled through her last dialled numbers, and hit the call button on Ava's name. It rang only a couple of times before her call was cancelled. She immediately dialled again.

"Don't you dare hang up!" she hissed, as soon as Ava answered.

"Elsa, can I call you back?" Ava asked feebly. "I'm really busy."

"No! Bloody talk to me, Ava!" Elsa demanded angrily.

"I'm sorry, Else…it was for your own good. Please don't hate me?"

"Come over tonight," Elsa demanded. "I'm not taking no for an answer, or you will pay! And bring wine…*expensive* wine!"

"I will…" Ava promised, and Elsa quickly hit the button to end the call before she got even angrier.

Elsa was in the kitchen when she heard the little car scrunch to a halt in the yard, and breathed a sigh of relief. Ava stepped out, clutching a bottle of wine. She straightened her jacket, took a deep breath and hurried to the door.

Elsa tried to be furious. Part of her *wanted* to still be furious, but then she remembered how good Frederick's touch had felt and all her fury melted instantly away. She flung open the door before Ava had even had a chance to knock.

"Oh!" Ava jumped back in surprise, and studied Elsa's expression for a brief second before deciding she was safe. She thrust the bottle of wine towards her. "Peace offering?"

"Why did you do it to me, Ava?" Elsa demanded, her hands on hips as she tried to take the moral high ground.

For a moment Ava looked like she was going to fight, but

she simply shrugged. "Because no one can get through to him, Elsa," she replied, running her hand through her loose hair. "I've always been able to, but he's been so distant recently. Now he's being nasty to his staff, and they won't put up with it. They work hard for him, they won't be treated like shit."

"And what's that got to do with me?"

"Because I thought, if I could persuade you to go there – under false pretences, I know, because you would never have agreed otherwise…" she trailed off. "Well, I thought I could kill two birds with one stone."

Elsa glared at her. "How did you even know I had a day off…which I didn't, by the way, when I woke up that morning?"

Ava had the decency to look embarrassed. "Because I called Sophia and asked her to give you a day off."

"You *what*?" Elsa gawped. "Ava, you can't do that!"

"She said you were having a quiet day. I told her you needed cheering up after the recent events so could I take you shopping, and maybe we'd stop off at a wine bar on the way home."

"So her offering to feed for me in the morning wasn't because she thought I'd be snuggled up in bed with Frederick?"

"No, Elsa!" Ava fought back.

"Why are you even wasting so much of your time hatching these disastrous plans for me, anyway?" Elsa demanded.

"Because you are both as stubborn as arseholes!" Ava went on, meeting her square in the eye. "I can see how you feel about him, and he about you. And it's not the hatred you want everyone to think it is, is it, Elsa? You are meant to be together."

"Yea, well, we won't be now." Elsa sighed.

"Don't tell me you've messed up again?" Ava declared, brushing past her and into the kitchen. She wasted no time in retrieving two wine glasses from the cupboard, and pouring them both a generous glass.

"I must admit I had high hopes that my little plan had paid off," she paused from pouring and gave Elsa a wink. "I was informed about how long your car was parked in our yard. People were suspicious about who it belonged to, and where the owner might have been."

"Oh, for God's sake!" Elsa rolled her eyes, feeling her cheeks reddening, and she had to turn away.

"No way!" she beamed, observing her sudden silence. "You did, didn't you? So, you slept with him and you *still* messed up? Seriously, Elsa!" Ava implored. She passed her a glass and Elsa pretty much snatched it from her, taking a long, much-needed gulp.

"What was it *like*?" she giggled, making her own way through to the living room and making herself comfy on the sofa, ready to hear the *whole* story.

Elsa couldn't face it yet, and went to the kitchen to put the pizza in the oven; her feeble attempt at providing dinner for the friend who probably didn't deserve any at all.

"Well, I'm glad you find it so funny," she said, upon her return.

"Oh, I do…" Ava giggled, but quickly broke off. "But I also don't. Because I know how much you like him."

"I don't."

"Oh, you do. A blind man could see that you do. So, tell me what happened? Maybe I could help put it right?" she looked hopeful.

"I think you've done enough, don't you?" Elsa glared at her.

Cecil barked, his tail thumping against the wall as he stared towards the kitchen door, and Elsa looked up with a frown as she waited for the sound of the knock.

"Must be Sophia," she said, dragging herself from the sofa. Cecil would not be wagging his tail so enthusiastically were it anyone else. "Please don't tell her anything, Ava? She doesn't know a thing."

"Hey!" Sophia called into the kitchen. "OK to come in?"

"Of course," Elsa called back, going through to meet her.

"I didn't want to interrupt," she followed Elsa through to the living room, and leaned down to give Ava a hug. "But I saw Ava's car on the drive and thought I'd try and make up for standing you guy's up last time," she held out a bottle of wine, certain that would be enough to seal the deal. "I did bring wine!"

"Ah, we're going to need lots of wine tonight!" Ava laughed, giving Elsa a wink even though her cold stare implored her to be quiet. "Elsa's got herself in a bit of a pickle, haven't you, Else?"

"Got *herself*?" Elsa retorted. "You've got a bloody cheek!"

"Right, come on," Sophia stood in the centre between them, hands on hips. "What have I missed?"

Ava patted the sofa space beside her, as she dragged herself up. "You sit down and Elsa will tell you all about it," she laughed. "I'll get you a glass of wine."

"Right, so the way you are shooting daggers at her, and she is clearly loving it," Sophia began, settling down opposite her Head Girl. "I'd say this has something to do with Clement or Frederick."

"Maybe both!" Ava roared with laughter from the kitchen.

"I almost regret inviting her over." Elsa winced.

"No, you don't!" Ava declared, returning quickly with a glass of wine for Sophia, and placing a sharing platter of hot, slightly browned pizza on the coffee table. "Although I must admit, I was petrified of coming over. I thought she was going to *crucify* me, Soph. You'd think a certain someone would be happy after getting laid *yet again* by Freddy Twemlow."

"You *didn't*?" Sophia's hands flew to her mouth, but Elsa's reddening cheeks gave her all the confirmation she needed. "Oh my *God*!" she clasped her hands together excitedly. "Tell us *everything*!"

"*Everything*?" Ava winced. "Are you sure you want to hear *everything*?"

"Too bloody right!" Sophia tucked into a slice of pizza. "So, get cracking."

With a hearty sigh, Elsa sunk back into her sofa, and Cecil immediately jumped onto her lap, his disapproval of Frederick Twemlow etched across his shaggy face. "Well, *she* set me up," she began, her finger pointing accusingly at Ava.

"It was for her own good," Ava shrugged innocently at Sophia. "Neither of them were going to get on with it unless someone intervened."

"Oh, my *God*!" Sophia exclaimed. "This gets better! I knew you were up to something more serious than just shopping when you called me!"

Elsa dragged herself from her bed with a foggy head the next morning. She wasn't sure what time she had eventually gone to bed, but it wasn't early enough in her opinion. Her mind was still spinning with a mixture of wine, emotions and all of Ava's and Sophia's suggestions of how she could win Frederick Twemlow back, although she wasn't convinced by any of them. She gave Ava a shake on the sofa as she passed on her way to the kitchen, and Ava stretched and yawned.

"Do you have to get to work?" Elsa asked, as she emptied a tin of dog food into Cecil's bowl before all hell broke loose.

"No," Ava replied in between yawns. "Day off, so stick the kettle on, will you?"

"Coffee? Strong, black?"

"Ah, you know me so well," Ava smiled blissfully, closing her eyes. Suddenly she opened them again in excitement. "Have you got a busy day, or can we go for a ride?"

"We can go for a ride, sure!" Elsa smiled, already looking forward to it.

"Awesome!" Ava hauled herself to her feet. "I'll help you with your jobs first."

There was nothing better to clear the fog of a hangover than a canter along the valley and the crisp, morning breeze in your face.

Ava sat astride her old favourite, Dusty, while Elsa accompanied Candy, and the pair matched each other's stride well as they ate up the firm ground. Candy may have been small, but she really went for it when Elsa opened up the throttle.

"Have you spoken to Clement…since…well, you know?" Ava probed as they pulled up, already knowing from Clement that she hadn't.

"No," Elsa replied. "I know I should have, but I couldn't bring myself to. I felt awful."

"There'll be no hard feelings," Ava shrugged. "You should just pick up the phone. He's pretty easy going."

Elsa nodded. Everything about him would have been ideal, she just wished she fancied him. She couldn't imagine ever having the feelings she had for Frederick, for anyone else. The lust, the passion, the emotions he stirred within her just by looking at her. He made her feel a million dollars, and she had enjoyed every moment in his company of her impromptu visit. She just wished it could be permanent.

"Has he called?" Ava asked her casually, studying her, and Elsa didn't need to check who she was talking about. She hesitated before slowly shaking her head.

"Wow," Ava murmured. "Did it really go *that* tits up?"

"I didn't think so," Elsa shrugged. "I thought it was glorious. What's happened to him, Ava?"

"I've no idea," Ava replied thoughtfully, with a sigh. "I've really no idea. Come on, let's trot."

Before Elsa could argue, she had gathered up Dusty's reins and trotted ahead. Candy lunged forward, determined not to be left behind. They trotted the length of the narrow lane, before turning off onto a grass track that led around a neighbour's sheep field, and they pushed their horses into a fast canter, which certainly brought the colour back into their cheeks.

"Ava," Elsa began quietly, as they eased to a walk. "While I was there…Portia came knocking," she paused, and took a deep breath, not sure she wanted to hear the answer. "Are she and him…you *know*…together?"

"Oh, I don't know, Else," Ava sighed, twisting a lock of mane between her fingers as she thought over her answer carefully. "I thought they were, then was certain they weren't, then I suspected they were…" she broke off, and eventually turned to look at her. "But he wouldn't have slept with you, Else, if he was with her. That's really not his style."

"You're sure?" Elsa probed, suddenly feeling dizzy.

She hesitated before nodding. "Certain."

Elsa sighed as she retrieved Connor from the sand paddock, and observed the state he had got himself in in the half hour he had been turned out. She tied him in the yard and ignored his constant pawing at the ground as she took a brush to him.

She looked up at the sound of a vehicle, and smiled as Harry's pickup cruised to a halt outside the stable block.

"I've come to see my patient," he told her, as he climbed out.

"Oh?" Elsa smiled. "Sophia looked fine to me."

He went to speak but quickly stopped himself. Elsa watched his cheeks reddening, and grinned at how easy it was to wind the two of them up. Elsa thought they were so cute, and while she was ecstatically happy for the pair of them when they'd finally got together, she was also a little jealous that she had not found the happiness that they both shared.

Not yet, Sophia had told her, when Elsa had accidentally raised the subject with her one evening. *But you will, soon,* she promised. But Elsa wasn't too sure as she felt the goalposts moving further and further away.

Harry's smile was wide as Sophia approached. He put his arm around her and kissed her forehead, before she led him off towards Drop Kick. She was almost skipping with happiness, and Elsa smiled.

Elsa was brushing off Cali when she heard the pickup departing, and she gave him a wave as he made his way out the drive.

"He said I might get him out to an event before the end of the season," Sophia clasped her hands together in glee. "Depending on his fitness, of course. I might not risk it, we'll see how it goes. But he said his legs will stand up to it!"

"That's great!" Elsa beamed, this being just the kind of news they needed.

"Will you join me in celebrating, in accompanying me to the gallops? You can bring Timber."

"Sounds like a plan!" Elsa beamed, dashing to get her tack.

Bear was fresh, and wanted to show Elsa just *how* fresh at every opportunity she could.

"She doesn't give up, does she?" Sophia smiled, watching her athleticism and hoping that Cali didn't get any ideas.

"She'd be boring if she did," Elsa replied, sitting expertly to another huge buck and wondering how she would ever hold her once they reached the neighbour's gallops.

They pushed on into a trot, and Timber Bear settled as Elsa rode her into her bridle, refusing to take any more of her silliness. Cali was eager to show that she was the better horse, and Elsa could almost feel her looking down on them with disapproval. They turned onto the sand gallop, and side-by-side set-off at a steady canter. Bear launched forward, hauling Elsa out of the saddle, but her reins were bridged across her neck and she anchored her feisty mare to stop her getting away from her as she leaned forwards to get the weight off her back.

Cali cantered strongly, and her stride was naturally longer than Timber's, so Elsa's little mare needed some persuasion that her companion wasn't trying to get away from her on purpose. They gradually eased up when they saw the end nearing, and while Bear was breathing fast and sweating, Cali didn't look like she'd barely started. They lengthened their reins and sat back in the saddle, as they turned to walk back down to the start.

"Elsa," Sophia began, and immediately paused, as if uncertain of her question. "Please will you accompany me as my plus one to the Roxwell's ball?"

Elsa couldn't think of anything worse. The Roxwell's were a wealthy family and although Elsa had never been to one of their balls, they were much talked about within the eventing community - being extravagant affairs. Events like that were well out of Elsa's comfort zone, and Sophia knew that.

"Is Harry not free?" she stammered, fiddling with her reins.

"He's already invited. *Please*? I promise not to ditch you for him as soon as we get there. Plus, Ava will be there."

"And Ava will be there I assume because Frederick will be there?" Elsa sighed.

"Come on, Elsa, the Roxwell's are his biggest backers. Of course he'll be there, but you can't avoid him forever."

"I can if people would bloody let me!" Elsa huffed. "I managed to avoid him very well, left to my own devices!"

And he me, too, she thought, with a tint of sadness. Still he had not called, and she couldn't honestly expect him to now. Nor would she call him. She had made her feelings perfectly clear by the succession of their antics between his crisp, luxurious bed sheets, and she would not chase him. He knew where she was, were he remotely interested, and she took from his silence that he most definitely wasn't.

She let out an involuntary sigh.

"I wish I could help," Sophia told her sadly.

"I know you mean well, you and Ava," Elsa replied. "But you need to stop trying to help. Although in hindsight I am very grateful that she *did* try to set me up with Frederick - and everything that happened, I have no regrets over - it hasn't really done any good in the long run, has it? I think actually, after the episode with Clement, I was happier hating him, than I am now constantly remembering the feel of his touch, his kisses, his..." she trailed off as she looked out across the valley. "Well, you know; everything in between."

Sophia smiled. "I try not to feel too sorry for you; most girls would kill to have Frederick Twemlow even so much as *look* at them."

"Well, I don't need or want your sympathy," Elsa smiled back. "I look around here, and look at what I've got, and I often already feel like the luckiest girl in the world."

"That is sweet," Sophia smiled, following her gaze. "We are lucky. But how about Clement?"

"No, Sophia," Elsa cut her off sharply with a glare.

"What?" she replied innocently. "You have no idea what I was going to say."

"I have a very good idea, actually, and you can wipe all those wild thoughts from your mind. I'm staying well away, from both of them. Hell, maybe even just men in general."

They reached the start of the gallop; both horses and riders having resumed their normal breathing. Sophia decided she would not push her, and instead shortened her reins.

"Ready?" she beamed.

"Oh *yes*," Elsa grinned, and she leaned forward in the saddle, the wind in her face brushing all her ill-thoughts away as Bear quickly ate up the ground.

Elsa always believed that the best thing to stop the mind from wandering and over-thinking was to throw yourself into your work - which was all very well when she had plenty to be doing. But the next couple of days were quiet, and Elsa debated what to do with Timber Bear to fill the void.

"Schooling, or a hack over the hills?" she murmured as she scratched behind the chestnut's ear, knowing which option both of them would prefer.

She was making her way across the yard when she felt her phone ringing in her jeans pocket. She hesitantly observed the display, wondering what on earth she was going to say. She knew she still owed him an explanation, but she had been putting it off for so long now.

"Hey, Clement," she smiled.

"Elsa..." he purred. "I thought for a second you wouldn't answer."

"I was just...you know...had my hands full," she stammered guiltily. "You know how it is. What can I do for you?"

"Well, I have a cheeky, young gelding who has been racking up a cricket score in the showjumping phase recently, and I was thinking of taking him on an impromptu trip to Victoria Farm for a couple of rounds." He paused. "I wondered if you and your little mare would like to join me? I can pick you up on the way."

"When?" Elsa gulped, these being the last words she expected him to say.

"Now," he replied. "Ava already has him loaded, if you start getting ready now, you should be ready in the time it takes me to drive to you, yes?"

"Should I?"

"Well, it depends how good your grooming skills are, doesn't it?"

She could almost feel his smile through the phone. "Is that a challenge?" she smiled back. "Because I accept!"

She hugged her phone to her chest for a moment after the call had ended. Clement acting like nothing awkward had happened between them was just what she needed, and she already felt the spring in her step as she jogged to catch up with Sophia.

"Do you mind if I..." she began, but Sophia rose a hand to stop her.

"Do what you want," she smiled.

"But you don't know what I'm going to ask yet!" Elsa implored, hands on hips.

"I've nothing planned, Else, you know that. So, what is it?"

"Clement's picking me up to take me and Timber Bear show jumping," she beamed, suddenly excited.

"Well, best you go get ready, then!" Sophia laughed. "Need a hand?"

"Ah! Could you?" Elsa smiled gratefully. "You're a *darling*!"

Sophia retrieved Bear from her paddock - grumpy that her turnout had been cut short - while Elsa turned the tack room upside down trying to locate her black jacket and a clean show shirt.

"This is all a bit short notice, isn't it?" Sophia enquired, as she brushed the minimal patches of dry mud from Bear's chestnut coat, as clothing located, Elsa finally joined her.

"He did say it was impromptu, but yea." Elsa replied, wondering why he had asked her. But she was happy, and hoped a day in his company would stop her from thinking about Frederick-bloody-gorgeous-Twemlow any longer.

She ran a brush through Bear's tail, grateful that it had not rained on the unrugged mare for a couple of days, and it was quickly bandaged. By the time Clement's lorry pulled into the yard, both Elsa and Bear were preened and ready to travel.

"Wow, impressive!" Clement smiled at their readiness as he jumped from the cab, and even Sophia felt herself go a little weak at the knees as she watched him lowering the ramp and sorting the lorry.

"Promise me one thing," Sophia whispered, certain they were out of earshot.

"What?" Elsa narrowed her eyes at her suspiciously.

"If he is doing all this because he likes you, and I mean *really* likes you, please just forget all about Frederick and make a move on him?" she paused, sensing Elsa's hesitation. "I mean, *look* at him!" Sophia implored. "He really is bloody gorgeous, isn't he?"

Slowly Elsa nodded. "And kind, and funny, and thoughtful, and…" she trailed off.

"And what?" Sophia demanded, her voice dangerously above a whisper.

"A *tremendously* good kisser," Elsa sighed, and they both embraced in laughter.

"So, what's stopping you, then?" Sophia asked, once they had eventually calmed, and Clement stopped glancing suspiciously at them.

"Because you can't just turn feelings on for someone, can you?" Elsa asked her seriously. "The same as you can't just turn them off for someone, even if I wish I could."

Sophia detected the sadness in her voice, and wished she could turn it to happiness. "Well try, won't you?" she said gently. "Please?"

"I promise I'll *try,*" she smiled, as Clement approached them.

"Your carriage awaits, *madam,*" his eyes sparkled.

"Gee, *thanks,*" she grinned, enthusiastically untying her little mare and leading her up the ramp. Bear nickered at her new friend, sniffing noses with him through the grill before her shrill squeal and the stamp of her hoof echoed through the lorry. The ramp was quickly shut, her equipment was loaded and Elsa joined him in the cab.

"No groom," she observed, glancing teasingly around as they turned onto the country lanes. "Are you sure you'll manage without one today?"

"No, not at all," Clement smiled. "That's why I've picked one up on my way."

"You cheeky git! I knew there couldn't be any other reason that you'd want my company," she told him, with a bite of her lip. "But you'd better be nice to me, or I might go on strike."

"Ha!" he sniggered. "Strike? You lot will never do

industrial action quite like the French. We know how to strike."

He smiled, but kept his eyes firmly on the road. He could be so easily distracted by her. Half an hour later he pulled into the Victoria Farm lorry park, and Elsa climbed through the lorry to check their horses. He was relieved she had agreed to accompany him. Small talk came easily, as if nothing had ever happened between them, and he was glad. He could never have forgiven himself had he already jeopardised a potentially blossoming friendship.

"Shall I go and sort the entries, and you get the horses out?" he called up to her as he lowered the ramp, but he knew it was pointless asking. Elsa would have everything under control, even though this morning she had no idea this was how her day would pan out. He thought if he left her to it, she could sort the entries *and* have both horses sparkling and ready, he would just have to turn up and ride. It was all second nature to her, she would think nothing of it, but he liked to consider himself a little useful, too.

"Sure!" she called back, untying Timber Bear and leading her down the ramp. Her little hooves were on springs, and she towered above Elsa as she danced around her. "Is yours OK to be left tied to the lorry?" she shouted between prancing hooves. "I might need to load her back up to tack up."

"He's fine," Clement waved his hand breezily. "Need a hand?"

"No, you go and get the entries in," she smiled, and paused before narrowing her eyes at him. "But don't you dare go entering me for any big classes; the likes of me and Timber Bear can't handle these technical, pure show jumping tracks."

"I'm sure you'll give it a good shot!" he replied with a laugh, and hurried off, leaving her momentarily worried for what the day would bring. She sensed it had disaster written all over it.

To unsettle her even more, Timber Bear stood like a rock

once Elsa tied her to the lorry; her new friend seeming to have a calming effect on her. By the time Clement returned, both horses had been stripped of their travel gear and had a brush run over them, and Bear was dozing with her head lowered and her bottom lip flapping.

"I thought you said she was crazy?" Clement's words stole her attention back, and she saw Bear's ear flicker at his arrival.

"She seems to like your gelding," Elsa replied thoughtfully. "Perhaps that's what she needs to keep her sane at events; a quiet travel companion."

"Well, every crazy girl needs a decent, sane, quiet guy, hey?" he gave her a wink, and she felt her gaze lingering on him longer than she should allow it. He was so smiley. She prized her eyes away as she lifted her saddle onto Timber's back.

"You're in the novice," he told her, unperturbed by her silence. "I think they're starting soon in Ring Two, do you want to go walk the course?"

She smiled appreciatively. The *novice*. She could cope with that, hopefully.

Elsa was relieved to discover that the course suited the true novice; straightforward with nice inviting fences. There were no odd lines or tight turns that should catch Bear off guard, unless of course they made it into the jump-off, but she wouldn't hold out much hope for that.

Bear came alive as soon as Elsa's bum hit the saddle, prancing and snorting like a dragon and refusing to settle.

"Do you need a hand warming up?" came a familiar voice behind her, and Elsa spun round to see Craig Ellis, wisely keeping his distance from her over enthusiastic beast.

"Craig…Hi," she smiled, wondering if he remembered her or whether he was just polite and helpful to all those who looked like they needed it the most. "What are you doing here?"

"I came to help Clement," he replied friendlily. "He's riding a young horse of mine."

"Oh, the quiet gelding is yours?" she asked in surprise.

"Sure is," he nodded, arms folded across his chest. "Bred to show jump, but doesn't look like it, does he?" he laughed as they nodded at the chunky, snoozing bay. "I thought he might prefer to try eventing. And I was right; his flatwork is decent and he's nailed the cross country, but his show jumping leaves a lot to be desired."

"All three of my phases leave a lot to be desired," Elsa replied.

"Nonsense!" Craig replied, turning away. "Come on. As I'm here early, I may as well get you both off to the best start."

Where walking beside Frederick at a low level horse trials turned heads – Elsa remembered fondly – she soon discovered that walking beside the one and only Craig Ellis at a low-key show jumping event had the same affect.

Elsa felt much like she was back at one of his clinics, but instead fending off horses and riders coming at her from all angles, and having to shout at the top of her lungs when she was going to attempt the practice fence, to warn others away. She quickly decided that eventers' appeared to have much more spatial awareness than any of her fellow competitors here, and Bear's ginger ears were pinned back a few times when others dared venture too close.

"Should have a red ribbon in its tail if it's going to kick," someone told her snootily, as they brushed past her with only a whisker between them.

"You'd kick if someone did that to *your* arse!" Elsa fought back, and the woman looked at her in disgust before trotting on.

"That's my girl!" Craig beamed. "Stand your ground! Now, come at the cross pole again."

Bear had been fighting her as soon as they'd entered the warm-up arena, and refused to focus on her rider, but instead went around with her neck up like a giraffe and her eyes out on stalks.

"This is just what she needs," Craig encouraged her. "Lots going on. She'll settle soon enough."

Elsa sure hoped so, as her muscles were being stretched in each and every direction. Her trot had been haphazard, and cantering a near disaster, as every other stride was laced with an eager fly buck in protest that Elsa wouldn't let her go. Craig had her cantering circles, and turning her for the tiny warm up jump when she was least anticipating it. The first two attempts Timber sent plastic poles flying everywhere, but quickly decided that wasn't wise and began to snap her legs up very nicely.

"Forty-seven, you're next!" shouted the steward, and Elsa felt her stomach churn.

"Good luck!" Craig gave her a thumbs up as she walked to the collecting ring, and Elsa could only grimace.

She was called in, and the bell went. Elsa cantered a couple of circles, but Bear wasn't really focusing on her. She backed off the first fence, and for a horrifying moment Elsa thought they weren't going to get anywhere near it, until Bear launched herself over it two strides early.

Elsa slipped her reins and did well to get them back quick enough for the fast approaching second. She wasn't used to such highly decorated and inventive showjumping fences in the eventing field.

Bear was worse when she came out, clearly anticipating that the cross country was next and working herself up in excitement.

"I've put you down for the next one," Craig told her, and she looked at him agape. "Get her back in there while she thinks she's heading out onto the cross country next, and she'll quickly stop getting so excited by it."

The next class was bigger and Elsa watched with a churning stomach as they raised the fences. Go under them, maybe, but *over* them? He had to be joking?

She felt sick to the pit of her stomach when the steward called her number. She gathered her reins and only half-heartedly nudged Bear forward, before quickly telling herself to pull herself together and get on with it. She had an international show jumper believing she could do it - he had even told her *how* to do it - so why didn't she believe him? When had she even stopped believing in herself? Didn't she want to prove to Craig, to Clement, to Sophia, to *herself* that she could do it? That it had been worth her coming here? She didn't know what had come over her recently, seeing failure before it had even happened, but she wished it would go away.

She gave Bear's neck a rub and trotted her confidently into the ring. This course was not aimed at novices this time; instead it was big, upright, and had a couple of twisty turns. But she could do it. She cantered her around once, and immediately felt her settle.

No cross country? Timber Bear seemed to say. *You want me to jump again?*

"Yes!" Elsa replied, and at the ring of the bell, she turned her towards the start.

"Next in, we have Elsa Aldridge riding Timber Bear," the judge boomed across the loud speaker.

Are you sure you're sure? Bear hesitated. *We've just done this...we never do this twice...*

Elsa dug her heels in and Timber Bear shot forward.

OK, she gave in. *I've got this!*

She flew the first, and Elsa immediately felt better. She couldn't deny her little mare had plenty of scope, she just needed to figure out how to channel her energy. The time was tight, and Elsa decided to use Bear's speed to her advantage, and raced down the long side, taking a pull for the upright wavy planks that commanded respect. And as she got braver, she even took a turn inside jump two to reach jump seven on just two strides, and Bear snapped her little legs up as though she'd been doing this all her life, wiping a couple of seconds at least off her expected time. Elsa was glad she had recently been making the time to do polework at home, and she was clear as she headed to the last. She couldn't quite believe it, and she let herself relax.

We're finished? Bear asked, slowing.

"No!" Elsa hissed, realising her mistake, but her rhythm had faltered and it was too late to sort her stride out. Bear had to put in an extra stride, got too close to the oxer and knocked the front rail off as she took off.

Elsa was furious at herself as she landed, silently calling herself every name under the sun as she patted her little mare's neck.

"You gave up," Craig shrugged, meeting her as she left the arena.

"I couldn't quite believe I got round," Elsa replied.

"You thought you had it in the bag, so you stopped riding," Craig told her with a wry smile. "Rookie mistake, but you'll learn."

She nodded, knowing he was right. It was a hard pill to swallow, knowing how hard Bear had worked, but if she knew one for sure, it was that she would never make that mistake again.

"Every day is a school day, huh?" Clement winked. "It was bad luck, don't dwell on it."

"It wasn't bad luck," she told him bitterly. "It was me being bloody awful, as usual."

"Don't say that," he replied, trotting off to have a final practice jump before he was called in.

Elsa walked Bear off while Clement did his round. He met each jump perfectly, getting all his distances, and the gelding only had one baby moment, getting his hooves in a tangle which meant Clement couldn't make the turn to save seconds, but he finished on a sound clear.

"I thought you said he wasn't very good at show jumping?" Elsa looked to Craig with raised eyebrows.

"I might have to snatch him back, but I think Clement will put up a good fight to keep him!" Craig laughed, clearly over the moon with the gelding's performance. "Well done today," he told her sincerely. "There are a lot of positives for you to take home with you."

Elsa smiled gratefully, and Craig left them to it while they cooled down.

"Quite good fun, this show jumping malarkey, don't you think?" Clement smiled, as they walked side by side back to the lorry.

"I guess I could be persuaded to come with you again, if that's what you mean," she nodded.

He watched as she unsaddled and brushed off that little pony of hers, looking deep in thought as she did everything on autopilot, and his heart suddenly swelled with pride. He could see the pure love she had for the little mare, even though things weren't really coming together yet, he knew they would do shortly, and he was so happy he had asked her to join him today. As Timber Bear nuzzled her, she gave her velvet nose a rub and produced a mint for her. She was still furious at herself, he could see that easily.

"Why don't we debrief our rounds over dinner?" he found himself saying.

She looked up suddenly, unsure of what to say. Her latest memories of going to dinner with a guy were still painful, and ones she did not wish to repeat.

"It's OK," he forced a smile at her silence. "It was bad idea, sorry."

"No," she quickly stopped him. "It wasn't a bad idea, it's just…" she gulped, deciding to take the easy route out. "It's been a long day, that's all. I need to get back to Cecil."

"I understand," he nodded, hoping he hadn't overstepped the friendship barrier *again*.

"I'm so grateful for Craig taking the time to help me," she smiled as they loaded their horses. "Thank you for that."

"It's all about who you know," Clement gave her a wink, closing the ramp. "I was joking about dinner, by the way."

She spun to face him, and frowned.

"I mean, not joking *exactly,*" he replied thoughtfully, biting down on his lip as he studied her. "Of course, I would love it if you would join me, but I knew you would say no. I just wanted to double check; I heard some of what you and Sophia were talking about when we left."

"Shit, sorry," she replied awkwardly. "We're not very tactful, are we?"

"Don't be sorry," he smiled. "I can take rejection. I mean, it doesn't happen often, but I'll manage," he winked.

"I'm sorry I never called," she told him, feeling anxious as she touched on the elephant that had been in the room all day. "I know I owed you an explanation, but I just didn't know what to say."

"No, I'm sorry, I should have manned up and called," he shrugged. "But I didn't want to tread on any toes."

"There are no toes to be trodden on," Elsa sighed, rubbing her temples. "I'm young, free and single - I guess there is so much I should be happy about, right?"

"You are young, for sure, and while you may be free and single in theory, your heart is not, is it?"

Her brow furrowed as she glared at him, but she didn't have to ask him to explain.

"Your heart is not free and single, is it, Elsa?" he tried again, knowing she would be much happier if she would just admit it. "I know there is something between you two," he told her quietly. "And I want you to know that I do not wish to come between it."

"Honestly, there is nothing to come between," her voice was shaking.

"Why are you lying to us?"

Because I'm in love with your boss, her eyes implored him. *There, I've admitted it to myself.* It was easier than she had thought it would be, and she took a deep breath.

"I love him," she whispered eventually, feeling her eyes welling up.

"I know," he nodded, gently reaching for her hand. "I can see that. But the question is, what are you going to do about it?"

Chapter Twelve

When Elsa thought nothing was worse than attending the Roxwell's fancy ball in the first place, she quickly decided that having to try on and purchase a suitable dress for it, was far worse.

"I've got loads you can borrow," Ava told her, as she accompanied her on a rare shopping trip.

"I want to buy one," Elsa snapped.

"Why?" Ava demanded. "You *hate* shopping!"

"I don't *hate* it," Elsa retaliated. "I just prefer it from the social safety of my computer, when I don't have to fight through crowds of people and queue up for changing rooms."

"So why won't you wear one of mine?" Ava tried again.

"Do you have any dresses suitable for this ball, that Frederick hasn't already seen you in?" Elsa stopped in exasperation and span to face her, hands on hips.

"No, probably not," Ava frowned.

"Exactly!" Elsa told her, marching on again. "That is *exactly* why I can't borrow one."

Ava followed her, smiling. This revelation was news in itself, and sent her mind into overdrive. Even after everything that had gone wrong between them, the spark was evidently still there. It just needed help in igniting a flame and the two of them would be good to go.

Elsa wasn't quite sure why people tried on dresses as entertainment, as she had had enough by the second and couldn't think of anything she'd rather do less with her day off.

"The Roxwell's always put on a good bash, Elsa," Ava told her as she watched her swirl before her in an emerald green, silky v-neck that was tight around her waist and splayed out over her hips. "This one is gorgeous. You're going to wear your hair down, aren't you?"

"Yea, I guess," Elsa replied absentmindedly, as she examined herself in the full-length mirror. "I think I'll take this one."

"You *think*?" Ava replied, not bothering to stand up. "You don't sound too sure? I mean it's lovely but you have to be one hundred percent certain. Do you want to keep shopping until you find *the one*?"

"No way," she replied, stepping back into the changing room. "It's just a dress; I'm not bloody getting married."

Ava rolled her eyes and folded her arms across her chest. She would never grab Frederick's attention from his recent depths of despair if that was her attitude. She needed to be dressing and behaving like *the one*.

Elsa already knew it was going to be a long day, before she rolled out of bed at five o'clock in the morning, fed the horses as usual and began brushing off Ruby and Merlin ready for their day out at Bealey. She loaded them up and Sophia joined her in the cab.

Sophia had drawn early times, quite close together, so it was all go as soon as the lorry pulled to a halt. Ruby was up first for the dressage, and somehow had managed to rub half her plaits out on the lorry. Elsa fumbled through them hurriedly, pricking her thumb with the threading needing at least twice while the little mare whinnied at the top of her lungs to her new friends in the lorry park. Elsa's ears were ringing by the time she waved the pair of them off to warm up.

Ruby settled brilliantly despite her inexperience, giving a fine display and shooting Sophia straight into contention for her section. Elsa didn't get a chance to watch, as Merlin was in soon after for his Novice test, but she was waiting with sugar lumps for when Ruby came out, took her reins and legged Sophia straight up onto Merlin, leaving them to warm up while she walked Ruby off. Merlin tried his best at his Novice test, but he found dressage difficult and pulled like a train, just wanting to get it over with and move onto the showjumping.

Young Ruby was still cautious over coloured poles and Sophia had to really ride her forward. Elsa caught glimpses of her round as she walked Merlin around. The time was generous, but even then Ruby would struggle to make it. She needed time to settle on the approach to fences, to suss out what the fence was about and build her confidence. She was taking her time to come on and build her confidence, but they felt certain that with a couple more seasons under her saddle, she would be capable of tackling the biggest courses. But today she had had the first part of the triple down, and the upright planks when she became a little unbalanced on the corner, but Sophia left the arena with a smile on her face nonetheless.

"Derek would be furious at me for those mistakes," Sophia told Elsa as she slid from the saddle. "Good job he was busy today!"

"You should have given her a pull on the corner," Elsa agreed. "She got her legs in a muddle. But she still tried for you; she didn't stop."

"She's a good girl," Sophia gave her a hearty pat, taking Elsa's observations on board. The pair of them had been friends for so long now that Elsa's criticism and praise - being the experienced eye from the ground - were fundamental to the progression of Sophia's career.

She found a quiet corner of the warm up arena to try and contain Merlin's excitement for the cross country and popped him over the practice fences without fault, and they were ready to go.

He bolted from the start box and flew the first with a youthful exuberance. The early fences were well spaced out, and if she used his long stride to her advantage here, she didn't need to hurry him home when he was tiring towards the end.

He flew over the picnic table, and bounded enthusiastically over the row of tyres. She steadied him down the incline and he met the first brush fence easily, but he was on a long stride for the second element and he had to stretch to make it. Sophia slipped her reins, and was torn between patting him and gathering them back up when she realised they'd landed safely. She didn't manage to get him back to her in time for the ditch, and she felt his eyes widen and him back off from six strides out. She helplessly dug her heels in, but they had lost momentum and Merlin was never going to take off.

"It's OK," she reassured him, as she gathered her contact back up and turned him in a circle. She established her balanced canter again, looked for her stride, and with a sense of determination he met it perfectly.

Ava was waiting for him at the finish while Elsa tried to keep Ruby settled, and watched them from a distance.

"Way to go!" the Australian high-fived the jockey as together they stripped Merlin's tack off and set about cooling him down. "He's a really nice little horse!"

"He is, isn't he?" Sophia beamed. "Although he does always think he knows the course better than I do!" she added, with a roll of her eyes.

"Must be the pony in him!" Ava laughed, giving him a hearty pat as he cheekily nuzzled her for more treats.

"I'll walk him back to the lorry," Ava told her, after they had thrown a couple of buckets of water over his steaming body and scraped off the excess and sweat. "You go get your next one worked in."

"Are you sure?" Sophia hesitated. "You must have a million things to do."

"I'm a *groom,*" Ava winked. "I am therefore a queen of multi-tasking. Plus, Frederick is in-between rides and we have a new kid on a trial day for us who would get down on her knees for him and spit polish his boots if she'd let him…" she trailed off with another roll of her eyes. "*Plus,* this pony is quite sweet, I rather like him, *and* Elsa told me how much of a warm up your next one needs, so yes I am sure." She turned Merlin away from her and turned towards the lorry park. "So, go get cracking!"

"Thanks!" Sophia called gratefully after her. "I owe you!"

Ava waved her away with a smile. There was no *owing* each other as far as she was concerned. What else were friends for?

Sophia wished Derek hadn't been busy elsewhere today, as she struggled along the fine line of warming Ruby up enough to settle her, but not too much to tire her out before she'd even started.

The young mare baulked at the practice brush fence, and Sophia knew she needed to get her act together were the two of them to get round. The brush fence was the easiest fence the two of them had ever cleared, yet Ruby's eyes were on stalks as though she'd never seen one before. She was so cautious; if she wasn't one hundred percent certain she could easily clear a fence, then she wouldn't take off. Sophia gave her a pat and tried the brush fence a couple of more times, until Ruby jumped it without hesitation, and then turned her towards the roll-top. Her eyes flicked and her tail switched, but she took confidence from Sophia that it was OK, and she cleared it even though she would have probably rather have refused. Sophia gave her a pat and brought her back to a walk with a resigned sigh. She guessed to the unknowing spectator, they probably looked like they had never tackled a cross country course before in their lives, yet this was Ruby's second season out on the circuit, and that was after a full season of hunting and many cross-country schooling clinics with top riders.

Ruby snorted like a dragon as Sophia pushed her into the start box. She patted her neck which was already lathered in sweat, and pushed her on.

"Three...two....one...Go! Good luck!" The starter called, and with her ears pricked, Ruby leapt from the box.

"Go on girl!" Sophia murmured encouragingly. "We've got this!"

Ruby sure had, and Elsa watched her confidence grow with each stride, as she gave the first a foot to spare, not daring to touch it. She trusted her rider completely, and was fully focused on every contact on Sophia's reins, every touch of her heel, distribution of her weight in the saddle as she manoeuvred for the best line and perfect stride. As she picked off each fence as though they were trotting poles, Elsa knew they would go far, but the mare's carefulness worried her, too. It used up so much of her energy, giving every single fence much more than it needed, that she was really flagging towards the end of the course. Sophia dropped her down a gear; time not mattering to her as long as she got her young mare home safe and clear. She threw her reins at her over the last, and cantered steadily through the finish to an almighty cheer from Elsa and Ava.

"What a little trooper!" Ava grinned, helping to quickly strip her tack while Elsa walked her around. Ruby was blowing hard, despite being one of the fitter horses in their yard.

"Reckon she might have placed, with that round," Elsa agreed, unfastening her bridle and not even breaking pace as she swapped it for the mare's headcollar.

"I'm not sure," Sophia replied, tipping a bucket of water over Ruby's flanks. "We must have got a few time faults."

"Not many," Elsa told her. "And others have been racking up penalties all the way around."

"Guys, I've got to go! One of Freddie's working pupil is up soon," Ava told them, holding up Ruby's tack. "I'll chuck this in your lorry on my way past."

"Thanks so much for your help," Sophia told her gratefully, scraping water and sweat from Ruby's lathered body.

"Any time! See you later for fun at the Roxwell's!" Ava called with a wink, and laughed as she was met by Elsa's grimace.

"What a great day," Sophia beamed clutching her fifth place rosette, as they turned out of the lorry park.

"Very pleasing," Elsa agreed, easing the lorry into a higher gear as they hit the road. "We have such a good stable yard of horses at the moment. It has been a great day," she paused, and her smile suddenly turned to a scowl. "So I guess it's all downhill from here, right?"

"Hey, curb your pessimism, girl!" Sophia scolded her with a smile. "The Roxwell's party is going to be fabulous!"

There was still a yard full of horses to contend with before heaving herself into her new dress, and she turned Ruby and Merlin out in the sand paddock while she bedded down the stables ready to bring everything in.

"We're going to be hung over in the morning, aren't we?" Sophia mentioned thoughtfully on passing Connor's stable.

"More than likely, yes," Elsa replied. She intended on drinking copious amounts of super-strength alcohol to see her through the evening.

"Should we just leave them all out tonight?"

"Makes sense," Elsa nodded. She would put a lightweight sheet on them all to keep the evening chill off their clipped out coats, and chuck them all some hay even though they probably wouldn't touch it while they had grass instead.

She gave Ruby and Merlin a thorough groom, and a final check of their legs gave no sign of heat, swelling or grazes. She put their protective boots on them before turning them out. Satisfied her work was done, she showered and pulled on her tracksuit, and made her way over to Sophia's bedroom to get ready.

"It'll be *fun*, Else," Sophia tried to encourage her as she curled her hair for her.

"I know," Elsa sighed. "It's just..." she broke off, ran her hand through her hair without thinking.

"Don't do that!" Sophia cursed her, watching her good

work literally uncoil before her. "I haven't put hairspray in that yet!"

"Geez, sorry," Elsa rolled her eyes.

"Well, you want to look your best, don't you?"

"I think I could turn up naked and Frederick wouldn't notice me," Elsa replied with a sigh, as she struggled hauling up the zip to her dress, despite having breathed in as much as she could. She thought at this rate she may well *have* to turn up naked.

The Roxwell's house was grand, but nowhere near as grand as Frederick's, Elsa thought, stealing glances around the impressive hallway as they waited to be welcomed. The stairway was about the width of Elsa's cottage, splitting halfway up to go in two directions, as seemed to be customary in these stately homes. A bronze horse head graced each side of the banister, and Elsa wondered if they replicated any famous horse in particular. The Roxwell's were prolific owners in both horse racing and eventing, shown by the photographs that lined the wood-panelled walls all around them, of either horse and rider flying huge fences or standing with Mr and Mrs Roxwell in the winners enclosure.

Mrs Roxwell was over the top as she rushed to greet them, trying to mask her expression of not recognising them at all as Sophia eagerly extended her hand to her. She wore a massive, burgundy gown that hung off her shoulders and showed lots of cleavage. Her make-up was excessive, as if she was desperate to hold onto her youth.

"Mrs Roxwell," Sophia beamed. "I am Sophia Hamilton."

"Of course, of course!" Mrs Roxwell enthusiastically shook her hand, and looked to Elsa, too polite to ask who she also was.

"This is Elsa, she is my Head Girl," Sophia introduced her.

"How *lovely*," Mrs Roxwell gushed. "My husband and I are *so* glad you both could make it. It's lovely to hold these functions and catch up with old faces, and meet new ones, don't you think?"

"Absolutely," Sophia agreed, as they followed her through to the main hall where a band played sedately in the corner. People milled together in clusters, drinking, chatting and sampling canapés.

This is so posh, Elsa thought, feeling desperately out of place. A waiter stopped as he passed her, seeing she had an empty hand.

"Drink?" he purred, and Elsa eagerly grabbed two wine glasses. It was a deliciously chilled pinot grigio, but she would have happily drank anything right now to settle her nerves, and she took a long glug of her own as she passed the other to Sophia.

Sophia quickly located Harry, and he slipped an arm around her as he planted a tender kiss on her hair, and introduced his girlfriend and the best Head Girl the eventing community had ever had – which made Elsa roll her eyes and blush immensely – to his group of acquaintances.

Elsa felt her heart swell as she noticed the way Harry looked at his darling Sophia, and was so happy that the two of them had finally plucked up the courage to get together. They made the most perfect couple, and Elsa only hoped she could replicate their happiness one day with the man of her own dreams.

She saw him across the hallway; the blonde beauty who all too often was the very man of her dreams. He looked even more beautiful now in the flesh than he did every time he came into her mind – which was often. He stood casually leaning against the great fireplace, and he looked so smart and well-groomed in his evening suit that he brought butterflies to her stomach. He stood talking to his mother – Elsa recognised Lady Twemlow from when she had awarded her the coveted Turnbridge Cup at Napier. She was elegant, well-groomed and extremely stylish in her expensive, designer dress, and just looking at her made Elsa feel inferior. It was easy to see where Frederick got his looks from, it was literally as though he had inherited all of his parents good looks equally, and none of their bad.

"Makes you sick, doesn't it?" Sophia laughed, following her gaze. "How can someone be born so perfect?"

"Fuck knows," Elsa sighed. She watched as Portia approached him and handed him a glass of wine. Her hand lingered on his arm and her long eyelashes fluttered shamelessly up at him as his mother continued to talk animatedly to them both.

"Thank God this isn't a sit-down dinner," Sophia murmured, as another waiter paused at them and they helped themselves to canapes. "Can you imagine being stuck on a table with some of these people?"

"I think you'd pull it off very well," Elsa smiled.

"Harry would have them eating out the palm of his hand," Sophia rolled her eyes, "but I'm not sure about me." She paused and looked around her. "This place needs livening up; shall we go and dance?"

"Why not?" Elsa grinned with a shrug, feeling much better now she'd got a couple of glasses of wine down her and the music had upped its pace.

Frederick had noticed her as soon as she'd walked in. Well, on his second glance, anyway. He hadn't recognised her at first; her hair was curled perfectly around her face, and he'd never seen her with curled hair before. He thought she looked spectacular, and he licked his lips as he soaked in the full sight of her. Her dress was a beautiful emerald green with thin shoulder straps and enough low cut to get his pulse racing, yet modest enough to be classy. It hugged her in all the right places, and he imagined slipping his hand around her dainty waist and taking her off to dance. He thought she was the most beautiful women in here, and he stole a glance in her direction whenever he was able. He had heard that Sophia was invited - and attending - but had assumed she would be bringing Harry. Ava must have known, yet she had not said a word to him. Or maybe this was another of her plans? He only wished he could allow himself to go along with them. He had been weak before, invited her easily to bed and enjoyed every minute of it, but he knew he couldn't allow that to happen ever again. Not if he wanted to salvage his career, and that was what he wanted more than anything, wasn't it?

He was trying to listen to whatever his mother was saying, but he was finding it increasingly impossible as Portia clung to his side, her arms around him sucking the life from him. He felt irritable and claustrophobic from her touch.

"How are you getting on at Frederick's, Portia, darling?" Yet another acquaintance asked her, snapping him from his thoughts.

"Oh, simply *fabulous*!" she replied, all smiles and sweetness that it made him feel a bit queasy. "I'm learning *so* much, and Frederick has been absolutely great, haven't you, Fred?" she fluttered her long lashes at him *again*.

He prized his eyes from Elsa, as he realised she was talking to him.

"Hmmm? Yes," he replied absentmindedly.

Elsa stole glances at him, even over Sophia's shoulder. She had not locked eyes with him even once, so she felt certain he hadn't even noticed her. He seemed so absorbed in that wretch hanging off his arm; who looked as though she'd quickly dispose of anyone who dared as to even glance at him. Elsa duly noted that of course she looked absolutely stunning, too. Her smile made Elsa feel sick; so fake and man-eating. Elsa had seen what the venomous madam was capable of, behind that sweet front, and she had no wish to associate with her.

"May I steal your dance partner?" Harry smiled at Elsa, slipping his arm around her shoulder as he leaned in and kissed Sophia's forehead.

"Of course," she replied without hesitation. Her feet were killing her already, and she didn't envisage herself lasting long in these heels. Of course, Sophia had insisted that they had to be worn as they matched beautifully with her dress, but what was the point in that if she couldn't even walk?

She stepped aside, and grabbed another passing wine. She leaned back against the wall as she took a sip, enjoying this time to herself to people watch. As she scanned the room, she wondered were Ava was. Her eyes fell on many recognisable faces; those she knew just by sight, others she knew by name, and many that she would exchange a polite *hello* with while crossing paths at events. The horse world was really quite small, after all.

"Will you dance with me?" Clement held out his hand, breaking her from his thoughts.

"I'd love to," she replied honestly, placing her hand in his. "If my feet can handle it. Thank you."

"No, thank *you,*" he murmured.

She had not seen him wearing black tie before, and it really quite suited him. His dark hair was freshly cut, and he looked as though he'd had a cut-throat razor shave. Were her mind not always elsewhere, she decided he really would be most appealing. She was certain he must fend off his own share of female advances.

"I thought it best to make an effort when invited to these fancy dances," he told her, watching her eyes as they observed him, and making her blush.

"You scrub up alright," she teased.

"And you yourself, look *beautiful,*" he whispered, leaning closer to her ear.

"I don't need you to feel sorry for me," she told him with a smile, as she fell into step easily with him. "I'm not lonely; I was just resting my feet." It quickly transpired that neither of them were great movers, and so she felt quite comfortable with him.

"I don't feel sorry for you," he smiled. "I just wish you'd take your eyes off him and stop putting yourself through such turmoil."

She felt her blush deepening, because she knew he was right. "I can't help myself," she whispered.

"I noticed, but you're not alone. Most members of the strange female species just continuously gaze at him."

She sighed as she helplessly stole another glance at him.

"No, Elsa!" he gave her a gentle shake, jolting her attention back to him. "*Don't* look at him. That is where the problem begins! What is the saying you lot have...out of sight, out of mind?"

"I can't take you seriously when you say *you lot*," she grinned. "As if it doesn't include you? Come on, Clement, you are the least-French Frenchman I've ever known!"

"How many Frenchmen have you known?" he quizzed her.

She didn't reply, just smiled. Smiled and gazed straight into his well-clothed chest, anything to keep her eyes from wandering.

"You are so beautiful when you smile," he murmured, taking her by surprise. "You know that, don't you? Please, don't waste your happiness and beauty on someone who does not appear to return it. Equally, do not waste it on someone who can never mean much to you. And please stop looking so uncomfortable with me," he added with a wink.

"I'm not," she smiled genuinely. "I only look uncomfortable because everything you say is right. I would *love* to feel about someone else, how I feel about *him* right now."

She felt the tears threaten, and he pulled her into his chest so that no one would see. She felt safe in his warm cocoon.

"Let's go outside," he murmured, "and get some air."

She nodded and allowed him to lead her out onto the patio. The fresh air quickly did its job, and she felt so stupid at still feeling this way. The Roxwell garden was expansive; but a small, stone wall enclosed the patio area. Clement took her hand and led her to the farthest, quiet corner. He sat down on the wall and patted beside him.

"You try your hardest to make me see sense, even though I'm a lost cause."Elsa murmured as she sat down, wiping her eyes and praying she hadn't smudged her makeup.

"Don't be silly," he smiled, his eyes scanning hers with nothing but fondness. "I hear you had a good day at the office today?"

Elsa quickly nodded, remembering her earlier jubilation at Sophia's results. "They both went brilliantly."

"That's great, isn't it?" Clement nodded. "Puts her right in contention for Cromwell."

"I know, it's brilliant. Although sad, too," she shrugged. "As it marks the end of our season."

"Well, if you get bored at home and need something to do, you can always come show jumping with me?" he winked. "My gelding took a shine to your little mare."

"That's very kind," she laughed. "And I may just take you up on that offer."

"How is your little mare?" he asked curiously.

"She's still feisty, opinionated, and *furious* that I made her do a round of show jumping without following it up with cross country."

"She sounds like my type of girl," Clement laughed. "You wouldn't have her any other way, would you?"

"No," Elsa whispered. "I wouldn't change much at all about my life, to be honest. Except of course, one thing…"

He quickly put his finger to her lip. "Shhh," he told her. "Stop thinking about it." His lips were dangerously close, but as she studied him she saw nothing but friendship, and hoped it may long continue.

"I hope you find someone nice." She murmured aloud, not meaning to.

"I hope you are not taking pity on me? I am not desperate," he winked. "I am fine on my own. Plus, I live by my own advice, and do not settle for second best."

"I wish I had your willpower," she winked back, and they laughed as he put his arm around her and pulled her into his chest.

"You know..." she began thoughtfully, feeling mischievous. "Ava is single."

"Yes, I am well aware of that," he replied, with a bite to his lip.

"How are you aware?" she prompted. "Did she tell you, or did you have to find out?"

"A bit of both," he shrugged. "She made me subtly aware, and I did a little probing just to be sure."

"Aha!" she gently nudged him in the chest, triumphant. "So, you *are* interested?"

"As if I would tell you," he grinned, "so you can go running straight back to her to tell her? I have heard about your *girl code*. I am not stupid, Elsa."

"She's interested," Elsa told him, not wishing to beat around the bush where two of her good friends' happiness was concerned. "Why don't you ask her out? You have nothing to lose."

"How sure are you?" he looked thoughtful. He narrowed his eyes at her, uncertain whether she was teasing him.

"Trust me; ask her out!" she gave him a prompting shove in the chest, and as she shivered in the crisp, evening air he stood up and guided her thoughtfully back inside.

"Ah, Clement!" A gentleman greeted him in the doorway, and as Clement shot her an apologetic smile as he shook the gentleman's hand, Elsa left him to it.

When she finally spotted Ava sitting at the Twemlow table, she hesitated at joining her. Frederick and Portia sat at the other end of the table, deep in conversation with another couple who Elsa did not recognise, and she contemplated turning and going straight back outside.

But Ava had already spotted her, and waved her over. Elsa

pulled out a chair beside her and angled it so that her back was slightly towards Frederick and she couldn't catch glimpses of him even if she wanted to.

"How was your dance?" Ava grinned, nodding in Clement's direction.

"Lovely," Elsa smiled, nodding as she followed her friends gaze. "He's a lovely guy."

"He's lush, isn't he?" Ava gushed, and Elsa didn't think she had ever seen her friend talk so fondly about a guy. "I hope you put in a good word for me?" she winked.

"Why don't you go and ask him to dance?" Elsa suggested, desperate to move away from here, unable to block Portia's voice out behind her.

"Oh God, *no*, I couldn't!" Ava laughed.

"Where have you been, anyway?" Elsa asked her. "I've been waiting for you for ages."

"Got held up at the yard," Ava rolled her eyes. "Then got stuck in the hallway chatting to some owners." She lowered her voice as she looked at Elsa in disapproval. "Talk of the devil; have you heard Little-Miss-Clingy behind us? I doubt she's parted from him all night. Bet she'd even have to take him to the toilet with her. Seriously don't know how he puts up with it, Else."

She broke off as Lady Twemlow approached them, and Ava gave her sweetest smile to her boss's mother who she was on very good terms with. Lady Twemlow glanced over Elsa with a polite smile, but no sense of recognition.

"Enjoying the ball, Ava?" she purred.

"Oh, yes, Mrs T!" she replied, her Australian accent gaining strength whenever she conversed with someone even slightly posh. "It's fab, isn't it?"

Lady Twemlow gave her a pat on the shoulder as she brushed past them to join her son. Elsa couldn't help but look, out the corner of her eye she saw Frederick standing to greet his mother, and she thought he looked almost relieved that this forced Portia's hand to be momentarily removed from him. She frowned; she couldn't imagine him ever being comfortable with such public displays of affection, that she wondered why he was tolerating it so well.

"You two look *so* adorable!" Lady Twemlow beamed at them, taking Portia's hand in hers. "I'm so glad Frederick met you, I was beginning to get quite worried about him!"

Elsa took a deep breath, trying her hardest to stare ahead. *Don't look at them,* she told herself. *Stay strong.* But she was hopeless at staying strong where Frederick was concerned.

"The pleasure is *all* mine, Mrs Twemlow," Portia purred, and Elsa had a sudden flashback to when she'd brought the crop down on poor, helpless Nobby, and she wanted to jump from her seat and launch her across this grand table and smack that smugness right out of her pretty face.

"I really have my Uncle to thank for putting in a word for me," she went on, causing Elsa to jolt around, just as Mr Roxwell put his hand on Portia's shoulder.

"Talk of the devil!" Portia laughed, turning to greet him.

When Elsa's eyes rested on Frederick, she realised he was looking straight at her. She had given up trying to read him, but she could tell he was far from happy. *This explains so much,* she suddenly realised. Frederick's hospitality towards the cretin, his refusal to believe she could do anything wrong. His patience at having her draped all over him, even when he looked so uncomfortable. The Roxwell's were his biggest backers; upsetting their niece could prove fatal to his career.

Gently, Ava took Elsa's hand in hers, and gave her a reassuring squeeze.

"I think I'm going to get some air," she breathed, tugging her eyes from Frederick.

"You've only just been outside," Ava replied, holding her hand firm.

"You can never have too much air, Ava!" Elsa insisted, tugging her hand free and getting to her feet. She would much prefer a breath of fresh, crisp, cold air, than to continue looking into those pained, blue eyes, and she hastily made for the door.

Sophia sat on the patio wall. Her legs were crossed, a glass of wine in one hand as she sat smiling at nothing in particular.

"Hey!" she beamed, locking eyes with Elsa. "Having fun?"

Elsa gulped, and forced herself to nod. "Marvellous."

"Told you you'd enjoy yourself," Sophia insisted. "Bloody boiling in there though, isn't it?"

She nodded as she sat down beside her.

"Everything OK?" Sophia frowned, immediately sensing that it was anything but. Elsa didn't reply, and Sophia could understand her turmoil. "If it's any consolation, I don't think many people can stand the conceited, nasty, privileged, little rich girl," she told her gently.

"Frederick apparently can," Elsa replied hastily.

"More to it than meets the eye though, isn't there?"

Elsa nodded, not wanting to think about it. "So, how is your night?"

"Great, actually!" Sophia beamed, deciding a change of the subject was a good tactic. "I've been wanting to talk to you."

"You have?" Elsa looked up in surprise.

"Yes! I've been chatting to Craig Ellis. Someone has told him there was a nice young mare jumping at Bealey today. Apparently she shows promise show jumping, but not so much across country..." she trailed off with a laugh.

"Ruby?" Elsa gaped at her.

"You guessed it!" Sophia was giggling.

"How bloody dare they say such things about our little star!" Elsa smiled.

"Actually, they were quite complimentary," Sophia took a sip of her wine. "Apparently they liked her scope, her carefulness, her technique...*Oh!* The list was *endless*! Craig has suggested that you take her show jumping over winter with he and Clement, and Timber Bear, of course, and he'll be there to help you out."

"Serious?" Elsa gaped.

"Yes!"

"Wow!" Elsa breathed. Compliments and offers like that from Craig Ellis were not to be taken lightly, and Elsa's heart swelled with pride that he felt her worthy of his precious time.

"And you'd...*let me*?" Elsa double-checked.

"Of course I bloody would!" Sophia laughed. "We might have a show jumping superstar in our stable yard, but how will we ever know unless we get her out there!"

She trailed off, and Elsa followed her gaze to the doorway where Frederick stood, his ocean blue eyes watching the pair of them.

"I'm going to...erm...go back inside..." Sophia got awkwardly to her feet. "Leave you two to it."

"What? *No*!" Elsa reached for her arm, panicking. "I'll come with you!"

She hurried after her, but while Sophia slipped easily inside, Frederick blocked her way, and she ran blindly into his chest.

"Elsa," he smiled awkwardly, a firm hand holding each of her arms. His touch on her bare skin sent her senses into turmoil, and she felt like she might faint if he didn't keep hold of her.

She narrowed her eyes at him as she looked over his shoulder for any sign of his hanger-on. "Does she actually let you out alone?"

"I just needed some air." He told her, his expression unchanged.

"Well, don't let me stop you," she snapped, trying half-heartedly to shake him off.

"Elsa…" he held onto her easily. "We should talk."

"Oh, so *now* you want to talk?" she turned on him. He smelled glorious, that familiar aftershave that reminded her of such happy times, and she warned herself to remain angry.

He thought she looked even more beautiful up close than she did from across the main hall. Her eyes were lined with kohl, and the dark look she gave him made him stir within, even though he was certain she wanted it to have the opposite effect.

He backed her away from the doorway and across the patio. She stopped him when she felt the stone wall grazing the backs of her knees, and she sat down. He hovered above her, and she wished more than anything that she could kiss him once again; right here, right now.

"Look, Frederick," she sighed, running her hands through her curls now that Sophia wasn't here to tell her off. "I don't know what's going on with you, what fucked up game you're trying to play with me. I know half the blame lies with me, but…well, it doesn't matter. I just want to tell you that I want no part of it anymore. I'm sick and tired of the way you make me feel."

"How about how you felt when we were lying in bed together?" his question caught her off-guard. "Or in my shower?" Oh, what he would give to repeat those tender moments.

"Oh, brilliant," she told him coldly, "But it was how you made me feel in the silence that followed that hurts me the most."

He wanted to say sorry, but he felt that his apologies were worthless when he was throwing them about so often with her. "I never wanted to hurt you, Elsa," he whispered.

"You always say that," she countered, "yet you always *do* hurt me. It's like you just can't help yourself."

He studied her, and for the first time she allowed herself to study him properly. Behind the mask of the gorgeous man she wanted to see, she saw his tiredness, his confusion, his *hurt*.

What's going on with you? She wanted to demand of him, to shake him. But instead she folded her arms across her chest, determined to make her own closure.

"You should go," Elsa told him. "The wicked witch will be out looking for you in a minute, and I don't want to be on the receiving end of *her*."

Me neither, Frederick thought, wanting to run off into the darkness of the garden with her instead and never look back.

"And you don't want to upset the precious *niece* of your best owners, do you?" Elsa demanded, hating her bitterness.

"I wish things could be different, Elsa," he whispered, taking her by surprise. His hands dropped from her and she suddenly felt very cold.

"So do I," she whispered back, and she watched as he turned and went back inside.

Elsa hoped the crisp evening air would help steady her fast-beating heart. She wasn't sure if she was shivering because of the cold, or simply because she was so wound up. She stayed rooted to the spot as she watched people step outside for air or to smoke. No one looked in her direction; she was half-shrouded in darkness. She had no desire to go back inside; she just wanted to go home now.

But her attention piqued at the next couple who fell out through the door. Hand in hand, they laughed as Ava caught her heel on the door step, and Clement held her up. His arms were around her as he guided into the darkness of the garden, and Elsa smiled as Ava giddily fell into him and their lips met.

"I've been wanting to do that for ages," she heard Clement murmur, and she smiled. And then they were kissing and laughing again and Elsa peeled her eyes away with a sigh, wishing a waiter would venture outside with a bottle of wine just for her.

They were so happily absorbed in each other that they didn't notice their spectator watching silently from the wall. Eventually they parted, and Ava mentioned they should go back inside before people started wondering about them. Elsa sat long after they'd gone, wishing her head would focus and help her make sense of things. She wished it would stop giving a damn, but God knew she'd tried.

She stared helplessly at the patio slabs, wishing they'd stop spinning. She next looked up a few minutes later, when Clement appeared in the doorway.

"We've been looking for you," he smiled, crouching down before her. "Had a bit too much to drink, have we?"

"Not nearly enough," she responded with a roll of her bleary eyes. Clement took his jacket off, and placed it around her shoulders, and she smiled gratefully.

"I think we're heading home soon," he told her gently. "Have you got a lift home arranged or do you want to come back with us?"

"I'm fine; I'm getting a cab with Sophia." She nodded. "I think Harry is staying over hers tonight, so that will be a fun cab ride home for me."

"Don't be bitter," he teased her.

"That's OK for you to say," she replied with a wink. "Enjoying yourself over by the flower beds, were you?"

His smiled immediately fell. "You saw?"

"I sure did," she grinned.

"Blimey, I thought I was good at being discreet!" he laughed, straightening up and offering his hand to her. "Listen, you won't say anything, will you? Fred's been...well, frosty lately. Ava and I have to work together, and I don't want things to be awkward on the yard."

"Of course I won't," she replied, accepting his hand. "But you're both adults."

"I know, it's just..." he trailed off, struggling to explain his worries.

"I won't say anything," she promised, and he put his arm around her and gave her an appreciative squeeze as he guided her back inside.

As Elsa climbed into bed alone, she wondered whether Portia were accompanying Frederick to his, and fought back bitter tears. She wished she could make her feelings go away, and just forget about him – not care what he was getting up to or with whom. But every time she closed her eyes, she saw him. She saw him standing across her room, in just his boxers; that perfectly sculpted body that had graced her bed and made her feel on top of the world, if only for one night.

Cecil snuggled up against her. He tried to lick her face and stretched out across her bed when she pushed him away, in his show of insistence that there was no room for any other man around here but him. But deep down, she knew she had lost him anyway, and she didn't see how she could ever get him back. She had lost him to that awful, cruel, two-faced creature Portia, and that made her angrier than anything. How he couldn't see straight through her flakiness to the vile person that she was, she would never understand. And to top it all off, the discovery that she was a Roxwell chilled her to her core. Elsa could never compete with that. And even though she knew she shouldn't waste a single tear on him, she couldn't stop them as they started to flow. She buried her head in her pillow and pulled Cecil close, as her mind whirred with raw emotions and alcohol, she slowly and painfully succumbed to sleep.

Chapter Thirteen

"How are you feeling?" Sophia asked cautiously when she emerged the following morning.

"I've got a sore head," Elsa sighed, not pausing from bedding down Drop Kick's stall.

"Me too," Sophia nodded. "But aside from that?"

She turned to look at her, and while Sophia thought she may try and deny anything was wrong, she just sighed in defeat.

"Hurt, beaten, angry…"

"Angry at who?" Sophia gently probed.

"*Him,*" Elsa winced. "Myself."

"Not Ava and Clement?" Sophia nervously enquired.

"Of course not Ava and Clement!" Elsa declared. "I couldn't be happier for them."

"Oh good!" Sophia breathed an audible sigh of relief. "They are a match made in heaven, aren't they?"

"Yup," Elsa resolutely agreed. "Just like you and Harry."

"Oh, *stop*!" Sophia demanded coyly, then quickly broke off at her insensitivity. "We'll find you someone, Else. Someone kind, gorgeous and most of all, *deserving*. Someone who will treat you like the Queen that you deserve."

"I don't want *someone,*" Elsa shrugged. "I don't even want *him* anymore. I'm over it; the witch is welcome to him. I've got Cecil and my horses, and that's enough for me for now."

Sophia gave her a reassuring smile, but she knew she didn't mean it. She could see her best friends heart break a little more each time that she couldn't bear to even say his name. She wished she could grab hold of Frederick and give him a piece of her mind.

Elsa knew she had to push her thoughts of him aside for once and for all, and focus on what was important. The end of the season was almost upon them, and Elsa was both relieved and sad. It would soon be time to rough the horses off; pull their shoes off and put them out at grass for a few weeks. It was the time to get all the maintenance jobs done on the yard, make sure all the leatherwork was repaired and put away in order for the start of next season. And although Elsa was glad that no events meant less chance of bumping into *him*, it also meant she had less excuses to hang out with Ava, to share BBQ's and beer in the lorry park. It would be a good opportunity to check-in with her mum, though, and face the tirade of abuse she would receive on her first visit for having neglected her daughter duties the last few months.

She looked around her tack room in dismay, and suddenly couldn't wait to give it a thorough deep clean. She wondered why, that every time she felt her heart snapping a little, she always turned to her tack room for comfort?

She flipped the switch on the kettle, and peered around the door out onto the yard.

"Tea?" she called.

"Oh, yes *please*!" Sophia called back. "You're an angel."

"I know!" she replied, smiling as she took Cali and Dusty's bridles off the peg and began taking them apart ready to clean. They had a full lorry travelling to their season finale at Cromwell at the weekend, and Elsa had lots of preparation to get done.

Although there were a handful of smaller events after Cromwell, it was the finale of the season for most of the top eventers', and Sophia had decided that it would also be theirs. She had Cali entered in the eight year old class, and Dusty entered in the special young rider class; a big ask for her still relatively-new rides. The young rider class was destined to showcase the country's young talent with international potential, and those who came out on top benefitted from bursaries and training with top international trainers to help them get established on the international scene. She had hoped to run Drop Kick in the Intermediate, but his stock-fencing injury had meant he'd been unable to do his preparation runs, so it was too risky. Instead she had decided to try Merlin in his first Intermediate after his promising run at Bealey, and Connor - back fit again after his time off with an abscess - was trying his hooves at the Novice before going out to grass for the winter and trying again next year.

Elsa loved going to Cromwell, and they put on a massive schedule to accommodate a variety of levels. The smaller classes started at the beginning of the week, with the big three-star class and the age classes concluding at the weekend. It promised to be a really good week away, but a very busy one.

The weather had been good in the run-up to Cromwell, and Elsa was pleased. Spending a week in temporary stabling in a muddy field could be a disaster if the weather decided not to hold out. Elsa drove the lorry to Cromwell alone, with Sophia arriving later. She loved driving the more modern lorry that Michael Patricks had provided them, much more than Sophia's old one. But a shiver still ran down her spine every time she turned onto the motorway, and she spent most of her journeys these days trying to reassure herself that she could not smell smoke. But as Cecil always sat in the cab beside her, she knew that he'd be the first to tell her were there anything wrong.

The journey was long, and as Elsa parked the lorry, all she wanted was to find her allocated stabling as quickly as possible, get her horses settled and get her head down. It had been a long day already, and she was nowhere near finished.

She was dismayed to find that she had been allocated stables as far away from the lorry as they could possibly be, and it would take several trips back and forth to get all her equipment and horses over to where they needed to be. She left the horses on the lorry while she took the bedding over, and bedded down their stalls with a deep bed, knowing they'd all be desperate for a roll.

"Hey!" Paige the New Zealander waved from across the aisle. "I swear we are always stabled together."

"It appears so!" Elsa laughed, waving back. "How's it going?"

"Well, we're all settled in," she smiled. "Brett decided to bring some youngsters with him, so it's going to be a long week. Think that's me done for today. Do you need a hand before I go?"

"That would be *awesome,*" Elsa sighed, replying quickly before she had a chance to retract her offer.

"They couldn't have stabled us further away if they tried, could they?" Paige commented as they walked back to the lorry together.

"I guess we obviously don't tip them enough," Elsa laughed, unloading her horses and passing her Cali and Dusty. She joined her with Merlin and Connor, and they began the long walk back again.

"You here for the week too, then?" Paige asked her.

"Yea," Elsa smiled. "It's our last event of the season."

"Us, too," Paige told her sadly. "Sophia got anyone in the three-star?"

Elsa shook her head. "Ours are all quite young. But at least I'll have a quiet moment so I should get to watch who takes the honours." She was looking forward to that, and deep down she hoped it was Frederick. "How many has Brett got in it?"

"Two," Paige smiled. "It'll be all hands on for me."

"Well, let me know if you need a hand," Elsa offered. Perhaps it would be best if she was too busy to idly watch Frederick, after all.

Elsa stabled her horses and quickly stripped their rugs and boots off before she let them roll. Cali had sweated up during the journey, and Elsa would need to give her a thorough groom before she retired to bed. She offered them all water and tied haynets, and then she went back for her equipment. By the time the lorry was unloaded of the essentials, and she was certain her horses were settled, she was absolutely exhausted. She fell down on the bench seat and allowed her eyes to shut as she pulled Cecil into her chest. He barked just before there was a tap on the door, and with a groan Elsa dragged herself to her feet.

"Thought I saw you return," Ava winked, holding out a can of beer to her. "Drink?"

"Ava..." she hesitated, with a bite to her lip. "I'm shattered."

"Even more reason to have a beer," Ava told her, forcing her to move aside as she climbed the steps. "Drink."

It was not a question this time, more of a demand, and Elsa gently broke into a smile.

"I'll drink, on one condition."

"Which is?" Ava frowned.

Elsa shoved her into the living area before she could back away. "You tell me *all* about *Clement,*" she laughed, falling back onto the seat and taking a long swig of beer.

"Oh *geez,* I've walked into this one, haven't I?" Ava fell down beside her, and Cecil jumped excitedly onto her lap.

"So, how's it going?" Elsa poked her in the ribs, unable to wait a moment longer. She knew it was good, Ava had broken into a wide smile as soon as Elsa had mentioned his name.

"Good," she admitted coyly.

"Just good?" Elsa probed with a grin.

Ava's cheeks reddened and she couldn't meet her eye. "It's lovely, you know? *He's* lovely. And he's *such* a good kisser," she sighed.

"He is," Elsa agreed, and they both fell around laughing as Ava launched a cushion at her, and Cecil leapt away with a yelp.

"He makes me laugh," Ava told her with a shrug. "I'm too busy for anything serious, but I like hanging out with him. He treats me like I'm the only one that matters. He's thoughtful and a true gentleman. He's everything I thought I didn't want."

"He sounds perfect," Elsa told her, and she meant it.

"You could have had him, Else," Ava told her, swigging from her own beer. "You've missed out there."

"Ah, no way," Elsa replied quietly. "He's not for me."

"Someone out there is," Ava told her seriously. "And he'll make you feel a million dollars, and he certainly won't ever make you cry. You'll enjoy hanging out with him, sharing a beer and pizza. And, most importantly, Cecil will *love* him."

"I know," Elsa replied, her voice barely above a whisper. But right now, she couldn't even bear to think about it.

Elsa fed breakfast at six o'clock, only a little earlier than she would do at home, and was grateful that Sophia wasn't due to arrive for a few more hours. A beer with Ava had turned into five, and although the late night had been a whole load of fun, it hadn't done much for her sleep deprivation and she was well aware of the black bags bulging underneath her eyes.

The stabling area was already a flurry of activity as Elsa quickly mucked out. She changed rugs and replenished haynets, then took Cali and Dusty out for a walk first and a pick of grass. When she had eventually retrieved Cecil from his latest rabbit scent, she returned the horses to their stables, locked Cecil in the lorry, and began saddling Merlin ready for a hack with Ava and Clement. Ava had invited her the evening before, and although Elsa had been reluctant to gatecrash their little thing that they had going on, Ava had insisted as apparently three wasn't a crowd when there were technically six of you.

Michael Patricks appeared over the stall door just as Elsa was picking out Merlin's feet.

"Hey!" she beamed. "Lovely to see you! How are you?"

"Very well, thank you," he nodded. He stepped aside, and

she noticed the man that stood beside him. They were of a similar stamp; both extremely well dressed and well groomed, with a similar haircut. "This is my partner, Philip."

Philip extended his hand over the stall door to her, as she shook it she couldn't help noticing how well manicured his nails were, a world away from the mud and grime that were underneath hers. And his hands were *so* soft that she concluded he did not work outside like she did.

"Partner?" she repeated. "As in...business partner?"

"No..." Michael replied, looking a little embarrassed. He coughed to clear his throat. "Partner as in...*life* partner?" he reached for his hand, and Philip took it with a smile.

Elsa followed their action, and her eyes widened with realisation. "Oh, I see! Oh, Ava will be upset!" she exclaimed, and immediately clamped her hand tight over her big mouth as she cursed herself. How could she be so tactless?

"I'm sorry?" he peered at her in amusement.

"I'm so sorry," she replied, her cheeks flaming red, and she vowed never again to begin an event on such little sleep. "The tiredness is getting to me. I just...didn't realise."

"I hide it well," he told her with a wink, immediately putting her at ease a little.

"I really am sorry," she told him, looking from him to Philip and back again. "It's none of my business. But it really is lovely to meet you."

"This is my first event," Philip clasped his hands together. "And I am *so* looking forward to it."

"Me too," Elsa beamed. "Our horses are going very well at the moment, and Sophia is really confident this weekend. Talking of Sophia, she's not due to arrive until later this afternoon, and Cali and Dusty don't do their dressage until tomorrow."

"Actually, we have friends in the area," Michael smiled. "So we thought we'd make a little holiday of it. Especially as it is Philip's first event, I wanted to introduce him to every aspect of it. I do apologise for dropping in on you unannounced."

"Oh, any time!" Elsa waved his apology away. "I really don't mind. I was just about to take this one out on a hack, show him the sights of the estate." She ran her hand down Merlin's neck, and he peered at her with a look that indicated he did not want to be parted from his haynet under any circumstances.

"Well, don't let us keep you," Michael smiled. "We'll catch up with you tomorrow." He went to walk away, and paused outside Cali's stable. "My horses are looking fantastic by the way," he told her sincerely. "Thank you."

Elsa beamed with pride as she watched them stride down the aisle. She felt a long way past the days of Christine Forrester finding fault with every single way Elsa turned out her horses, and she didn't ever wish to go back to those dark days.

"Did you *know* that Michael Patricks is *gay*?" Elsa demanded, as she joined Clement and Ava on their hack, and they left the stabling area.

"No *way*?" Ava spun around in the saddle to face her, to determine whether she was joking.

"I'm serious!" Elsa told her. "I've just met his *boyfriend*!"

"Bloody hell!" Ava exclaimed. "Well, I didn't see that coming! I am heartbroken!"

"I know, right! Thank God you found Clement, hey?" she replied with a wink.

"Yes, isn't she lucky!" Clement laughed, and Elsa pushed Merlin into a trot before Clemet could try and pull her off her horse.

Hacking routes were clearly marked around the estate, and they made the most of them for the hour that they were out, chatting easily about events that had passed, as well as the week to come. Elsa was so glad that the two of them had hit it off; they got along so easily, and she felt privileged to call them both friends.

Sophia arrived in the afternoon with Merlin's owner Rosie, who was unbelievably excited to be attending Merlin's biggest test to date. Rosie sneaked him slices of carrots when she thought Elsa wasn't looking; she was always being warned about it encouraging him to bite. She removed his rugs and ran a body brush over his sleek bay coat, and Elsa watched with amusement from Connor's stall, thinking she'd let Rosie get on with it and tidy the poor boy up later.

Rosie stepped back and allowed Elsa to tack up when Derek arrived to put Sophia and Merlin through their paces; she knew Sophia was meticulous about how her tack fitted and there was no way she could replicate any of Elsa's grooming and horse care skills.

Elsa waited until they had departed for their lesson, and saddled Connor. Paige had mentioned wanting company on her hack, and together they headed off around the estate.

Connor was up early the next morning for his dressage, and Elsa was rather glad that his owner Gilly didn't do early mornings and she was instead able to prepare her horse in peace. Rosie had already started drinking - to quell her nerves at Merlin's impending test - and Elsa was easily able to divert her to the owners' hospitality marquee whenever she got too much for her.

Connor worked in beautifully, and Elsa had a good feeling about this week. He was extremely focused in the warm-up, refusing to get distracted when another horse came too close or when there was a loud noise or sharp movement nearby, and Elsa felt so proud of him before he even went into the collecting ring.

Gilly was gripping the rails to the arena, and her knuckles were white by the time Elsa joined her. They embraced in a quick hug, and turned to watch Connor's test. He entered the arena with a bold trot, his halt was perfectly square, his paces expressive, and Elsa felt her own heart melting as he tried his heart out throughout his test. She was not surprised that the judges found admirably in his favour, and Gilly threw her arms around Elsa as they dashed to meet him at the exit.

Merlin was up not long after, but Elsa would not get to watch his test as she had to get Cali and Dusty ready to trot up before the judges, all part of the rigmarole of getting them prepared for international competition. As Elsa saddled Merlin and sent him on his way with Rosie and Sophia, she settled Connor back into his stall and set about brushing off Cali and Dusty. She had a feeling this was going to be a really good week, but first she needed to eat.

She leaned against the counter of the chip wagon, convinced she was going to pass out if he didn't serve her soon. It had been a busy morning, and both Connor and Merlin had excelled themselves in their tests, putting them in a good position for the show jumping and cross country tomorrow. Cali and Dusty had also passed the trot up and the vet check, ready for their dressage the following afternoon, so it was a good start all around.

"Ah, *shit*," Ava cursed, dragging her from her thoughts. "I forgot to order for Frederick." She signalled the chip attendant for another scoop of chips.

Elsa forced herself to keep breathing upon Ava's mention of his name. She had not had time to think about him recently, and for that she was glad. She had crossed paths with Portia a couple of times already at Cromwell, and had happily looked the other way, not even exchanging glances. She was not used to being so unsociable, but where Portia was concerned, Elsa hoped to keep it that way.

Elsa troughed her chips in the manner of a groom who had not had a chance to stop to eat since she'd climbed out of bed that morning. She stretched out, exhausted, across Ava's expansive bed in the plush Twemlow lorry. She already knew from Ava that Frederick was staying in a hotel in town, and she wasn't sure she wanted to know about Portia's sleeping arrangements, so they had the whole lorry to themselves. Ava had the start sheets for their classes laid out before her, and they went through them in detail, discussing the chances of all the important entrants.

"How is Sophia feeling about her entries?" Ava asked excitedly.

"Confident," Elsa nodded, unable to contain her smile. "We've found a few events across Europe that she might contest next season, but we're trying not to get too excited until we see how today goes."

"They will probably be the same ones as us," Ava beamed. "Wouldn't it be awesome if we could travel together?"

"It would be the best!" Elsa agreed.

Eventually they peeled themselves off the bed, as one of the Twemlow working pupils required Ava's assistance, and Elsa thought she really should get her horses out for a pick of grass. She changed their rugs and put overreach boots on Cali and Dusty, and took them for a walk across the lorry park to find the best grass, keeping her eyes peeled for the arrival of Clement's lorry, which would also signal the arrival of her best boy. She noticed it pull in half an hour later and quickly returned her horses, sprinting back to the lorry park before anyone beat her to it.

"Need a hand?" she fluttered her eyelashes at the handsome Frenchman as he lowered the ramp.

"I thought you wouldn't be too far away," he grinned back at her as he unfastened the first partition.

She waited with anticipation, hoping from foot to foot until he handed her a leadrope.

"I assume this one is for you?" he asked her, as she practically snatched it from him and threw her arms around the neck of the big bay it belonged to.

"Nobby!" she breathed. "It's *so* good to see you!"

He nuzzled her pockets expectantly, and pawed at the ground until she produced a slice of carrot for him. He hauled her down the ramp for a pick of grass, and she giggled and gave him a pat, over the moon to see him looking and feeling so well.

"How do you think he'll fair in the big class?" Elsa smiled, as Clement unloaded another bay and handed her the leadrope while he went back inside to retrieve the final occupant.

"Fred's feeling confident," Clement smiled, as they made their way to the stabling with the three of them. "Otherwise he'd have left him at home."

"He'll be glad to be out," Elsa gave him another pat. She showed him into his stable, and he circled the deep shavings bed wanting to roll, but she made him wait until she'd removed his boots and rugs.

"You trying to steal my job?" Ava grinned over the stall door, Clement having left her to it to go and clear out his lorry.

"As much as I'd love to get him ready for his trot up," Elsa replied, giving him a parting hug. "I'd best get back to my own horses."

She was stopped by the sound of familiar voices in the aisle, and she looked up as Frederick and his mother approached. She stood shielded by Nobby's broad shoulder, not wanting to see him, nor him to see her, and the awkward conversation that would undoubtedly flow between them. Ava gave her an encouraging smile, but Elsa gave her just a scowl in return.

"Did they travel well?" Frederick asked his groom.

"Like a dream, apparently," Ava replied.

Lady Twemlow had her arm linked through his, as she totally disregarded Nobby and led him straight to Cobra's stall, an impressive young, black stallion who was Frederick's second entry in the big class.

"Doesn't he look *fabulous*?" Lady Twemlow declared. "Mr and Mrs Roxwell would be so glad of a win, especially as Cavalier was so close to taking the title last week. And it would be thoroughly well-deserved for the both of you."

"Nobby's been going well, too," Ava piped up, desperate for Frederick to look over and lock eyes with Elsa, despite knowing that Elsa was shooting daggers into her turned back.

"Oh, he's not really of the same calibre," Lady Twemlow waved her away. "That Forrester woman is a bit of a dreamer, isn't she? That animal has the pedigree of a donkey and hardly any ability. How he's made it even *this* far is beyond me."

"Mother..." Frederick tried to stop her, having the decency to look embarrassed, if only in front of his loyal groom who had heard much worse before from his tyrant mother.

"No, darling," Lady Twemlow was insistent. "It's the Roxwell horses you have to concentrate on. Portia and you make such a *darling* couple, you have a chance to be a real power couple in the eventing world, you know? Mr and Mrs Roxwell are delighted for you, they would set you up with horsepower for life if you would just..."

"Sophia used to get along just fine with Nobby as her top horse, didn't she, Else?" Ava cut them off, turning to peer over Nobby's stall door.

Elsa peered over Nobby's withers at them, clutching his mane for support as she genuinely felt she might be sick. She saw the fear fill Frederick's face as he followed Ava's gaze to her, and Elsa wished the ground would just open and swallow her whole.

"Elsa..." he breathed, unable to conceal his guilt.

"Are you a new groom?" Lady Twemlow peered at her.

"No," Elsa forced the words out. She realised they were not going to stop staring at her until she spoke.

"Well, what are you doing in our stalls?" Lady Twemlow demanded.

"Mother, leave it..." Frederick told her, shrugging off her suddenly overbearing grip.

"No, I will not, Freddy!" she retorted. "With the calibre of horses that you are campaigning, you have to get a bit tighter with your security! You can't have any old waif and stray wandering into your stalls, even if it just Nobby's!"

"Elsa is not a waif or a stray," Frederick insisted, through gritted teeth. "And Nobby is just as valuable as any of my other horses."

"I think Portia would have something to say about that," Lady Twemlow folded her arms firmly across her chest. "But of course, when you and Portia are set up properly, she will be running the yard as a tight ship, and no doubt will be vetting *everything* that comes into the stable," she broke off and winked at Ava as she added, "horses *and* grooms."

Ava forced a smile. Frederick was more than capable of vetting his grooms himself, before that wretched Portia had got her claws into him and brought an unwelcome atmosphere with her to the yard. It was unfortunate that Lady Twemlow appeared to *adore* her.

"You need a good, strong woman like her, and I am relieved you have finally found one!" Lady Twemlow went on, gaining momentum. "God knows it's taken you long enough! I'm sure Clement would happily take the likes of Nobby off your hands, and good riddance, I say! You won't have time to be messing around with low-grade horses when you and her are…"

"Mother, *stop*!" Frederick growled, bringing her to an abrupt halt. He ran his hands through his blonde curls, and Elsa actually felt sorry for him, which was difficult for her after all the heartache he had caused her.

"Whatever has got into you?" Lady Twemlow peered at him closely, looking as though she suddenly might cry, and Elsa rolled her eyes. She had heard all about the over-bearing mother before, guilt-tripping him into always behaving how *she* wanted, but never until now seen her approaching her best.

Elsa wished they'd all move away down the aisle, so that she could escape from this stall without making any more of a scene. She needed to get out of here.

"I'm going…to go….now," she stammered, fumbling with the bolt to the door as she tried desperately not to make eye contact. Ava opened it for her, and gave her arm a gentle squeeze as she passed her.

Frederick watched her go, unable to form any words that could justify stopping her. He wished he could escape with her, but he didn't deserve her.

"Was it something I said?" Lady Twemlow murmured.

"She's got a manic schedule today," Ava forced a polite smile, remembering who paid her wages.

Elsa took a long walk around the lorry park, forcing herself to calm down before she returned to her own horses. She kept her head down, watching as her tatty boots scuffed at the grass with each stride she took.

"Elsa," he made her jump as he stepped out from behind a lorry.

"Geez, Frederick," she clutched her palm against her chest, her heart racing. "Must you do that?"

"Sorry," he shrugged. "I thought you wouldn't stop if you saw me first."

"My life doesn't revolve around you," she told him coldly. "I don't spend it trying to avoid you, nor do I spend it trying to run into you."

"I have never expected that you would," he replied with a wry smile.

They lingered for a moment in an awkward silence, and Elsa waited for him to speak, desperately trying to avoid his handsome eyes as they scanned her face.

"My mother is not very tactful," he began. "She would not have meant to hurt your feelings, if she knew how much Nobby meant to you."

"I feel certain that a woman like her would not have held back, had even Christine Forrester been standing in the aisle," Elsa retorted. "But I suppose that would have done you a favour? You obviously can't wait to get rid of all your horses that may not be potential Olympic superstars, and instead have a Roxwell exclusive stableyard?"

"That's not true," Frederick replied quietly.

"That's clearly your mother and Portia's plan?" Elsa pressed. It was a question, but she was certain she knew the answer, nonetheless.

Frederick's gaze dropped to the floor, his hands shoved deep into his pockets as he struggled for words. Eventually he looked up. "She's not a nasty person," he shrugged.

"I've seen *exactly* what a nasty, cruel person she is," Elsa snarled, jabbing him in the chest with her pointed finger. "And I wouldn't wish her behaviour to be inflicted on any animal, whether it had Olympic potential or happened to be a beach donkey!"

Frederick stepped back, beaten. When he knew he should be rising up and fighting for his beliefs, the wrong women had beaten him down, and he was so ashamed of himself for allowing it to happen. But there was nothing he could do anymore. He was trying to run a business; he needed to earn money, and if Portia was the key to that, then so be it.

"You've changed," she whispered, her hands on her hips and even though he were taller than her, he felt as though she was looking down on him. "The Frederick who Ava described to me, when I very first met you, is not the Frederick that is standing before me now. What has happened to you?"

"I don't know," he replied, his voice barely audible. "And I wish that Frederick could come back, but I don't think he ever can." And he hated himself for it. He hated himself for what he had allowed people to sculpt him to be, and he knew that she must hate him for it, too. And she had every right to. He had done nothing right by her, and that pained him more than anything.

"As far as I can see, you've got a beautiful, over-powering mother who has got you - whether you like it or not - to where you are today," she shrugged, not wanting to hear any of his turmoil. "Now you've got a beautiful, wealthy woman hanging off your arm, which you are doing nothing to discourage, and clearly you believe that is going to raise you up even further to the top of your game. Yet you're walking around as though you have the weight of the world resting on your shoulders. And do you know what? I don't care anymore, Frederick, because I'm only in this game for the horses. You've made your bed, you need to go lie in it."

Her words stung him like a wasp, but he knew that he deserved them. And he needed to hear them. He felt like he had been burying his head in the sand for far too long now. He needed someone to tell him what they really thought, and he needed it to be her.

"I just wish you didn't have Nobby, because he is the most genuine horse I've ever met, and it breaks my heart to see him put up with…with…*eurgh*!" she broke off before she insulted his new girlfriend any further. She knew it wasn't attractive, that it didn't make her a better person to insult someone that he was sharing his life with, but there was no way she could ever warm to her.

"You do not need to worry about Nobby," he told her. "He is blissfully unaware of what my mother calls him, or what she thinks about. And as for Portia, well she never wants to lay eyes on him again, so you can rest assured she won't be going near him. He has Ava, and in Ava he has everything that he needs. Ava treats all our horses like they are the most valuable horses in the world. Because to her, they are."

"And what about to you?" her question took him by surprise. "Are any of them valuable, or are they all just as indispensable as the last one?"

"Believe it or not, Elsa," he narrowed his eyes at her. "I am in this game only for the horses, too. They all touch me a bit in their own way, leave a little bit behind when they pass through my yard - some good, some bad. Some I wish I could keep, some I wish to never return. But I am grateful to them all."

"I wish I could believe you, Frederick. I really do." With a shake of her head, she folded her arms defiantly across her chest and turned away, knowing he would not follow her, and not wanting him to, either.

Elsa was slower mucking out than normal, and looked at the faces Cecil was giving her from Cali's stall doorway as he whined and wondered how much longer he had to wait until he could go for his walk. She grabbed Cali's tack from the locker, needing to get out to the peace and quiet and feel the fresh air in her face. She mounted from her tack box and headed out across the lorry park, frowning at the big bay that trotted to catch her up.

"Mind if I join you?" Ava asked cautiously from astride Nobby.

"Sure," Elsa smiled, not surprised they'd both had the same idea.

"No hard feelings?" Ava double-checked.

"No hard feelings." Elsa reassured her.

"I'm sorry," Ava told her, with a bite to her lip. "But it would have been worse if they hadn't have known you were there. I thought I should stop her early. Mrs T can be quite...*vicious*."

"You're not kidding?" Elsa retorted, keeping an eye on Cecil as he ran ahead in search of rabbits. "It's hard to imagine they're cut from the same cloth, isn't it?"

"In everything aside from looks, yes, it is," Ava agreed. "They look identical, but in every other trait, Fred may as well be adopted."

"Do you ever feel sorry for him?" Elsa asked her quietly.

"All the time," Ava nodded, without hesitation. "She's worse at home; every day she is out on the yard finding fault with everything he does, because she has nothing better to do. She tells me it makes him a stronger person, instils fight in him to succeed, but I am not so sure," she trailed off, and they walked a few more steps in silence. "I can easily stop myself feeling sorry for him, though. I remind myself of his wealth, his influence, his power, and that he could just walk away and start afresh if he detested it so much. But he stays and fights, so maybe Mrs T is right."

Elsa slowly nodded. She wished she could understand, but her own life was a world away from that of Frederick Twemlow.

"I guess it's not as easy as just walking away, is it?" she added thoughtfully. "It's hard to leave so much behind, when you have everything. It would be easy for us, of course, as we have nothing."

"Else, he may have more than we will ever have, but I wouldn't swap places with Freddy Twemlow for anything in the world."

Elsa wondered if he wished he could trade places with them, though. She had detected from the looks at him she had stolen, that he most definitely would.

"Come on," Ava said, gathering up her reins before Elsa had time to give it too much thought. "Let's have a canter."

Chapter Fourteen

Elsa's horses were as ready as they were ever going to be by the time their start times rolled round the next morning, and she and Sophia had a full day ahead of them. Considering all the thoughts and feelings that had been whirring around her head when it finally hit her pillow, she had had a brilliant night's sleep, and was raring to go. She reminded herself that this was what it was all about; they had a really good yard of horses and she couldn't wait to get them out on course.

Elsa thought nothing could wipe the smile from her face, until she walked Connor out of his stall and he didn't look to be walking sound. She felt her heart sink as she turned him on a circle and led him down the aisle, running backwards slightly in front of him as she tried to trot him up *and* look at what the problem is. At the end of the aisle she pulled him up and walked him back.

"Paige?" she called, running a hand through her hair in exasperation. "Please could you trot him up for me?"

"Sure," the Kiwi groom appeared from her stall and took the lead rope from her.

She jogged down the aisle with Connor enthusiastically trotting at her side. *Near hind*, Elsa thought, observing how his back end shuffled rather than moved freely.

"Your turn," she said, handing the lead rope back, and she watched while Elsa jogged him down the aisle again, turned and jogged back.

"Near hind," Paige confirmed. She ran her hand down both of his hind legs, and Connor lifted them in turn and turned his head to watch her, as if wondering what all the fuss was about.

"No heat or swelling," she said, straightening back up. "Maybe he'll walk it off?"

"Maybe," Elsa replied desolately, but they were running out of time for him to do that, and there was no way he could be asked to show jump on only three legs.

Sophia arrived and led him out with Merlin for a pick of grass and in an attempt to walk off his mystery, subtle lameness, while Elsa mucked out the stalls.

"I'll get him worked in," Sophia told her when she returned, half-heartedly reaching for his tack. "He is walking on it better; I'll get Harry to take a look at it when he gets here."

Elsa smiled at the mention of his name. "Quite convenient dating a vet, hey?"

"It has its perks."

The stabling was getting busy as Elsa groomed and plaited Merlin, and she looked up with a frown as thirty minutes later Sophia halted Connor before her, and slid from the saddle.

"Harry may be a really good vet," she said with a sigh. "But he's no miracle worker. Looks like Connor has caught himself in the night; Harry has found the *tiniest* nick on his leg, and Connor is being such a drama queen about it, so I've had to withdraw."

"Oh, *babe,*" Elsa put her arm around her, unable to hide her own disappointment. She tried to pull herself together, for Sophia. "It's fine," she told her. "There'll be other events."

"But this is like the *worst* possible start to *this* event," Sophia whined, putting her arms around Connor nonetheless. "And do you know what really pisses me off the most?"

Elsa waited.

"That *this* horse," she rubbed his face affectionately. "Is the *biggest* hypochondriac. If this was Nobby…*Nobby* would have to have half his leg hanging off before he showed any sign of lameness. But if anyone so much as *sneezes* too close to Connor, then suddenly he thinks he's on deaths door."

Elsa couldn't help but laugh, for it was very true. "Come on," she said as she began untacking him. "He's sensitive, he can't help that. Some guys *are* sensitive, I guess? But let's not make a big deal out of it; we don't want to ruin his street credit in front of all these other horses."

Sophia giggled as she removed his bridle and watched as he walked straight into his stable with no sign of lameness at all and tucked greedily into his haynet.

"I could *kill* him," she said, with a shake of her head.

"No time," Elsa smiled, closing his stall door behind him. "Merlin's almost ready and there is no way he is withdrawing!"

The plus side of not having two horses to juggle meant that Elsa at least got to stay and watch Merlin's round. Derek warmed the pair up, and Rosie clutched her wine glass with shaking hands as she watched beside Elsa.

"He'll be fine," Elsa tried to reassure her, wondering how she had ever thought that being a groom was about looking after *only* horses. Sometimes it was the people involved that made it most stressful. "*They* will be fine."

"This is a massive track," Rosie replied, unconvinced. "As if this show jumping isn't bad enough, have you *seen* the cross country?"

Elsa nodded. She had walked it last night imagining she were on Timber Bear. She'd had two refusals at the picnic table, ran out at the first brush fence, been chucked off spectacularly at the water and thrown in the towel at the solid rail oxer because she could see the lorry park and she was dying for a drink.

"I thought it looked lovely," she smiled sweetly. "There's nothing out there that Merlin hasn't tackled before."

"Doesn't make you worry any less though, does it?"

Merlin was called into the collecting ring, and Elsa thought they looked more than ready. As Sophia cantered around she was so focused, and Merlin concentrated entirely on her.

The bell sounded, and Sophia turned to the first fence, a simple upright. But Merlin's head shot up as distraction finally got the better of him and he began to rush. Sophia didn't have time to correct him and he brought the top rail down with his knees.

He landed on the incorrect leg-lead, and swished his tail when Sophia asked him to change. But even Elsa could see the apologetic look on his face as Sophia gave him a firm half-halt, and he promised to try harder. He was much more focused as he thundered towards the second, and it could have been two foot higher and he still would have cleared it. Sophia eased up on him as he continued to soar clear; distraction only returning when she had to ride him deep into the far corner to get the correct stride for the triple. There was one stride between the first two elements, and a long two strides to the third element which Merlin had to stretch for, but there was no way he was going to let himself miss it after letting Sophia down so badly at the first. They flew around jump six, keeping it tight to their left and getting the perfect stride for the final fence, and landing safely he thundered through the finish with just the four faults.

"He got better with every fence," Elsa told Rosie as they rushed to meet them. It was hard to be annoyed with him for his mistake at the first when he had showed such promise over the following fourteen jumping efforts.

"It was just so unlucky!" Rosie agreed, giving him a hearty pat as he walked from the ring on a loose rein, looking as pleased as punch.

"He's going to be great," Sophia was unable to hide her smile as she slid from the saddle and loosened his girth. "I can't wait to take him cross country!"

Elsa took him for a walk while Sophia joined Derek to get herself mentally prepared. When she was ready Elsa legged her back into the saddle and left them to warm up while she got on with some jobs. She had at least time to muck out before Sophia went to the start.

Sophia took Merlin to the start early, making use of her

time to keep him walking and settled. She walked him into the start box a few times, frustrated that he was one of her most experienced horses since the departure of Nobby, yet he still had moments when he was so easily distracted. But he gave her the impression that he was equally annoyed at himself, and promised to make it up to her.

The starter counted them down, and Merlin bounded from the start box. He clattered up to the first, and cleared it easily. Elsa watched them clear the first five until they went out of sight, and she started walking up towards the end of the course, so that she could see them coming back and ready to grab him at the finish. She could hear from the loudspeaker that they were bang on track and doing everything right. She held her breath until she heard that they were safely through the water, and then she waited to see them gallop back up the hill.

He was absolutely flying as Sophia steadied him up for the brush fence with a hideous drop on landing, and Elsa almost thought he wasn't going to listen to her. He jumped much too forward, and Elsa's heart was in her mouth as she watched him jam on his brakes upon landing, as if clocking the drop at the very last minute, and he descended at a hair raising pace - but clear - and that was all that mattered as he galloped on to the huge table. He flew over that, as he did the final three, and Elsa could hardly contain herself as he flew through the finish full of running, and well-within the tight time.

Sophia flung her arms around the gelding's neck as soon as Elsa had his reins. "He was fantastic!" she beamed, as he hoovered up the sugar lumps from his groom's palm.

"He was!" Elsa agreed, keeping him walking as she patted him heartily.

Sophia slid to the ground and quickly removed her saddle. Rosie was quickly beside them, her wine glass discarded as she grabbed the saddle from Sophia.

"That was one of the best rounds of the class!" Rosie told

them, having kept a close eye on the scores throughout the three phases. "Real shame about the pole in the show jumping, otherwise you could have won!"

"Merlin asked if we could forget about the pole," Sophia laughed, scraping the sweat from him. "He's worried I'm going to dock it from his hay allowance!"

"Oh, *darling*!" Rosie rubbed his face as Elsa paused to offer him more water. "We'd never do that to you!"

When Merlin was sufficiently cooled, Elsa returned him to his stable, and he tucked gratefully into his hay as she wrapped up his legs.

"He was awesome, wasn't he?" Paige beamed, as she returned leading one of Brett's youngsters.

"Yea, he was!" Elsa replied, unable to stop smiling. "Shame about the pole, but that aside, it was just the start we needed after Connor being withdrawn."

"I've high hopes for you this weekend," Paige told her with a wink.

"I hope you're right," Elsa replied. But where horses were concerned, it was so easy for everything to go wrong at the drop of a hat.

"Ava invited me over to her lorry tonight," Paige broke her from her thoughts. "Are you coming?"

"Unfortunately not," Elsa let herself out of Merlin's stall. "I'm driving these two back tonight. No point in them being stabled here for three days when they could be at home in the field."

"Ah, unlucky," Paige replied. "I managed to delegate that job to someone else!"

"Well, I am a one man band," Elsa laughed. "I get all the jobs – good and bad."

"Yea, I'm not sure how you do it!"

But as Elsa swung the lorry from the show ground and out onto the open road, she couldn't imagine doing anything else. While Merlin knew he had done well and was full of himself for it, she could sense Connor's disappointment that he was heading home before he'd even had a chance to play. It was these emotions that sealed it for Elsa, that she simply had the best job in the world. When she struggled to drag herself from bed in the mornings when it still felt like the middle of the night, it was the thought of her loyal horses depending on her that hauled her to her feet. And while she knew people worried about her being lonely, she was anything but. At work she was surrounded by her best friends.

She was so glad to finally turn onto the familiar country lanes that signalled that home was around only a few more corners. As soon as they were unloaded, Connor and Merlin were turned straight out into the sand paddocks. Elsa was grateful to see that Colin had already hayed and watered everything and saved her from the job. She slipped into Timber Bear's paddock with a carrot before retiring to bed with Cecil.

When her bedside alarm sounded, it really was still the middle of the night, but Dusty and Cali were due for the vet inspection at eight o'clock, and Elsa still had to get them presentable. Cromwell was quite some distance away, and felt even more so while driving a lorry that had a top speed of not very fast. But the early start was worth it as Cali and Dusty passed the vet inspection with flying colours, as Sophia and Elsa had suspected that they would.

"Morning!" came a cheerful voice over Cali's stable door, as Elsa stood inside plaiting her ready for dressage. She removed the needle and thread from between her teeth and broke into a smile.

"Lovely to see you again," she told Michael and Philip, as they watched her work.

"Are they settled in now?" Michael enquired.

"Yes, it definitely did them good getting here early. We've been hacking around the estate lots, so hopefully they've seen all the sights and sounds."

"I can't wait to see them in action," Michael clasped his hands together. "In the meantime, we're off to get some breakfast. Can we bring you back anything?"

"Not for me, thanks," Elsa replied gratefully. "I'll grab myself a coffee on the go, but I won't have time to eat until these two both have their dressage out the way."

"That is dedication," Phillip looked at her in awe.

No, this is just my life, Elsa thought, as she watched them stride away. She wondered whether she should have tried harder at school, performed a little better in her exams and got an office job that promised her better working conditions of an air conditioned office in the summer, and heated in the winter, a little more money, and the opportunity to get more hours sleep. But the thought was absurd; office workers didn't get to experience the nerves and emotions of preparing two promising young horses for their international debut, even if it was only short format. Although she suspected they didn't get through half as much hand cream as she did.

Cali was up first, and she looked immaculate as Elsa legged Sophia into the saddle and walked with her to the warm up. She was a flashy, forward going horse and perfectly suited to dressage. She found no difficulty in pulling off expressive paces, and she had it nailed as soon as Sophia turned her down the centre line. It was almost as though Cali thought that everyone at the entire showground was here to see just her, and now was her chance to shine.

Although Sophia had been having extensive dressage lessons at home to try and nail the new moves she would have to ride in international competition, Elsa could see how tense she was. Sophia hid it well to those who did not know her well, and both Michael and her mother had insisted that there was no pressure; that she should use Cromwell as a practice run, train hard over winter and really hit the ground running next season. But Sophia was concentrating hard and really going for it. If she were to be overly critical, Elsa thought she could collect more for the collected movements, and she thought that although the shoulder-in was a little wobbly, the judges were overly harsh in their scoring. Cali got impressive marks for her extended movements, and half-passes were her party piece where she was duly awarded. As she was hard to contain, Elsa thought her rhythm lacked consistency, and she had the habit of holding herself a little tight - made worse during this test by Sophia being so tense, but Elsa knew they would relax over time.

Cali was very hot by the time she left the arena, and Elsa threw a sweatsheet over her and walked her off while Sophia went through the test with Michael and Phillip, who were determined to get to grips with all the movements and terminology.

"It's so much more complicated than the jumping, isn't it?" Phillip laughed. "If they clear the fence, no penalties. Simple, really?"

Elsa smiled; she couldn't imagine even the best riders describing a three-star cross country course as *simple*.

Dusty was excited at the return of his stable mate, but it would be short lived. As soon as Elsa had stripped Cali's tack and made her comfortable, it would be Dusty's turn to show the world what he could do. His mane was thick and coarse and took much longer to plait than Cali's. Elsa was convinced he had a high dose of pony blood in him somewhere.

She removed his rugs, ran a brush over his dark coat and splashed oil on his hooves, grateful that by nature he was such a clean horse. He was quickly becoming one of her favourites, although of course she would never admit it. But he reminded her a lot of Nobby.

Where Cali found the more expressive movements easy, Dusty struggled with his extensions, but pulled off the collected movement easily. He really shortened his frame for Sophia, and was lithe and springy despite being on the chunky side when it came to stamps of horse. He was a little sticky on his half-passes, and did not score great for his circles, but he otherwise tried his heart out for his nervous, inexperienced rider, and that was all that they could ask for.

"I feel awful," Sophia murmured to Elsa as she accompanied her from the ring. She wiped her hands over her face in frustration. "If we score lowly it was totally my fault. There's so much pressure to not let Michael down; he could be such a good owner for us."

"There is *no* pressure," Elsa reminded her. "He knows you are not very experienced at this level, and he doesn't expect you to go straight out and win."

"Nobby..." Sophia began, but Elsa cut her off sharply.

"Nobby was a totally different kettle of fish. You brought him through the ranks yourself, and knew each other inside out. That is not going to happen with these two over night, and Michael knows and respects that."

"I know, I guess," Sophia sighed, the pain on her face evident, but she didn't say anything more as she saw them both approaching, and slid from the saddle to greet them.

"That was *fab*!" Michael beamed, patting Dusty's sweaty neck and sliding his other arm around Sophia's shoulder, and Elsa felt any apprehension fade away. They had nothing to worry about; she just needed Sophia to see that, and *relax*.

Elsa got them both settled in their stables as quickly as she could, desperate to get to the grooms canteen and see what they had left to eat, and then she needed a power nap. She was used to surviving now on very little sleep, but Cromwell was a long away-stay, and today she was struggling.

"Elsa!"

She heard the shout, and her stride briefly altered, but she did not stop.

"Elsa!" he tried again.

"Get lost, Frederick!" she shouted back, wondering what the hell he wanted. She tried to tell herself she didn't care, but of course it was a lie. With a sigh, she stopped, and spun around, her hands on her hips. "What do you want?"

"Nothing, this time," he replied, pointing to the ground between them. "You dropped your sweatsheet; it fell from your rucksack."

Shit. She stayed still, wanting to believe it wasn't hers, that he had tossed it down just to get her to stop, so he could talk to her. But as she allowed herself to glance over the navy blue netting, she could see the gold trim of the embroidered lettering of Sophia's initials.

"Thanks," she mumbled, bending down to hide her reddening cheeks as she gathered it into her arms.

"No problem," he smiled, taking in the sight of her. He was normally so focused at events, so absorbed in his own world pre-competition that not even a bomb being dropped could distract him. Yet he had noticed her when she should have blended in so easily with the other grooms going about their work. He had seen the sweatsheet come loose from where she'd swung it over her strap; he had willed it to become looser with every stride so that it would fall to the floor and he'd have reason to call after her. His prayer had been answered. Yet now he had her attention, and she didn't look quite so furious at him, he had no idea what to say.

"Nobby is feeling well," he murmured, knowing that could now be the only weapon he had left to get her on side.

"I should think he is," she replied curtly, "if he's running in a three-star. Otherwise you'd have left him at home."

"Well, yes of course," he replied, his amusement tugging at his lips. He could already see her mellowing just at the pure mention of her favourite horse, even if she didn't allow her voice to show it.

"Right, well, catch you later." She turned to continue on her way.

"But he's feeling *really* well," he called after her, his words making her stop. "As in he could win."

She felt her heart skip a beat, as she absorbed his words. If

Frederick Twemlow said a horse was ready to win, then he was to be taken very seriously.

"He deserves to win," it came out as a whisper, as she turned back around to face him. She could not hide her surprise that he had strode closer and she had not even heard him. He stood only a couple of feet from her, her heart pounding in her ears as his eyes searched hers.

"I know." He replied. "Would it make you happy if we won?"

"Of course it would. I could be the happiest girl alive."

"Then we shall win." He smiled, as if that sealed the deal. *As simple as that.*

"We're going to win this title - Nobby and I - for you. I promise."

"You shouldn't make promises you can't keep, Frederick," she warned him.

Oh, he was going to keep it even if it killed him.

The short format classes ran the cross-country and show jumping in the reverse order than a traditional three day event, and was not necessarily split over three days. Cali was running first, on the Saturday. She was drawn early for show jumping, then there was just a short wait before she ran across country. Then the highlight of the day was the main class, the three-star ran the cross country on the Saturday, with the show jumping on the Sunday afternoon. Elsa's own event would be finished by then, as Dusty would have show jumped and gone cross country by Sunday lunchtime. The classes were packed in non-stop, often with different phases at the different levels running concurrently, so grooms and riders with multiple entries in different classes barely had a chance to stop and draw breath.

Elsa loved being busy, but she also loved the opportunity to watch the competition and see what she could learn to take home from the country's best. She was looking forward to that after Cali had done her best for them.

The chestnut mare refused to stand still while Elsa plaited her mane again, but Elsa refused to give up. It was her job to have Sophia's horses looking immaculate, and there was no way Cali was leaving her stall looking anything less.

Eventually satisfied, Elsa saddled her up and jumped on, walking her the long way through the calm of the estate to the warm up areas, where she began working Cali in until Sophia appeared to take over.

Despite the mare's certain fieriness, she knuckled down when it mattered, and Elsa couldn't have been prouder as she watched her navigate the show jumping course as though she'd been competing at this level for years, to pull off a clear round two seconds within the time limit.

"Could the pair of you have done that *any* better?" Michael beamed, as he met them exiting the ring.

"She is on fire!" Sophia told them modestly. "I barely had to do anything!"

Elsa took her back to her stable as she had some time before the cross country. She stripped her tack off, took her plaits out and ran a brush over her and gave her some hay. She took Dusty out for a pick of grass and let Cecil out of the lorry on her way past. Cecil was quite accustomed to being a lorry dog, and went back inside without any arguments when Elsa told him to.

Sophia came to collect her when it was time for cross country. Elsa knew she would have already had a talk with Derek, and then gone off for a walk around the estate to settle her nerves. Now she paced outside Cali's box, not saying a word as Elsa tacked her up and led her from the stable. She legged her up into the saddle and tightened her girths.

"Want me to walk with you?" Elsa asked, knowing she'd probably want to walk alone. She sensed the huge weight resting on Sophia's shoulders to do well. A good, clear run across country would put her in the placings, and Elsa didn't know anyone who deserved it more.

"I'll be alright," she murmured, smiling appreciatively.

Elsa nodded and watched her go. She would muck out the stable now that it was empty, and she would have time to tidy her tack trunk before going to the start.

As Elsa watched Cali bound excitedly from the start box, she had feelings that she had never experienced before. Normally she knew her horses strengths and weaknesses; she knew where Sophia could let them run, and the fences which they would find a bit more testing and need extra help. But Cali and Dusty were unknown to them, and Elsa felt uneasy. Of course she just wished they would come home safely, but she really wanted Sophia to go for it. A young rider on a new, unknown horse - yet one that had previously been associated with none other than Frederick Twemlow - galloping into the placings would certainly put their name on the map for next season. It may even bring her to the attention of potential owners and sponsors, which would make their bold and expensive adventure to the big, European classes even more achievable.

But Elsa hoped that Sophia didn't let the pressure get to her. She was stony faced as she galloped to the first, and Cali took off a stride too early and launched over it. Sophia suddenly looked tiny, perched in the saddle, but she quickly recovered and gathered up her reins for the second. Elsa saw every stride with her, her heart in her mouth at every fence until they were safely landed. She tripped landing into the first water combination, and any lesser rider could so easily have received a drenching, but Sophia sat up and kicked on. She *wanted* this, Elsa realised, as much as she herself wanted it. Sophia *needed* this more than anything, to round off what had really been quite a shoddy season.

Elsa was bouncing up and down as she shouted them home. She thought people must think she was mad, but she didn't care. As they cleared the last, she was so happy she thought she could cry. The pair of them had been foot perfect the whole way round. Elsa had been watching the clock, and she knew they had done enough. As she cooled Cali off, she didn't veer too far away from the finish. Sophia was lying fourth, and there were only five more riders to come who could take that away from her. But they all - except one - encountered troubles on their way round, and the class finished with Sophia in fifth place.

Elsa thought she may burst with pride as she re-saddled Cali for the prize giving. The mare quickly decided that this was her favourite part of the day, preferring to show off rather than stand though the presentation and getting a little full of herself during her lap of honour. When the steward directed everyone except the winner to leave the ring, Cali objected rather haughtily, believing she should be allowed to career around with the winner, also. Sophia laughed and gave her a pat, and Michael told his brave mare that that was more incentive for her to win next time.

Elsa took them both out for a pick of grass and iced Cali's legs. Michael and Philip had taken Sophia and Petra out for a late, celebratory lunch to which Elsa had been invited too, but she had politely declined. Although she didn't like to leave her horses for too long - especially after a cross country run - she had an ulterior motive for staying, and she made her way back to the cross country course, where the three-star competition was getting underway.

She spotted Frederick and Nobby across the far side of the warm up arena, Frederick's tall frame making the bay gelding look little more than a pony. The pair had pulled off Nobby's test of a lifetime to put them straight into the lead, and while Elsa expected to feel a little bitter that her favourite boy was achieving these results with someone else other than Sophia, she actually felt nothing but pride.

She hung back as Frederick was called to the start box, not wanting him to see her. But Frederick looked one hundred and one percent focused on the job at hand, as did Nobby. Ava had done a sterling job with him, and Elsa was pleased that of all the people Caroline Forrester could have sent him to, it was them. Despite the pain it had caused her to say goodbye to him, she was grateful that he was not lacking opportunities. Noble Mission had the world at his feet with Frederick aboard him.

He was counted down, and he leapt from the box; his long stride easily eating up the ground. He had always been such an awesome cross country horse, and Elsa expected this round to be no different. She was so absorbed in following his round that she did not hear the footsteps behind her, and jumped as an arm was slipped through hers.

"I thought you wouldn't be too far away!" Ava laughed, not taking her eyes from the big bay as he cleared the first real question. "Doesn't he look great?"

"They both do," Elsa replied, the words leaving her mouth before she had a chance to stop them.

Ava gave her a fleeting, knowing look, and they both began running along the rope that marked the course, as Nobby jumped clear over the double of logs and disappeared down the hill. They saw him carefully navigate the brush fence combination which were on an angle at the bottom of the hill, and fly the table on his way back up, and then he disappeared into the woodland. He emerged twenty seconds later and flew over the trailer adorned with bright flowers, which Elsa thought Timber Bear would probably stop and try to eat. Then he disappeared back into a section of the woodland to navigate a series of ditches. Neither of them could stand still as they waited for him to come back out. Ava checked her watch as he galloped on towards the water complex.

"He's bang on the time," she told Elsa excitedly, as they craned to see. They could not see him clear the fences now, but as long as Elsa could still see Frederick's head bobbing above that of the spectators', then she would know they were still going. There were claps as they left the water complex behind them, and she knew it should all be easy from here.

"He's so fit," Elsa commented.

"We've been galloping him a lot," Ava replied, assuming she must be talking about Nobby. "One of the working pupils takes him out twice a week with a local racehorse trainers string; they both love it."

"I bet!" Elsa agreed, her heart in her mouth for what felt like the hundredth time this week, as she watched them clear the huge picnic table. Eventing was her life, but she wasn't sure her nerves could take much more of this, as they were running along the rope again towards the finish, while Nobby made mincemeat of the final four questions.

"Come on!" Ava shouted over her shoulder, as she felt Elsa back off, as they both knew what came next. "Come and help me – you've nothing else to do!"

It was true, Elsa thought, jogging to catch up with her. She couldn't keep avoiding him.

Frederick stopped his watch as he galloped through the finish, and knew he was spot on. A flawless round meant no penalties to be added to his score, and he would maintain his first place position. He could not stop smiling as he eased Nobby to a trot and turned him to face his groom running to catch them.

"Way to go, Boss!" Ava beamed breathlessly, slapping Nobby's lathered neck. "You aced it!"

"We certainly did," Frederick replied, his eyes firmly fixed on the figure jogging up behind her.

He slid from the saddle as she came to a stop before him. She froze, taking in the sight of this man who did not look like he had just galloped three miles, and instead was gazing at her with those adoring puppy dog eyes. She felt the butterflies in her stomach stirring. She wished she could launch into action, but Ava already had his horse and was removing his saddle, and she instead just stood rooted, staring helplessly back at him.

"I told you, Elsa," Frederick murmured. "We're going to win this. For you."

She went to reply; she felt so emotional at what he and Nobby could achieve that she wanted to throw her arms around him and sob delighted tears into his shoulder. But the microphone shoved in Frederick's face stopped her from doing anything to him at all.

"Mr Twemlow," the reporter beamed, his cameraman waiting patiently beside him. "Mind if we get a few words?"

Yes, I do bloody mind! His mind screamed. *I need to talk to* her! In private! Instead he watched her smile, her helpless shrug as she turned and helped his horse. She pulled the sweatsheet from Ava's rucksack and slung it over her shoulders ready for when she'd cooled him. She slung a bucket of water over him and began scraping it away from his coat while Ava kept Nobby walking. The perfect team; they were a picture of dedication. Frederick thought the reporter would be better off talking to them if he wanted to get a real idea of what made their sport so unique. He had been brought up in the limelight, but he didn't deserve it. They were the lifeblood behind it all - the unsung heroes.

"Not at all," Frederick found himself answering.

Chapter Fifteen

The arena crowd erupted into a deafening applause as Frederick and Nobby cleared the final show jump that stood between them and the title, and Elsa thought she could cry. She wanted to grab Nobby as he left the ring and throw her arms around him, but she reminded herself that he wasn't her horse. She didn't care though, because seeing him so happy and reaching these glorious heights all but made up for it. The crowd were going crazy for him, she thought they'd mob him if they could. But she didn't need to worry about not being able to get close to him, because Frederick's gorgeous blue eyes were fixed on her as he left the ring. He stopped beside her and reached for her hand, and she duly reached up to him.

"I told you, Elsa," his voice was husky. "We were going to win it for you - and he did."

And then he laughed, and it was the most beautiful sounding laugh she thought she had ever heard. He was beautiful, as he gazed down at her she thought she might melt. But then he reached down and scooped her up in just one, strong arm, pulling her onto the saddle with him.

"Join me for the lap of honour?" he asked her, as if she could object now. And before she knew it, she was galloping around the arena with him, his arm tight around her waist holding her close to him. She ran her fingers through Nobby's mane, which had somehow grown over night to be a foot long, but Elsa knew she didn't need to hold on. Nobby would never dump her, nor would Frederick ever let her go. She had never felt more certain of anything in her life, as she felt Frederick's damp, full lips kissing her neck, and she squirmed gloriously against him as the crowd went wild...

The most awful stench roused her from her deep sleep, and she screwed up her face as she prized open her eyes.

"Have you farted again, Cec?"

Cecil stood on the end of her bed, his pointy paws digging into her ankles, his hackles raised as he growled at her, showing her his sharp teeth.

"How did you know it was him I was dreaming about?" she yawned, leaning forward to give him a scratch behind his ears, and watched him relax. "You really don't like him, do you?" she murmured. *And he has good reason,* she remembered.

"It was quite a nice dream, though," she added, shoving the duvet to one side and getting to her feet. "Hopefully it will play out for real this afternoon."

Cecil yawned and pattered to the door. She opened it and watched him jump from the lorry.

"Don't go far!" she warned him, her eyes narrowed.

Yea, yea, whatever, his shaggy face seemed to say.

Even though it was so early, she was not the first one up, and she greeted the various people she passed on her way to the stables. She gave Cali and Dusty a light feed, and removed Cali's bandages. She was pleased that there appeared to be no heat, bumps or swelling as she ran her hands down each leg in turn.

"Hey!" Paige beamed, arriving at her stables carrying a full English breakfast squashed into a polystyrene food container. She smiled as she sank back into the pile of rugs outside her stable and tucked in. "It's going to be a long day for me today; need to eat while I can!"

"Yea, tell me about it." Elsa replied, adding with a wink, "I can't wait to watch Nobby take the title this afternoon, though!"

"Brett will be doing his best to make sure that doesn't happen," Paige laughed.

Elsa smiled. "Could you just watch while I trot Cali up?"

"Sure," Paige replied, not breaking from her eating as she watched Elsa trot Cali briskly down the aisle, turning at the bottom and trotting back up and past her.

"Sound as," Paige confirmed.

"Thanks, I thought she would be."

"Let's hope the same can be said for my two," Paige grimaced, tossing the empty food container aside and letting herself into her stall.

"They'll be fine," Elsa reassured her, referring to their impending second horse inspection, where they were required to trot up for the judge and be passed before they were allowed to show jump – a formality at long format international events.

"I hope so," Paige told her with a wink, as she affectionately gave her big bay a pat. "Binky here is lying in second; he has the best opportunity to knock Freddy Twemlow off the top spot!"

Elsa laughed as she removed Dusty's rug and brushed him down. She watched as Paige quickly brushed off her already groomed and plaited three-star horses, put their bridles on and led them away ready for the horse inspection .

"Good luck!" Elsa called after her.

"Thanks!" Paige beamed. "And good luck to you, too, if I don't see you again before your cross country."

Elsa felt her heart stop as the news filtered back to the stables. Noble Mission, the overnight leader of the three-star class, had been sent to the holding box when presented to the Ground Jury. Frederick had re-presented, adamant that there was nothing wrong with his horse, but the Ground Jury had decided otherwise and failed him. Nobby had been eliminated from the competition, putting an abrupt end to his title hopes.

Elsa couldn't believe it. While fellow competitors may have been secretly relieved, many were heartbroken for Frederick, and echoed his insistence that there was nothing noticeably wrong with Nobby. He appealed, but the Ground Jury's decision was held, and Nobby would play no further part in the event.

Elsa edged towards their area of stabling with caution. She knew there was nothing she could do, but she needed to see for herself. She watched from a distance as - at Frederick's instruction - Ava trotted Nobby down the aisle for the umpteenth time, looking close to tears. Elsa knew that horse better than anyone, and even at this distance she would have happily put her life on there being nothing wrong with him. But the Ground Jury must have seen something that she could not, to have made such a crucial decision.

"There's nothing wrong with him!" Frederick implored to all those gathered around, echoing her thoughts. He was red in the face and stressed. He looked beaten, as though he was on the verge of giving up, and she'd never seen him like that before. At events, he was so resilient. Even when things were not going his way, he always maintained his composure and used everything thrown at him as a learning curve. That was part of the reason he was on top of his game. But not this morning. He dropped his head into his hands, unable to make anything of the situation he found himself in.

"Oh, put the bloody horse away now, will you?" Portia snapped at Ava, and slid her arm around Frederick's shoulder.

Elsa wanted to run up to her and shake her, or worse. How *dare* she be so insensitive? She wanted to cry for poor Nobby, even if he was totally oblivious to everything that was happening, but it was Frederick's heartbroken look that unexpectedly pained her the most.

"You've still got Cobra," Portia soothed him, when he tried and failed to shrug her away.

"He's a young horse, Portia," Frederick retorted. "He doesn't stand a bloody chance!"

"Hey, don't let my Aunty and Uncle hear you say that!" she tried to laugh it off. "He is the future of their breeding operation."

"Yes, the *future,*" Frederick replied, unable to conceal his snarl. "*Today* was Nobby's day. We were going to win that title."

Portia's hands were on her hips as she glared at him, as if the mere mention of Nobby having any success at all offended her. "Actually," she replied pointedly. "Cobra is in fourth place, how can you say that is not having a bloody chance? If they all have a pole, you finish second. If Brett has *two* poles, then you win the title."

"Yes, I am very aware of how it *works*, Portia!" Frederick turned on her, and immediately stopped himself. He took a deep breath. "But it's just not the point."

"What the point is, Fred, is that my Uncle and Aunty are ploughing hundreds of thousands into our venture, and their venture, and you are losing focus on some washed up beach donkey that quite frankly should have stayed with that rubbish young rider he was previously with!"

Frederick could not listen to any more of this, and he turned quickly on his haunches before he said something he lived to regret. Elsa pinned herself back against the side of the end stable as he flew blindly towards her, holding her breath until he was safely past without noticing her. She clenched her fists, her heart pounding hard, as she summoned all her restraint to stop herself from marching right up to Portia and giving her a piece of her mind. But she hadn't achieved much last time, she realised, or at least she had for Nobby, as Portia had hated him ever since.

She went back to her horses and led Cali out for a walk around the estate to loosen her up, help prevent any swelling, but most importantly to try and clear her own head with the fresh air. She wondered where Frederick had gone. Half of her had wanted to go after him, but she doubted that would do either of them any good, either. She tried to shove thoughts of him aside; reminding herself that he obviously didn't want her to be involved in his life, and he needed to sort his own problems out with the people that were creating them for him.

It was not her battle to fight.

She returned Cali to her stable and tacked Dusty up. It was almost time for him to prove to everyone what a fantastic cross-country horse he could be, and Elsa jumped on him and ambled the long route to the warm up arenas.

Where Cali was forward going and hauled Sophia into her fences, Dusty was much more reserved and wanted a chance to weigh up the situation before he left the ground. Michael was full of praise for Frederick having brought Dusty out of his shell. When connections had told him Dusty was a total waste of money and would never go eventing because he was too shy, Frederick had had faith in him and built him up very slowly, building his confidence over every fence.

Realistically, Elsa wondered if he needed more speed and boldness to ever make it to the big tracks in eventing, but she knew he definitely had enough heart. As she slid from the saddle, she gave his face a gentle rub, and he reached out and sniffed her face, before curling back his top lip as though laughing at her.

"OK, OK," she giggled, arching her back away from him as he tried to lick her. "I believe you; you can do it!"

She legged Sophia into the saddle and wiped the slight mud and grass from her polished boots.

"I hope you've woke him up for me," she beamed down at her groom.

"I may be a bloody good groom, Soph," she laughed in reply. "But I'm no miracle worker!"

She watched the pair of them stride away to the far side of the warm up, where Derek had already arranged a series of raised poles designed to get Dusty to think about where he was putting his feet. She left them to it and made her way back to Cali, who had become a little unsettled at her stable companion leaving her, despite being surrounded by other horses. She would lead her out for another walk and some grass, and hopefully have her settled in time to return and watch Dusty's round.

She greased Dusty's legs, checked his studs and boots, and he was ready to head to the start. Derek's exercises had certainly put him on his toes, and he hauled Sophia into the start box as the starter began to count them down.

"Three...two...one...Good luck!" he called, and they were underway.

Dusty thundered to the first, his ears pricked as he sized it up from several strides out. Sophia allowed him to steady and look without altering his rhythm, and he cleared it easily. She gave him a pat as they galloped away, and Dusty responded by accelerating. Derek had insisted that if he made the most of his big stride in between the fences, he could be forgiven for taking so much time to jump each actual fence, but as Elsa checked her watch at about quarter of the way, they were already behind on the time.

Dusty chipped in an extra stride for the first element of the brush combination, and Sophia struggled to set him up correctly for the second element, on a dog-leg line. He hesitated, and then took off early, throwing her off balance a little. But he seemed to gain confidence from having cleared it, and got away quickly. Elsa knew the distance between the hidden ditches was short, and wondered if Sophia would be able to collect him enough to hit it perfectly, but as she nervously waited and watched, they emerged from the woodland in one piece.

Elsa's breath caught at the big picnic table, when Dusty needed to stretch, instead he shortened, flicking his ears back and forth as if double checking with Sophia it was OK.

"It's *OK*!" Sophia insisted, kicking with all her might to reach her stride, and Dusty cleared it with just enough room.

Elsa stopped worrying about him getting home safely; he would be no record breaker, but he had all the carefulness in the world. To Elsa's delight, he scurried through the finish only eight seconds over the time, when she had estimated it would be more. He had gained confidence and got faster as he'd progressed around the course.

"Not bad!" Elsa exclaimed, running beside him patting his lathered neck until Sophia brought him to a walk.

"He is a darling, isn't he?" Sophia beamed, as Petra, Michael and Philip quickly joined them. "He really, *really* wants to try for me, he is just petrified of getting it wrong."

"He'll come right," Michael told her, unable to hide his smile. "I'm sure of it."

There was no time for Sophia to debrief them, as she was whisked away to the media tent for an interview to discuss her future competition plans for next season. Elsa was delighted for her; classes like this were designed to get the younger riders media coverage and bring them into the public eye, to the attention of potential sponsors and owners.

Petra helped to cool off Dusty, and then Elsa walked him back alone. He was blowing quite hard, and Elsa concluded that he put a lot more effort into his work than what it looked like.

"You did good, mate," she told him fondly as he wandered duly by her side and she gave his cheek a scratch.

She kept a close eye on the score board as she washed him off and rugged him up, to see how the other competitors were fairing. Her interest was piqued as she noted a number of them were clocking up faults around the course.

"That course was a bigger test than it first looked," Paige commented from across the aisle, as Elsa finally put Dusty away.

Elsa nodded, and observed Paige's horse standing looking sorry for himself, his filthy and soaked tack dripping in the aisle.

"Brett took a dunking at the water," Paige screwed up her face. "He was less than impressed. But he's even more determined to take the title this afternoon. At least our other horse is in the lead now after...well, you know."

Elsa nodded. Poor Nobby, and poor Frederick. *But poor Brett,* she laughed. "I hope he's brought some spare breeches!"

Elsa was packing up her equipment when the lorry door swung open and Sophia peered in, breaking her from her thoughts of how much washing she would have to do once she got home.

"Hey," she forced a gentle smile. "Everything OK?"

"Sure." Elsa replied half-heartedly, and Sophia mirrored her disappointment. Although Dusty had tried his hardest, his time faults had left him in ninth place; a huge achievement for his and Sophia's first outing over a testing track, but unfortunately he was not required for the prize giving. It would have been lovely to see him stomp around the arena to the applause of the crowd. And Sophia knew Elsa had been looking forward to Nobby maybe pulling off his biggest win to date, but that just wasn't to be either. Except that nobody could make much out of that mystery, as Nobby was looking and behaving like one of the fittest and healthiest horses on the showground.

But despite this turmoil, Sophia had something she needed to discuss with her treasured, loyal groom, and it just couldn't wait any longer.

She took a deep breath. "Do you want to take a walk? We need to have a chat."

Elsa gulped at her serious tone. She observed how Sophia was nervously wringing her hands, and wouldn't meet her eye. Slowly she got to her feet, and grabbed Cecil's lead. He was already waiting at the door, and he jumped from the lorry ahead of them. They followed him through the lorry park to Wellington's expansive, open parkland at their mercy.

"It's been a long week, hasn't it?" Sophia began eventually, struggling to form a sentence to get this heavy weight from her chest.

"Yes, but a successful one nonetheless," Elsa replied with

an encouraging smile. There was a lot of good to take home from this event to improve on over winter and come back even stronger next season. "So, I assume you want to talk to me about something good; something promising?"

"Yes, and no," Sophia bit down on her lower lip, and took a deep breath. "I've been talking to Jannik Dietrich the last couple of weeks. He made me an offer which has taken a considerable amount of thinking about, and now I think I've made a decision."

With a nod, Elsa waited. Jannik Dietrich was one of Germany's top event riders, still competing successfully on the international circuit with his protégé competing against him, and sometimes even beating him.

Sophia took a deep breath. "He's asked me if I would like to be based with him next season for training; in Germany."

Slowly, Elsa nodded. She felt her heart slow, and she gazed after Cecil as he sniffed for rabbits in the undergrowth, as she processed the information.

"My results this week have really cemented his offer." Sophia told her. "He was very impressed."

"As well he should be," Elsa told her with a smile. "It's a fantastic opportunity."

"It is, isn't it?" Sophia affirmed, cautious. Deep down she knew she could never have got this far without Elsa by her side every step of the way, and she was not naive enough to think this opportunity that had arisen couldn't jeopardise their potential future partnership.

"Absolutely," Elsa grinned, feeling somewhat relieved that the news being delivered wasn't awful. "This is *great* news, Sophia! So why do you sound so sad?"

"Because of you, Elsa," she shrugged helplessly. "We are best friends and I couldn't be without you. Would you come? You can come, you know? But I know you have commitments here, what with Cecil, Timber Bear and family. Jannik said I can share his grooms if you decide not to come. But we wouldn't kick you out, Elsa. The cottage will always be yours, and Mum will need help with the youngsters. Michael Patricks is really keen that I take his two with me, and I would like to take Drop Kick and Merlin. The others...well, I'm not sure of the finer arrangements, yet."

"You will think of something," Elsa smiled.

"Yes, and I'm not worried, because I am in control of them. But you, Elsa...I would really like you to come, but I know I can't make you. I want you to do what *you* want, and I will respect whatever decision you make. Promise me you'll think about it?"

"Of course I will," Elsa smiled. "I am *so* happy for you though. You know that, don't you?"

"I do," she grinned. "And I am *so* excited. But it's a massive step. I promise it's just for a season, though. It will be invaluable training, but I am determined to come back the following year and build my own yard up with everything that I have learnt, and I can't do that without you."

Elsa nodded. She wanted that more than anything, too, but she had so many thoughts and options whirring around her tired mind. There was so much to weigh up and think about.

"I'm going to leave you to it," Sophia told her. "I'm heading back with Mum now, I'm teaching this afternoon. Take your time to head back, though? Stay and watch the show jumping, if you want?"

Elsa nodded. She couldn't wait to see the great finale, but it just wouldn't be the same without Nobby in it. She sighed and carried on ambling as Sophia strode away. She whistled Cecil back and knelt down to gave him a scratch behind the ears.

What do we do, Cec? She silently asked of him. But she knew there was only one thing she could do. Her life was here, and it would be a lot of upheaval to move, even if it was only for a season. Just when things were starting to look up with Timber Bear, it would set them right back. She would have to put her out on loan - or even worse - sell her. And she couldn't imagine how her main man Cecil would feel about leaving his comfy cottage to live in Germany, and this provided the first of many potential stumbling blocks.

Chapter Sixteen

Elsa shut Cecil back in the lorry and went to check her horses. The stable yards were emptying out quickly now; a flurry of activity as people packed up and prepared to go home. The earlier classes had concluded, and the three-star show jumping was underway.

Elsa reapplied Dusty's bandages, and checked they weren't too hot under their rugs, as they were both getting a little worked up at the amount of horses passing by their stable on their way to the arenas or to the lorry park. Elsa suspected they were just agitated in general and wanted to go home, and she couldn't blame them. It had been a long week for them, but she was happy that it was the right thing bringing them to the event early so that they had plenty of time to get accustomed to their surroundings.

She packed up a trunk of equipment to drop off at the lorry on her way past, checked they both had plenty of water and full haynets, and then she made her way to the main arena.

She sat down in the grass behind the white rope of the warm up, and studied from a distance the top ten horses and riders as they started to get worked in. She didn't think she could ever get bored of watching any of them ride, even though she had her favourites, and others had styles that she didn't particularly agree with - she learned something from them all. She noticed Paige at the far side, adjusting Brett's girth and then adjusting the height of the practice jump for him, and could only imagine the pressure she was feeling having her horse in the lead.

She noticed Frederick before he'd even made it to the warm up arena; his huge, young, black stallion was impressive and stood out above all the others. Elsa suspected he carried the same blood lines as another of Frederick's top rides, Cavalier.

They were very much similar in looks, presence and ability, and of course were both bred by the Roxwell's. Her heart panged at Nobby's absence. She let out a sigh as she reflected on Sophia's season of ups and downs, and realised she wouldn't have changed any of it for the world. At the beginning of their season, this class had been Sophia's aim with Nobby, and neither of them dreamed that prospect would be taken away from them. But when one door closed, another always opened - maybe not with a compromise, but the chance of another challenge - which they both relished. Sophia's German opportunity made Elsa feel so proud of everything they'd achieved, even though she knew in her heart of hearts she would not be included in that part of Sophia's eventing journey.

Frederick had Elsa's undivided attention as he pushed the young stallion into a trot. Elsa knew from Ava that Frederick hadn't really thought him to be ready for this class, but that the Roxwell's had absolutely insisted he campaign at least one of their horses in the main class - preferably two, but as Nobby had taken the other spot that was even more fuel for Portia to hate him. It took weeks of preparation to get a horse ready for a class like this, and Frederick decided it would be Cobra that had to step up to mark and carry the Roxwell flag.

Elsa grimaced as she observed Portia enter the warm up arena on foot with Ava. She felt small joy in the fact that Portia had not qualified to ride at Cromwell - being new to eventing and not yet having attended enough events to gain the required mileage - however she was not quiet about how she believed she had the ability to, and the rules were grossly unfair to her. If Elsa were in charge, she would take great pleasure in twisting the rules so that Portia were never allowed near another horse again.

However, Elsa wasn't in charge, so instead she watched in silence as Portia waved her arms around animatedly as she shouted across at Frederick her instructions on what he had to do. He changed rein along the diagonal of the arena, pushing the stallion out of earshot of her. She glared after him, her hands on her slender hips. Elsa shook her head in disbelief of the woman, wondering how any of them put up with it.

Ava was lowering a practice fence from a straight bar to a steep cross pole. When Portia noticed, she marched over and said something to Ava that sent her away looking furious, and put the jump back up to a straight bar. Elsa waved, trying to catch her eye without catching anyone else's, and Elsa immediately saw the relief flash onto her tired face.

"You have the patience of a saint," Elsa told her, as she slumped down in the grass beside her.

"I'm not sure I can take much more of this, Elsa," Ava replied, and she meant it. "If this all goes wrong for Fred, it will be totally her fault, yet Fred will solely get the blame. It's all going to end in tears, Else. I know Fred, I know how he likes to prepare for an event, and this isn't it. He goes into himself, he needs to be left alone."

They watched as Frederick cantered circles at the end furthest away from Portia, evidently ignoring her as she shouted at him to turn for the jump.

"What is her problem?" Elsa shook her head.

"This is *her* discipline, isn't it?" Ava rolled her eyes. "She thinks having show jumped internationally gives her the authority to shout her instructions at Fred as soon as a coloured pole is mentioned. She may have some good results under her belt, granted, but she's never show jumped a horse that galloped around a three-star cross country course the day before. No one knows what to do better than Fred."

"So, why doesn't he tell her, then?" Elsa scowled.

"Oh, come on, Elsa!" Ava rolled her eyes again. "Look at her!"

"Yes, I see a pent up little ball of arrogant, rude, fury that needs knocking down a peg or two!" Elsa retorted.

"So I do," Ava agreed. "But that's obviously not what Fred

sees, is it?"

Elsa shrugged. She had no idea what went on in that beautiful head of his, but she wished he would stand up to her and put an end to the obvious misery her presence was causing him. She was broken from her thoughts as Frederick brought the beautiful stallion to an abrupt halt and slid from the saddle.

"*Ava*!" he shouted, looking around for her.

"Shit," Ava hauled herself to her feet and ran quickly to him, taking Cobra's reins.

"I'm going to watch a couple jump," he told her, wanting to be left alone. "Keep him walking round; I'll jump him when I come back."

"Sure," she nodded, leading the stallion away.

"Where are you *going*?" Portia shouted after him, and Frederick made himself take a deep breath before he turned around to face her.

"Portia, darling," he replied, his patience wearing thin. "I'm going to watch a couple of rounds."

"*Why*?" she demanded. "You know the course by now, don't you? You need to jump him, Fred. What's got into you?"

What's got into me? His inner self implored, as he clenched his fists by his side. *I need to be left alone, I need to focus!* So, why couldn't he just tell her? Instead he said nothing, and carried on walking.

He heard her light footsteps as she jogged to catch him up, and tried his hardest to stop himself from snapping at her. He slid his finger along the inside of his collar, suddenly feeling as though it were trying to strangle him. He liked to stay focused in private when there was pressure resting on his shoulders. He liked to find a quiet corner of the collecting ring and keep his horse walking and settled. But this girl was really getting him worked up, and he could feel the young stallion getting agitated the more he rode him so he had had no option but to get off.

He hadn't expected to be anywhere near the leader board with Cobra; he had just meant to be the pathfinder and out for the experience. Frederick had no idea he would eat up the ground so quickly, tackle all the jumping questions so easily. This was meant to be Nobby's moment; Portia was meant to spend the day sulking and avoiding him because she was so annoyed that the Roxwell's didn't play a part in the leader board. He was meant to have been able to get on in peace – with only Ava by his side – just like how it always used to be. As he tried to block out the droning of her voice as she insisted on watching beside him, he remembered her derogatory words just before he'd headed out on cross country with Nobby. Instead of encouraging him, he knew she'd intended for them to prevent him from tackling the course with the ferociously he'd intended. And when he'd waited to show jump a non-Roxwell horse in one of the earlier classes, her attitude had been much the same. Yet he'd manage to ignore her then, so why couldn't he now? If he lost focus, he had only himself to blame. He had been trained to not allow things like that to affect him, so if he let them now he would never forgive himself. He'd wanted the title with Nobby more than anything – for Sophia, for *Elsa* – and the whole mystery surrounding his elimination left a bitter taste in his mouth.

He turned on his haunches and marched back to the warm up before he'd even stayed long enough to watch one competitor jump the whole course. He *needed* to get away from her.

"Where are you going *now*?" Portia whined, exasperated at his behaviour as she turned to follow him.

Elsa walked beside Ava and the gentle Cobra, watching as Portia followed him around like a little lost puppy dog.

"This is all getting a bit embarrassing now, don't you think?" Ava commented, as they approached.

"Definitely," Elsa nodded. "I'm going to let you get on with it. I'll see you in the collecting ring."

"Gee, thanks," Ava replied sarcastically, wishing right now she worked for anyone *other than* Frederick Twemlow.

Elsa dashed the other side of the rope before they had the chance to see her. She watched as Ava reached to give him a leg-up into the saddle, but she was pushed aside by Portia. Frederick couldn't do anything about it now, but he admired Ava's patience. He just worried about how long it could last. He felt his life spiralling out of control, and he knew he needed to put a stop to it, *fast*. But not right now – all he had to think about now was bringing the Cromwell title home. If the three above him incurred faults, it was well within his grasp. He had stayed cool and achieved similar feats before, so why couldn't he focus now?

"You need to turn inside the oxer to the final fence," Portia told him. It was a demand rather than a suggestion. She grabbed hold of his rein, her other hand on his knee, not letting him go until he'd indicated he'd listened.

"It's too risky," Frederick shook his head, circling him and wishing she'd let go of his rein. Reckless riding of a young, promising horse went against everything he stood for. "He's a young horse who I just aimed to get round clear."

"My Aunty and Uncle are not in this sport to *get round*, Frederick," she belittled him. "And there's the chance this horse might not leave the poles up – if that was a certainty then he'd be out doing *serious* show jumping with me, not playing around here with you. You need to take the risk."

"She's right, Frederick," Lady Twemlow joined him, and Frederick wasn't sure how much longer his patience could hold out. But never before had he been so glad to see his mother and he wished she'd take Portia away.

He looked up over their heads, and locked eyes with Elsa. His beautiful, understanding, clever Elsa. But she was too clever for him, he knew that. He was resigned to spending his life with Portia; his mother had it all worked out for him. She had been in many a deep conversation with the Roxwell's, arranging his future for him, to ensure a steady supply of top-class horses. They had power-couple written all over them; she the international up and coming showjumper, he gracing the eventing throne. They would have sponsors and owners falling at their feet, so why did the prospect make his blood run cold?

"I am *so* glad he met you," he heard his mother purr at Portia, as he pushed the stallion into a canter and Ava adjusted the practice jump to a cross-pole for him. "You are so right for him."

"I know, I feel *exactly* the same way," Portia gushed, her bad mood miraculously draining away. "And won't we have such *beautiful* children?" she giggled, and Frederick thought he was going to be sick.

Elsa thought she could watch the glorious black stallion jump all day, as Ava raised the practice jump and he cleared it effortlessly from a ten-metre circle from both directions. He was so agile, she felt certain he would jump clear and put pressure on the leaders, and she desperately wanted him to, despite a win giving Portia - as a Roxwell - the lime light she craved.

She hung back as Ava accompanied him to the collecting ring, and she waited for him to be called into the main arena before she joined her.

The crowd erupted into applause as one of their favourites cantered in. Frederick halted before the judges and tipped his cap, and Elsa wasn't sure why her heart was pounding quite so hard as the bell rang.

Frederick collected Cobra beautifully and let him stretch down the long side as he headed for the start. The first fence was a simple upright, and Cobra cleared it effortlessly. He tracked left and got his five strides to the second, and the stallion gave a flick of his hind hooves on landing as if he found this much too easy.

"He's beautiful," Elsa murmured.

"I absolutely adore him," Ava agreed, suddenly realising how much she would actually leave behind if Portia ever got the better of her and she walked out. The idea was simply inconceivable, and she swallowed hard.

A sharp right turn, and Frederick sat deep for the double. And that was where it all started to fall apart. All he could see, as he tried to focus on his stride, was Portia's perfectly made-up face, sneering into his. He tried to shake her off, but she was persistent, and poor young Cobra didn't stand a chance of getting his stride right when he was getting zero help from his jockey. He clouted the top pole with his knees, and lost his confidence for the second, crashing through it on one and a half strides.

He tried to give Cobra a tug, but the poor stallion had lost his mind, and Frederick wasn't surprised as he brought the fourth fence down, too.

What the fuck are you doing? Portia sneered in his face, and he closed his eyes to try and rid himself of her. But she was suddenly being pushed from his vision by something even more daunting; by Elsa, refusing to give in to tears as she listened to his mother ramble on about how good he and Portia were together. He felt his heart snap in two as he remembered every contour of her perfect, beautiful face, shaped by her soft, caramel locks. But her eyes almost killed him, as no one could mistake the sadness that clouded over them at the realisation of how cruelly he had treated her. He knew it, as did she, and now so did Cobra as he missed his turn inside the sixth fence. But it didn't matter now, anyway. It all seemed so unimportant compared to the total fuck up that was his life, being ruled by strong, vicious woman when the only one that mattered was the kindest soul, and he had treated her so badly. He tried to focus, but his mind was not having any of it as he saw Portia in a standoff with Elsa over and over again... He tried to blink them away and kick on.

His round was all about damage limitation now, trying to salvage his reputation. He knew he should just retire. But he couldn't face leaving the ring like that; facing *her*.

Elsa's heart broke a little for him with every pole that fell, as Ava grasped hold of her arm, her mouth wide open in disbelief that this was happening to them. *Mr Cool was losing it.*

"What the *fuck* is he doing?" Portia snarled furiously from further along the rail. "I'm sorry, Mrs T, it's just… we've been through this - time and *time* again!"

"Don't apologise," Lady Twemlow retorted. "I quite agree; what on earth is he playing at? We don't invest all this time and money into him for him to throw in the towel."

Frederick turned to the oxer, and a word of encouragement and Cobra snapped his legs up tightly over it. Frederick gave him a pat, told him it would be OK and they'd both live to see another day.

Elsa tried to block out their words as she watched him land safely over the up-to-height wavy planks, she waited for him to shift his weight to the left.

You're a fucking disgrace! Portia snarled in his face, and he wobbled to get away from her. But he was looking right, and so was his weight, and Cobra followed his lead. Elsa's hands flew to her mouth, her eyes wide as he aimed Cobra at the wrong upright.

Frederick only realised his mistake when it was too late. Cobra was locked onto his fence, and he may as well let him jump it. It was over. He cleared it beautifully and pulled up as the bell rang.

"Unfortunately, that's elimination for Frederick Twemlow and Cobra," the commentator sounded heartbroken, "having taken the wrong course."

"I can't bloody believe it!" Portia shook her head in fury, hands resting on perfectly refined hips. "I gave him instructions down to the infinite detail, and he totally disobeyed me. He's thrown it all away. You wait until I get my hands on him!"

Frederick trotted Cobra from the ring at a spanking pace. With his head lowered, he looked as though he'd mow down anyone that dared try get in his way, his spurs stuck in the side of the stallion whenever it looked like slowing.

Elsa stood rock still. She tried to read his expression - even from this distance - but it was impossible. She didn't even notice Ava leave her side as the Australian sprinted after him, her rucksack bouncing on her back and her arms full with a headcollar and sweat rugs. Ava caught up and ran alongside him, her hands shaking as she grabbed hold of Cobra's reins, wondering what the hell had just happened but not daring to ask. Eventually Frederick allowed Cobra to fall to a walk, and Ava was grateful as she wasn't sure how much longer she could run alongside him.

Everyone was speechless, mouths open as they gawped at their King falling from his eventing throne. Elsa's heart broke, but especially for Ava - she had been *so* excited about their round, and she had just watched weeks of hard work evaporate before her eyes.

People were gravitating towards him, but Cobra was becoming worked up at the sudden flurry of activity surrounding him. Elsa recognised some of them; Frederick's parents, his owners, his sponsors. *Portia*. Portia especially, looked furious.

Frederick ensured that Ava's shaking hands had a firm grasp of his reins before he slid from the saddle, and with not even a second glance back at his horse or his groom, he was power walking to the lorry park. Elsa watched people call out to him, trying to catch up with him, and he broke into a jog to get away from them.

Elsa didn't move at first as she struggled to comprehend what the hell had just happened, but then she started to follow the crowd of people desperate to know, also.

"The stallion looks fine," she heard people mutter, as she passed them crowding Ava. "Is it Frederick – has he been taken ill?"

No one was following him now; they were pre-occupied with finding something wrong with Cobra, as if that were the only answer they would accept.

"Elsa!" she felt the hand reach for her trailing arm, but she pulled it away in time.

"Elsa!" Clement called after her again, in exasperation.

"I can't stop!" she shouted back over her shoulder.

"Don't go to him!" he pleaded. "Leave him be!"

"I *need* to go to him," she shouted, barely breaking from her stride. "I *need* to see him!" *And he needs to see me,* she told herself.

Elsa broke into a sprint. She wasn't sure if she'd catch him, or what she'd even say if she did, but she had to try. She couldn't even imagine how he was feeling, or where he was planning on going. She just knew that she had to see him.

"Frederick!" she shouted after him, and although he must have heard her, he ignored her like he ignored everyone else.

He jumped into his Range Rover and slammed the door. The engine started just as she reached it, but she would not be deterred. He hadn't seen her as he put his foot to the accelerator, and she grabbed hold of the door handle as it began to move.

He slammed his foot on the brakes as he noticed her. She frantically tried the door handle, but it was locked. He wouldn't meet her eye as she stepped back and he went to move away again. But she hung on, shimmying along the paintwork to the bonnet.

She waited, looking right at him. But he still wouldn't meet her eye as he ran his hands over his face. She felt her heart pounding, threatening to rip right through her chest, and knew that curious people were not far away as they were quickly bearing down on them. She didn't want to make a scene for him, but she didn't want to leave him on his own in this state. She didn't care if he didn't want her, but she couldn't let him drive off like this and have it on her conscience if he came to harm.

He wound down the window. "Get out of my way, Elsa," he sighed, running the back of his hand over his forehead.

"Let me in." She told him firmly.

"No," he shook his head, his face red and angry. "Please leave me alone." He started to shut the window, and she frantically banged on it, daring him to look at her, *daring* him not to disobey her.

"Let me fucking in, will you?" she demanded, hanging off the door handle as he attempted to move again.

"Are you trying to get yourself killed?" he shouted furiously, the car jerking forward as he slammed on the brake.

"Let me in! I'm not letting go, so you're either going to have to let me in, or run me over."

He sighed, ran his hand through his ruffled hair, and she heard the doors unlock. She didn't take her eyes from him as she cautiously and quickly moved around to the passenger side.

The pursuing group had caught up just as Elsa slammed her door shut. She braved a look towards the confused face of Lady Twemlow, and the furious look on Portia's immaculately made-up face, and the Range Rover lurched forward as Frederick put his foot to the floor in his haste to get away from the event ground.

"What do you want?" he asked her gently as they bounded across the uneven field.

"Where are you going?" she ignored him as a steward waved them out of the lorry park and they turned left onto the country road. He sighed and rammed his foot down, and the Range Rover roared with such power that she felt like she was sitting in a fighter jet with a pilot about to wage war on the world.

She waited, desperately wanting to ask him what the hell had just happened, but knowing he wouldn't appreciate it. She hoped he would tell her in his own time. He had let her in the car at least, and that was enough for her for now. Just being here with him, to provide some comfort, was enough.

They drove on in silence. Frederick had one hand on the steering wheel, his elbow on the window with his head in his hand. Elsa stole a glance at him every few seconds, and thought he looked ready to break down and cry at any minute. She glanced out the window, and watched the fields pass by in a blur as she realised her own tears were close. She had no idea where they were going, but the town was signposted and she wondered if Frederick were heading somewhere in particular, or just driving anywhere to get away from all the people he had just let down.

The roar subsided and she felt the Range Rover slowing. She turned back to look at him, watched him push the indicator and he turned off the road and came to a halt in a layby. He switched off the engine and stared straight ahead, and she just waited.

"I just lost the title, Elsa." He told her eventually, his voice threatening to crack.

"That's horses for you." She replied feebly, and she wondered if she would be better off staying silent. If she couldn't even think of anything comforting to say, he really might have been better speeding off alone.

"No, it wasn't." He shook his head. "That was me riding like a total twat."

Why? She silently implored him. *What happened back there?*

"It happens," she shrugged.

"Not in my life, it doesn't!" He roared, making her jump as he slammed his fists against the steering wheel.

She gently bit her lip. "Happens in my life all the time," she replied, her voice little more than a whisper. "I'm always riding like a total twat."

"That's a lie," he murmured, looking out the window onto the road as he bit down on his thumb nail. "I've seen you ride."

She thought calm had restored itself, and he suddenly rammed his fists against the steering wheel again. "I've *never* taken the wrong show jumping course in my life!"

She waited again, her heart rate threatening to go through the roof. And then he looked across at her, for the first time since she had climbed in beside him. He looked as beautiful as ever, but his hair was a little longer than normal, and his blue eyes had lost their piercing spark. He looked worn and beaten.

"What's funny?" he frowned, and she hadn't realised her smile hadn't been secret.

"I was just thinking," she replied, "how funny would it be if you slammed that too hard, and the air bag inflated and shot you through to the back seat."

He gave a gentle laugh, and she was surprised. He twisted in his seat to face her, and reached across for her hand. He held one in both of his, and she jumped as his thumbs brushed softly over her knuckles.

"You always say the right things." He murmured, looking right at her.

"Really?" she looked doubtful.

"Yes," he outstretched his arm to her, and in the huge interior of the Range Rover she could have easily moved out of his reach, but she stayed stock still as he brushed her escaped strands of hair back behind her ears. She dreaded to think what she must look like right now, but he didn't seem to care as his blue eyes drank in the sight of her. His hand lingered, as he traced his finger around her ear and brushed his thumb across her cheek. She stayed deadly still, her oversensitive skin tingling to his every touch. His eyes searched hers, gradually roaming down her nose, and resting on her lips. His thumb followed, brushing over her bottom lip, and she slightly parted them in anticipation of his lips following. She waited, refusing to make the first move. She had given everything to him before, and look where that had got her.

"What went wrong?" she murmured.

He looked up, his smile gone. "Between us? Or in the show jumping?" His hand fell from her face, and she silently cursed herself.

"Both," she whispered.

He took her hand again, and brushed his thumb tenderly over her knuckles as he chose his words. "Do you know why I had all those fences down in the show Jumping?"

She slowly shook her head. He did not meet her eye, instead staring down at her hand in his as he struggled with his words.

"Because all I could see, the whole way around, was the hurt on your face when you heard my mother declaring to the world how good Portia and I would be together, and I hate myself for not grabbing you there and then and banishing that hurt forever. Every corner I turned, every jump I presented for, all I could see was *your hurt*!" he dropped her hand and banged his fists on the steering wheel again, and Elsa winced.

She had a million questions. *Are you two an item? Why didn't you grab hold of me? Will we ever have our happy ever after?* But she wasn't sure she wanted to know the answers to any of them.

"Elsa," he breathed eventually. "I was going back to my hotel for some peace and quiet and…reflection. Please, will you come with me?"

"You didn't want me to come with you at first," she murmured. "In fact, you were quite adamant I leave you be. But now you are asking me?"

He didn't answer, yet she found herself slowly nodding, against all her willpower. The voices in her head were screaming at her to get him to take her right back to the lorry park so that she could pack up and go home, that she should never have got in the car with him. But now that she was in here, it felt like the most natural thing in the world.

He started the engine and she wondered if he had observed her nod. She wondered whether she should speak up, to confirm she had said yes, in case there was any doubt. But then was it bad if he thought she had declined and drove her back with this tender moment never to be spoken about again. He eased the Range Rover forward to turn back onto the road, and she waited to see which way he'd turn.

She only let out her breath when he eased the Range Rover left - towards town - and she felt a warm feeling in the pit of her stomach, the feeling of launching into the unknown with this mysterious figure who she thought she'd previously shared so much with.

She sat in silence for the ten minute journey that felt much longer, until he eased to a halt in the carpark of an upmarket hotel. There would be no seedy motels with Frederick; and she should have guessed as much. Yet through her excitement, she hated herself for saying yes.

He climbed out from the Range Rover, and she nervously followed. He didn't look at her, not even as he held the entrance door open for her and she brushed past him. She stole a glance, and he looked as though his mind were not really here at all. She didn't feel like it was personal, she felt like she could stand naked before him and he wouldn't even notice right now.

His huge stride ate up the lobby floor as he made for the lift, and she struggled to keep up. He waited until she was safely inside before pressing the button to take them to the fourth floor. He leaned back against the glass side of the lift, his arms behind his back as he stared blankly at the ceiling. She just wanted to throw her arms around him and tell him it would all be OK, but she wasn't even sure he was inside his lifeless body.

The lift beeped, breaking her from her thoughts, and he

silently indicated she exit first. With a nod she followed his guide, feeling his palm brush her back and wishing he'd slip it around her waist and pull her into that delicious body.

He stopped her outside the door to his room, and hesitated, as if giving her another chance to flee. She tried to slow her breathing as she waited. Eventually he unlocked the door, and pushed it open, allowing her to walk in first. His hotel room was spacious and luxurious, as if she'd expect anything less. A huge bed graced the middle of the room; with standard hotel cream sheets and too many pillows. The huge curtained window looked out over the car park - probably one of the better views the boring little town of Cromwell had to offer - and Elsa wondered what had possessed someone to build such a grand hotel here in the first place. When she turned back around, Frederick had already removed his spurs and boots and tossed them by the door. He laid back on the pristine, made bed, stretching out and staring blankly up at the ceiling with the back of his hand guarding half of his weary face. She loitered for a bit, wondering what she could say to make him feel any better. Her heart was breaking for him, and temporarily banished were the memories of how he'd hurt her. Right now she just wanted to be there for him with whatever turmoil he was going through. She slipped out of her grubby boots and slowly made her way to the bed. She lied down beside him and let out a deep sigh at the welcoming comfort of the soft mattress. She rolled over so that she was on her side, her head propped up on her elbow as she watched him, waiting.

"Do you know, some days I could happily just walk away and leave all this behind. And I would never look back." He murmured eventually.

"You don't mean that." She frowned.

"Don't I?"

"The guy that has absolutely everything, would leave it all behind?" she gave a gentle laugh at the absurdness. "Some would say that's ungrateful."

"Those who know me wouldn't." He grunted.

"If you're looking for an ego boost, you're asking the wrong person."

He turned his head slightly to look at her, and drank in the full sight of her. She looked so naturally beautiful; wisps of wind-swept hair escaped from her pony tail, her t-shirt and jeans were grubby. But she was still the most beautiful little thing he'd ever laid eyes on. Yet he didn't deserve her, and he knew that. He'd hurt her, he could still see it in her eyes if he looked close enough, and it tore his heart in two. He'd had no right to hurt her; and it had been the last thing on earth he'd wanted to do. He was surprised she'd agreed to accompanying him here. Whether she truly wanted to be here or not, he couldn't quite tell, but he was grateful that she was. There was no one he wanted to see right now, except her.

"Have you got your filthy yard clothes draped over my pristine bed?" he murmured, a smile tugging at his lips.

She glanced down her outstretched body, her mud-splattered jeans, bits of hay stuck to her t-shirt, and nodded. "Too right I have."

"Good girl," he smiled, and looked away again, back at the ceiling where she could not read his expression.

"Come on, talk to me," she pressed. "What happened? What's wrong?"

"I should have had that title, Elsa," he murmured. "I could have had it. I'm furious at myself."

"Just at yourself?" she pressed.

"And you," he whispered.

Excuse me? "Me?" she glared at him.

"Yes, you." He replied, his voice cracking as he turned to look at her again. Their lips were just inches away, and she had an overwhelming urge to kiss him, but something stopped her.

"You say I have everything," he whispered, reaching over

and trailing a tender finger down her soft cheek. "But I don't have you, do I?"

"Don't talk nonsense," she told him shakily, his touch knocking her off guard. "You didn't want me, remember?" She could still remember the humiliation of him slamming the door in her face, as though it were only yesterday. The happy, lust-filled times they had shared since, followed by the hollow silence.

"I always want you," he closed his eyes as though it were too painful to look at her. "Without you, I don't have anything, do I?"

"Stop asking me; I won't agree with you," she told him, forcing back a tear. "We can't be together."

His silence spoke volumes as he stared at her, his piercing blue eyes making her melt a little inside.

"You hurt me, and I think I probably hurt you." She whispered, and she could not prevent the solitary tear that rolled down her cheek.

"And you never forgive people who hurt you?" He murmured, his thumb skimming across her soft skin and taking the tear with it.

"Not easily," she admitted. "We were both in the wrong, Frederick."

"Well, at least we're even." He whispered huskily, his lips moving closer and she sensed his hesitation before they finally met hers.

She arched to meet him, desperate to feel his hard body pressed against her as his tongue hungrily roamed her mouth, forcing her to open wider. She had forgotten how good he tasted, and even though the voices screamed at her stop, her body betrayed her. She wanted him badly, and she knew she could never get enough of him.

"But two wrongs don't make a right, Frederick!" she tried helplessly again, pulling away. "I won't be second best – if I am even *that*!"

He ran his tongue along his lower lip, looking thoughtful. He could forgive her for anything; any hurt she'd caused him was really nothing compared to having her back in his arms. He had some serious making up to do if he was ever going to win her around, but it was all out of his reach now.

"Why did you punch Clement?" she asked a moment later, feeling this was the best opportunity she was ever likely to have for them to get things off their chest.

"Geez, Elsa," he sighed and ran his hand through his curls as he reluctantly remembered his moment of madness. "I know I had no right, but…when I *saw* him with you…I just flipped."

"Your anger – whatever you felt – was nothing to do with him."

"I know, and he's a good guy, but I just saw red." He held her gaze. "I've never fought over a girl before." He traced his hand across her cheek, down into the groove of her neck, praying she wouldn't stop him as he lifted her t-shirt off over her head. "Did you like him?"

"Is this an appropriate topic to be talking away, while I'm *almost* in bed with someone else?" Elsa queried, her cheeks reddening.

"Probably not," Frederick shrugged. "But I need to know, nonetheless."

Slowly, Elsa nodded. "If you'd have let me, I could have, yes," she told him truthfully. "But it will never happen now."

He slowly nodded, and she wondered what that look was that flickered across his face. *Relief?*

"He's a good guy," he murmured, even more certain now she wouldn't stop him as he unbuckled her jeans and slid them down her hips. "I'm grateful he stuck around; I half expected him to pack his bags and leave."

"He has thought about it." Elsa took a deep breath, barely moving as she kicked her jeans off over her feet and let them drop to the floor. She turned to face him, wishing his touch wouldn't do such crazy things to her as he skimmed his palm along her thigh. "And so has Ava."

"They have?" he froze, knowing she wouldn't lie to him. "Clement because of the whole...*incident*, I guess," he screwed his face up as he was forced to remember it again. "But *Ava*? Why?"

"Grooms work bloody hard, and get paid a pittance."

"I treat my staff well, Elsa, so I hope we're not going over this old ground again."

"*You* might," Elsa responded.

"What's that supposed to mean?" he challenged her.

She could barely bring herself to think about her, let alone *talk* about her, but she had to. "The wicked witch of the show jumping world who has been swanning around yours like she bloody owns the place, making Ava's life hell."

"What?" he glared at her, incredulous. "She has never said."

"She has *tried*, Frederick, but you are bloody oblivious!" She almost felt sorry for him. "That witch has well and truly pulled the wool over your eyes, hasn't she?"

His sudden refusal to meet her eye sent alarm bells ringing throughout her, and she suddenly knew she should get herself a million miles away from him. She shifted subtly away, distancing herself as much as she could while lying in bed almost naked beside someone so magnetic. But she needn't have bothered; his hand on her hip was enough to stop her. She wondered if she would ever be strong enough to walk away from him.

"She's a good groom." Elsa added, her voice shaky as she tried to pull the duvet over her.

"My best." He murmured, his tender hand tracing every contour of her body.

"So, she could easily find work somewhere else," Elsa fought back threatening tears, furious at her lack of self-control. "Remember that, Frederick."

He half expected her to shove him away, tell him she never wanted to see him again and flee as fast as she could. And he wouldn't blame her. He wasn't sure what he had done to deserve her laying here beside him, looking so glorious in her plain, beige bra with the tiniest lace trim detail and plain, navy blue knickers. He wanted nothing more than to peel them from her, but he could sense her backing away, and it broke his heart to see her look so hurt.

"You're so beautiful," he whispered. "You drive me crazy, and you make me fall apart. How do you do that?"

Slowly she shook her head. "I don't mean to," she whispered.

She didn't move as he reached out to her again, his fingers gently trailing down her cheek, his thumb skimming over her chin. She licked her lips, her eyes following his hand, and then it was around the back of her head, pulling her to him, and any strength she'd had was gone. She dissolved in his arms as his lips met hers.

She arched her body against him; as his hands ran all over her, feeling every inch of her soft, smooth skin. He unclasped her bra and her breasts sat upright, looking him right in the face, and his lips parted from her so that he could sit back and get a better look. But he couldn't keep his hands from her, and he brushed his palms against them. Her breath caught, a tingling sensation shooting to her groin as her nipples immediately stood to attention. He gently tilted her body towards him, and his mouth was around a hardened nipple, sucking at it and causing her to let out a low groan as she fell helplessly into his arms.

"I've missed you so much, Elsa," he whispered, looking her straight in the eye. "But I will just keep hurting you. I wish I could stop, but it's not in my power. Everything is planned out for me, and it will just involve hurting you over and over."

She battled helplessly with her demons as she ignored his

words and slowly climbed astride him. As she felt his erection poking against his breeches, she thought she would let him do anything right now.

"Well, if that's the case," she replied, needing him. "You could at least make love to me first?"

He did not need asking twice. His lips were so gentle as they brushed over her nipples in turn, and she felt how wet she was for him already. She fell into his hard chest as he slid her knickers from her. They weren't even attractive knickers, either, she realised with a regretful sigh, they were very much her *I'm going to be working outside all day doing manual work* knickers. If he noticed, he didn't say anything, and she bet Portia had a whole drawer of sexy, lacy underwear at her disposal. She inwardly cursed herself for thinking about her. But she didn't think anything could ruin this moment, and she slowly and teasingly unbuckled his belt, her fingers moving nimbly over the buttons of his breeches. He lifted her buttocks, allowing her to slide his breeches and pants down in one, and she prized herself away from his strong grip and climbed from him as she slipped his long socks and breeches off over his ankles. And then she kissed him, starting at his ankle and tantalisingly slowly moving her lips up his calf, across his knee, along the inside of his thigh as she glanced up every now and then to see his erection rising up before her. She stopped just as she reached it, and he let out a groan.

With a teasing smile she gently took the throbbing shades of purple between her lips, and he grabbed a fistful of the bedsheets as she swirled her tongue the length of his thick shaft, tasting the saltiness. Something told her this may be her last chance to devour him, and she wanted to go all out.

He resisted the deep urge to grab her hair and drive himself deep into her mouth. Just the thought of her often made him lose control, yet he wanted to treat her like the Princess that she deserved. He had thought he would never get to relive this moment again, yet somehow they had found their way into each other's arms again, and he didn't want it to ever end. He adored her; he never wanted to hurt her.

She licked the entire length of his rock hard cock, and with a deep breath she took him as deep as her mouth would allow. She waited with a pounding heart for him to stop her, to tell her that they shouldn't be doing this. But he didn't. He was blissfully silent, his blue eyes never leaving her. He felt the back of her throat, and groaned.

Cromwell was almost forgotten as he watched her head bob up and down at his crotch, her hand and tongue working in unison. He was in frenzy and he hadn't even touched her yet. He knew he was dangerously close to coming already, and he sat up, cupping her face in his hands.

"*Stop,*" he breathed, desperate to last longer.

She lifted her head, biting down on her bottom lip as she moved back just out of his reach, trailing wet kisses along the inside of his thighs. He propped himself up on his elbows as he watched her, until he could take no more.

"Come to me, Elsa," he murmured. "*Please*?"

She nodded, sliding a knee either side of him as she crawled up his body. There was no way she would deny him.

"I've missed you so much," he whispered as he trailed his finger along her opening. She gasped as he pushed a finger inside her, and pushed her whole body against him. He just wanted to make her happy, but he wasn't sure it would be for any longer than this moment they were in bed together.

But he didn't want to think about that right now as he withdrew his finger from her and fumbled around on the bedside table. She watched him as he slid the condom on with hands that didn't shake anywhere near as much as hers were right now. He grasped her butt cheeks as he positioned her above him. And then he was quickly inside her, and he felt all his troubles evaporate as she met his every thrust.

She let out a low moan as she felt herself stretching for him. She wondered, if she were to sleep with him a hundred times, would this sensation ever wear off? She hoped not, and she smiled as she met his soft blue eyes staring up at her.

She felt her pressure mounting and she knew he felt it, too. She closed her eyes and bit down on her lip as her hips bucked vigorously against him. She could not hold on for much longer and as he sat up and took her in his arms, hungrily kissing her neck, she let go. Her orgasm shook her to the core, and he held her tightly as she came back down to earth. He didn't part from her as he rolled her onto her back, and she eagerly spread her legs wider for him as he drove into her with a hungry need, mesmerised by her bouncing breasts as she gazed at him above them.

Her hands were running desperately through his thick, blonde hair and as he bit down on her neck he couldn't wait any longer, and she wrapped her legs around him as his orgasm took over him.

They held each other as they caught their breath, and he let out a groan as he withdrew from her. He stretched out beside her and pulled into his chest, and she snuggled contentedly against his damp skin. He didn't say a word as he stroked her caramel hair, and she listened to his loud, beating heart.

She smiled as she realised that had Frederick jumped clear, he may well be the Cromwell champion but he wouldn't be here with her. She had never realised there was so much happiness to be obtained from taking the wrong course, even if it was only bound to last while they lay in this bed. She remembered the fuming look on Portia's perfectly made-up face, and felt a small triumph that it was not her that was currently gracing Frederick's bed and making him feel better. But then she remembered they would have to face the music, once they stepped outside of these four walls and back into the feel world.

"*Fred...* Are you in there?" came the hiss through the thick wood, hotel room door.

The shiver that ran down Elsa's spine chilled her to the

core. Even though her ears were muffled by Frederick's strong arms and chest, she could tell it was definitely Portia; there was no mistaking the snarl of her voice.

"Open the bloody door!" she demanded furiously, banging her hand against it. "I know you're in there!"

"Frederick..." Elsa began, her shaking voice barely audible.

"Shhh," Frederick cut her off, his voice soothing.

"Maybe he's sleeping!" They heard Lady Twemlow suggest, and she sounded exasperated.

"He won't be sleeping when I've bloody finished with him!" Portia spat, banging on the door again. "Does he know how humiliating this is for us and our yard?"

Elsa's eyebrows rose at the use of *our,* and her heart was beating over time. She distanced her head from Frederick a little so that she at least got a chance to look him in the eye.

"Is this her room, too?" she croaked. "Are you and her...you know?"

"No, Elsa," he replied with a sigh, gently stroking her hair. "She'll get bored in a moment and leave us alone."

Part of her wanted to rise from the bed, march naked to the door and tell Portia to bugger off and leave them alone. But she lay frozen, as she suddenly realised there was much more to it than she would ever know.

"Maybe he's gone out?" Lady Twemlow tried again.

"His car is parked downstairs!" Portia raged, and Elsa heard her pacing outside the door until she calmed a little. "I'm going down to reception to get a key for the room! You can't hide in there forever, Fred! I will find you, and we *will* talk about this."

Elsa froze in fear, unable to imagine the fight that were to break out if Portia let herself in and *did* find them in bed together, but Frederick was unmoved.

"I should go," she murmured, trying half-heartedly to tug herself from his grip.

"No," he insisted gently, stilling her and pulling the duvet around them. "They won't give her a key; I warned them not to. She will leave and take my mother with her; trust me."

Trust me. Why did the words send alarm bells ringing through her, even as she tried her best to ignore them? She heard the footsteps of them leaving as she snuggled into his chest, feeling safe in this cocoon, and took a deep breath of his sweet aftershave masked with sweat. She gently closed her eyes, thinking she could stay here lying in his arms forever, but knowing that she shouldn't.

"It's you that I keep coming back to, Elsa," he told her gently. "What does that tell you?"

"That you're hopeless, you're pathetic and you're a fraud," she replied sadly, wondering if there was supposed to be a compliment in there somewhere.

He sighed. He'd walked into that and he deserved every word.

"And so am I." She whispered.

He brushed his lips across her forehead, and she opened her eyes to see his beautiful, blue gaze scanning her face. He skimmed his finger tips down her soft cheek, and traced his thumb over her damp lips. She trembled as he stirred her feelings welcomingly awake, and she willed him to kiss her.

"Please, stay with me?" he murmured.

She bit down on her lower lip, so tempted, but remembering her horses waiting for her back at the show ground. They wouldn't be missing her yet; they had plenty of hay and water to keep them going for another few hours, but she needed to hit the road and get them home. The thought of her cosy little cottage and home comforts beckoning her would have normally had her heading to the door, but she stuck to Frederick's warm body like glue, wishing this moment didn't have to end.

"I can't," she reluctantly murmured. "I have to get the horses back."

"Of course," he sighed, wondering if it was for the best. "It was rude of me to even ask."

Chapter Seventeen

Elsa could see the showground entrance only one hundred yards ahead, when Frederick pulled the Range Rover off the road of the normally sleepy village. He cut the engine, and Elsa knew this was her cue to leave.

"I've missed you," he murmured, stilling her hand as she reached for the door handle.

She jumped at his touch, as if not expecting it to be so soft, but he did not let her go. He *needed* her to know. *I'm a prick,* his gorgeous blue eyes conveyed*, but it's not my fault!* He wished things could be different, but he didn't see how they ever could be. She deserved better than to be messed around by him; he knew he had to do the right thing for both of them and not see her again. He couldn't bear to bring her anymore heartache.

Slowly she nodded, as if in agreement with the pain and emotions whirring around his jumbled mind. It was almost as if she mirrored him, and he had never felt so connected to someone in all his life - while at the same time feeling so far, far away from her. She had missed him more than words could ever describe, but she knew there was more standing in the way of them than she could ever begin to understand.

"I'm going to head back to my hotel, and drive back in the morning, face the music." He told her, even though she had not asked.

"Drive safely, yea?" she couldn't hide the pleading sound from her voice. She worried about him; *really* worried about him.

"Elsa?" he gently tugged her towards him, and brushed his lips against hers. He stopped, not trusting himself to resist anymore.

His touch sent pulses racing through her, and she longed to

demand he turn right back around and take her back to his hotel with him. She forced herself to think of Portia; anything to make the passion dissolve and her be furious at him, instead.

"Thank you," he murmured. "For everything."

She nodded as his blue eyes searched her. He softly brushed his lips against hers again. But it was different this time; more of a tender goodbye than a promise of more to come, and Elsa felt her heart breaking.

"Bye, Frederick," she forced a smile, her voice cracking.

She didn't mean to *slam* the door shut behind her, but the adrenaline raging through her made sure that she did. She didn't dare look back; instead she kept her head down, her arms folded tightly across her chest as she walked fast towards the show ground entrance. She barely broke her stride as she flashed her wrist band at the steward and the he moved aside to let her pass.

She marched straight to the stabling, needing to busy herself in her work. It was the only way to stop thinking about him. She knew if she stopped for even just a minute the tears would flow and she would be a helpless mess for everyone to see. She needed to get home; back to the glorious familiarity of home and its comforts, notably Cecil curled up on her lap while she nursed that bottle of white she'd left in the fridge and watched a shitty film.

Cali whinnied as she saw Elsa approaching, and that immediately lifted her spirits a little. Horses really were the best medicine for *anything*. She sighed as she peered over her stall door, and realised the mare had hardly eaten any of hay. Too preoccupied by all the packing up and removing of horses all around her, she had instead pulled most of it from her haynet and walked it into her shitty bed. Dusty dutifully tucked into his own haynet like the good boy that he was, not really understanding what his stable companion was making such a fuss about.

The Kiwi party opposite looked like they were having a shindig, with empty plastic champagne glasses perched on a plastic table as Paige and her fellow grooms chatted animatedly as they tried to tidy up.

"We won the bloody class!" she beamed at Elsa, embracing her in an enthusiastic hug.

"Oh my God!" Elsa's happiness was genuine. She had spent all afternoon trying to get Frederick to forget about the class, that in turn she had forgotten all about it herself. "That's great! Congratulations!"

"Thanks! This is the perfect end to our season. Brett is away celebrating with the owners! We had a little tipple," she nodded to the empty glasses, and pulled a face. "But none for me as I'm driving the lorry back."

Elsa leaned across the stall door and gave the big, bay champion a pat. "I hope there'll be extra carrots for you tonight, hey boy?"

"You bet!" Paige laughed. "He can have all the carrots in the world if it means he keeps on jumping like he did today!"

With a parting pat, Elsa left them to their packing up and celebrations. It would be a jubilant drive home for them. And Elsa and Sophia themselves had had a very positive weekend, she reminded herself through the turmoil and mix of emotions of this afternoons events. Elsa let herself into Cali's stall and peeled back her rug. To her expectation, the mare had worked herself up to a sweat. She cursed herself for being away so long. Sophia paid her wages to be a groom; her first priority should have been her horses and she'd let them down. She grabbed a sponge and bucket of water and quickly washed the mare down and dried her off.

"Come on, girl," she scratched her neck. "Let's get you and your buddy home." It was a long drive, and the quicker she got going - after her unscheduled delayed - the better.

"Where the bloody hell have you been?" Ava demanded, glaring in over the stall door.

Elsa didn't reply. She spent a bit longer adjusting Cali's rug straps while she tried to regain her composure before turning to face her friend.

"She'd kicked her water over twice," Ava told her, nodding towards the chestnut but her eyes never leaving Elsa. "But don't worry, I filled it up."

"*Shit*!" Elsa finally met her eye. "Sorry, Ava. I shouldn't have left her, and you shouldn't have had to do that. I'm sorry."

"It's not your horse I was worried about, "Ava still glared at her coldly. "I'll always keep an eye on them, you know that. It was you I was most concerned about, last seen haring off after my boss!"

Elsa grabbed a travel boot and knelt down in the shavings, her back to her as she fumbled to put it on. She knew it was pointless trying to hide anything from her, but she would be so disappointed if she knew the truth.

"Fred won't answer his phone." Ava said a moment longer, refusing to let it go.

With a sigh, Elsa got to her feet and turned to face her. "He's driving," she shrugged.

"Which is when he's most likely to be contactable by phone," Ava sighed, her hands on her hips. She narrowed her eyes at her. "Where did you two go?"

"To his hotel room," Elsa replied, unable to meet her eye.

"No, no, *no*, Elsa!" Ava shouted, making Cali flinch. She ran her hands through her hair in exasperation, and gave the poor chestnut an apologetic scratch. "Why do you do this to yourself? You *need* to stay away from him."

"Nothing happened!" she fought back, forcing herself to look at her. She hated lying to her, but she couldn't talk about this right now.

"Well, what did happen, then? You need to tell me, Elsa. I'm really worried about him."

"We talked," she shrugged. "Just talked. He was really cut

up."

"That's inevitable, he rode the *shittest* round of his life. I didn't realise things were so bad."

"What things?" Now it was Elsa's turn to narrow her eyes accusingly.

"I don't know, but I'm determined to find out. In the meantime, I think you should stay away from him. What with his current state of mind, someone's going to get hurt and I don't want it to be either of you. You need to be careful, Elsa."

Elsa looked at her in confusion. *Careful?* Ava was always the one encouraging her.

"I'm warning you because I know him." Ava went on. "He's always so in control and focused. This is a different Fred, one I've never seen before and one that scares me. He's not focused and not in control. Some people were looking around the yards last week and I don't think they were owners. Something's happening," she affirmed, "and I don't like the feel of it."

Elsa felt numb as she loaded her horses and got ready to set off. Her stuff was packed and her stables cleaned out. Most of the people had left now; the stables were emptying and the trade stands packing up. Her stomach rumbled, and she wondered if there was any chance of a tray of chips for the long journey. Her rations in the lorry were running low. She dashed to the canteen and begged them to scrape out what was left in the fryer, certain it was only heading for the bin anyway. She loved crunchy chips, and she smothered them in sauce as she added her lorry to the queue to get off the show ground, and into the traffic that would probably crawl along at a snail's pace for a good few miles to the motorway, and only then would she feel like she was on her way home.

It was well-past midnight when Elsa swung the lorry into the yard, and almost got blinded as the security lights flashed on. She was grateful that her cargo was so tired they had travelled peacefully all the way home. While Dusty was happy while he had a haynet, and Cecil as long as he had somewhere warm to curl up for a nap, Cali could get rather impatient on the lorry and start thrashing about until someone gave her some attention. She left the lorry parked in the middle of the yard and quickly unloaded her horses, peeling off their rugs and turning them out into the sand paddocks for a few minutes so that they could stretch their legs and have a roll. She was grateful to see their deep beds already down in their stables, and their feed and hay waiting for them in the corner manger. She couldn't wait to get inside to the comfort and familiarity of her own bed and lay her head on her *own* pillow.

She retrieved a reluctant Cali and Dusty from the sand paddock, promising them a day off in the field the following day. She quickly ran a brush over them to remove the sand and dirt, and then rugged them up and put them to bed. As she let out a long yawn, she shut the lorry up, made sure the stable doors were bolted, and slipping Timber Bear a carrot on her way past, she switched the lights off and made her way the few steps to her welcoming cottage.

Elsa wasn't sure she'd ever been this exhausted in her whole life, but still she couldn't sleep. She tossed and turned in her bed as her mind battled what felt like every emotion she'd ever known. Cecil growled every time the duvet moved, and peered at her with large, accusing eyes.

"I'm sorry, Cec," she pulled him close and kissed his head, ignoring the fact that he desperately needed a bath. "I just feel..." she trailed off. How did she feel? *Out of control.* She sighed. She was used to running a tight ship, throwing herself into her work and being totally in control of it all. But now, for the first time since she'd started working for Sophia, she felt anything but. Things were changing, and she didn't like it one bit. All thoughts of Frederick aside, she knew a big upheaval was coming to her life, and she was really struggling at the prospect of it.

"We can't go to Germany, Cec," she sighed, tugging on his ear.

He yawned and glared at her some more, as if wishing she would figure it out quickly and let him sleep. "But what will we do?"

He allowed her to hold him tightly to her, even though she knew he didn't really like it. She closed her eyes.

"We can't go..." she murmured, before drifting quickly off to sleep.

A constant banging at the door roused Elsa from her deep sleep, and she squinted into the sunlight pouring in through her open curtains. She fumbled around blindly on her dresser for her phone, and let out a deep groan when she finally found it and realised she had majorly overslept. The banging was still sounding, and Elsa wished it would shut up. She rose slowly from her bed and moved to her open window, to see Cali looking none the worse for wear for her long, late night journey as she pounded her knees against her stable door.

Elsa pulled on her jeans and a t-shirt, and hurried downstairs. The banging had stopped, and she peered out of her cottage to see Sophia enter the stable with a fresh haynet. She pulled on her boots and tiptoed to her.

"I'm so sorry," she told her. "I must have fallen asleep before I even set my alarm."

Elsa couldn't remember falling asleep - all she could remember was not being able to - but her mind had been far too preoccupied to remember to set her alarm.

"It's fine," Sophia laughed, tying the net up for the impatient mare. "You should have stayed in bed longer; there's really no hurry."

"You should have woken me."

"It's *fine,*" Sophia insisted. "The morning stables are done now, anyway."

"Already?"

"Elsa, it is almost lunch time!" Sophia laughed. "Cali and Dusty have had a few hours out in the paddock. Timber Bear is fine too, by the way. And all the others."

"Right, well, guess I should start clearing out the lorry," Elsa shrugged, feeling helpless.

"It can wait until this afternoon," Sophia replied. "I've got to nip out in it in a minute and pick up Banjo. Do you remember the naughty little piebald we had in for schooling last year?"

Elsa nodded. She had been very fond of the little pony and sad to see him go. "He was awful."

"Apparently he's back up to his old tricks," Sophia rolled her eyes, her smile wide as she had been as fond of him as Elsa. "They want him to come here for a couple of weeks before I go," she hesitated, trying to gauge Elsa's reaction, but her groom was giving nothing away.

"Of course, it makes sense."

Sophia could sense her decision without even having to ask, but she wouldn't press her on it; there was plenty of time for them to discuss it. Right now she had a more pressing matter to bring up.

"Harry stayed over last night," she began tentatively. "He stayed to watch the jumping yesterday, too. He told me all about the carnage that followed. Apparently a certain someone was the talk of the lorry park; a mysterious girl chasing after Frederick Twemlow as he sped off in his Range Rover."

Elsa felt her cheeks reddening. *Shit!* How could she honestly have been so naive to think no one would have noticed; every single set of eyes in that showground had been pinned on Frederick Twemlow. "That didn't take long to get round, did it?"

"Oh, come on Elsa," Sophia smiled gently. "The horse world is very small; the eventing world even smaller. Portia was livid."

"Good," Elsa scowled, turning towards the feed shed.

"It's not the first time you've been talk of the show ground at one of my events, is it?" Sophia teased, following her. "You're beginning to make quite a habit of it; people will be wondering what you're going to pull off next season."

"Shut up!" Elsa snapped, but it only made Sophia laugh.

"Seriously though, you do know that any girl in that showground would have given their right arm to be the girl in Frederick's Range Rover?"

Slowly, Elsa nodded. "But maybe it's not all it's cracked up to be?" she countered, referring to the tears that getting so involved had forced her to cry, the longing and lust she felt for him, yet deep down knowing he would never be hers.

"What happened?" Sophia pressed, concerned. "Are you back on?"

"Were we ever *on*?" Elsa gave it some thought.

Sophia watched her as she threw the feed bowls out across the feed shed floor, lining them up in two rows to run in order of the horses housed on the yard.

"Has he called?"

"He won't call." Elsa insisted. Of that at least, she was certain.

"Give it time."

"Time is irrelevant. He won't call."

Elsa made the feeds up and retired to her little cottage, desperate for a shower and a strong coffee. She emerged feeling a lot more awake and optimistic when she heard the roar of the lorry in the lane. It was quickly parked and the ramp lowered, and cheeky Banjo tried to take a lump from Elsa's arm as she led him out.

"Did you *see* that?" she yelped, jumping out of his reach just in time.

His tiny ears pricked forward, gazing innocently at Elsa as if he had no idea what she was on about.

"I see he's still got bags of character!" Sophia laughed, keeping her distance as Elsa led the unruly gelding to a spare stable.

"So, what's he been up to?" Elsa asked, releasing the headcollar and jumping quickly out of the way as he pummelled the stable wall with both his hind legs. "If I even need to ask?"

"Exactly that..." Sophia replied, with a bite to her lip. "Kicking, biting, bucking her off. He's up to date with dentist, back, farrier. So, we'll see if we make any progress, but I think I'll get Harry to test him for being a rig."

Elsa nodded in agreement, remembering the chaos he'd caused last time he'd visited; breaking through fences to get to the mares. He may have only been a little over thirteen hands high, but he had the strength of an ox and a huge character.

"Want to head out for a hack?" Sophia asked, as Banjo eventually finished checking out his new surroundings and dived into his hay. "Then I'll help you with the packing away?"

Elsa nodded, desperately needing some fresh, valley air. Now that their season was over, the horses would be allowed to wind down. They would have some walks before being turned out to grass. But as neither of them liked to have not much to do, Banjo was just the first of their impending schooling liveries Sophia had crammed in to keep them both busy until she departed, and then Elsa would have to find her own entertainment.

Frederick wasn't sure at which point he'd started to dread stepping foot into his own yard, but he suspected it had been a while before his monumental cock-up at Cromwell. Of course, his own mother had taken great delight in informing him that this wasn't his own yard, and that this area of the Twemlow estate had better start paying for itself, rather than embarrassing the family like he had done at Cromwell. There was nothing like kicking a man when he was down and piling on the pressure.

"Fred?"

His whole body tensed, and he took a moment to realise it was Just Ava, and he relaxed a little.

"Sorry, I thought you were..." he broke off and looked away, forcing the words back.

"You thought I was her, didn't you?" the bold Australian was not one to hold back. "You flinched like I was about to beat you up or something."

"Don't be silly," Frederick snapped, but he would not meet her eye.

She sighed and ran a hand through her hair, her deep worry for him evident. "What's going on, Fred?"

"Where would you like me to begin?" he gave her a wry look.

"Wherever you feel best appropriate."

He didn't reply, just looked out across the yard as he tried to pinpoint exactly where it had all started to go wrong.

"I know you, Frederick. I know you are driven, determined, you *normally* speak your mind." Ava refused to let it go.

He nodded, and slowly swirled his tongue across his lips. He felt nervous under her gaze, because she was right, she did *know* him - better than anyone - and if anyone could see through his thick skin to the inner turmoil he was trying to secretly harbour, it would be her. He looked out to the manège where Portia was forcing a five year old into such a tight outline that it made him cringe. He wanted to launch across there and yank her from the poor horse, but he couldn't. Firstly, because he was too much of a coward, and secondly, because he wouldn't be left with any horses to ride if he did.

Ava followed his gaze. "OK, let's start with her. What on earth is all *that* about?"

It wasn't in his nature to say unkind things about anyone,

and he had always been taught that if nothing nice sprang to mind, then don't say anything at all. But that wouldn't wash with Ava, and he tore his eyes away, trying to think of anything to form a sentence.

"She's...pretty."

Ava rolled her eyes. "Don't fob me off with that bullshit. You can have any pretty girl that you like, so why would you pick such a nasty one?"

But of course she knew why, before she'd even asked him. "I admit I was struggling with understanding it before, but not so much since the Roxwell's ball. I mean, you kept that one quiet, didn't you?"

He hadn't meant to deliberately mislead her, but of course it was the only reason why Portia was on his yard. He would never have entertained the idea otherwise. He needed working pupils who pulled their weight and were genuinely here to learn, but she had not lifted a finger since she had first pulled into the yard and clicked her fingers for a groom to come and unload her horse. He'd known right from the first minute this was a bad idea, but what other choice did he have when her Aunty and Uncle owned most of the horses that graced his yard?

"Well, regardless of the real reason, I assume it also has a lot to do with the anonymous visitors who have been shown around the place recently?"

"Everything will be OK, Ava," he told her, although in his heart of hearts he couldn't see how it could. Maybe he should just give it all up now, before it started getting out of hand. "We've been friends for a long while now, haven't we?"

"You're much more than just a boss to me, Fred, you know that."

He nodded. He needed her, probably a lot more than she needed him.

"I'm your Head Girl, which means I'm in touch with everything that goes on around here; horse-wise and personal.

My cottage looks out over the yard, but also out over your front door. I've seen and heard her visiting you a lot recently. I need to know who I answer to," she paused, the thought of ever having to answer to Portia making her feel sick. "I don't miss anything that goes on, Fred. So, please don't keep me in the dark."

"Neither do I, remember?" he winked, resisting from breaking into a smile. "So, you make sure that your young Frenchman knows that, too."

He watched the crimson tint flush her gently freckled cheeks. She felt her heart stop. *How could he possibly know?* They had been so careful that no one would see them.

"Don't worry, no one else knows," he gave a gentle laugh. "Your face! Seriously, Ava, you make a nice couple. Please do tell him to stop being so scared of me, though."

"He thought he was being subtle. But he is always walking on eggshells around you, ever since..."

"Tell him to chill out," Fred cut her off quickly, before she gladly relayed one of his less finer moments. "There's no hard feelings. I like the guy, I just wasn't thinking straight."

"Not sure you ever are when it comes to her, are you? So, tell me. Did you sleep with her? Elsa, I mean, that time at Cromwell when you both disappeared for hours on end, and were the talk of the showground."

He hesitated. If she was asking him, then Elsa can't have already told her, and he knew they must have spoken about it. They were always talking to each other about whatever it was girls spoke about. "No. I bloody wanted to, though."

Ava took a deep breath. She didn't believe him for a second; she could tell that he had. "So, what did you do, then?"

He shrugged. "Talked. *Just* talked."

"And you can do that with her, easily?"

"About as easily as I can with you, yes."

"Except, she means a lot more to you, doesn't she?" Ava

probed. "Because you don't see her just a friend, do you?"

He shook his head. "It's a feeling I would struggle to describe no matter what company I was in."

"It's *love,* Fred!" Ava implored impatiently. "You *love* her!"

Love. He took a deep breath, and felt a huge weight being lifted off his shoulders at the fact that someone could see straight through him. *A problem shared is a problem halved,* he realised. *You should have told someone sooner, preferably Elsa.*

He stood staring blankly ahead, as if his mind were far away in a much better world than this one here. And as the weariness began to lift from his face, she saw the faintest of smiles tugging at the corner of his lips.

"Not going to deny it, then?" she folded her arms across her chest, looking triumphant.

"Why would I?" he replied simply, with a shrug. "It's a bit of a problem though, isn't it?"

"Not half."

"Frederick!" The shout tore through the pair of them, and they span to see Portia halted at the manège fence, glaring at them. "Are you going to adjust these poles for me, or not?"

He let out a sigh, unable to hide his weariness even though he knew he should at least try.

"Why the *fuck* are you shacked up with her when really you want Elsa, and you know she wants you, too?"

"Because it's not as easy as that," he murmured.

"Why can't it be?"

"Oh, you couldn't even begin to understand."

"Then *tell* me!" she pleaded.

He didn't reply; just stared after Portia while trying to hide his feelings of absolute contempt. Oh, he wished it were that easy, more than anyone. But whatever it was stopping him from getting what he wanted, Ava knew it must be bad.

"I'll go," she told him softly.

"No," he reached for her arm, stopping her.

"But it's my job," she shrugged. "To put up with you and

all your...*baggage.*"

"No, you didn't sign up for this." *No one did,* he realised, as he ran his hand through his soft, blond curls and turned and began walking towards the snarling Princess. *Not even me.*

Chapter Eighteen

Elsa turned Banjo out into the sand paddock to kick up some dirt before she attempted to work him. As she watched him belt from one end to the other, letting out non-stop bucks on his way, she decided she was quite looking forward to it. She chucked hay over stable doors as she made her way back down the row of stables to the tack room. Boots, rugs and numnahs were spread out all across the floor as Elsa attempted to sort them. The washing machine had been going non-stop all morning, and Elsa was glad that the weather had stayed fine and she could just lay them all out on the post and rail fencing to dry. She flipped the switch on the back of the kettle, just as the washing machine finished its spin cycle, and she pulled out the white saddlecloths and loaded it up with its next wash of filthy brushing boots. Cecil growled half heartedly, his tail wagging as Minty the yard cat jumped down from the roof rafters, his face covered in thick cobwebs.

"You still don't like that washing machine, do you?" Elsa laughed, picking the cobwebs from him as he sat beside the kettle, glaring tauntingly down at Cecil.

Elsa's mobile phone started ringing just as the kettle boiled. She was gasping for a drink, and contemplated silencing the call in favour of her long-awaited cup of tea.

She answered just before it cut to voicemail. "Ava, hey!" she pressed her ear to her shoulder to anchor the phone while she splashed boiling water on the teabag.

"Else, I didn't want to tell you, but it appears you may have done something to compromise the situation of me being able to keep a secret from you."

"What is it?"Elsa pressed, struggling to make sense of her. She pushed the tea away, giving Ava her undivided attention.

"You slept with Fred, didn't you?"

Elsa closed her eyes and leaned against the worktop. Her silence was all the confirmation that her friend needed.

"Well, I didn't want to tell you, but I have no choice now," Ava went on. "Portia and Fred are living together. At first I thought this whole thing is infatuation on her part, and I still want to believe that, but he is doing nothing to discourage her, as far as I can see. She moved in a couple of weeks ago, and she doesn't appear to have moved out after...well, you know. So either she doesn't know about it, or she's determined to keep her claws in him no matter what."

"Oh, *God*!" she groaned. "What have I done? And what the fuck was he thinking?"

"Probably thinking with his cock, Elsa, like most guys," Ava replied evenly.

"Why are you telling me this now?"

"I would have told you before, had you told me you slept with him."

"Did he tell you?"

"He didn't have to, Elsa. Just please be careful? I meant what I said before; I am worried about him. And you."

"You don't need to be worried about me," Elsa took a deep breath.

"I would love to *not* have to be worried about you," Ava told her quietly. "But I know what you're like when it comes to him."

Elsa wished she could say she would stay away from him, but she couldn't lie to her. She had seen how quickly she had changed his mind at Cromwell; she couldn't help feeling that he did *need* her, after all. She knew that if he called, she wouldn't ignore him. But if what Ava was saying was true, and she had no reason to suspect it wasn't, he wouldn't call. She needed to concentrate on herself; she had enough problems and uncertainties to sort out in her own life, without worrying about him.

Once the lorry was emptied, the boots and numnahs dried

and packed away ready for their new season, Elsa took a moment to slump in the tackroom and reflect on their season. Cecil clambered onto her lap and she gave him a rub behind his shaggy ears.

It had started on such a high; Nobby coming in from his winter break looking a million dollars. He had thrown himself into his work, and Sophia knew that in the upcoming three-star classes he was entered in, he had every chance of being right up there on the leader board. She had wanted to take him abroad, but Petra had persuaded her to concentrate on the home circuit this season, and widen her horizons the following season when hopefully they had some placings under their belt. Little had they known at that point, that Christine Forrester had other ideas for her star horse, and she had ripped him away from them and sent him to Frederick Twemlow. And that of course, had been where Elsa's turmoil had all started. She had so desperately wanted to hate him, but instead the opposite had happened, and she just wished she could make her feelings disappear.

She pulled herself to her feet and put Cali and Dusty on the horsewalker while she mucked out their stables. They had had a couple of days off in the field following their successful Cromwell, but they were otherwise being kept in work so that they stayed fit for their impending move to Germany. She knew they both had a lot of show jumping classes lined up for them over winter. Elsa still had not spoken to Sophia properly about the situation, and she made a mental note to invite her over for dinner one evening so that they could talk about it over a bottle of wine.

She retrieved Candy from the paddock and put her into her stable beside Timber Bear, and fetched Cali and Dusty from the horsewalker. Elsa wasn't sure about Sophia's plans with her new, young mare, who was also still in work having not yet done enough to warrant having a holiday.

She fetched the pony stock saddle from the tackroom and

went to Banjo's stable. He looked at her quizzically from his hay as she put in on his stable door and went in to him. He stretched out his neck and sniffed at the leather.

"I have a feeling I'm going to need that saddle," she smiled, scratching his neck as she slid the headcollar on him.

While Sophia was still making a name for herself, most of the horses and ponies she took in for schooling were unruly, including those no one else would touch. Back in the early days when Elsa had got fed up with eating the dirt after being bucked off one too many times, someone had suggested trying a stock saddle, and she had never looked back. It's deep seat and padded knee rolls meant Elsa could sit to most shenanigans in it. Now that Sophia was becoming well known in the eventing world and general equestrian community she could pick and choose which horses she took in, but Elsa knew she would never have declined helping Banjo. He belonged to the young daughter of a local farmer who absolutely adored him, and Elsa had seen exactly why the first time he'd stepped foot onto their yard.

She led him outside and tied him in the yard. He had untied himself within seconds and was trotting off across the yard towards the nearest patch of grass.

"You little *bugger*!" Elsa hollered, sprinting after him, and as she grabbed his lead rope she was certain he scowled at her. She re-tied him with a knot that any scout leader proud of.

"There!" she smiled triumphantly. "You'll have to take the wall with you before you get out of that one!"

"Don't encourage him," Sophia commented as she joined them. "I wouldn't put it past him."

Elsa quickly brushed him off before he could try anything else, bribing him with treats to get him to eventually lift each foot so that she could pick them out. She was exhausted before she'd even got his tack on him.

"Got our work cut out with him, haven't we?" Sophia could

not stop laughing as she watched the little piebald running rings around her.

They tacked him up and led him to the manège. Elsa tied his reins up and threaded the lunge line through his bridle, and sent him out on a circle. She hoped she'd tightened his girth as he went straight into canter and proceeded to launch in the air and kick out towards her, and she pointed the lunge whip at him to drive him away from her.

"Shotgun not getting on him first!" Sophia called from the gate.

Quickly tiring, the little round pony brought himself back to a trot, but Elsa kept him moving until *she* wanted him to slow. He had barely got his breath back before she asked him to canter again, and he responded with a swish of his tail, this time with fewer airs above the ground. Once he was settled and trotting and cantering sensibly and listening to her, she brought him to a halt.

"Little sod, isn't he?" Sophia commented, walking to give her a leg up.

Elsa nodded in agreement as she adjusted her stirrups and asked him to walk on.

He ignored her, his ears flicking back as he stood stock still, considering his work to be done for the day.

"Walk *on*!" Sophia got behind him with the lunge whip, and he leapt into a trot, taking Elsa by surprise.

Feeling he had unbalanced her, he let out a series of bucks down the long side of the school, but it took a lot to unseat Elsa these days, and she drove him onto a circle at the far end of the manège. By the time Elsa had finished with him forty minutes later, she felt as though both arms had been pulled from their sockets, and she had used muscles she wasn't aware she had. Although the stock saddle was comfy, she had not ridden in it in a while, and that had certainly been put through its paces, too. It was hard to believe a pony so small could possess such strength.

"Anyone who looks at ponies and thinks they're cute, cuddly and innocent *and* perfect for children, needs their head seen to," Elsa breathed as she slid from the saddle and prayed that her knees held her up.

"Well, he *is* cute and cuddly," Sophia responded, slipping him a treat as he beamed at her as though butter wouldn't melt. "He's just not getting enough work."

"*And* he's being allowed to get his own way too much," Elsa added. She stripped his tack off him as they walked, and quickly hosed him down before turning him out in the sand paddock for a roll. He stared across at the grass-filled neighbouring paddocks with envy, and Elsa quickly retrieved him before he could calculate how to scale their fencing *again*.

"I may suggest they get someone over a couple of times a week to exercise him," Sophia told her as she saddled Candy. "He's being ridden less now the kids are back at school, and it's only going to get worse as the dark nights and shit weather set in, and he gets less and less turnout."

Elsa nodded, in full agreement. Ponies like Banjo were built to survive on very little food and work very hard, and most benefitted from an occasional adult rider to give them a few firm reminders and keep them suitable for the children they belonged to.

"Need me to stay and help you with poles or anything?" Elsa asked, as she legged Sophia up onto Candy.

"No, we'll just do some flatwork today."

"In that case," Elsa replied, "I'm going to take Timber Bear for a wander down the valley. I fear once I sit down, I'll never get up again."

Sophia laughed as she nudged Candy on. Despite Elsa's aching muscles, she knew she wouldn't have let Sophia take Banjo away from her – she'd been having far too much fun.

Returning Timber Bear to her paddock and finishing up her afternoon stables, Elsa returned to her cottage and spent much longer than normal in the shower. She wished she had a bath

– she could kill for a long soak right now – but the water cascading fast onto her aching shoulders was welcome relief for now. Wandering downstairs in just a towel, she searched the freezer for something for dinner. She reluctantly took out a pizza to defrost, noting that she really needed to go shopping. She poured herself a glass of chilled white wine and slumped down on the sofa, Cecil immediately clambering onto her lap. She was grateful that it was Sophia's turn to do evening stables today, and she didn't need to go back out again. She contemplated calling Ava for a chat, as she had not spoken to her all week as they had both been busy. She loved being busy; it gave her less time to over think things. She wasn't sure she wanted to hear the latest about Portia and Frederick and all the happenings in their yard just yet. She needed some more wine inside her before then, and she tossed her phone aside as she realised she had not given Frederick one single thought all day, and she drained her glass in triumph.

Cecil was not impressed at being shoved aside for her to get up to refill her wine glass, and he relocated to the floor by the patio door in protest. Her phone rang just as she reached the wine bottle, and she was momentarily torn between the two.

"Hey, mind reader!" She smiled, quickly pouring and then choosing the phone. "I was just about to call you."

"Else!" The Australian boomed down the receiver. "Feels like ages, doesn't it? It's just a quickie; I'll call you tomorrow for a proper chat."

"You sound like you're in a hurry?" Elsa probed.

"Me and Clem are going *out*...eeek!" she squealed like an excited teenager.

"On like a *date*?" Elsa replied, laughing.

"*Yes*! Else I'm *so* excited, can you tell?"

"Just a tad," Elsa replied, leaning back on the sideboard she took a sip of her wine. "Where are you going?"

"Well, we're going to the cinema, and then he's taking me to dinner. He won't tell me where, but I'll assume it's French!"

she babbled excitedly. "What do they even *eat*?"

"I've no idea," Elsa replied. "Snails and horses, right?"

"Well, we definitely *won't* be eating any of *them*!" Ava retorted. "But Elsa I need your help. I'm not sure if what I'm wearing is OK, and we're leaving in ten minutes. I have plenty of fancy dresses hanging up for when we go to balls and awards things and the like, and loads of tiny little numbers for the rare occasion that I ever get to go clubbing..."

"Calm down," Elsa smiled. "Take a breath."

"I'm sorry," Ava sighed. "I'm not really used to this."

"Me neither," Elsa reminded her. "What are you wearing at the moment?"

"Oooooh," Ava giggled. "You sound like one of those phone sex lines that charge the earth for dirty talk!"

"Ava! How much wine have you had?"

"*Loads* more than you, apparently," she paused and took a deep breath. "OK, I'm wearing a purple knee-length dress with three-quarter length sleeves. It has sequins around the top, and it's not too tight but not too...*floaty*. It's quite summery, I guess?"

"Summery sounds good," Elsa agreed.

"I've got black pumps on – I thought heels were a bit OTT for the cinema. And my slate-grey jacket; you know the one that looks a bit military style with the big gold buttons?"

Elsa nodded. "And what have you done with your hair?"

"Well, I washed it," Ava replied hesitantly. "I only just came in off the yard half an hour ago. I can't do everything, Else."

Elsa rolled her eyes.

"Don't roll your bloody eyes at me!" Ava scolded her. "I know you are, Else. Right, I'm going to send you a pic, OK? I'll message it to you and you tell me if I look OK, or just average, or way over the top, OK?"

"Sure, but calm down, OK?" Elsa smiled. "Play it cool. It's just dinner with Clement, no big deal, OK?"

"I *am* calm!" Ava insisted, feeling the least calm she had ever been.

"I will remind you of this moment when you next take the piss out of me," Elsa warned her. "Right, send me the picture over. And promise to call me tomorrow to tell me all about it, OK?"

"I will," Ava promised. "Wish me luck, Else!"

"Good luck!" Elsa beamed.

"Oh...one more thing! I almost forgot the massive news I have for you!"

"What?" Elsa waited, hoping it wasn't anything bad.

Ava took a deep breath. "Christine Forrester came to the yard earlier to talk about Nobby's future. She was *less* than impressed with Fred's performance at Cromwell, putting it politely."

Elsa was holding her breath as she waited for her next words.

"Fred has lost the ride on him."

"Oh *no*," Elsa's heart sank, feeling a black cloud ascend on her evening. "Poor Nobby!" Ava was the best groom he could have asked for, and now he would be shipped off into the unknown before he'd even had a chance to settle. "And poor Frederick," she added as if an afterthought. "But I assume he's got all the Roxwell horses propping him up, so he won't be too bothered."

"He is fond of him," Ava told her gently. "Despite what you may think of him. And I think he would rather have Nobby over *any* of the Roxwell horses, if it meant he never saw another bloody Roxwell in his life."

"You told me he and Portia were living together!" Elsa exclaimed, hating how much it still hurt her heart.

"They are, but there's more to it than meets the eye. But anyway, it's not all bad – listen!" Ava was hurrying now. "So Christine saw Clem riding while she was at the yard, and she offered Nobby to him."

"I am *so* happy!" Elsa declared, feeling the black cloud drift past. "For Nobby *and* for Clement."

"But mostly for Nobby?" Ava giggled.

"Of course!" Elsa replied shamelessly. "Clement makes his own destiny, but Nobby has to put up with whoever he is landed upon, and I am glad that he won't be leaving your yard."

"I will still be his groom," Elsa could feel her smile through the phone. "Which I am very happy about, so I just wanted to let you know before you heard it first somewhere else and only got half the story."

"Thank you," Elsa told her, from the bottom of her heart.

"Now I really am going! I'll call you tomorrow!"

The call was cut and Elsa held her phone to her chest as she waited for it to beep. While she wished Nobby could come back, she knew it wouldn't be possible anymore with Sophia off to pastures new, so the ride being given to Clement was the best outcome she could have wished for. She was sorry for Frederick, but mainly relieved that it meant Portia could never get her claws into poor Nobby again.

Elsa glanced at the uninspiring pizza on the side, not wanting to cook it despite her stomach rumbling in protest. She suddenly wished her mother lived closer and she could pop round for dinner. Her mother was always trying to feed her up as soon as she walked through the door, telling her she looked pasty and thin before even asking how she was.

She half wished she had someone who could whisk her off to the cinema and dinner, but then she imagined the agro that could come with that, and she wasn't sure she minded so much only having herself to answer to.

Beep beep.

She opened up the picture to see Ava grimacing as she took a photo of herself standing before her full length mirror.

Please be honest if I look awful? Xx

Elsa hit reply. *You look stunning! Have fun and smile! Xx*. And she meant it; Clement would think all his birthdays and

Christmases had come at once.

She snuggled up on the sofa alongside Cecil, who seeing that her wine glass was full again, had now deemed it safe to return. She tried to focus on the TV, but she had missed half of whatever program this was and her eyelids were beginning to droop.

Ring ring.

She jolted awake and sloshed wine on her wrist. She had no idea how long she had been asleep, but Cecil was still keeping her warm, and although she had dropped her wine glass it was miraculously wedged upright between her arm, the sofa arm and Cecil's hind legs.

"Aha!" she beamed triumphantly, snatching it back up. "I do have talents!"

She licked the wine from her wrist and searched for her phone underneath the cushions, as the persistent ringing reminded her of why she had woken up in the first place. She squinted as she read the caller display, certain her eyes were deceiving her. She got to her feet and paced the tiny living room, her finger hovering over the answer button. She knew she should decline, but did she have the willpower? She took a deep breath and ran her hand through her loose hair as she hit the answer button.

"Hi."

"Can I come over?" Frederick's abruptness knocked her off guard. No *"Hello, Elsa, how are you?"* She sensed the urgency in his voice, and it left her feeling intrigued but also a little scared.

Her mind danced as she thought over the information Ava had recently shared with her. So he had slept with her while he was seeing someone else. And he couldn't deny he was seeing her then, because he was now living with her and things did not move that quickly in anyone's relationship. Elsa felt sick at the thought of it. *How could he do that to her?*

But sadly it didn't change the way she felt about him, and

she hated herself for it. But now he just expected to be able to call her after a long silence and she would bow to him? Did he honestly think that low of her?

"No," she eventually replied. There was no way she was allowing herself to be alone in her house with him. She wasn't sure she would be able to keep her hands from him, and she hated herself even more. She hated herself for still letting him hurt her. Why couldn't she just cut all ties?

"Please, Elsa? It's important and I need to see you."

"I don't think that's a good idea," she told him through gritted teeth, ignoring the pleading, weary tone of his voice.

"Come over mine?" he asked, but he knew that was probably out of the question, too.

"What the fuck do you want, Frederick?" she snapped. *Leave me alone!* She wanted to plead with him. *Stop doing this to me!* But she didn't want him to have the satisfaction of knowing that just the thought of him did things to her.

"How about we go to dinner?" he countered, ignoring her question.

"Frederick, dinners with you have never ended well for me. I wonder why I get the feeling this one would be no different?" She told him, certain even he could hear her growling stomach. She walked through to the kitchen and saw her pizza on the side. Well, it should have been a pizza, but now it had fully defrosted it was just a sloppy mess.

Go to dinner with him! Her stomach pleaded with her.

"Please, Elsa?" he whispered, and she sensed the urgency in his voice.

"Why, Frederick?" she sighed. "We go over and over old ground, and get nowhere."

"I know, but it's different this time. I can't talk about anything like this over the phone with you. I need to see you."

"I'm not coming to meet you," she insisted. "Not in a million years."

The restaurant he'd chosen was small and intimate, and she stood outside knowing this was her last chance to duck out, before taking a deep breath and gently pushing open the door, and stepping inside.

Candles flickered on the centre of each and every table, and her first impression was of how romantic the place looked, and she wondered if that had been his intention.

She had got ready in record time, and now knew exactly how Ava had felt earlier. She felt like all eyes were on her as she entered, and she wondered if she looked too casual or far too over the top. She had decided against wearing a dress, because she thought that signalled that she was on a date, and she wanted to feel that this was anything but. She couldn't cope with getting her hopes up anymore to be left broken hearted. She had instead settled for smart, black jeans and her comfortable suede boots, with a long-sleeved, dark green satin top.

Frederick sat two tables back from the door, and he stood to greet her. His eyes had been fixated on the door, willing her to push it open. And now that she had, he wasn't quite sure what he was going to say.

Well, at least I am not going to get stood up, she told herself, the sight of him taking her breath away. He looked so casually beautiful in a checked shirt and beige trousers, with polished brown shoes. He ruffled his hair and she could tell that he was nervous. At first she couldn't place it, but he was definitely nervous.

"You look beautiful," he told her.

"Please don't say things like that," she told him coldly, sitting down opposite him before he had a chance to come round and pull the chair out for her.

But it's true, he thought, but he didn't retaliate. He didn't want her to feel uncomfortable, even though he knew that was inevitable.

The waiter was beside them before he could say anything

else. He passed them their menus, and she tried her best to smile.

"What can I get you to drink?"

"Just a water for me, thanks." She replied.

"I'll have a beer," Frederick smiled, although she guessed that was as forced as hers was. "You can have a glass of wine, can't you, Elsa?"

"I've already had too much," the sharpness of her voice did not go unnoticed on him. "Just a water is fine."

With a nod, the waiter left them to it. The flame of the candle flickered between them, and she desperately wanted to blow it out.

"I've heard the calamari here is excellent," Frederick said gently, hating the silence between them.

Elsa tossed her menu onto the table and folded her arms across her chest. "What do you want from me, Frederick?" she asked him, and not for the first time. "Why have you dragged me here?"

Dragged? Was she back to hating him that much? He took a deep breath. He would have to get used to her hating him, as he didn't see there could ever be a way of going back, after tonight.

"To talk to you," he shrugged feebly. "I was very...*messed up*, when I last saw you."

"Is that supposed to make me feel better?" she held him gaze. "You've come to tell me you wouldn't have slept with me had you not been so *messed up*?"

"No, not at all." Quite the opposite, in fact. If he wasn't so messed up he might have been able to find the inner strength to kick all his problems aside, take her in his arms instead and sleep with her every day for the rest of his life. Why couldn't it be that easy? Why did family and politics, money and horses have to get in the way?

He let out a breath he didn't realise he had been holding. He had brought her here to talk, that much was true, but he just couldn't seem to string together a sentence. Everything he formed in his head seemed so stupid that he couldn't bear for the words to leave his mouth. So silence shrouded them, and as the waiter returned, Elsa took a welcome sip of her ice cold water.

"Can I get you anything to start?"

"I'll try the calamari," Elsa smiled sweetly, having not even looked at the menu. "Someone told me it's really good, but he's a lying wanker and I don't believe a word he says, so I guess I should find out for myself, right?"

"Very well," the waiter hid his amusement well as he scribbled it down on his pad. "Can I get anything for you, Sir?"

"Can you er...give us a minute?" Frederick asked, his embarrassment evident.

"Sure, just give me a signal when you wish me to return," the waiter gave them a curt nod, not wishing to risk walking back into their obvious domestic too early.

"Elsa, what was that about?" Frederick asked gently, once he had left.

Elsa felt her cheeks flaming red as she struggled not to meet his eye. She wondered how the hell he could make her feel like the bad guy, when he was the one who had monumentally fucked up here. She bit back her anger as she tried to answer him civilly.

"That was about me finding out that you slept with me while you were shacked up with someone else," she thought she did well to fight back her rage which was threatening to boil over at any moment. "How could you, Frederick?"

"It's not what it looks like," he replied, looking regretful, but he knew it was helpless. She was unlikely to believe anything he said, and even more so after he had delivered her the news he desperately needed to get off his chest.

He reached across the table for her hand, and she flinched as he took it in his, but did not try to move it away. Elsa took a deep breath. She could feel her heart pounding in her chest, and she wondered if he felt it, too, as he tenderly brushed his fingers over her knuckles.

"Elsa, I have something to tell you," Frederick began.

He was finally going to tell her, he had seen sense and couldn't live without her, the voices in her head danced, but she quashed their ridiculousness.

"What is it?" she managed to croak the words out, even though her mouth was bone dry. She wondered if in a moment she might be able to kiss him. She had missed him so much.

"It's quite important, and not many people know, but for some reason I felt like you should be one of the first," he forced a wry smile, and eventually met her eye. Her heart quickened, but as he quickly looked back down at her hands she felt it slow.

"Oh go on, hit me with it," she told him, sensing there would be no opportunity for kissing, or anything more that she wanted. "It's not as if my life can get any worse, is it?"

She watched his gaze drop to the table, and fear flooded through her.

"Oh God," her voice was shaky. "Tell me it can't, can it?"

He didn't reply, and she knew she wasn't going to like whatever he had to say. He dropped her hand, and rubbed his fingers along his temples.

"What is it?" she urged, fear rising within her. But she already felt her world stop around her, as she knew exactly what he was going to say. Even as her ears were filled with the hard pounding of her heart, his words hit her loud and clear.

He took a deep breath. "Elsa," he began, unable to meet her eye. "I am getting married."

About the Author

Laurie Twizel lives and breathes horses. When not writing, she can often be found roaming the beautiful countryside of her current home in the South East of England, with or without a horse!

Follow her on social media for all the latest book releases
"Laurie Twizel - Author"
@LaurieTwizel
Blog - http://laurietwizel.blogspot.co.uk

If you enjoyed this book, please let your friends know! Laurie would also love your feedback; you can drop her an email
at laurie.twizel@gmail.com

Printed in Germany
by Amazon Distribution
GmbH, Leipzig